Abbie Taylor lives in Dublin. She works as a doctor and has two daughters.

www.penguin.co.uk

Also by Abbie Taylor

Emma's Baby

and published by Bantam Books

THE DILEMMA

Abbie Taylor

BANTAM BOOKS

LONDON • TORONTO • SYDNEY • AUCKLAND • JOHANNESBURG

TRANSWORLD PUBLISHERS
61–63 Uxbridge Road, London W5 5SA
www.penguin.co.uk

Transworld is part of the Penguin Random House group of companies
whose addresses can be found at global.penguinrandomhouse.com

Penguin
Random House
UK

First published in Great Britain in 2011 as *In Safe Hands* by
Bantam Books, an imprint of Transworld Publishers
Bantam edition reissued as *The Dilemma* 2018

A CIP catalogue record for this book
is available from the British Library.

ISBN
9780857503763

Typeset in 11/14½ pt Sabon by Kestrel Data, Exeter, Devon.
Printed and bound by Clays Ltd, Bungay, Suffolk.

Penguin Random House is committed to a sustainable
future for our business, our readers and our planet. This book
is made from Forest Stewardship Council® certified paper.

MIX
Paper from
responsible sources
FSC® C018179

1 3 5 7 9 10 8 6 4 2

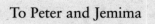

To Peter and Jemima

Acknowledgements

Sincere thanks to Marianne Gunn O'Connor, Pat Lynch, Vicki Satlow and Jessica Broughton.

Chapter One

'Nurse!'

The shout came from somewhere out on the ward.

Sister Dawn Torridge glanced towards the door of the side room. Someone wanting a glass of water, most likely, or the commode. Clive and Elspeth were both out there. One of them would see to it.

She turned back to her patient.

'All right, Mrs Walker?' She smiled at the elderly lady propped up on her bank of pillows. She was helping Mrs Walker to drink, holding the cup to her lips, supporting her head so that she could swallow. 'How are you getting on with that tea?'

Mrs Walker wasn't in a position to answer but it was clear from the way she sucked at the cup that the dark brown liquid, tepid and unpleasant as it must be, was very welcome. From outside the window, six floors down, came the distant rattle of a train hurtling over the railway bridge, but up here in the little room all was peaceful, the only sounds the little gasps between mouthfuls as Mrs Walker drank her tea and the regular *beep* of the antibiotic pump beside her bed. Mrs Walker's lips were dry, cracked and sore-looking. How long had she been lying here like that with the cup on her bedside table just out of her reach? Dawn made a mental note to remind the junior staff to check that the patients were able to feed themselves before leaving them alone with food or drinks.

'*Nurse!*'

That shout again from the ward. Something in the tone of it. Dawn frowned and lifted her head.

'NURSE!' The panic was unmistakeable. 'Somebody! Come quick!'

Dawn jerked the cup of tea back on to its saucer.

'Just a moment,' she said to Mrs Walker.

She put the saucer down and hurried to the door.

Clive and Elspeth were nowhere to be seen. Halfway down the long, high ward with its rows of blue-curtained cubicles, a man in brown pyjamas was kneeling on his bed, peering towards the nurse's desk. As soon as he saw Dawn, he raised his arms over his head and began to semaphore wildly.

'Sister!' He jabbed his finger towards the curtains around bed eleven. 'In there. Quick!'

Dawn was already running down the ward. Her mind flew ahead, recalling what she knew about the patient in bed eleven. Mr Jack Benson, aged seventy-two. Post-op thyroid surgery earlier that morning. He had been perfectly stable when she'd last seen him, not two hours before.

'Keep a close eye on him,' she had warned Clive, the senior staff nurse. 'Thyroids can be dangerous. I've got a budget meeting to go to, but any problems, just page me and I'll come straight back.'

The budget meeting had gone on longer than expected but there had been no word from Clive which Dawn had taken to mean that all was well. Now, as she approached the bed, a harsh, scraping noise, *Huuuh*, *huuuh*, from behind the curtains made her heart shrink back towards her spine. *Oh no, please. Not this!* She hadn't heard that sound in years, but you only needed to hear it once to know immediately what it was. She grabbed the curtains and flung them back.

Jack Benson was sitting upright against his pillows. The buttons of his paisley pyjama jacket were open to the chest. Studded around his neck, like a gruesome, Frankenstein-monster necklace, was the row of metal staples from his thyroid surgery that morning. But that was not what made Dawn step back in shock. Mr Benson's neck had swollen to twice its normal size. It looked as if a giant, mottled, inflatable tyre had wrapped itself around his throat, throttling him, squeezing the air from his lungs. The pressure of it made his eyes bulge. He was clutching at his neck, gasping for breath.

Dawn acted immediately. She jabbed her finger on the emergency button over the bed. As the high-pitched jangle sounded over the ward, she yanked the oxygen mask from the wall and stretched the elastic around the patient's head.

'All right, Mr Benson.' She forced her voice to sound calm. 'Breathe this.'

Jack Benson pressed the mask to his face with both hands, sucking frantically at the oxygen. *Huuuh, huuuh*. The plastic of the mask fogged and cleared, fogged and cleared. Then he looked at Dawn, his eyes wide with terror. *It's not working. Do something.*

Running feet sounded outside the cubicle. Clive and Elspeth appeared around the curtains.

'Oh God.' At the sight of the swelling, Elspeth put her hand to her mouth.

'He's haemorrhaging,' Dawn said. 'The pressure is blocking his airway. Clive, get the crash trolley. Elspeth, you stay with him while I page the surgeon.'

She ran to the nurse's desk and punched the pager numbers into the phone. Hurry. Hurry. Over by the bed, Elspeth stood twisting her fingers around each other. '*Take his BP*,' Dawn mouthed at her. The phone rang. She snatched up the receiver.

'Coulton here.' A bored drawl.

One of the new registrars. Dawn couldn't put a face

to the name. She wasted no time filling him in. 'This is Sister Torridge, from Forest Ward. The post-op thyroid in bed eleven is haemorrhaging.'

A sigh from the phone. 'You mean there is a slight bleed from his wound.'

'No. I mean there's a major—'

Dr Coulton interrupted her. 'What's his blood pressure?'

'We haven't done it yet, but—'

'Well, Nurse, surely that would be the first thing? I'm up to my eyes here in A&E. If you could make sure to have the *complete* information next time you call, that would be extremely helpful.'

Dawn blinked. Did this patronizing-sounding junior doctor seriously think that a ward sister was incapable of recognizing a seriously ill patient when she saw one?

She kept her tone neutral. 'Dr Coulton, you may not be aware, but Mr Benson had his thyroid removed only this morning. The haemorrhage is now pressing on his trachea. If something is not done about it in the next ten minutes, I am warning you, Doctor, he will die.'

She didn't wait for him to argue but put the phone down and hurried back to the bed. Even in the couple of minutes she had been away the swelling in Mr Benson's neck had increased. His face was dark red, suffused with blood; the pressure was blocking his circulation as well as his breathing. He was scrabbling at his neck as if to literally tear the flesh away from his airway. *Huuuh, huuuh*. His shoulders heaved with the effort; it must have been like trying to suck air through a tiny straw. Dawn dropped her gaze to his bedside locker, searching quickly through the objects there for what she wanted. A bottle of purple grape juice. A pair of glasses, folded on top of a book. A sheet of paper, folded in half, covered with shaky green print: *Get well soon Grandad*. Then she saw it: a set of staple-cutters, still in their sterile packaging. The strict rule on Dawn's ward was that a set of these cutters was kept beside every thyroid patient at all times so that in an emergency no one would have to hunt for them. The only way to release the intense pressure in Jack Benson's neck was to cut the staples in his wound. Open it up so that the haemorrhage could escape. She snatched the cutters from the locker and ripped them from their package, ready to hand them to Dr Coulton as soon as he arrived.

They waited in a tense semicircle around the bed, Dawn gripping the cutters, Clive parking the crash trolley, Elspeth still with her hands to her face. Dawn looked towards the doors of the ward. Any minute now, Dr Coulton would be here. He would have known from her phone call to drop whatever he was doing and run. Jack Benson continued to struggle. *Huuuh, huuuh*. Sweat rolled down his face. Veins like blue worms bulged on his temples. He was leaning forward, supporting himself by gripping his hands on his thighs, concentrating utterly on each breath. The oxygen mask sat askew, the elastic pushing his grey hair into spikes around his face. He stared wildly around the circle of nurses. *Help me. For God's sake. Why are you all just standing there?* It was extremely distressing to watch. Dawn straightened the mask, turned the oxygen up further, cranked the back of the bed upright to give him some extra support. 'The doctor's on his way now,' she said. 'He'll be here any second.'

She hoped. Something poked hard against her shin. The corner of the crash trolley, dislodged by Clive.

'Not doing too well, is he?' Clive said as Dawn looked at him.

She couldn't help herself. 'Weren't you watching him, like I asked you to?'

Clive folded his arms, jutting his jaw forward. 'Didn't get a chance, did I? Ward's been mayhem all day.'

The ward was not busy and Dawn was sure she had seen him and Elspeth come from the direction of the coffee room just a few minutes ago. But now was not the time. The doors to the ward were still closed. Where *was* Dr Coulton? Jack Benson was getting worse by the minute. The longer that pressure remained around his trachea, the more it would be crushed until eventually the entire airway would swell up and close. If that happened, no matter what they did it would be too late to save him.

'Page that doctor again, please,' she told Clive. The skin on Mr Benson's neck was bulging between the staples. Dawn felt the spring of the cutters in her hand. She could cut the staples herself, quite easily. Nurses removed stitches every day. But this was no normal wound. Opening it would release the massive pressure, not just on the airway but on the haemorrhage itself. With no surgeon or equipment to control it Mr Benson might well bleed to death. The strict rule, handed down from Professor Kneebone himself, was that it had to be a doctor who made the decision.

Mr Benson's hands slipped on his thighs. He fell back against his pillows. Had his breathing begun to quieten? The harsh *Huuuh, huuuh* sound begun to fade? He lay motionless, appearing to stare at something ahead of him in the distance, the terror in his eyes replaced by a filmy gaze.

'He's getting better.' Elspeth clasped her hands to her chest.

Dawn did not correct her. Mr Benson was not getting better. The fading breath sounds meant that hardly any air was getting through to his lungs. He was exhausted. In a few more minutes the sheer effort would become too much for him. When it did, he would lose consciousness and it would all be over.

'Go on home,' Dawn had advised his wife and

daughter only that morning. 'Try to get some rest. He'll sleep here for most of the day.'

'Are you sure, Sister?' His wife, a slim, well-dressed woman in her sixties, looked as if she herself hadn't had much sleep the previous night. 'It was such a big operation. I don't like to leave him.'

'He'll be fine.' Dawn had looked her straight in the eye. 'I promise. He's in good hands here.'

And so they had left him just three hours ago, trusting her that he would be safe.

She looked again from the staple-cutters to the doors. No matter what she did, the odds were against her. Open the wound: Jack Benson might bleed to death. Do nothing and he would suffocate right here in front of her eyes. Behind her, Clive, back from the phone, said with relish, 'Very grey, isn't he? I don't think he's going to make it.'

Dawn stood straighter and gripped the cutters. 'Yes. Yes, he is.'

She couldn't wait any longer. Rules or no rules, this man's life was in her hands. She was the Matron; he was her responsibility. If she made the wrong decision, so be it. But she would not stand here, do nothing and watch him die.

Her hands were steadier than she would have expected as she placed the cutters over the first staple. The clip was almost buried in the swollen skin but she managed to prise one of the blades beneath it. Mr

Benson didn't react. He was beyond feeling anything now. Dawn brought the handles of the cutters together.

Snap! The first staple cracked in two. She moved on to the next.

Snap! Snap! Snap! No going back now. One by one, the staples flew apart. The wound opened. A wave of scarlet gushed down over Mr Benson's chest.

'Jack.' Dawn shook his shoulder. 'Can you hear me? Can you breathe?' His eyes remained shut. Was his chest still moving? She leaned forward to listen. Anything? Any air coming out? She shook him again. '*Jack!*'

A tiny flutter, like a heartbeat, at her side. She looked down. The flutter was Mr Benson's hand, moving in the air. The hand groped for her arm, found it, gave it a feeble squeeze.

Dawn took his hand and gripped it back. 'All right,' she whispered. 'All right. Well done.'

He *was* breathing. She could hear him now. The massive pressure had left his trachea; the air could flow through it again. But now they had a new problem. The blood was still pouring from his neck, soaking into his pyjamas. Grimly, Dawn eyed the widening crimson circle on the sheets. They needed to get that stopped; needed to get him to theatre as soon as possible. How much blood was in the bed now? One litre? Two?

'Call transfusion,' she said to Elspeth. 'Tell them Mr Benson needs six units.' She turned the spigot up on his bag of saline so that the fluid stopped dripping and poured into his arm like a tap.

With a rattle, the curtains swished back further. Standing in the gap was a tall, thin, balding man in a gleaming white coat. Dr Coulton, Dawn presumed. His eyes held a bored, supercilious expression: *This had better be good.* One look at Mr Benson, however, and the superciliousness was wiped from his face.

'What's happened here?'

'I cut the clips,' Dawn said.

'You cut the *clips*? What the hell—?'

He pushed past her, rushing at the patient, feeling his hands, pulling his eyelids down, barking out orders. 'What's the Hb? Let's get some blood up here. Now! Have we called theatre? *Tsk*, Nurse.' He spun to Dawn. 'I hope for your sake that what you've done here was necessary.'

If he had bothered to come up sooner he could have seen for himself whether it was necessary. But Dawn didn't attempt to argue. It was she who had made the decision to open the neck. If she had been wrong, she would deal with the consequences. Right now, the most important person here was the patient. She returned to the phone and quickly made the calls necessary to organize theatre, transport, ITU. Then, as the theatre porters crashed through the doors with the trolley, she gathered up everything Mr Benson would need for his trip: oxygen tank, monitor, spare bags of saline, jets of adrenaline.

The last thing she did, so that the team would not have to pause for even those precious few seconds, was to walk ahead of them to open the heavy wooden doors.

Light streamed from the ward into the hall. Down the corridor they flew, the two porters in their dark green theatre scrubs; the pompous new registrar, his white coat flapping importantly; Mr Benson, pale and still in his pool of scarlet. Dawn watched him on his way, motionless in her navy uniform, her long shadow lying before her as she stood between the doors of her ward.

'The airway was almost completely crushed,' Francine, the ITU sister, reported later that afternoon. 'Another few minutes and it would have been too late.'

Around them, the rows of heart monitors and dialysis machines clicked and beeped. In his high bed, Mr Benson lay unconscious, his head and neck wrapped up with long strips of gauze, covering every part of his face except his nose. From somewhere in the middle, his breathing tube stuck out, connected by a plastic hose to the ventilator. He looked like a giant white mummy. But after a fraught three-hour battle in theatre to get the bleeding under control, he was finally safe.

Francine was adjusting the flow on the blood bag over his bed. 'Professor Kneebone told the theatre staff that if that wound hadn't been opened when it was, he would have died.' She nudged Dawn with her elbow. 'Well done, Dawn. The only reason he's still here is because of you.'

Mr Benson's hand lay white and still outside his sheet. 'It should never have got that far.' Dawn touched the waxy skin. 'I thought I could trust Clive to watch him. If the patient in bed ten hadn't looked round his curtain to borrow some headphones . . .' She shuddered.

Francine quirked an eyebrow at her. 'Cuppa?'

'Yeah, lovely.'

In the tiny, toast-smelling ITU kitchen, Francine switched on the kettle and spooned powdered coffee into mugs.

'Clive's that new nurse, isn't he?' she called from the draining-board. 'Scruffy-looking bloke? Looks like he could do with a good wash? Maybe he didn't realize how serious it was.'

'But he's a senior grade.' Dawn was crouched by the fridge, hunting for the milk. 'And it wasn't just Mr Benson. Other patients were neglected as well, left all morning with nothing to drink. I don't know, Fran.' She found the milk and stood up, closing the fridge door with her hip. 'Clive's been here for over two months now, but he doesn't seem to have any interest at all.'

It was a relief after all the drama to be able to let off steam. Dawn and Francine went back a long way. They were both sisters on the same floor, Francine on the ITU, Dawn on the surgical ward. Francine, a slim blonde, was as silvery and delicate as the porcelain dolls you saw in toy shops, wrapped in tissue paper. Her dainty appearance, however – all willowy slenderness and glamorous chignon – masked the fact that she was a shrewd ward manager who was perfectly capable of getting her own way when required. The time last year that she and Dawn had both gone for the Surgical Matron position, there'd been very little to choose between them. Dawn often wondered if the reason she had been successful was because Francine had come across in the interview as just too fragile for the post.

'Some of the junior staff these days, you've really got to wonder,' Francine was saying. 'We had one recently who absolutely refused to wash her hands between patients. No matter how many times I reminded her, she'd just widen her eyes and go, "Ooh, sorry, Sister, I forgot." Then one day she was eating her sandwich in here and kept saying there was a funny taste, and it was only when the last bite had gone in that she realized she'd got poo on her fingers.'

'Blimey.' Dawn almost choked on her mouthful of coffee.

'Yes, well. Standards these days aren't the same as yours or mine – especially yours, Dawn. The trouble is, the patients keep coming faster than ever and we're so short-staffed. You've got to bite your lip sometimes, don't you? Give this Clive person a chance. You don't want to have to do everything yourself.'

'No. That's true.'

Dawn finished her coffee and got up to wash her cup. Francine watched her from the small round table in the corner.

'Dawn – are you all right?'

'Of course. Why?'

'You look tired. You've not been yourself for a while. Doing a full day's work here, then going home to care for your gran on your own all night too. It can't have been easy.'

'It wasn't so bad.' Dawn squirted washing-up liquid into the mug. 'Anyway, Dora refused point blank to come in to hospital. She said it was no place for the old.'

'Well, she was lucky to have you, then,' Francine said. 'But you were back at work the day after the funeral. The *day* after! That's not right, Dawn. Not healthy. Why don't you take a break now it's all over? Give yourself a chance to recover?'

23

'I will do, Fran. It's just, the ward's quite busy at the moment. Now's not the best time—'

A frightened-looking face appeared around the door.

'Sister Hartnett, can you come? Bed nine's just pulled out his breathing tube.'

'I'll be right with you, Seema.' When the nurse had gone, Francine said, 'Look. I know where you're coming from. I'm exactly the same. We're both a bit . . . obsessive, I suppose. You have to be, or you'd never keep on top of this job. But you need something outside, too. You need to keep your perspective. Don't give your life up for the hospital. All right, Seema.' She was standing up from the table. 'All right. On my way now.'

On the bus home, looking out over the swaying trees on Wandsworth Common, Dawn thought again about what Francine had said. She had meant well, but now really wasn't a good time to take a break. The hospital was going through a busy patch and only a couple of months ago Priya, one of her best staff, had gone on maternity leave. Clive had been hired from an agency to replace her but Dawn had never been entirely happy with him and today hadn't helped. There was no way she could go off on holiday and leave him in charge.

Anyway, she wasn't tired. Far from it. In fact, she

hadn't mentioned it yet to Francine, but only recently the idea had come to her for a huge new project. One of the biggest and most complex she had ever taken on, but one which, when completed, she was convinced would be of unprecedented importance to the hospital.

At number 59 Crocus Road, Milly came panting to the gate to greet her.

'Hey, girl.' Dawn bent to pat her. 'How are things? How was your day?'

Milly barked and twisted in circles, trying to present every part of her stubby body to Dawn at once. Her dark muzzle was smudged with grey but the bright, triangular Labrador eyes were still shiny and alert.

'Poor old girl.' Dawn scratched the furry chest. 'On your own here all day. You miss Dora, don't you?'

She missed Dora herself. It was still so strange, to open the door into the narrow, Regency-striped hall and see no Dora bustling from the kitchen to greet her with some joke or piece of gossip: 'Dawn, you'll never *believe* what the new young man at the chemist's said to Mrs Morton . . .' Because when she pictured her grandmother now, that was how she saw her, the way she had always been, plump and cheerful and active, not the withered, pain-racked skeleton she had become. The sitting-room was back to normal now, the bed and commode and sleeping pills cleared away, the tasselled lamps and gold-coloured three-piece suite restored. Just the way they had been the day Dawn had first come to live here when she was ten years old. No more Dora lying there, faded and wasted amidst the cushions, her thin face twisted with distress. Dawn closed the door and continued on her way to the kitchen.

After dinner, she spread the notes for her new project out over the kitchen table. The project was still in the very early stages. Still an enormous amount of work and research to do, but if it worked out as she hoped, the whole future of St Iberius could depend on it.

The idea had come to her a couple of months ago. It had been shortly after Dora's death. Priya had just gone on her maternity leave and Clive hadn't yet started his contract at St Iberius. The ward had been so short-staffed that Dawn had ended up working two shifts back to back. She had come home around midnight and collapsed into bed. Towards morning she'd had the dream.

St Iberius was on fire. Dense black smoke swirled in the corridor. The piercing shriek of the fire alarm echoed around the walls of the fire escape.

'This way. This way.' The fire officer ushered the panicking crowd towards the stairs. The patients shuffled along, leaning on the arms of the nurses, clutching their drips and oxygen masks to their chests.

Behind them came the faint cries of those patients still on the ward: 'Help! Don't leave us!'

'They can't walk,' Dawn said urgently. 'How are we going to get them out?'

'We can't,' the fire officer said. 'We're five flights up. We're going to have to leave them.'

Dawn pictured the patients struggling to escape from their beds: Mr Cantwell with his fractured spine, Mrs Murray with her emphysema, Mr Ugabe with his amputated leg. Tangled up in their blankets, unable to climb out, left with no choice but to lie there and watch in terror as the flames approached.

She had to go back. They were her responsibility; she could not leave them. She retreated from the stairwell and turned to grope her way back towards the ward.

'Sister,' the voices cried. 'Help us.'

'I'm coming. Hold on.' But the smoke was thicker now, charring her throat, stinging her eyes. She had to squeeze them shut and put her hands out to feel in front of her. Every time she touched something she thought she had reached the doors of the ward, but each time it turned out to be just another wall. Then the cries turned to screams as the flames reached the beds and Dawn cried out too.

She had been very agitated when she woke. The dream had seemed so real: the hot, stinging smoke, the feelings of panic and helplessness. But once she was up and sipping a cup of tea in the kitchen in her dressing gown with the sun pouring through the frosted-glass back door, her normal, practical self returned and she could see why she'd had the dream. The newspapers recently had been full of stories about pandemic flu. Questions had been raised in parliament: *Can Our Hospitals Cope?*

Dawn had been wondering that herself. Since being promoted to Matron, she was responsible not only for the day-to-day running of her ward but also the development of future services at St Iberius. The A&E was bursting at the seams as it was, the patients stacked in rows like tins of beans at a supermarket, operations being cancelled daily for lack of beds. If something happened and the numbers of patients suddenly mushroomed, how on earth would they cope?

St Iberius did have a Disaster Plan in place. Dawn took a copy of it home to study. But despite 200 pages of dense text, the main points it seemed to boil down to were: (1) call in extra staff and (2) divert excess patients to other hospitals. The whole approach stank of an ostrich burying its head in the sand. What if the entire city was affected and there *were* no other hospitals? Dawn pictured St Iberius overrun, the floors lined with groaning and bleeding patients and still more crushing through the doors. Ever since she'd had the dream, the strongest feeling had been with her. These things came in cycles. Something terrible was going to happen; it was only a matter of time. And when it did, it would be vital to be prepared.

She worked until late in the evening, reading up on accounts of disasters in other countries, making notes about equipment shortage, power failure, infection spread. At eleven o'clock, she yawned and tidied the papers away. Milly was waiting at the back door to be let out for her run.

The April night was damp and cool. The light from the kitchen window painted a bright yellow square on the lawn. From somewhere behind the houses, a dog barked, a lonesome sounding yip yip yip. Waiting on the step, Dawn thought again of Jack Benson, his terrified face under the oxygen mask, his harsh, desperate struggle for air, the split-second decision she'd had to make, which thankfully had turned out to be the right one. She hoped he would do OK.

Right then, if someone had asked her, she would have said that of all the patients she'd seen that day, Jack Benson would be the one she would have most reason to remember.

She would have been wrong.

Chapter Two

Dawn yawned, pressing the lift button for the fifth floor. These days it was getting harder and harder to climb out of bed. The cold, rainy weather did nothing to help; it was more like winter than the end of April. Glassy-eyed, as the lift doors closed, she took in the huge poster on the back wall: *St Iberius International Research Conference. Sponsored lunch. All staff invited.* For weeks, these posters had been up all over the hospital. St Iberius was extremely proud of its growing reputation as one of the top research centres of Europe. Dawn yawned again and looked at her watch: five past seven. Professor Kneebone would be just arriving for his round.

The ward round began, as always, in the side room at the top of the ward. The professor and Dawn entered first, followed by the usual phalanx of junior doctors, nurses and students.

'How are you today?' Professor Kneebone called, very loudly and clearly, from the end of the bed.

Mrs Ivy Walker, blinking out of her doze, stared in bewilderment at the crowd of people around her: Dawn, holding the large, red Rounds book; Professor Kneebone, short but immaculately dressed in his grey, fitted suit; Dr Coulton, the new registrar, in his pristine white coat, still with the supercilious expression on his face. Behind him was a cluster of medical students, some eager, some hiding yawns. Behind them again, the new nursing student, recognizable from her plain white tunic and trousers, stood almost flattened into the wall, plainly trying to make herself as invisible as possible.

Professor Kneebone leaned further over the bed.

'I said,' he shouted, 'HOW ARE YOU?'

Mrs Walker shrank back into her pillows, clutching the sheets to her chin. Her mouth moved. A tiny, quavery voice emerged. 'I want to go.'

'Go where?'

'To the South Pacific.'

Professor Kneebone raised his eyebrows at Dawn. She touched the old lady's thin shoulder.

'She always says that. That she wants to go somewhere. She finds it hard to tell us what she really means.'

'I see.' Professor Kneebone glanced at his watch.

'Well, Sister, we've had the results back from her scan. These pains she's been having in her nursing home . . .'

'Yes?' Dawn beckoned him closer to the door, a little way away from the bed.

'Bad news, I'm afraid. Ovarian cancer.'

Dawn looked quickly at Mrs Walker, but she didn't seem to have heard or understood. She was still gazing in confusion at the circle of faces.

'Poor thing,' Dawn said quietly. 'How long has she got?'

'A few months. At best.'

'What about surgery?' one of the medical students asked. 'Wouldn't that work?'

'Highly unlikely,' Professor Kneebone said. 'And the hospital isn't made of money. At her age . . . and with her Alzheimer's Disease . . .' He paused, glancing towards the bed. Then he crooked his finger for the medical student to step closer.

'The thing to realize,' he enunciated through barely moving lips, 'is that this woman died years ago. The only problem is, her heart is still beating.'

The students, still mostly young and idealistic, filled with dreams of saving the world, slid shocked glances at each other. But the callousness of the conversation was nothing new to Dawn. Geoffrey Kneebone was probably right about the prognosis, and whether anyone liked it or not, there *was* only so much money to go around. Today, however, for some reason, she found herself remembering a conversation she'd had with Dora. It was around the time her pain had begun to get worse.

'Please,' Dawn had begged her, 'come into hospital. Just for a while. There'll be much more we can do there to help.'

Dora had shaken her head. 'You're best in your own home. No one wants you in a hospital when you're my age.'

'Of course they do.' Dawn had sat beside her and stroked her hand. 'Why would you think that? You've got as much right to be there as anyone.'

But Dora had remained stubborn. 'I know the way people think. I won't go somewhere I'm seen as just a nuisance. I'd rather die here in my own house, where I belong.'

The medical team trooped out of the side room, already shuttling Mrs Walker to the very backs of their minds. Dawn was the last to leave. She looked at the elderly woman, lying there shrunken and discarded on her pillows.

'I'll be back,' she said softly. 'Don't worry. I'll look after you.'

After the round, Dawn took the new nursing student on a tour of the ward. Forest Ward, on the top floor of the old Victorian wing, had never been designed to be part of a hospital. St Iberius had originally been built in the 1800s as a workhouse for women and children. The long, high dormitory, with its iron-framed windows, was draughty and difficult to heat in the winter and the only privacy the thirty-odd patients had were the thin blue curtains around their beds. There was only one side room for infectious cases, well below the recommended number for a department of this size. Yet despite the inconveniences, Dawn had always loved working here. From the nurses' desk at the top of the ward you could see every patient at a glance and know what was happening in every corner. In eighteen months' time, the entire department was due to be relocated to the adjoining 1950s tower block as part of a multi-million-pound redevelopment programme. It would be better for the patients, of course – modern bathrooms, four people to a room instead of twenty. Still, Dawn thought, something would be lost: that feeling that you were a part of the hospital's history, walking in the steps of all the nurses who had gone before you, helping to make St Iberius what it had become today.

'This is the stock room.' She opened the door to show the student. 'Where we keep all our drugs and equipment. Over there is the Day Ward, where patients having minor surgery come in and go home again the same day.'

'Yes, Sister.' The student's voice was almost a whisper. She was a small, pale girl with brown hair cut in a feathery bob. Her thin, childlike face gave her a vapid, unfinished air. She seemed almost speechless with nerves at being shown around by the matron. Her name badge read, 'Trudy Dawes.'

Next to the stock room was the side room. The door had a pane of glass in the centre. Through it, Dawn saw Clive washing Mrs Walker with a sponge. The blankets were pulled all the way to the end of the bed. Mrs Walker lay shivering on the mattress, stark naked, for anyone passing to see.

Dawn frowned. She tapped on the door and put her head around it. 'Everything all right, Clive?'

Clive dunked the sponge back into its basin of water, splashing droplets all over the bed. He didn't look too happy to be interrupted. 'She's had an accident. I'm just cleaning her up.'

'Shouldn't you close the blinds? Mrs Walker might like some privacy.'

'Blinds are broken,' Clive said. 'Won't pull down all the way. Anyway, look at her.' He jerked his head towards the bed. 'Barmy as a fruitcake. Hasn't got a clue where she is.'

Dawn looked at Clive, at his sullen expression, his greasy hair straggling to his collar, the permanent three-day stubble like a dark rash around his mouth. It was people like Clive who had made Dora so afraid to come in to hospital. But it wasn't Dawn's policy to discipline staff in front of junior nurses or patients so all she said was, 'Mrs Walker looks uncomfortable. Has she had her painkiller today?'

'She had some morphine an hour ago.'

'Well, it doesn't seem to have worked. If you give me the morphine keys, we'll fetch some more.'

Dawn took the keys to the stock room next door. Trudy Dawes followed. Dawn pressed the light switch. The fluorescent ceiling bar buzzed and flickered, eventually casting a pallid gleam over the rows of spotless white surfaces, the drawers and cupboards filled with dressings, drugs, needles and syringes.

'Mrs Walker's tumour is pressing on her nerves,' Dawn explained to Trudy. 'That's why she's in so much pain. Have you seen morphine administered before?'

'No, Sister.'

'I'll show you.' Dawn was unlocking a metal cupboard beside the sink. 'Morphine is a controlled drug so there are strict rules about how it's kept. Each day a named nurse holds these keys. Two members of staff must be present every time the safe is opened and any morphine removed must be witnessed and signed for so we can keep track of where it's going.'

'Yes, Sister.'

Dawn held up a glass ampoule about the size of her thumb, filled with a clear liquid, like water.

'Notice anything?' Dawn asked.

Trudy frowned at the ampoule. 'There's no lid. It's made completely of glass. How do you open it?'

'You break the glass.' Dawn showed her where. 'It's to prevent anyone tampering with the contents. Go on, have a try. Just snap it in two.'

'Y-yes, Sister.'

Trudy fumbled with the ampoule, her fingers slithering over the sides. She really was the most nervous student Dawn had seen in quite a while. Had *she* been that terrified when she'd first started? She thought back to her first morning at St Iberius, to the eager girl of eighteen, so in awe of Sister Cranmer who had seemed so grim and old. Though the frightening thing was, she couldn't have been all that much older than Dawn was now. Seventeen years! Where on earth had they gone?

'Well done,' she said when Trudy finally managed to get the ampoule open. She drew the morphine up into a syringe and stuck a blue Opiate identification sticker on the side. Then she took the syringe back to Mrs Walker's room. Clive had finished and gone. Mrs Walker was dressed again in her printed hospital nightgown, the stiff cotton floating like a giant square on her thin frame. Perspiration shone on her forehead. Her wispy, see-through hair was plastered to her scalp. The green ECG spikes on the monitor above her bed raced along: *blip-blip-blip*. It was clear that she was in pain. She muttered something as Dawn approached the bed.

'What, sweetheart?' Dawn leaned in closer. 'What did you say?'

'I want to go!'

'Go where?'

'I want to go to Dagenham.'

'Dagenham, eh?' Dawn couldn't help a smile. 'Not quite as nice as the South Pacific, is it?'

Mrs Walker mumbled something as if in defeat. Dawn felt guilty at having made fun of her, however gently. Mrs Walker's gaze flitted constantly about the room, her eyes puzzled and unhappy, as if searching for someone. How terrible to be so alone, to find yourself in a strange place, unable to understand what was going on, surrounded by strangers, deserted by all your family and friends.

'I'm going to give you something for the pain,' Dawn told her. 'It should help in a few minutes.'

She beckoned Trudy over to watch her inject the morphine into Mrs Walker's drip.

'It's very important to make sure you give the right dose,' she explained. 'One third of all hospital complications are due to staff errors. If ever you are in doubt about something you are about to do to a patient, just remember the most basic rule of nursing: first do no harm.'

'First do no harm. No, Sister.'

While waiting for the morphine to work, Dawn held Mrs Walker's hand. It was like holding the cold, fragile wing of a bird. The hand was so wasted that Dawn could almost see the bones through her skin. The grey light from the window emphasized the bareness of the room. There was just the single plastic chair pushed into the corner, the bag of saline hanging from its stand, the ECG monitor mounted on its bracket over the bed. On the locker was a box of tissues and a glass of water with a set of dentures at the bottom. That was it. No books, no sweets, no home-made cards with *Get well soon, Grandma* printed on them. The world outside, it seemed, had forgotten that anyone was in here. Mrs Walker seemed to respond to the contact. Her frail body turned towards Dawn. The frantic *blip-blip-blip* on the monitor began to slow. Dawn felt the quiet, familiar satisfaction. She loved every part of her job: the technical side, the teaching, the managerial aspects. But this – just being with the patients – this was what it was really about.

'You'll probably want to give up your ward commitments now you've been promoted to Matron,' Claudia Lynch, the Nursing Director, had told her. 'You'll have enough on your plate with all the admin and meetings. Leave the hands-on work to someone else. You're above all that now.'

But Dawn had insisted on keeping her ward. Yes, it would mean a great deal of extra work. She'd have to do a lot of the admin and paperwork in her own time. But she didn't want to end up sitting in an office filling in forms, her time taken up with endless meetings, losing touch with what was happening at the bedside. She wanted to be out there on the front line, to . . . well, to keep her finger on the pulse, as it were. And surely the whole point of becoming a nurse in the first place was that you enjoyed working with the patients?

And if she had a favourite type of patient, it was the elderly. Younger patients tended to be confident and informed; they had the back-up and support of family and friends. The elderly, on the other hand, were so often vulnerable and alone, yet so stoic and unwilling to complain, determined not to be a bother or a nuisance to anyone.

Mrs Walker was gripping her hand, the way Dora had gripped at the end. Dora who had refused to come in to hospital where she could have been helped. But Mrs Walker *had* come in. She could help *her*. Gently, Dawn smoothed a strand of hair from the damp forehead.

'I'll make you comfortable,' she said. 'Don't worry. You're in safe hands here.'

Over the next few days, however, despite regular doses of morphine, Mrs Walker's pain seemed, if anything, to get worse. She was seized by attacks where she lay rigid and trembling in her bed, her eyes wide and staring, tiny shudders rolling all the way from her head to her toes. Dawn was increasingly drawn to her and troubled.

'There must be *something* we can do,' she said firmly one evening, collaring Professor Kneebone after the ward round.

Professor Kneebone's plump, ski-tanned face took on a hunted look. 'Like what? We're all in agreement here. Her cancer isn't for treatment.'

'But for the pain,' Dawn insisted. 'What about surgery? Would something like that help?'

'She's too frail for surgery,' Professor Kneebone said. 'She'd never survive it.'

They were interrupted by Dr Coulton who had been standing to one side, flicking through Mrs Walker's notes.

'It says here,' he announced, 'that she's on an extremely large dose of morphine. More than twice what she was on in the nursing home. I find it very strange that it's not working. Are you sure your nurses are actually giving it to her?'

Dawn counted to five in her head. What the hell did he think they were doing with it? Squirting it under the bed? Dr Coulton was relatively new here, she reminded herself. Give him a chance. He probably didn't realize that she was the matron.

'I have given the morphine to her myself,' she

said pleasantly. 'It does seem strange, I agree, but it definitely is not helping.'

'Maybe she's not in pain at all then,' Dr Coulton said. 'You do know she's . . .' He twirled his finger in the air beside his temple.

Dawn looked at him coldly. 'I am well aware of Mrs Walker's disability. It doesn't mean that she can't feel pain.'

He really was appalling. Francine, who normally got on well with all her colleagues, had no time for him either.

'Pompous git,' she had commented only the day before. 'Treats the patients like lab experiments and the nurses like servants. No bedside manner whatsoever. The junior staff call him Rude Ed.'

Dawn turned back to Kneebone. 'So what should we do?' she asked. 'If her cancer isn't for treatment?'

'Well, I don't know.' Professor Kneebone scratched the back of his head. 'The only reason we admitted her in the first place was to treat her pressure sore. Strictly speaking, the cancer is a side issue. Once the sore has improved, she'll be going back to her nursing home.'

'But we can't send her back like this. Look at her. She's in agony.'

'I'm sorry, Sister, but I don't see what else we can do. She can have her morphine at the home just as easily as here. No point her blocking a hospital bed that could be better used by someone else.'

Professor Kneebone was edging away, his eyes flicking towards the doors. Dawn knew perfectly well what was going through his mind. This sort of conversation was *not* why Geoffrey Kneebone had put himself through fourteen years of surgical training. To be fair, he was an excellent surgeon, but what he liked best was snipping away in a nice, sterile environment with Radio 4 playing in the background and the patient out cold. Actually having to deal with awake, messy people was a lot more tricky. He left that side of things to Dawn, which was why the two of them normally worked together very well. Now here she was, breaking the agreement, expecting him to deal with her half of the problem. He exited the ward as quickly as he could, a long line of white-coated doctors and students trailing behind him like spume from a motor boat. Dawn drummed her fingers on the desk. Of course she knew the pressure there was on beds. But still. Once a patient was actually *in* one, the least they could do was treat them properly. She had promised Mrs Walker that she would help her. There must be something she could do.

She took Mrs Walker's enormous chart from its pigeonhole and sat down to go through it in detail. For the past few years, Mrs Walker had been resident in a nursing home called The Beeches. Dawn knew the name. She had often heard Dora talk about it with her friends.

'Ethel Hickey had to go there after her operation,' one of them had said. 'They seemed to have different staff working there every week. They gave her the wrong pills, and when she tried to tell them they said it was all in her head.'

'Janice Whitfield's husband – you know, the one who used to be in the Army? He was sent there after his stroke. He had to go to the bathroom but they didn't have anyone to help him, and when he had an accident he had to sit in it for five hours.'

'The trouble is,' Dora said, 'I don't think they pay their staff very well. It can't be very pleasant, a young person like that having to clean us old ones up, can it?'

'No. No.'

They had shaken their heads and sat in silence, their cups of tea balanced on their knees, perched like thin brown birds around Dora's gold three-piece suite.

Dawn tightened her lips. They couldn't send Mrs Walker back there. By the sound of things, if The Beeches had only been giving her half the morphine she was on here, they hadn't even noticed she was in pain. What if they could find her a nicer home? The difficulty with that was, her family would have to be involved. No one had come to visit Mrs Walker on Forest Ward, and according to the letter from the

Beeches she never got any visitors there either. But it was worth a try.

From the notes, she discovered that Mrs Walker's next of kin was her niece, a Mrs Heather Warmington, of Kent. Dawn rang the number. A woman answered.

'Mrs Warmington?'

'Yes?'

'This is Sister Dawn Torridge, calling from St Iberius Hospital. It's about your aunt, Ivy Walker—'

'Dead, is she?'

'Well – no.' Dawn was taken aback. 'But she is in quite a lot of pain.'

'Oh dear. But what can *I* do about it? You're the nurse, aren't you?'

Dawn said gently, 'Would you like to come in and see her?'

Heather Warmington gave a curt-sounding laugh. 'Sister, you've seen her. What would be the point? She wouldn't know me from the bin man.'

Then, as if realizing how that sounded, she changed her tone. 'Look. It's not as if I ever even knew her that well. The only reason the social workers put me down as next of kin was because there wasn't anyone else.'

'She doesn't have any other family? No children?'

'My mum said she'd had one child but it died as a baby. And her husband's not been around for as long as I can remember. Like I said – I hardly knew her. She lived abroad for years, didn't keep in touch much with my mum or any of the family. And I live miles away now and I've got my own kids to think of, so . . .' She tailed off.

'I thought,' Dawn said, 'that if we changed her to another nursing home?'

'But that's the one the council said she had to go to,' Heather Warmington said. 'And if she doesn't know where she is, then what's the difference?'

Dawn said nothing.

Heather Warmington sighed. 'Look,' she said. 'I do know Ivy was a very independent woman in her day. She travelled the world when she was young – on her own, which not many women did back then. She'd have hated to see herself the way she is now. Lying in that bed all day, not able to feed herself, not knowing who anyone is. Where's the dignity in it? She's eighty-four years old, for God's sake. And now she's got cancer. What's the use in prolonging things? Can't you just . . . you know . . . give her something?'

'Mrs Warmington—'

'I know, Sister, I know. The sanctity of life, and all that. Look, I'm sorry but I can't stop to chat. I've got the kids to pick up at three.'

The line went dead.

'The old finish-them-off routine, eh?' Mandy, one of the other nurses was at the desk, refilling a stapler. 'Probably wants to get her hands on the money.'

'I doubt if there is any,' Dawn said.

'No?' Mandy snapped the stapler shut. 'Well, then perhaps she's got a point. Sometimes you've got to wonder, haven't you, where we're going with these very old ones. But where would it end, I suppose? Next thing we'd be bumping off the more annoying relatives. And then, who knows?' She glared towards the spot where Dr Coulton had been standing earlier. 'Maybe even the staff. Fancy that Rude Ed saying we weren't giving the morphine properly! Arrogant twat.'

Before her shift ended, Dawn went back to check on Mrs Walker again. Her pain still hadn't settled. A lot of the discomfort seemed to be in her back. Dawn tried everything she could think of: rolling her from one side to the other, placing pillows beneath the knobbly spine to take the weight off. Nothing helped. She was reluctant to leave her. The evening shift only had three staff on instead of the usual daytime four. Unless there was an emergency, everyone would be far too busy to spend time with Mrs Walker. Dawn decided to stay on for a while; check on Mrs Walker again in an hour. In the meantime, she could work in her office on the Disaster Plan.

Dawn's office, at the end of the ward, was just large enough for a desk, a narrow filing cabinet and two chairs. On the wall above her desk was a cork notice-board, pinned with cards. 'Dear Matron. Thank you

for being so kind to my father during his illness . . .'
'Dear Sister Torridge, I was dreading my operation
but you made it so easy . . .' 'Dear Matron, Thank you
for always seeming to know just what I needed even
when I was too ill to say it . . .' Normally Dawn liked
having the cards there, but this evening the grateful
messages seemed to mock her. She sat at her desk and
opened up the large red folder in which she kept all
her Disaster Plan notes. At the top of the pile was the
hospital's current plan.

In the event of a major incident, read the first page,
A&E patients should form an orderly queue.

Who on earth, Dawn wondered, had written this?
Clearly not someone who had ever actually worked
in an A&E. Dawn had no illusions about how a
panicked urban population would behave in a crisis.
Hobbesian principles would apply. The hospital would
be overwhelmed. There was every chance they'd have
to call in the Army. Dawn couldn't say for certain, not
being privy to top government policy, but she strongly
suspected that in a genuinely serious catastrophe,
with nationally depleted resources, the only people
eligible for treatment would be healthy, skilled men
and women who were of fertile age. Everyone else
would be left to take their chances. The thought gave
her an odd feeling. Under those criteria, in another
few years she herself would no longer be eligible for
treatment.

She put the thought away and busied herself pinning blank A3 pages around the walls of the office. She would use these to write up clear guidelines, easy to read in an emergency. She was going to assume minimal supplies, loss of electrical power, a skeleton staff. Far from being able to call in extra workers, the hospital would likely find that even those people who were supposed to be on duty would stay at home to look after their families. But for those who would still come in and want to do what they could, Dawn's plan would aim to guide them.

She was so preoccupied that she lost all track of the time. When she next looked at the clock over her desk, it was ten past seven. She leaped up, stuffing her notes back into the folder. Milly would be waiting for her evening walk.

Elspeth, on the late shift, was sitting at the nurse's desk, reading a copy of *Hello!* magazine. She nearly dropped the magazine on the floor when Dawn came out of her office.

'Oh, Sister.' She shoved the *Hello!* under an X-ray. 'You're still here.'

'Just leaving now.' Dawn kept her tone mild. 'Everything all right?'

'Yes, fine. Actually, I was just about to do a quick round.'

'All right then. Have a good night.'

Dawn continued to the side room, though not

before she caught Elspeth looking at her watch, an incredulous and slightly scornful expression on her smooth, tanned face. Mrs Walker lay against her pillows with her eyes closed, her head dropping forward so that her chin almost touched her chest. Her breath went in, held for a few seconds, then pushed out again with a little slump of her shoulders. The sleep was probably more due to exhaustion than to anything else, but it was better than nothing.

Outside, the evening was dim and drizzly. Dawn put up her umbrella by the blue and white NHS sign at the entrance. A breeze lifted the edge of yet another enormous, glossy poster advertising the upcoming International Research Conference. Thursday, 27 April. *Tomorrow*, Dawn realized. At the bottom of the hill, the railway bridge over the road clanked and rattled as a train shrieked overhead. From underneath came the hollow roar of traffic: cars, taxis, green and yellow fluorescent ambulances. The bus to Silham Vale was just approaching the stop on St John's Road. Dawn ran to meet it.

She had the top deck to herself. The windows gave off a dirty, metallic smell. From downstairs came the heavy *clunk clunk* of the windscreen wipers. Passing the common, heading south towards Croydon, Dawn spotted an old man shuffling over the wet grass, carrying a plastic shopping bag. She recognized him. He had been a patient at St Iberius a few months ago.

Perforated ulcer; very septic. There'd been a time when Dawn had wondered if he would even make it. But here he was now, she was pleased to see, shaky but out and about. She often recognized regulars in the parks and streets around the hospital. She always found herself checking to see how they looked, whether they were coping, if they were doing well. It was as if, having once been under her care, they were still her responsibility. She was still their guardian, watching over them from the windows as she passed, touching the glass with her fingers to keep them safe.

In the night, the silence woke her. Dawn sat up in bed. Something was wrong! The house was too quiet. Three years of listening out for Dora meant that she was out of bed and halfway down the stairs before she remembered that, of course, Dora wasn't there any more.

She shivered on the bottom step, feeling foolish. The carriage clock on the sitting-room mantelpiece *tick-ticked* into the silence. On the carpet, a dark shadow moved: Milly, come from her basket in the kitchen to investigate.

'I can't believe you're moving back there,' Kevin had complained three years ago, shortly after Dora's first stroke. 'Silham Vale's a hole. A dump! There's nothing in it.'

'Dora's my family,' Dawn had pleaded trying to

placate him. 'She brought me up. I can't abandon her now.'

'But what about our flat here? What about *us*?'

'It's just for a while,' Dawn had soothed. 'Just until she's back on her feet.'

But then had come the second stroke. And then the cancer. The best that could be said for that was that it only lasted a few months.

Towards the end, Dora had developed spasms where her face had twitched and her arms jerked of their own accord, sometimes for hours at a time. Distressed, Dawn had called Dr Barnes out again.

'Not long to go now,' he had said in his matter-of-fact way. 'You've done very well to keep her going this far.' He added, 'The spasms may mean that the tumour has spread to her brain. I should warn you, sometimes people can notice a personality change.'

Dora *had* changed. Her plump, kindly face had become thin and sharp and bitter.

'Call yourself a nurse,' she spat at Dawn. 'I thought you could help me. But you've done nothing. You've just left me here to suffer.'

'Dora—'

'Leave me alone.' Dora struggled to face away. 'You're useless. I want to die.'

Hours later, as it happened, a massive blood clot had put an end to it all.

In the sitting-room, on the cabinet, was a photo, its

silver frame lit by the orange glow from the street lamp outside. Dora in her back garden, her arm around a child of about eleven in a pink coat. Both of them were smiling. That had been a day to celebrate. The first time in almost a year that Dawn had smiled.

She had worn that coat the night she'd come down from Cumbria, the week of the accident. The social worker had driven around and around the housing estates north of Croydon, searching for Crocus Road. Dawn had sat huddled in the back seat, her hands, her face, her mind all so frozen with cold and misery and despair she thought she would never thaw again. Then the lozenge of yellow on the wet path, the plump figure in the doorway. Dora's warm arms around her. 'Welcome, Dawn love. Welcome home.'

You're useless. I want to die.

After a lifetime of love, the hardest thing to bear was that they were the last words Dora ever spoke.

Chapter Three

Dawn's alarm went off at five thirty the next morning, the harsh, croaky buzz drilling through the chilly air. The rain was pounding on the window. Dawn stuck her hand out to press the snooze button. Then she lay, face down, her hand still on the clock, feeling as exhausted as if she had climbed out of a mine. Normally she was a good riser, out of bed at the first alarm, her mind bursting with plans and ideas for the day. But this morning, even after her shower, her head felt as swollen and bloated as a pumpkin. She towelled her hair dry, trying to remember what she had timetabled for today. A pressure-sore audit to review. A meeting with a sales rep about a new type of portable cardiac Resus kit. She pulled on her Sister's uniform, ironed from the night before, and examined herself in the mirror on the back of the wardrobe door.

She smoothed down the uniform. The navy, short-sleeved, polyester dress reached to her knee, cinched in at the waist with a canvas belt. Underneath, she wore dark woollen tights and black, lace-up shoes. In a million years you couldn't call it a glamorous look – but when you were on your feet all day you didn't care so much about that. She clipped her ID badge to her breast pocket and straightened her collar. She re-fastened her belt, positioning it so that the buckle sat dead in the centre.

Then, all of a sudden, she sagged. What was the point? All of this – ward rounds, audits, high-tech equipment – but people still got sick, didn't they? You could prolong things, drag things out, but no matter what you did people still grew old and suffered and died. Francine was right. Who cared about standards any more? Nowadays people wanted trendy careers – media, sport, fashion. Living-in-the-moment sort of jobs, where you did things for yourself instead of striving for the impossible for someone else. Priya had been an excellent nurse, gentle and conscientious. But she had left now to have her baby, and who was to say she'd ever come back? And in her place; bored, lazy Elspeth and surly Clive. The best, apparently, that the nursing agency had to offer.

Dawn shook herself. What was with her today? One chilly morning and she was throwing in the towel. She collected her coat, bag and umbrella and went out into the dank dawn. Milly watched her to the gate before creeping back to curl up on her warm, fleece, paw-patterned rug in the porch.

Forest Ward was so quiet that Dawn wondered at first if she'd got the time wrong.

'Where is everyone?' she asked Lorna, the night nurse. Normally by this hour the overhead lights were all on, the patients out of bed and making their way to the bathrooms, the junior doctors beginning to trickle in for their rounds.

Lorna gave her a funny look. 'Today's that big meeting? The research one the posters've all been on about?'

The International Research Conference. Of course! She really wasn't with it today. It was the last thing she felt like doing but she really should go down there and put in an appearance. As the Matron she would be expected to be present, for the opening speakers at least.

'How was Mrs Walker last night?' she asked.

'Bad.' Lorna shook her head. 'Hardly got any sleep at all.'

Dawn sighed. 'I'll speak to Professor Kneebone again.'

'He's been in already,' Lorna said. 'Said she's to be discharged today.'

'Today? But . . .' Through the glass pane in the side-room door Mrs Walker could be seen, trembling and white-faced against her pillows. 'We can't possibly send her out today. Look at her.'

'Sorry, Sister.' Lorna pushed her bottom lip out in sympathy. 'He said to tell you he knows how you feel. But he's got a couple of urgent cases waiting and he really needs the bed.'

The auditorium was a sea of dark suits and white coats. Every seat was taken but still people came pushing through the doors, squeezing down the rows, standing along the walls at the back. Professor Kneebone, nattily dressed in a pinstriped suit and yellow silk tie, stood on the podium and spoke into the microphone.

'We are delighted,' he boomed, 'to welcome this morning some of the world's greatest experts in the field of Systemic Inflammation. St Iberius is proud of our own recent achievements in this field, some of which we hope to present to you today. Meanwhile, if we could all welcome our first guest speaker: Professor Robert Klinefelter from Philadelphia.'

Applause from the crowd. Professor Klinefelter, very stiff and serious with a tiny brown goatee, mounted the steps to the podium. He cleared his throat into the microphone.

'Good morning, ladies and gentlemen. My presentation, entitled "Apoptosis and the Neutrophil", will attempt to explain . . .'

Dawn tuned out. Her thoughts turned back to Mrs Walker, leaving them today to return to that understaffed home, where by all accounts she would lie alone and uncared-for in some bleak, dead room. The sense of failure was very strong. It went against all of her principles to discharge a patient in that condition. Not only had they done nothing to help her, she was, if anything, actually worse than when she'd been admitted. Her discomfort seemed to have increased by the day. Dawn gripped her hands together. What on earth was she doing, sitting here listening to someone drone on about lab experiments while all the time a real patient was in distress up on her ward? She had promised Mrs Walker that she would help her and now she only had a matter of hours left to think of something. She rose from her seat. As she made her way towards the exit, the people in her row had to turn sideways and pull their feet back to let her pass but no one complained. Everyone recognized and respected Dawn's navy uniform. In no time at all, she was on the steps, climbing to the doorway with the green Exit sign and out into the cool of the hall.

On Forest Ward, Clive was giving Mrs Walker her breakfast with his back to the glass pane in the door. Even at the best of times Clive never looked exactly thrilled to be at work, but today, if possible, he appeared even more aggrieved than usual. He sighed, rolling his head around on his neck, tapping his foot as he waited for Mrs Walker to be ready for her next spoonful. Watching him, Dawn thought: *He really hates this. Working here.* Once or twice she had tried to talk to him about it, to find out if there was something in particular bothering him, but he had been abrupt, seeming to resent her prying into his private business. The conversation had gone nowhere. Mrs Walker lay in bed, in her too-large nightgown, looking exhausted after her sleepless night. She twisted her head from side to side, doing her best to avoid the porridge that Clive was thrusting towards her.

'Eat it, can't you?' he snapped, shoving the spoon hard at her mouth.

That was when it happened.

Dawn had her hand on the door, about to enter the room. At the same moment, Mrs Walker lifted her hands to push the spoon away. A pillow became dislodged and she slithered down the bed. The spoon was catapulted from Clive's hand. A large splodge of grey purée spattered down the front of his tunic.

Clive flung the bowl down.

'For *Christ's* sake!'

As Dawn watched in disbelief, he grabbed Mrs Walker by the arms. Then he hauled her back up the pillows so violently that her head flew back and banged off the bars at the top of the bed. Her eyelids fluttered; she gave a cry of fright and pain.

Dawn pushed open the door.

'Clive.' A tightness in her chest, as if she couldn't quite catch her breath. 'A word, please.'

Outside the room, she said, '*What* just happened in there?'

Clive, red-faced and furious at having been caught, spread his hands out. 'Well, what was I supposed to do? She wouldn't eat the bloody stuff. Kept mumbling instead of getting on with it.'

'And you didn't try to find out what was wrong?'

'She doesn't *know* what's wrong.' Clive's lip lifted in a sneer. 'I haven't got the whole morning to spend on her. If she hasn't got a clue what's happening, she should just cooperate and let the staff get on with their jobs.'

'Clive. She has cancer. She is in *pain*. *Look* at her.'

Dawn's voice had risen. She was aware of Mandy hurrying over to see what was going on but her field of vision had narrowed, closing off the view around her until all she could see was Clive's porridge-spattered uniform, his sweaty face, the greasy hair he never seemed to wash. Why on earth was he working in a hospital? This was his eighth week here and he seemed to despise the place more every minute. Why do nursing if you hated it so much? Why come in here, day after day, and treat patients for whom you seemed to feel nothing but loathing and contempt?

She said, 'Get Mrs Walker her painkiller, please.'

'I'll get it when I'm ready.'

'*Excuse* me?'

A white dot had appeared on each of Clive's nostrils. 'Don't you tell me what to do. I am a professional nurse. I don't need you interfering, telling me how to go about my work.'

Dawn was tall enough so that her face was almost level with Clive's. She drew herself up further. In a loud, clear voice so that he would understand, she said, '*I* am in charge here. And you will do what I say.'

They faced each other, like cowboys in a Western. Clive's pupils were enormous, black and dilated with rage. For a moment, Dawn wondered what would happen. In all her time as a ward sister she had never reached this level of confrontation with a member of staff. Ever since Clive had started here he had made it plain that he had a problem taking orders from her – muttering under his breath or going about the work with deliberate slowness – but this was the first time he had displayed such open contempt for her authority. Well, he wasn't going to get away with it. How dare he treat a patient on her ward like that? How *dare* he! The anger rose in her again. It must have shown in her face because Clive backed down.

'I'll get the morphine,' he muttered.

'No.' Dawn had changed her mind. She didn't want him in there with Mrs Walker. 'You see to your other patients. I'll take over here.'

61

Clive said nothing but his eyes flattened again. He walked away without a word. The ward had gone silent. No one spoke; the breakfast trolleys had stopped squeaking; even the incessant ringing of the phones seemed to have been put on hold. Dawn was aware that she was shaking. What sort of impression was she creating, flushed and large in the middle of the ward? Clive had been out of order but the way she had handled the situation had been completely inappropriate. Humiliating a staff member like that in front of everyone. She'd never done that before, lost control like that. What on earth was the matter with her?

Mandy was beside her. 'Are you all right?' Concern in her voice, but a touch of glee also. This was news! The Matron having a meltdown. It would be all over the hospital by lunchtime.

'I'm fine.' Dawn made an enormous effort to sound calm. 'Thanks, Mandy. Have you got the morphine keys?'

In the stock room, Mandy opened the safe and took out an ampoule. She and Dawn signed for it in the ledger. Dawn took the morphine to the side room. Mrs Walker was shuddering and breathing hard, her hands to her face, the most agitated Dawn had ever seen her.

'I want to go,' she kept crying. 'I want to go.'

'I'm sorry. I'm so sorry. Shh. This will help.'

Dawn injected the morphine into her drip. But a full ten minutes later, Mrs Walker was still trembling, her face contorted, the *blip blip blip* on her monitor pelting along. Dawn held up the syringe and stared at it in frustration. What was *wrong* with this stuff? She might as well be giving water.

For the first time, something occurred to her. All along, she'd been assuming that the pain problem was due to Mrs Walker herself. Had she been looking at it from the wrong angle? Could it be the *morphine* that was the problem?

She returned to the fluorescent glare of the stock room. The two halves of the broken ampoule were still on the counter where she had left them. She picked them up and reread the label. She went through every single word, double-checking each detail. Correct drug. Check. Correct dose. Check. Not out of date . . . The glass had been intact when Mandy had removed the ampoule from the safe. Dawn had broken it open herself and had not left it unattended for one second between opening it and drawing the contents into the syringe. The company that supplied the drug was a reputable one. St Iberius had never had a problem with their products before.

No. The problem was not the morphine. Dawn shook her head and threw the fragments into the bin.

Back in the side room, she sat by Mrs Walker's bed.

'I don't know.' She gave a sigh. 'I really don't know what else I can do here.'

Rain spattered against the window. The roofs of the brown South London housing estates were smudged with cloud, as if the edges had been rubbed out by an eraser. As long as Mrs Walker was here, at least, Dawn could protect her from the Clives and Rude Eds of this world. But in a few hours she would be back at The Beeches where by the looks of that pressure sore she would be left to lie in the same spot day after day. Not one person would come to see her or comfort her or speak up for her. She would be abandoned, suffering and in pain, to live her last days out alone.

'I've let you down.' Dawn slumped her shoulders. 'I've been useless, haven't I?'

Mrs Walker moved in the bed.

'Please.' Her voice was a whisper. 'Please. I want to go.'

'Where would you like to go?' Dawn leaned forward and took her hands. 'You tell me, and I promise you, we'll go there.'

'I want to go to heaven.'

Mrs Walker was sitting up in her bed. The grey light from the window shone on her face. The lines around her eyes and down the sides of her mouth spoke of her exhaustion. For the first time, her gaze was not moving about, restlessly searching the room, but steady, looking straight at Dawn.

Dawn looked back at her.

She said, 'You want to go to heaven.'

'Yes.'

The drumming of the rain continued. Mrs Walker's eyes remained on Dawn's. Her eyes were wide and still, and the grey sky was in them.

Dawn felt as if she was in a dream. She squeezed Mrs Walker's hands. She whispered, 'Don't say any more.'

The stock room next door was dazzling, too bright. She had to wait for her vision to adjust so that she could see. The morphine, of course, was locked away and Mandy had the keys. But all the other drugs and medicines were in the big cupboard at the back where anybody could walk in and take them.

Hurry. Hurry. She stood before the shelves, looking along the rows of familiar bottles. She had never thought of any of them in this context before; but that wasn't a problem. It was just a matter of looking at things in a different way.

Two things were important.

First, it had to be quick. The Beeches staff might be here at any minute to collect her.

And second, it had to be painless. Mrs Walker had been through enough.

On the middle shelf sat a box of plastic vials. Around each vial was a scarlet label, a vivid splash of warning in the white.

Potassium Chloride.

In small doses, one of the most commonly used drugs on the ward. But a large dose, given quickly through a vein, would stop the heart within seconds. The only problem was, the injection could be painful. But she could add some local anaesthetic to the syringe.

Easy. Easy. When you knew what you were doing.

Dawn took two vials of potassium and drew them into a syringe. She added a couple of mls of local anaesthetic. Then she threw the empty vials into the sharps bin. She put the syringe in the pocket of her dress and stepped out of the room.

The ward was peaceful. Morning visiting hour was over. From here Dawn could see the rows of patients in their beds, dozing, reading, listening to headphones. At bed fourteen, Elspeth was showing Trudy the new student how to set up a nasogastric feed. Across the floor, in the Day Ward, Mandy was covering the steady stream of admissions and discharges. Clive had left. His shift had ended at twelve thirty. Dawn had seen him with his backpack on his shoulder, slamming through the doors to the hall. It had been a relief to see him go. Apart from the nurses on duty, no other staff were about. All the pharmacists, dieticians and physiotherapists were at the research conference. The ward was the quietest Dawn had ever seen it.

If she was a person who believed in signs, surely this would count as one?

The side room was dim, filled with the patter of rain and the *blip blip blip* of the ECG. Mrs Walker lay on her pillows with her eyes closed, her fists clenched on the sheets. Her breaths came out in a hiss: *Swishh*, *swishh*, like car tyres on a wet road. At the sound of the door she moved her head.

'It's all right,' Dawn said softly. 'It's only me.'

She closed the door. Then she went to pull the blinds down over the glass. She tugged at the cord but nothing happened.

Oh yes. Broken. Clive had said.

Dawn paused. It was a nuisance. Through the window, she could see Mandy in the Day Ward, busy with a patient. Her back was to Dawn. The Day Ward was quite a distance away, thirty feet at least. To the right, the main ward and Elspeth and Trudy were not visible from here. To the left, the double doors to the hall were tightly closed. There was no one to look in, no one to see her. And if there was, so what? She was the Matron. She had every right to be in here.

But the broken blind must have unsettled her, because as she approached the bed she tripped on the ECG cable. The lead was yanked from the monitor. Instantly the alarm shrieked: *BLEEE-BLEEE-BLEEE-BLEEEE*.

The high-pitched screech drove straight through

Dawn's head. She shot her finger out and stabbed the Alarm Silence button. The shrieking stopped. Hands shaking, she shoved the cable back into its socket. The ECG, silently now, resumed its green spiky progress across the screen. Dawn glanced again at the window. Mandy's back was still to her. No one had come running. No one seemed to have heard. But now, as though roused by the blast of sound, a cloud of doubts had risen to flap and wheel about inside her mind.

Was she really, seriously, thinking of doing this?

Of course she knew why this sort of thing was illegal. *Where would it end?* Mandy had asked, and she was right. You couldn't have just anyone allowed to go about killing patients. Most people simply did not have the ability – or the character – to be trusted to make that kind of decision. Imagine, heaven forbid, someone like Clive having that sort of power over people's lives!

But it was different for her.

There was no point in being modest. Dawn knew that she was an exceptional nurse. All through her training she had come top in her exams, had won the gold medal at her graduation. She was the youngest Matron ever to be appointed at St Iberius; she had won the post even over Francine who, in fact, had more experience. Over the years she had come to learn that in a crisis she could trust herself. She'd been faced with some difficult decisions, decisions that many other nurses might have hesitated to make. Jack Benson, for example, only a few days ago. He might so easily have died, but thanks to what Dawn had done his life had been saved. In all her years of nursing, her instincts had never let her down.

Mrs Walker's clenched fist lay on the blanket. Dawn touched the back of it.

'Ivy?'

Then she jumped back. Mrs Walker had answered with a sharp intake of breath. Her shoulders drove upwards until they were right under her ears. A deep line appeared between her eyes. She held the breath for a moment, then released it with a long sound, somewhere between a sob and a sigh: 'Aaaaah.' Dawn let her own breath out, and felt all her doubts fly with it. It was enough. Mrs Walker was dying anyway. Dying in great pain, and it would only get worse. She was her patient, her responsibility. She would not stand here and watch her suffer and do nothing.

She attached the syringe to the drip in Mrs Walker's arm. Then she pressed the plunger. The local anaesthetic had done its work. Mrs Walker did not flinch. Dawn pressed the plunger the rest of the way. Going in . . . going in . . . and now it was gone, it was in, it was done; it was over. Seconds left. If that.

At the last minute, as if for reassurance, even though

she knew that none was needed, she put her hand on Mrs Walker's.

She had never known Ivy Walker. Never would now. But she had nursed her enough to guess a few things about her. That delicate face, now drawn and taut, had known its share of laughter. You could see the tiny lines at the corners of her eyes. She had no one in the world now, but once she had been loved. Her husband had asked her to marry him. And pressed her to him with dizzy relief when she said, 'Yes.' She'd had a child once, who for a little while had been the whole world to her and she to him.

Mrs Walker's shoulders were relaxing. The ECG spikes on the monitor were flattening and slowing. The gaps between them came longer. Dawn should leave. She should leave now, while no one was around.

When she was thirty, Ivy Walker had stood on the gangplank of a ship, her suitcase at her feet, and gazed about her in the balmy, unfamiliar breeze. When she was twenty, men had turned to stare at her as she passed, and she had tossed her hair back and laughed and walked on. Because she had all the time in the world. And when she was two, she had sat on a kerb and played in the mud, and everyone who had seen her there with the sun in her hair and the world at her feet had felt a sharp wrench of hope and longing that they could hardly understand.

Dawn should leave. She really should leave now.

One final green spike on the monitor. A pause. Then the spiking ceased. All that was left were random, crazy loops trailing across the screen, like a thread fluttering in a breeze. Mrs Walker's shoulders sank from her chin. The deep lines of suffering faded from her face.

And still Dawn stayed, and still she held her hand. Because no one should die alone.

Chapter Four

It was still raining when the bus dropped her at Silham Vale. The sky was like a dark, dripping bowl upturned over London. Halfway down Crocus Road, the streetlights blinked on. The roofs of the 1930s houses, shining through the mist, appeared otherworldly, not quite real.

In the porch of number 59, Milly yawned and pushed herself up from her rug.

'Hey, girl. Hey, girl.' Dawn crouched beside her. Milly's chunky body was so warm and solid and safe. Still sleepy, Milly pushed the top of her head into Dawn's knees. They stayed like that for a while, Dawn pulling over and over at the floppy ears, Milly enjoying the unexpected massage. The tip was missing from her left ear where another dog in the home had chewed it off years ago before Dora had rescued her. After a couple of minutes, Dawn released her and stood up.

'Let's get you some dinner,' she said.

In the kitchen, however, the gleam of the fluorescent light on the white fridge and washing-machine made her pause. All of a sudden she was right back in the cold, clean stock room on Forest Ward.

No one had seen her leave Mrs Walker's side room. She had slipped into the stock room and thrown the empty potassium syringe into the sharps bin, making sure to push it right to the bottom. Then she had gone to her office and concentrated on her Disaster Plan.

The knock came an hour later: Mandy in her pale blue tunic and trousers, her frizzy blonde hair framing her face like a halo.

'Just to let you know, Dawn. Mrs Walker has passed away.'

'I see.'

The flowery thank-you cards, pinned to the board in front of her. *Dear Matron, You knew what I wanted, even when I was too ill to say it . . .*

'It was the new student who found her,' Mandy said. 'I sent her in to see if Mrs Walker needed anything and there she was just lying there, cold. The student's in hysterics. She came running out in a right state. She's gone to have a bawl in the toilets. Honestly,' Mandy rolled her eyes, 'you'd think no one ever died in a hospital.'

She added, 'I didn't call the crash team, is that all right? The notes said: *Do Not Resuscitate.*'

'No, that's fine.' Dawn's voice sounded much more casual than she had expected. In fact, all of this was happening so normally it was beginning to seem as if it was just one more natural death. Mandy, busy fixing her hair by the door, seemed so unperturbed. To her, Mrs Walker's death was nothing more than the natural end to a life that had run its course. Which, if you thought about it, was exactly what it was.

'Thanks, Mandy,' she said. 'I'll let Professor Knee-bone know.'

The one tricky moment had come during the phone call.

Professor Kneebone said, 'Well, it's for the best. Not going anywhere, was she? You'll let the family know, Sister?'

'Of course.'

Dawn was about to put down the phone when Professor Kneebone added, 'Oh, and Sister, will you inform them about the PM?'

A sharp rattle of rain on the window.

'The PM?'

'Yes. Quite a sudden departure, wasn't it? Interesting to pinpoint the cause.'

Dawn's hand had stiffened around the receiver. A post-mortem! The idea had never occurred to her. And why should it? Why on earth would anyone order a post-mortem on an elderly, terminally ill inpatient

74

who must have been seen by a dozen hospital staff in the weeks before she had died?

But of course Professor Kneebone would want a post-mortem! Of course he would want to know what had happened. It didn't look good that Mrs Walker had died on the very day he had said she was fit to leave the hospital.

As if from nowhere, Dawn heard her own voice, calmly addressing the receiver: 'Yes,' she said, 'yes, it *would* be interesting to know. Of course, if you think about it, there are several reasons why she might have died.'

'Well—'

'What with her being so elderly,' Dawn went on firmly, 'and with that cancer diagnosis.' She wasn't even thinking about what she was saying; her brain seemed to have gone on to autopilot, the way it often did in an emergency when there wasn't a second to be wasted. 'And she's been through so much already. All those tests and investigations she'd had before you came along and worked out what was going on.'

'Well, you know,' Professor Kneebone sounded pleased, 'ovarian cancer can be tricky.'

'And then, of course, the family . . .'

'Distressing for them, you're saying?' She could tell by Kneebone's tone that he was starting to lose interest. 'It's a good point, Sister. Well, we've got enough to go on, I suppose. End-stage metastatic cancer and advanced Alzheimer's Disease. That'll be plenty to put on the death cert.'

'Of course, Professor. Whatever you think.'

The air in the room seemed to glitter when she had hung up. She felt the way she had the time she'd gone up in the gondola on her very first skiing holiday with Kevin, and only realized when she had looked out half-way that they were suspended above a vertiginous drop down the valley. Although, now she thought about it, she remembered something: even if there had been a post-mortem, the potassium wouldn't have shown up anyway. Or no, wait. Wasn't it that it *would* have shown, but that a high potassium was so common in dying people that no one would think twice about it?

She couldn't remember now. It made no difference. There wasn't going to be one anyway.

She went to bed early that night. Usually she read for a little while before going to sleep but tonight she switched her lamp off as soon as she was under the duvet and lay gazing upwards into the dark.

She often did this after a difficult case: spent time going over the incident, picturing the events that had led up to it, wondering if there was anything she could have done differently. Tonight, though, it was odd, but when she tried to recall the events of the afternoon there were strange gaps in her memory, like a DVD that kept skipping. She could *see* what had happened, see herself moving about in her navy uniform, drawing the potassium into the syringe. But she couldn't seem to get inside herself, to remember how she had felt, what had impelled her to move on to each next step. It was as if the woman she was remembering was a completely different person altogether.

First Do No Harm.

Dawn shifted in the bed.

You had no choice in this, she told herself. *No choice!* She had been over and over it in her mind. Everything she could think of to help Mrs Walker she had tried. She had given the maximum possible dose of morphine, discussed alternative treatments with the surgeons, tried to get the family on board. None of them had worked. Mrs Walker's suffering had continued – and things would only have got worse for her. Dawn was not guessing; it was not speculation; she *knew*. She had watched Dora go through the very same thing until the pain had got so bad that Dora had said, 'I want to die.' Mrs Walker herself had wanted it to end. She had said to Dawn, 'I want to go to heaven.' How should Dawn have responded to that? Said, 'Shh, shh, you don't mean it,' and walked away?

Where would it end? Mandy had asked. Yes, the law was there for a reason. There had to be a taboo. The slope on the other side was much, much too slippery. Years of nursing had taught Dawn only too well how easy it was for hospital staff to get used to the deaths of other people, how appallingly quickly the justifications would arise as to why that sick, elderly person should not live too long, take up that hospital bed, sit on that inheritance.

But where did the law leave someone like Mrs Walker?

Dawn lay with her hands folded on her stomach, staring ahead of her at the bedroom window. Through the thin fabric of her curtains came the fuzzy orange glow from the streetlamp.

Sometimes, when you were responsible for someone – when you knew for a fact that you could trust your own abilities – you had to make a decision. And what she had done, she had done in Mrs Walker's best interests. Not for the family; not for the hospital; not for herself. But for the patient, and for the patient alone. In this one case, therefore, there was no slippery slope to apply.

Her muscles relaxed. Her limbs grew heavy, sinking into the sheets. It had been the right thing to do. It had. Mrs Walker was safe now, free of all pain. Dawn's eyelids drooped. The rain had started up again, a soft patter on the glass, soothing and pleasant, like the rushing of a stream.

Something made her open her eyes again. A car, turning down Crocus Road, going somewhere, perhaps important, in the night. First came the light from the headlamps, arcing between the gap in the curtains, sweeping over the ceiling. Then the hiss of wet tyres, swishing on the tarmac.

The stiff shoulders falling. The lines of suffering fading from her face. *Swishh, swishh.* It's all right now. How peaceful her face had been.

The St Iberius canteen was like a school gymnasium: vast, wooden-floored and slightly grubby, filled with rows of plastic chairs and melamine tables. A trellis and some ferns in china pots separated the staff seating areas from the main. At twelve thirty the noise was just building: cutlery rattling, chairs scraping, trays clashing. Staff poured through the doors in their tunics and trousers, the colours varying according to the speciality: ward nurses (pale blue), radiographers (purple), theatre staff (dark green). Giant steel vats gave off the smells of curry and goulash.

Dawn placed a sandwich on her tray and joined the queue for the till. Behind her, a voice said, 'Good afternoon, Sister.'

Dawn turned. To her surprise, the speaker was Dr Coulton.

'Hello,' she said politely. *What on earth did he want?* This was the first time she had heard him speak to a nurse other than to be patronizing or to snap out an order.

Everything about Dr Coulton was long and thin and pale: his bony limbs, his narrow, dolichocephalic head, his white coat, starched and pristine, despite the fact that hardly any of the other doctors wore them any more. Even his lips were little more than two white lines in his face. The light from the window gleamed on his forehead, making it seem even higher than it was. He looked like the stereotype of a mad scientist from a cartoon, plotting to blow up the world.

'You know,' he said. 'You and I appear to have got off to a bad start the other day. Perhaps we should try again.' He held his hand out. 'Edward Coulton.'

His smile showed too many teeth, as if his lips weren't quite used to the movement. Dawn took his hand.

'Dawn Torridge,' she said.

Dr Coulton's teeth showed again.

'I was very impressed,' he said, 'with what you did for Mr Benson the other day. It turns out you did exactly the right thing.'

'I see.'

'Yes. And you'll be pleased to hear he's doing very well now. He came off the ventilator this morning.'

'Well, that's good news.' It *was*. And it was good of Dr Coulton to tell her about it. He must have known how concerned she would be.

'Of course,' Dr Coulton added, 'Mr Benson isn't the only person for whom you've made a difference.

I also admire what you did very recently for another patient of ours.'

'Oh? Who was that?'

'Mrs Ivy Walker.'

Dawn looked sharply back at him but he didn't seem to notice. He had turned to the snack stand and was busy studying the sausage rolls and pasties.

'What do you mean?' she asked.

Dr Coulton selected a pastry and placed it on his tray. He turned back to Dawn.

'Hmm?' he said. He turned back to Dawn. 'Oh, the other day. On the ward round? When you asked Professor Kneebone what else could be done for her pain. I admired the way you were the only one of us who seemed to be thinking laterally about the issue.'

'The ward round . . .' Dawn became aware that the queue had moved forward. A large gap had opened up in front of her. The ward round! Of course! She shook her head at herself. Talk about paranoid. Clearly Dr Coulton was one of those people who couldn't help sounding menacing even when he was just trying to make perfectly civil conversation. In fact, this was the most pleasant she had ever seen him. Perhaps they had all misjudged him. His previous arrogance could simply have been due to shyness.

'Thank you.' She slid her tray forward again on the rack. 'It's just a shame that Mrs Walker couldn't have been helped.'

Dr Coulton followed her. 'But she can. I spoke to the pain team about her yesterday. They're coming to see her today.'

'Today?' Dawn stopped pushing the tray. 'But – Mrs Walker is dead.'

'Dead?' Dr Coulton's eyebrows climbed on his forehead.

'Yesterday afternoon. I thought you would have heard.'

'No one told me.' He seemed astonished. 'What happened? I examined her thoroughly myself, only yesterday morning. I wouldn't have thought she was anywhere close to dying.'

'She was just . . . found.' Dawn gripped the edge of her tray. 'We think it might have been a blood clot.'

'I see.'

'Anyway,' despite herself she had started to babble, 'I don't see how the pain team could have helped. Professor Kneebone said she was too frail for any kind of surgery . . . You heard him . . . He said she'd never survive it.'

Dr Coulton waved his hand dismissively. 'Palliative care isn't Professor Kneebone's area. The pain team is used to dealing with very frail people. They said there was plenty they could do. In fact, with proper pain management, she might have been fit enough for surgery. We might have had a shot at taking out that tumour . . .' His pale eyes were staring at her. 'I'm sorry, Sister. Are you all right?'

'Excuse me.' Dawn put her tray back on the trolley and made for the exit.

The Ladies was a few feet down the hall. Dawn pushed open the door. The room, with its row of sinks and plywood toilet cubicles, was garishly lit, smelling of disinfectant, and, thankfully, empty of people. Dawn leaned on the edge of the nearest sink. *With proper pain management, she might have had surgery* . . . Mrs Walker could have been cured! She'd got it all wrong. No! No, she hadn't. Rude Ed was the one who was wrong. Professor Kneebone was the senior consultant. If he said Mrs Walker was unsuitable for treatment, then . . .

It was with a shock that it came to her. Rude Ed and his diagnosis were not the issue here. The issue was that an elderly, ill, vulnerable woman had looked to her – the Matron – for help and protection. And what had Dawn done? She had gone to her room and deliberately injected her with a syringe full of poison. The edge of the sink was slimy beneath her fingers. First Do No Harm! What she had done went against everything she had ever learned, taught, practised as a nurse.

It was murder.

The floor seemed to tilt under her feet.

She had murdered someone. That was the reality.

No matter how she tried to justify it to herself, that was how others would see it. What in God's name had she done? What had possessed her? How had she ever thought it was OK?

The bathroom door clattered open. Dazed, Dawn swung to the taps. Two middle-aged women, festooned with umbrellas and raincoats, entered midway through a conversation: '. . . so he told her to keep her feet up, and she said, "Love, you try doing that when you've got three kids . . ."'

The women made for the mirrors, patting down their hair, wiping the rain from their faces. Dawn kept her head down, rubbing her hands over and over under the sloshing water. She had no idea which tap was hot and which cold.

'I said it to Denise,' one of the women shouted over the roar of the hand-drier. 'I said to her, "If it was me I'd have had out years ago."'

The other woman, standing next to Dawn, was looking at her with a curious expression. Dawn realized that she had been washing her hands continuously for the past five minutes. A streak of dried soap was smeared on the wall behind the sink. She pulled a paper towel from the dispenser and began to scrub at the smear.

The women nodded to each other.

'Good to see that,' one of them said. 'Standards. The return of the Matron.'

They exited the bathroom. The doors clattered closed, the talk and footsteps faded. Dawn turned the taps off and threw the paper towel in the bin. She placed her hands on the sink and stared at herself in the mirror. Her washed-out face and thin, fair hair were much too pale for her navy uniform. The spaces under her eyes were scooped-out, purplish shadows. She could be seventy-five, not thirty-five. Still, she looked normal enough to return to the ward. It was time to pull herself together and get on with her afternoon.

As soon as she saw the side room again, however, she knew she couldn't face looking at it for the rest of the day. The bed was stripped to its waterproof mattress, the bare, scrubbed surface a blatant reminder that someone had recently died on it. The ECG wires trailed over the monitor, dangling towards the ground like strands of dead ivy.

Dawn found Mandy in the staff room.

'Mandy, are we still quiet?'

'Quietest we've been for a while,' Mandy said cheerfully, rapping on the wooden arm of her chair. 'No real sickies today.'

'In that case,' Dawn said, 'I think I'll take off early.'

'Ooh.' Mandy stared. Dawn never left work early. 'Something nice planned?'

'No. I've got a headache.'

'Oh, poor you. You do look a bit peaky. Have you tried taking a paracetamol?'

'I will do,' Dawn said. 'In the meantime, I'll take some paperwork and do it from home. If you need me, I'll be on my mobile.'

'Yeah, course.' Dawn could feel Mandy still gaping after her as she went down to her office. She picked out a couple of bulging files from the cabinet and left the ward, turning her head away from the side room as she passed. She went along the hall to the changing-room, tapped the code into the security pad and opened the door. Then she stopped.

Her locker being one of those nearest to the entrance, she saw it right away. The metal door with her name on it swung open, the lock buckled and twisted on the floor. Her coat lay beside it in a crumpled heap. Her bag had been emptied and flung under a bench. The contents – keys, papers, her wallet – were scattered all over the room.

Dawn went straight to the phone on the wall and dialled the number for security. Within minutes, two large men in navy ribbed sweaters were prowling the room. This was a serious incident. A Matron didn't get burgled every day.

'Anything missing?' Jim Evans, the head of security asked, hoisting the radio-laden waistband of his trousers up under his belly.

'Just some cash.' Dawn had gathered her belongings back into her bag and checked the contents of her wallet. 'Maybe ten pounds.'

'Any other lockers affected?'

'No. Just mine, as far as I can see.'

Jim looked at the locker and clicked his tongue. 'Nearest the door. Unlucky. We've had a few incidents like this recently. Patients' bedside lockers being cleaned out while they're in theatre; nasty stuff like that. We've got our eye on a couple of members of the public but the trouble is proving anything. We need cameras on every floor, not just the main hall, but the problem is funding. There's always some doc needs a new scanner or kidney machine or something. Which I respect, Matron; but a hospital needs security as well. If you get a chance, you might mention that at your next meeting.'

The other man was examining the door.

'Look,' he said. 'This is how they got in.'

On the wall beside the security pad was printed a row of numbers in biro. Jim Evans shook his head. 'That's the junior staff doing that,' he said. 'So they remember the code. Trouble is, other people can see it as well. Gives them access to all sorts of places they shouldn't.'

'I'll send a memo around. Thanks, Jim.' Dawn just wanted to get home. She really did have a headache now. She went to put her arm into her coat and found the sleeve coming away in her hand. It had been ripped – or slashed – completely away from the shoulder.

Jim pursed his lips into a whistle shape. 'Now that's a new one. I've not seen that before. Normally they just take the money and scarper. This is nasty, this is. Damaging property like that. Take the money if you have to, but there's no need for that. Don't you worry, Matron. We'll get them.'

Behind the macho, eighteen-stone, radio-clad exterior was a genuine kindness and concern. To Jim Evans, this was just one more random, opportunistic burglary. But to Dawn, walking down the hill outside the hospital with her ruined coat on her arm, it was much more than that. In all the time she had worked here, nothing like this had ever happened to her before. It was as if St Iberius, the place where she had always felt wanted and needed, was sending her a warning: *Get out*.

Chapter Five

Mrs Walker's funeral took place on Saturday morning.

'Ten o'clock,' the brisk-sounding female manager of The Beeches had told Dawn on the phone. 'At Bixworth Park Crematorium. Do you know where that is?'

'I'll find it.' Dawn was writing the address into her notebook. 'Will it be in the chapel, or . . . ?'

'The chapel, yes. We're assuming Church of England . . . although, in fact, we're not actually sure . . . You wouldn't happen to know, would you, Matron?'

'No,' Dawn said. 'I'm sorry, but I didn't actually know Mrs Walker very well. I only met her when she was in with us.'

'Oh, right?' A hint of curiosity in the Beeches manager's tone. Hospital staff didn't normally attend the funerals of patients they hardly knew.

On her way to the crematorium, Dawn stopped at a florist's in Thornton Heath. The tiny shop was crammed with flowers: bright pink and yellow carnations, orange, sunshiny gerbera wrapped in cellophane, tall, purple irises in vases. The Sympathy section down at the back had a more sober, respectful colour scheme. Dawn spent several minutes looking over the muted cream and pale pink bouquets and chose the nicest arrangement she could see: a spray of white and red roses nestled in dark, waxy leaves.

'Red and white together.' Dora would have tutted. 'Very bad luck for an ill person.' But it could hardly matter now, and the roses were beautiful, luscious and velvety, dotted with tiny droplets of water. The air around them was filled with a delicate fragrance.

She was the first to arrive at the crematorium chapel. *Jerusalem* was playing on pan-pipes through a set of hidden speakers as she entered. The air smelled warm and scratchy – most likely due to the brown carpet tiles lining the walls and ceiling. Walking up the aisle between the rows of chairs, Dawn thought how much the room resembled one of those American courtrooms you saw on TV. Except for the coffin at the front.

The vicar, a middle-aged woman in a grey shirt and dog-collar, was at the lectern, adjusting the microphone. Dawn took a seat in the third row. The first row would be presumptuous; the family would want to sit there. She sat with the roses on her knee, feeling the dampness in her palms. Not for the first time she wondered what Heather Warmington would look like. She had to admit to herself now that one of the reasons she had come here was to meet Mrs Walker's niece. To talk to her about Ivy, maybe even go for a coffee afterwards and have a proper conversation about her. Dawn would gain some insight into what Mrs Walker had been like before she'd become ill. What sort of person she'd been – lively, curious, kind. What she might have thought about what had happened.

The sound of the chapel doors opening made her turn. A woman was hurrying down the aisle, dressed in trousers and a white blouse, clutching a large leather holdall to her chest. She looked to be somewhere in her forties. Breathing hard, she sat a few seats away from Dawn and began to rummage in the holdall. Her hair, shoulder-length, dark and thin, with strands of grey, fell down over her face.

Dawn leaned across the intervening seats. 'Mrs Warmington?'

The woman stopped rummaging and looked up. Smiling, Dawn held out her hand. 'My name is Dawn Torridge. I'm the Matron at St Iberius Hospital. I think we might have spoken on the phone the other day?'

The woman continued to stare at her, a faint crease between her eyes. Then the crease flattened out.

'Oh, I *see*,' she said. 'Oh no, no, no. I'm not the niece.'

She took Dawn's hand and gave it a hearty shake.

'Celia Dartson,' she said. 'Manager of The Beeches. I'm a bit late, I know, but with the weather today the traffic's been appalling. Bumper-to-bumper all the way from Morden.'

The vicar gave a small cough. 'Anyone else to come?'

'No,' Celia Dartson said. 'This is it.'

Dawn whispered, 'What about her niece?'

'Can't make it,' Celia Dartson said out of the side of her mouth. 'Phoned this morning to let us know.'

The vicar began the service. 'I am the Resurrection and the Life . . .'

Dawn looked around the empty chapel in dismay. Dora's funeral had not been large either: twenty-five people at the most, such elderly neighbours and relatives as could make it to the tiny St Saviour's Church in Silham Vale. Dawn's father had been Dora's only child. But the gathering, small as it was, had been infused with genuine emotion. Judy, Dawn's good friend from her nursing training days, had sat beside her and squeezed her arm. Francine had maintained a comforting presence on her other side. Afterwards in Crocus Road there had been tea and cake, speeches and reminiscences, even a sing-song. The guests had crowded around the piano to hear Eileen Warren from number 62 play, 'When You Were Sweet Sixteen' – the song that had been a hit the year Dora turned that age and which she had always loved.

But this. The rows of bare seats, the thin, cheap coffin, the harried-looking Beeches manager glancing at her watch.

I'm sorry. Dawn beamed the telepathic message forwards to the forlorn coffin on its wooden stand. *I'm so sorry.*

But Mrs Walker had *wanted* this. Hadn't she? She had looked so peaceful, her face free of suffering. She had said to Dawn, 'I want to go to heaven.'

But the truth was, Mrs Walker had not known what she was saying. Only a few days before that, she had told Dawn she wanted to go to Dagenham. Dagenham, heaven – it was probably all the same to her.

'O grave,' the vicar was asking, 'where is thy victory?'

If only they could have controlled her pain. *That* was what had rattled her. The way she'd been suffering, on and on, and it had been there all the time, no matter what they did.

But of course, they could have controlled it. That was exactly what the pain team was for. Only Dawn had never thought of contacting them. And the way Mrs Walker had looked so peaceful at the end . . . of course she had. Her pain was gone. Who knew? Without the constant discomfort she might have been more alert, more able to communicate. She might have asked to see her niece. Even at this late stage, they might have found a closeness. Mrs Walker would not have spent her final days with strangers, would not have been forced to endure this soulless ceremony alone.

The pan-pipes were playing 'Abide With Me'.

'Forasmuch as it hath pleased Almighty God . . .' The vicar had reached the committal stage of the service. The blue curtains in front of the coffin slid back to reveal a shadowy space behind.

'Earth to earth,' said the vicar. The coffin moved forward on its wooden platform. 'Ashes to ashes.' The coffin jerked, then stopped. It appeared to be stuck. No – there it went again. 'Dust to dust.' A final jolt and the coffin was through. '. . . in the sure and certain hope of Resurrection to eternal life. Amen.'

The blue curtains slid shut.

Abruptly, 'Abide With Me' was cut off.

'I've got to go.' Celia Dartson stood up and hoisted the leather holdall on to her shoulder. 'I'm going to be late for . . . er . . .'

She didn't bother to finish. She waved at Dawn and headed off down the aisle at a half-trot. The vicar left too, though more sedately, chatting to the chapel attendant about another service.

Dawn sat on in the muffled, carpet-tile silence. Twelve minutes. From beginning to end, that was how long the service had taken. The hands on the clock beside the blue curtains stood at eighteen minutes past ten. The spray of roses still lay across her knee. She hadn't had a chance to ask where to put them.

In the end, she got up, went forward and placed them on the wooden platform where the coffin had lain. The summer-garden scent of the flowers rose, drifting towards the curtains.

'I was trying to help you.' Dawn aimed the words towards anyone who might be behind them, listening in the darkness. 'I thought I was doing the right thing.'

But there was no answer. All she was talking to was a pair of dark blue curtains.

In the afternoon, she took Milly for her walk. They walked farther than usual, all the way up to Tooting with its curvy, crooked streets and red and white Victorian house fronts. As they passed the common, a giant drop of rain platched a star shape on the sleeve of Dawn's good black coat. The sky was low and threatening, vivid purple at the edges. Sometimes when Dawn was out walking like this, the light from the sky would fill up her eyes, the brightness making it seem as if something extraordinary was about to happen. But of course, nothing ever did.

The sky darkened further. All of a sudden it was more like night-time than the middle of the afternoon. Another giant star-shape on her sleeve. Then, as if at the dropping of a trapdoor, an incredible torrent, a solid wall of water, plunged from the sky. People scrambled and dashed for cover. Through the sheets of rain, Dawn glimpsed a blue-framed window with the words 'Café' and 'Eat-in or Take Away' printed in an arch on the glass. She found herself almost pushed through the door, propelled by the rush of bodies behind her.

'Phew,' a woman said, laughing and holding her arms out to let the drops fall.

Milly crawled under an empty table by the window. She was not a fan of the rain. Dawn followed her to the table and sat down. Her hair stuck to her forehead and dripped down her neck. The tables were laid with blue-checked cloths, steel milk jugs, large bottles of tomato ketchup. The laughing woman had settled herself at the next table along with a red-haired man and a toddler.

'Yes please?' A man with an apron over his jeans stood in front of Dawn. He had a pencil stuck behind his ear.

'Just a coffee, thanks,' Dawn said.

The man went away. Something touched Dawn's

knee: Milly, her wet chin leaving a dark patch on Dawn's trousers. Her kindly, triangular eyes gazed up at Dawn. *Look, I know there's something wrong. Why don't you tell me what it is?*

Dawn touched the damp head. 'My wise old friend.'

What would Milly think of her if she knew? The thing was, she had always assumed she was so exceptional at her job. With her gold medal and her early Matron promotion and all her grand ideas for the hospital. She had always seen herself as just that little bit better than the others, capable of taking decisions that no normal nurse in her right mind would dream of making. But the truth was, there was nothing exceptional about her. Nothing at all.

The café door opened again with a metallic *ching*. A splatter of water sounded from the street. A man came in, accompanied by a large, flustery red setter with its tongue hanging out. The setter promptly rushed over to sniff at Milly. She ignored him, keeping her head on Dawn's knee. But the little boy at the next table hung over the back of his seat in delight.

'Mine!' he shouted, pointing at the dog.

The red setter went down on its front paws and gave a *wuff* of excitement. His owner, a tall, untidy-looking man with glasses, came over.

'Boris,' he said, 'come here.'

'Sorry,' he added to Dawn, dragging the dog away.

The child wailed, stretching his arms after them. 'MINE!'

'Ben.' His father tried to make him turn around. 'Eat your sandwich.' There was no doubt that he was the father. Dawn had rarely seen two people look so alike. Both had the same cheery, freckled faces and gangly limbs, the same bright red hair. Unusual to see that shade of red in London. The father's intense pride in his son was obvious. It was there in the way he looked at him, touched his head, wiped a splotch of jam off his cheek. Dawn turned away from them, back to her own table.

No, she was not exceptional at all. She had failed to make Dora comfortable before she died. Failed to control Mrs Walker's pain. What else might she have missed over the years, always smugly thinking she was so right?

It was a shock, like looking in the mirror and seeing someone different from who you had always thought you were. Should she resign? Surely a person who could do what she had was not fit to be in charge of patients? But she shrank from the thought. What else would she do with her life? She'd been at St Iberius for almost twenty years; she knew the hospital better than any other person there. The smells of her ward, the sounds; she could stand at the top of it and close her eyes and still know what was happening in every part. If she left, who else would look after it so well? Who would make the difference that she knew she did every day?

But wasn't that the point? If she really wasn't the wonderful nurse she had always thought herself to be? If this so-called greatness of hers had been a delusion all along?

The child at the next table was still fussing.

'Mine,' he wailed. '*Mine!*' His father tried to distract him but there was the sound of a plate being flung across the table. The cries of 'Mine' degenerated into a scream. 'Miiiuuugghh.'

His mouth was full but he didn't let that stop him. The scream rose, climbing to a plateau, then tailed off, getting lower and lower, like an air-raid klaxon running down.

'Ben,' the father whispered fiercely. 'Ben, behave yourself.'

But Ben was only just getting started. He was just beginning to work himself up now. He took a deep breath, reloading himself with air. Out came a second scream, louder and longer than the first: 'UUUUU-URGGH.' Then he took another breath, a deeper one this time. The café patrons braced themselves.

But nothing happened.

Where a penetrating shriek should have set the knives rattling on every table there was an unexpected, throbbing silence. Dawn could almost feel her eardrums uncurling, peering around themselves, starting to relax.

Then came the sharp scrape of a chair.

'Ben?'

Another scrape.

'Ben!'

Something in the voice. Dawn turned. The red-haired father was out of his seat. He had his back to Dawn and seemed to be struggling with the child in his chair. Across the table, the mother had risen too.

'Ben,' she said.

Her hands were to her mouth. Her face had sagged, like a round of dough that had collapsed, like a cake that had been taken too soon from the oven.

Her face was like the painting *The Scream*.

Dawn swivelled back to look at the father. He still had his back to her. She couldn't work out what he was doing. From the jerking of his shoulders he seemed to be making some violent, repetitive movement. Was he hitting the child? Shaking him? Before she could make it out, the father straightened and swung with the child in his arms, staring around him. The child's arms stuck straight out from his sides. His mouth was shaped like an O, his eyes round and glassy as beads. There was something odd about his face. Dawn thought at first that it was the greyish light from the window.

'It's stuck.' The father's voice was hoarse. 'It's stuck, and it won't come out.'

That was when Dawn got it. That was when she knew. The loud wail, the full mouth. The deep inhalation and the sudden silence. The child was choking. Even as she thought it, he went limp. His arms flopped to his sides. His head fell back, his eyes rolled up and his face . . .

His face was dark blue.

Dawn stood up.

'Call an ambulance,' she said.

Nobody moved. Startled faces bobbed in the gloom.

Dawn said it again, louder. 'Someone call an ambulance. *Now.*'

The tall man with the red setter was beside her, tapping into his phone. 'OK,' he said. 'I've got it.'

To the father, Dawn said, 'I'm a nurse. Can I help?'

He answered by thrusting the child into her arms. It was so unexpected; she caught him, but the weight made her stagger backwards, catching her knees on the edge of her chair.

'Do something,' the father said in a voice that sounded as if there was a knot in his windpipe.

Dawn had plopped on to her chair. The child's head sank back on her arm. His hair hung down, soft and spiky like a tiny red crown. He was wearing a green

T-shirt with a picture of a train on it. Under the T-shirt his chest heaved but he made no sound. No air passed in or out through his lips. Dawn felt her own breaths come faster and shallower, as if to compensate. She was not a paediatric nurse. Children were not the same as adults. They were a different species, as different from an adult as a human was from a hamster. She had no equipment here. No oxygen, no defibrillator, no adrenaline. The ambulance would have all of these things on board. But it would never reach them in time.

She was it. She was all they had.

She worked her hand to the side of the child's neck. To her utter relief, a rapid beat fluttered under the skin.

'Is he dead?' the mother cried.

Dawn said, 'He's not dead.'

But if he didn't breathe soon, he would be. She had three minutes. Five at most. The child's lips grew darker. No nurse could ever see that colour without a leaping of her heartbeat, an urgent, primal surging in her veins: *Do something. Do something. Now. Now. Now.* Every cardiac arrest tutorial she had ever taught or attended flew through her head: the legless rubber dolls with their disposable lips, the torsos with compression monitors attached. The real patients she had helped to resuscitate in A&E and the cardiac ward. All of them adults, every one.

She sat the child up. Then she leaned him forward, over her arm. With the heel of her hand she slapped him sharply, twice, between the shoulder blades. Was that right? Was that what you did for a child? She slapped him again. Nothing. Now what? Feel around in his mouth? Try to remove whatever it was he was choking on? No. No. You weren't supposed to do that if you couldn't see it. You might push the thing in more.

The tiny body trembled in her hands. Three minutes. Three minutes. Three minutes.

Then something happened.

Everything around her seemed to slow and fade. Her own thoughts continued as normal, but the surrounding café went still. The rain stopped running down the windows, the bobbing faces froze in the gloom. The voices disappeared until all she could hear was her own heartbeat, strong and clear, *tick tick tick*, in her ears.

You know, Dawn. You know what to do.

She turned the child on her knee so that he faced away from her. Then she put her arms around him. Her fist was on his tummy, just higher than his belly button. Her other hand was on top of the fist. Then she pushed with both hands, inwards and upwards. A single push, quick and firm. Had there been something? A sound? A rush of air from his lips? She pushed again.

Huuuh. The child's arms windmilled. His head flew back, almost hitting Dawn in the mouth. Something was there. There, glistening, just behind his teeth. She reached in, hooked the object with her finger, swept it out.

The child inhaled. A long, raucous, rattling whoop. Then he coughed. He doubled over Dawn's arm and coughed and coughed and coughed. Alarmingly, his blue colour darkened even further. Under the mop of bright hair, his round face looked like a blueberry.

Then he inhaled again.

And then finally, like the shriek of a long-awaited train hurtling in to the platform, came the scream.

The noise made Dawn's ears pop. Around her, everything sped up again to its normal pace, the sobbing mother, the whispering customers, the hammering of the rain on the window. The sounds were loud and echoing, as if she had just surfaced from underwater.

'Aaaaaghhh.' The child screamed again. His mother was beside them, screaming too.

'Ben. Oh, Ben, Ben, Ben.' She was grabbing him from Dawn's knees. His soft hair brushed off Dawn's arms as he was dragged away. The mother clutched him to her, rocking the two of them from side to side. Then she held him away again, up in front of her.

'Never do that,' she screamed at him. 'Never do that again!'

The child bawled louder. He kicked his feet in terror, trying to get back to her. The mother pulled him to her again. Sobbing, they clung to each other. The child's face was buried in her shoulder but the skin on his legs had changed from blue back to a bright, healthy pink.

'Thank you.' The father was in front of Dawn. 'Nurse, thank you. Thank you.'

His face was green. All his blood was in his feet. He tried to shake Dawn's hand but his own hands were shaking so hard that he had to use both of them just to grip hers.

'I'm just glad I could help,' Dawn said. The practical, common-sense Matron calming everything down.

'I thought . . . I thought . . .'

'I know. I know what you thought. But he's fine. Look at him. He's going to be fine.'

A siren blooped in the street. The rainy window turned green and yellow. Blue lights flashed through the blurry glass. Two men in overalls came charging in with a large red box.

'Collapsed child?' one of them shouted.

'He was choking,' Dawn said. 'But we've got it out.' She showed them the soggy lump which had flown through the air and landed on the next table. A half-chewed crust of bread.

They took him anyway, the mother leading the way with the child in her arms, the green father following with their bags and coats. The ambulance delivered a final bloop and pulled away. More people were pushing through the doors to escape the rain. Several of the customers were still looking over at Dawn, whispering and craning their necks, but the queues at the door were blocking their view. The staff were back at work, clearing tables and taking orders. The excitement was over, the moment of drama slipped already into the past.

Dawn picked up her bag from the floor.

'Come on, Milly, let's go.'

But when she went to stand, her legs wouldn't work. Her knees were weak and flubbery, as if about to fold in half the wrong way. She'd have to give it a few minutes. She sat down again. Beside her table a bulky shape was hovering, blocking the light from the window.

'I'm just going,' Dawn told the shape. 'You can have the table in one minute.'

'I'm not waiting for the table,' the shape said.

She looked up. It was the tall man with the flustery red setter. The one who had called the ambulance.

'Are you all right?' he asked.

Chapter Six

For a moment, she couldn't answer. The man loomed over the table, peering at her in a concerned way through thick-framed rectangular glasses. He was a large man about her own age, not fat but bulky, with broad shoulders that strained at his navy jacket. He had thin, straight, light-brown hair. Despite her agitation, something about him struck Dawn as familiar. She had seen him somewhere before. Either that or he had one of those very ordinary faces that you saw on the street all the time.

'Are you all right?' the man asked again.

'Yes. Thank you.' Dawn's voice came out at a higher pitch than normal. The effect of the adrenaline on her vocal cords.

'I can't believe it.' The man's eyes were round and staring behind the glasses. 'What you did . . . I mean . . .' He waved his hands, seeming to search for a dramatic enough way to describe what had happened. Then he gave up, gesturing instead towards the soggy lump of bread on the next table.

'He could have died,' he said.

It sounded more intense than Dawn could cope with right now.

'He wouldn't have died,' she said. 'What I did was just basic first aid.'

'Are you a doctor? Nurse?'

'Nurse.'

'Incredible.' The man shook his head. 'Incredible.'

He kept repeating it. He wasn't as confident as Dawn had first thought. She'd had the vague impression when he'd called the ambulance of a powerful, capable man but this man, large as he was, had the hunched shoulders and stooping posture of a person who habitually tried to avoid drawing attention to himself. His glasses had a dated appearance, as though he had found them in some charity shop from the 1970s. They seemed too big for his face. He kept having to poke them back up his nose with his finger. He had an anxious expression. Not, Dawn guessed, the sort of person who normally struck up random conversations with strangers. It occurred to her that he was actually quite shocked.

She said in a kinder tone, 'Well, it was you who called the ambulance.'

'But it wouldn't have got here in time.'

The man was interrupted by the red setter tipping

his head back and emitting a long, high-pitched yowl. He was fed up of staring at Milly and being ignored. Milly lay across Dawn's feet, pressing into her legs, gazing up at her from time to time in a worried way to check that all was well.

'Boris. Take it easy.' The man crouched beside the dog and put a hand on his head. Boris sat back and panted.

'What a beautiful dog,' Dawn said, as much to put his owner at ease as anything else. The setter *was* a beauty; all quivering energy and movement, balanced on the very tips of his paws as if ready to leap off somewhere at any moment. His distinctive, bright blue collar contrasted vividly with his orange coat. London seemed full of redheads today.

'He belongs to a friend,' the man said. 'He can't walk him at the moment so I'm doing it for him.'

Milly thumped her tail on the wooden floor. The man looked down at her. 'Your dog's nice too,' he said. 'Friendly.'

'She loves being with people,' Dawn said. 'She spends a lot of the day on her own.'

The tall man's agitation seemed to be settling. The small talk about the dogs had brought the colour back to his face. It was a cliché, but it always was the largest men who were the most squeamish. They came in to the clinics, all stiff upper lips and grim waving away of any offers of comfort: 'Nah, mate, I'm fine,' then slid to the floor at the first glint of a needle. The man knelt on one knee, pulling at Boris's ears until the dog's eyes half closed and his paws began to slip on the floor. Dawn thought he seemed to glance at her a couple of times, but when she caught his eye he looked quickly away again as if afraid of being thought rude.

'This might sound strange,' he said, 'but I think I recognize you.'

'Oh?'

'Yes, I think you were at the same school as me.'

'Oh, really?' Dawn was intrigued. 'A King's graduate!' No wonder he had looked familiar. Which of her classes had he been in? The Croydon King's Academy had been enormous. In Dawn's year alone there had been 500 pupils. At least a quarter of them, she had never known their names.

But the man was shaking his head, returning his attention to Boris's long ears.

'No,' he said. 'I'm wrong, then. I was at school in Cumbria.'

'Cumbria?' Dawn sat up. 'But – I did live there. Until I was ten. You don't mean the Red Barrow School near Buttermere?'

The man looked up at her again, the skin around his eyes crinkling in a sudden smile that altered his whole appearance, making the square, sombre face look almost merry.

'That's the one,' he said.

That's the woon. His accent! How had she missed it? The measured Northern speech, the long vowels. A vivid memory assailed her: the slate schoolhouse on Sheepclose Lane with its pointed roofs and gables. The sloping wooden desks, the bottles of milk with their bright red straws at break time.

'Were you in my class?' she asked.

'I think you might have been a couple of years behind me.' The man poked his glasses back up his nose. 'Your name's Torridge, isn't it?'

'Yes. Dawn Torridge.'

He nodded. 'The reason I remember is because your family had that farm – on Crummock, wasn't it?'

'That's it.' Dawn was staring at him. 'That was us.'

'Ours was a few miles away,' he said. 'In the hills.'

Now she knew him! There'd been a couple of farms on Crummock. The highest and most isolated had been about six miles from theirs, right up on its own. There'd been a child there, a boy – she hadn't known him well. A tall, solitary, fair-haired boy, always out in the fields. He'd been a couple of years older than she was, which when you were nine or ten was the equivalent of a vast social gulf.

'Will . . .' she remembered.

'That's right!'

It *was* him! She couldn't believe it. She'd been in

his kitchen! She'd gone there once at Christmas with her father. There'd been a stone floor and pots hanging from the ceiling. The range had smelled of bacon and hot fruit. Will's mother had given Dawn a slice of cake. She had talked about her son. 'We never see him. Gone from morning to night he is, always out with his dog.' She'd been a nice woman. Mrs . . . Mrs . . . She couldn't think of the name.

'I'm sorry,' she said, 'I can't remember your surname.'

'It's Coombs.' The tall man stood up. 'Will Coombs.' He shook her hand. His was the huge, rough-edged hand of a farmer.

'Sit. Sit down.' Dawn pushed a chair out. This was so strange! Will Coombs, from Sparrowhawk Farm. Here in Tooting, of all places, sitting across the table from her in this damp, blue café. The fair hair had darkened to light brown, but the height was the same, and the solitary air she remembered. The squareness of his face was emphasized by his fringe which was cut very straight across his forehead, as if he'd done it himself. In the nicest possible way he looked like Lurch from *The Addams Family*.

'It was lovely up there.' Dawn pictured the sloping fields, the grey cottages with their tiny windows. 'Really lovely. I haven't been there for years but I often think about it.'

'Not bad, is it?' Now that he was seated, Will seemed

uncomfortable again, sitting too upright, jammed into the space between the chair and the table. He looked awkward and out of place here, too large for this small café, this tiny table. 'Shambling' was the word that came to mind. A big, shambling man.

'What are you doing in London?' Dawn asked.

Will shrugged. 'More jobs in the city in my field.'

'As a *farmer*?'

'No. I'm in IT.'

'Oh.' She didn't know why she should find that so surprising. Why shouldn't he be in IT? It was just that somehow, if she'd ever thought about him, the boy he'd been, she would have seen him as always being there, out in the fields with his dog, tramping up a muddy track, the acid-green, sheep-dotted hillside rising behind him through the drizzle.

'My parents sold the farm,' Will explained. 'They moved to Cockermouth years ago, before they died.'

'I'm sorry.'

He shrugged again. 'They weren't the only ones. Not much money in it any more.'

It was true. Dawn recalled Dora's dismay on her behalf at how little had been left over when her own parents' farm had been sold. The café had brightened now. A silver light came streaming through the window.

'My father,' she said, 'thought the Lake District was the most beautiful place he'd ever seen. The summer

113

he left school he went up there on a hiking trip. He got lost and put his tent up on my mother's family's farm. She came out in her wellies and told him off. Said she'd set the dogs on him if he came round there again. They were married eight months later.'

A loud clatter from the next table. Boris leaped back in a feathery fluster. Milk from the overturned jug came dripping over the edge of the tablecloth.

'Boris.' Will squeezed up out of his seat. 'What are you up to now?'

The silver light had disappeared. Will's big shoulders were blocking the window. He tried to clean up the mess but his general air of being too large and clumsy for everything led to the tiny napkin promptly soaking through and disintegrating, dripping milk all over his trousers. Boris sank on to his front paws, a series of tiny groans escaping from his throat.

'He wants to get going,' Will said, abandoning the napkin. 'We'd just got started when the rain came.' He glanced at the window. 'Stopped now, though.'

So it had. The splattering from the street had ceased. Patches of blue splotched the lifting sky. The soaking pavements glittered.

'I'd best take him on,' Will said. The awkwardness was back. 'Will you be all right here if we leave?'

'Of course. I'll be fine.'

But she felt a pang. Not in a thousand years after that sad, bleak little ceremony at Bixworth Park

Crematorium would she have thought that this would be how she would spend her afternoon, reminiscing about the mountains and muddy lanes of her childhood. Will's slow, deep speech had opened a window in her mind that would close again when he left, leaving her isolated in her gloom. Should she suggest that they meet again? But what would they talk about? Will was a nice man but he was no conversationalist. Despite the fact that it was he who had approached her, Dawn had ended up doing most of the talking. Will had sat there and stared at the tomato ketchup, failing to ask her anything about herself or her family. Probably it had been the adrenaline that had made him so sociable at first. She'd felt the effects of it herself. But once the shock had worn off, Will's conversational skills had quickly dried up. One of those shy, eccentric men, Dawn guessed, who were ill at ease with other people and most comfortable on their own. Their meeting each other like this had been a pleasant surprise but it was probably best to leave it at that.

Will clipped Boris's lead to his bright blue collar. Under the table, Milly clambered to her feet, her claws scrabbling on the damp boards. Dawn said, 'Oh, no, Mill, we're not leaving just yet,' at the same time as Will said, 'I think Boris has made a friend.'

Dawn laughed, stroking Milly's bitten ear.

'She likes the company,' she said. 'She's on her own

115

all day while I'm at work. She's used to having people around. It's not ideal, but at the moment I don't know what else I can do.'

Will was hovering again, appearing preoccupied with something under his thumbnail.

'Do you live near here?' he asked.

'Just outside Croydon. Why?'

'I'm in Streatham.' He hesitated. 'Look . . . if you'd like . . . I could walk her for you sometime.'

'Walk Milly?'

'I don't mean to pressure you,' he said quickly. 'I just mean the same way I walk Boris. It's hard to have a dog in a city flat. I like having a dog to walk; your dog could do with the company. Simple as that.' His square face had flushed, or perhaps it was just the reflection of his maroon T-shirt on his skin.

'No, of course,' Dawn reassured him. 'I know what you meant.' Milly and Boris were sniffing at each other under the table. 'Look,' she said, 'why don't you give me your phone number? I don't know what my plans are yet, but at least that way I'll know how to reach you.'

Will fumbled about in his pockets for a pen. Dawn took one from her bag and handed it to him, along with a clean napkin from the dispenser. Will scribbled something on the napkin. From a series of squiggles Dawn deciphered the words 'Will Coombs' and a phone number.

She smiled at him as he slid the napkin towards her. 'Thank you,' she said. 'It's a kind offer. I'll definitely bear it in mind.'

Will nodded, as if relieved.

He was at the door with Boris, his hand on the glass, when he stopped again and turned back.

'What you did . . .' he said, not quite looking at Dawn. 'You saved that boy's life. You should be very proud.'

Abruptly, they were gone. The door slammed with its tinny *ching*. The café, without Will and Boris in it, seemed to expand to twice its size. Through the window, the shiny pavements reflected the red and white shop fronts, the colourful vegetable stalls, the hard, yellow gleam of sun. Will and Boris were sharp silhouettes on the dazzling road. Boris hauled on the lead to reach a bin. Patiently, Will stepped over a puddle to let him have a sniff. His gait was slightly uneven; the gait of a person with a limp or an injury of some kind. Or just the clumsiness sometimes seen in large, shy men.

You saved that boy's life. You should be very proud.

The gleam from the window moved over the table, the silver milk jug, the blue and white squares on the cloth.

She *had* saved his life. There had been nothing at her disposal. Just a frantic father and a rag-doll child, thrust in her arms. But she had coped. What she had done was basic first aid. Not rocket science, not even advanced nursing of any kind. But in the moment of crisis, when she needed it most, her training and experience had not let her down.

She *was* a good nurse. But that was all she was. She was not God.

Milly's dark head bumped at her knee. She said quietly, 'No more killing, Milly, eh?'

The window in her mind was still open. She saw a white, bright day, a waterfall foaming down to a brown, frothy river. She was on her father's shoulders and Jock, her grandfather's sheepdog, was scrambling up the bank. Her mother stood at the kissing-gate, smiling up at them, the wind blowing her long blonde hair over her face.

Chapter Seven

Monday was Theatre Day, the busiest day of the week. As well as all the day-to-day tasks of running a ward – dressings, feeding, giving medications – there was the stream of pre-ops to wash, shave, fast and consent and send off to theatre in the right order with their lab results and X-rays securely attached and the correct limb or kidney marked with indelible ink. On a Monday, Dawn didn't have a minute to herself and for now that suited her just fine. Over the weekend she had done her best to distract herself with various activities – walking Milly, hoovering the house, writing up a staff appraisal – but time and again, just as she was in the middle of something, Mrs Walker would rise up into her thoughts, forcing her to stop what she was doing, leaving her stranded uneasily in a vacuum. It was a relief to be back at work, to be too busy to sit and think. She occupied herself with arranging an ITU bed for a post-op, flushing a blocked chest drain, showing Elspeth how to set up a haemodialysis circuit – and the more her attention was taken up by the frantic, familiar routine of her ward, the less room there was in her head for anything else.

At one point, her arms full of linen, she found herself walking past the side room. An admission was expected later in the afternoon – a teenager who had fractured his leg in a forklift accident – but for now the room was unoccupied. Automatically, as she passed, Dawn looked away. Then she caught herself. This was ridiculous. Sooner or later the new patient would be in there and she'd have to go in and see to him. *It's an empty room*, she told herself. *Nothing more.*

She made herself stop and look through the door. And in fact, once she did, the room didn't look half as desolate as it had on Friday. The bed was made up in a welcoming way, the green mattress covered with a clean sheet, the corner of the blanket turned down, two fresh towels folded on the end of the bed. The locker was scrubbed and clean, the ECG leads folded and ready on the monitor. The weather had picked up since the weekend. Through the window came a shaft of sunshine, lighting up the empty bed opposite. By some odd effect, a knot or flaw in the glass had focused a vivid yellow circle on to the pillow. The creases and shadows of the fabric formed the shape of a nose, a downturned mouth. A face, pale and still, with closed, peaceful eyes.

'Nurse.'

Dawn almost dropped the pile of sheets.

'*Nurse!*' A man in a cream striped dressing gown was waving at her from a nearby bed. 'I need the commode.'

'Just a moment, Mr Price.' Matrons didn't normally deal with commodes but the other staff were rushed off their feet. She wouldn't keep the elderly man waiting. Before she left, she glanced back for a final time. The shaft of sunlight had faded. The face on the pillow had dimmed to a pale, ghostly blob.

Walking down the ward to the linen room, Dawn delivered herself a firm lecture. This had to stop. Ghostly faces on pillows indeed! If she went on like this she would cause herself harm. What was done now was done; obsessing about it would not change anything. What she had done – she had thought it was the right thing to do. Not the correct thing maybe, but the *right* thing. But she had got it very wrong. Still, no matter how much she might wish it, the clock could not be turned back. *You've got to move on*, she told herself. *Push Mrs Walker from your mind, concentrate on what you're supposed to be doing.* There were other patients here who needed her. She had to focus on them now.

And there was another reason she needed to pull

herself together. There was another serious matter weighing on her mind today, one that, unlike Mrs Walker, she knew she could not put off dealing with any longer.

Clive.

All morning she had been wondering how to approach him. As the Matron, she could not ignore the way he had treated Mrs Walker. Swearing at her like that and banging her head on the bars. It had been appalling to see. Every time she thought about it she felt angry all over again. How many other patients had he done that to? To let it go would be to put other elderly people at risk.

In the warm, detergent-scented linen room she stacked the sheets on the shelves. The most obvious way to deal with Clive would be to organize a disciplinary meeting and have him dismissed. And why not? She had never been happy with his work or his attitude. And the way he had openly defied her the other day and been rude to her, in front of the entire ward . . . No. She couldn't deny it, she'd be very glad to see the back of him. There was something she just didn't like about him and that was that.

When the last sheet was stacked, she went to the sluice room to fetch the commode.

'Good morning, Mr Price.' She parked the commode by his bed, flipping the brake on to steady it. 'How's your hip today?'

'Still very stiff, Sister. But improving.'

'That's good.' She helped Mr Price out of bed and got him settled on the seat. Afterwards, still thinking about Clive, she wheeled the commode back down the ward.

Sacking a nurse. It would be the first time she had ever done anything like that. It was an enormous step to take. What if there'd been a reason for Clive to behave the way he had? Perhaps he had been under stress that morning. He might have problems in his private life he hadn't told anyone about. Everyone was entitled to a bad day.

Dawn shook her head, rinsing the commode pan in the long steel sink. People did get stressed; of course they did. But not everyone consistently despised the patients, and certainly not everyone frankly abused them. And if your personality meant that you were the sort of person who took your stress out on vulnerable, ill people, then you shouldn't be working with them. It was as simple as that.

She placed the commode pan in the washer and turned it on. The giant machine hummed and juddered. Dawn sighed. She knew what the real problem was. She was reluctant to go back over the details of that day. She pictured the disciplinary meeting: the HR people, Clive and his union rep, all sitting around the table in the HR conference room, dressed in suits, sipping from glasses of water. 'Now,

Matron, if we could just run through the story again. What exactly was Mrs Walker's condition at the time? Did she seem upset by Mr Geen's actions? When you spoke with her afterwards, what did she have to say?'

No. She wasn't ready to go through that all over again.

Clive was clearly worried as well. Today was his first shift since the incident and he had been keeping a low profile all morning, staying well out of Dawn's way and spending far more time with the patients than usual. Now that the theatre rush had calmed down a little she realized she hadn't spoken to him since the handover round.

'Seen Clive anywhere?' she asked Mandy, rattling past with the BP trolley.

Mandy stopped.

'He was somewhere about a minute ago,' she said. She glanced over her shoulder. Then she sank her voice to a whisper. 'Very *quiet* today, isn't he? Guilty conscience if you ask me.'

'Because of Thursday, you mean?'

'Well, yes. Wouldn't you? I mean . . . that old lady. Found dead like that only a couple of hours after he'd left her. How hard do you think he did bash her head off those bars?'

Mandy tapped the side of her nose with her finger. Then she rattled on down the ward with her trolley, leaving Dawn rigid, face to face with a row of bed-pans.

Clive blamed for Mrs Walker's death! The idea had simply never occurred to her. The disciplinary meeting rose again in her mind, only now with a far more menacing aspect to it. 'You are saying, Matron, that you witnessed Mr Geen abusing this patient. Committing a physical assault. And a short time later she was found unexpectedly dead in her bed.' The conclusion they'd come to was as obvious as a brick in the face. Before Clive knew where he was, the police would be involved. He might find himself facing a charge of manslaughter.

She finally tracked him down in the stock room, most unusually for him, busy changing over the sharps bins, sealing the full one for disposal and opening up a fresh one. It was unlike Clive to do something he hadn't specifically been asked to do. He was obviously making a huge effort today.

'If you've got a moment,' Dawn said, 'could we have a talk?'

Clive's eyelids lowered, turning his eyes into hooded, hostile slits. But he said nothing. He peeled off his gloves and followed Dawn to her office. There was just enough room to close the door. Dawn cleared a pile of *Nursing Today* journals from the only spare chair and placed them on the filing cabinet.

'Please,' she said, 'sit down.'

Clive sat on the very edge of the seat, barely touching it, as if the plastic might scald his rear. Down the front of his tunic hung a silver chain with a large, chunky medallion on the end. His lips were so thin they had all but disappeared into his face. Despite her anger, Dawn felt almost sorry for him. After hearing about Mrs Walker's death last week, the chances were he had passed a very unpleasant weekend.

'I'm sure you know why I've asked you in here,' she said. 'It's about what happened on Thursday. With Mrs Walker.'

Clive said nothing but his lips vanished even further into his face.

'I've been thinking hard about it,' Dawn said, 'as I'm sure you have, too. And I've come to a decision. Provided nothing like this happens again, I don't intend to take things any further.'

Clive's taut expression didn't change. But the drop in his shoulders showed that he had suddenly exhaled. Definite relief. Surprise too. Dawn caught the flash as his eyebrows lifted.

She said firmly, 'That's *provided* nothing similar happens again. Any further mistreatment of a patient will be taken much more seriously. If you're busy and finding it difficult to cope, then ask someone for help, or come and speak to me about it. But you don't take your problems out on the patients. Do you understand?'

'Yes, Sister.'

Definitely meeker than usual. Close up, Dawn saw that he had shaved off all his stubble. His face looked much less unhygienic than usual. His hair was washed and tied back in a ponytail instead of straggling down over his collar. The only jarring note was the chunky medallion dangling on the front of his tunic. She might as well deal with that as well. Get everything sorted out while they were here.

She said, 'Clive, I'm sorry, but there's one more thing. That chain will have to go. I've seen it touching the patients when you're treating them. It's an infection risk. The policy on the ward clearly states minimal jewellery only.'

Clive's head came up. 'But it's my allergy chain.'

'Your what?'

'I'm allergic to penicillin.' He lifted the medallion to show her. 'See?'

On the front of the medallion, the words *Penicillin Allergy* were engraved around a central, raised carving of a skull.

'I didn't know you were allergic to penicillin.' Dawn tapped her pen on the desk.

'Yeah, well, I am. And my allergy specialist said it's vital I keep this warning on me at all times.'

Dawn was familiar with the concept of allergy alerts. Lots of people carried them. Just not normally so ostentatiously.

127

'Couldn't it be something smaller?' she asked. 'A bracelet? Or a thinner chain?'

'A thinner chain might break,' Clive said. 'Anyway, it *has* to be big. That's the whole point. It's a serious allergy. I could die.'

He spoke in a very earnest tone but deep in his eyes was a triumphant smirk. *This will show you. Don't think you're going to have it all your way.* HR would back him up on this one and they both knew it. You couldn't argue with an employee telling you they could die.

Dawn kept her tone neutral. 'Fine,' she said. 'If you need to wear it, I don't have a problem with that. But try to keep it inside your tunic. It shouldn't need to dangle over the patients.'

'No, Sister.'

The air seemed cleaner and fresher when he had left. Dawn exhaled, blowing out her cheeks. So *that* was over. Let Clive have his victory over the chain. His hygiene and attitude had improved and that was the main thing. She doubted very much that he would abuse a patient on her ward again. But she'd be keeping a close eye on him from now on. Either he treated the patients with courtesy and respect or he lapsed again and he was out. It was entirely up to him.

Even with the windows open, the sun beat through the glass into the bus, trapping a stifling heat in the seats. The passengers, caught by surprise, were carrying their coats on their arms. It was the first of May and, overnight, summer had arrived. Wandsworth Common was filled with people sitting with their trousers rolled up, their faces to the sky. Couples lay sideways on the grass, giggling and playing with each other's fingers.

Whether it was the change in the weather or the relief of having dealt with Clive, Dawn didn't know, but the dragging sense of sadness and unease that had weighed her down over the past few days seemed, very slightly, to have lifted. Looking out over the dappled grass, it was as if she'd had a revelation. She could see now how all of this trouble had started. How the incident had happened with Mrs Walker. She'd been too caught up with things at work. With nothing going on outside of the hospital to distract her, her sense of her own importance had inflated until things had got completely out of hand.

Francine's warning: *You need something outside, too. You need to keep your perspective.*

The thing was, it crept up on you. Work. For a start, there'd been all that preparation for the Matron interview. You didn't just walk into a post like that off the street. There'd been courses to attend, journal articles to read, management exams to pass. Then when she'd finally got the job, there'd been all the extra hours at the hospital, finding her feet in the role.

And in her spare time, of course, there'd been Dora.

Dora's first stroke had happened three years ago, one windy morning in March. She'd been in the garden hanging her washing out, when with no warning at all, a hidden blood clot in her neck had broken free, floated upwards and lodged in her brain. She was found by a neighbour, hours later, lying on the grass, unable to move or speak.

Dawn, summoned urgently from the London flat she'd been sharing with Kevin, her boyfriend, had rushed on to the ward to be greeted by Dora, almost swallowed up by her giant, inflatable, anti-pressure-sore mattress, looking tiny and terrified and half the size Dawn had always known her. Strong, independent Dora who had raised her young son single-handedly after being widowed at the age of twenty-three, who in her fifties had started all over again, taking on the full-time care of an orphaned granddaughter, now lay slumped and helpless to one side of the bed because her muscles refused to support her. The corner of her mouth hung down, dripping saliva on to her chin. Dawn, hiding her distress, clutched her hand. Dora's speech sounded as if someone had stuffed a large dishcloth in her mouth, but with a little effort Dawn could understand her.

'I'll be all right,' Dora kept saying. 'I'll be better in a week or two. Don't worry about me.'

The consultant sat down with them to discuss her prognosis.

'The scan shows a lot of damage, I'm afraid,' he said. 'Mrs Torridge may make some recovery as time goes on, but . . .' He hesitated. 'Do you live on your own?'

He was speaking to Dora but it was Dawn that he looked at.

'Yes,' Dawn said, 'she does.'

'Have either of you considered the possibility of long-term care?'

Active, busy Dora tried to hide her shock.

'Fine,' she said. 'If that's what I've got to do, then I'll do it.'

But Dawn knew that one of her grandmother's greatest fears had always been to lose her independence, to have to go into a home or a hospital. When the doctor had left, Dawn tried to console her. 'We'll work it out, don't worry. We'll keep you in Crocus Road.' And Dora, breaking down at last, had cried and tried to touch Dawn's cheek with her hand.

Dawn moved back to her childhood bedroom in Silham Vale.

'Just for a few weeks,' she assured Kevin. 'Just until we sort things out.'

There was a lot to organize. Dawn arranged for carers to call during the day while she was at work to get Dora out of bed and help her with her lunch. In the evenings, Dawn took over. She fed Dora, washed her and changed her, gave her all her medications. Dora objected to the amount of time Dawn was spending with her.

'Go back to your flat,' she kept saying. 'I'll be all right here with the carers.' But she was still very shocked and teary and Dawn knew that, for now, she was the one who made Dora the most comfortable. She was so used to doing it for the patients on her ward. She gently cleaned Dora's eyes and ears, brushed her teeth, lifted her in and out of bed, insisted on her doing all her physio exercises. And gradually it became clear that it was working. Dora began to improve. The movement returned to her leg and right arm, her speech became more intelligible. She could manoeuvre herself around in her wheelchair and ask for what she wanted instead of having to slur and point at things with her eyes. It was going to work. Despite all the doctor's fears, Dora was going to manage at home.

But Kevin was growing more and more irritated.

'This is crazy,' he complained when Dawn phoned, yet again, to say that she couldn't make it up to London because Dora was running a chest infection. 'Are we in a relationship or aren't we?'

Kevin. Dark, lively, football-mad. The man Dawn had once assumed she was going to marry.

She had met him when she was twenty-nine, at

a party in Judy's boyfriend's flat. The blokes from
Andy's Tuesday-night football team had been
attempting to form a human pyramid on the kitchen
table which had collapsed in a heap with Kevin at
the bottom. He had landed in a funny way and done
something to his wrist. Dawn, hustled urgently over
by the panicking footballers to check it out, had
covered it with a plastic Waitrose bag filled with ice.
Kevin had made her laugh with some corny comment
about needing to be hospitalized for the rise in his
pulse. The following day they had met for lunch in
Camden market. The week after that he had taken
her to see *Les Miserables* and things had gone on
from there.

It had been a very happy time; Dawn still thought
that even now. Lots of people about – not many of
their friends had children then. There were parties,
dinners, a skiing holiday for eighteen in Andorra.
After a year, Dawn and Kevin decided to move in
together. Dawn moved all her stuff to Kevin's rented
place near Waterloo, a one-bedroomed flat with a
tiny garden on the roof. The flat was a short walk
from the South Bank and the British Film Institute;
a couple of tube stops from Oxford Street and the
West End. On summer evenings they ate dinner on the
roof where they could see the top of the London Eye
revolving above the chimneys. Dawn would put her
bare feet up on the sun-warmed wall and tell Kevin

about the various funny or hair-raising experiences she'd had at work that day.

'We couldn't find Mr Cromwell's dentures anywhere. Then the student suggested looking in the commode . . .'

The topic of their buying a place arose. Inevitably, this led to arguments. Kevin wanted to stay in Central London. Dawn thought it might be nice to move out a bit where they could have a garden and escape the crowds at weekends. Details. Friends said, 'You two will be married in no time.' The thought made Dawn feel content and secure. She and Kevin were good together. They enjoyed doing the same things – going for winter walks along the Regent's Canal or summer strolls by the Thames at Richmond. Eating out at Indian and Lebanese restaurants – which Kevin particularly liked because you could order a whole selection of dishes instead of having to settle for just one.

Occasionally Kevin could be moody.

'Thank God that's over,' he grumbled one evening on the way home from a drink with Dawn's nursing friends. 'Can't you lot talk about anything but patients and hospitals and diseases?'

'Of course we can.'

'Well then, why don't you? I've been sat there for the last three hours listening to Michelle describing the colour of someone's leg ulcer and your other mate

Judy bleat on and on about the time she nearly got two types of antibiotic mixed up. I don't mind saying it, Dawn, I was bored out of my bloody mind.'

The harshness of the attack surprised her. 'That's not all we talk about.'

'It *is* all you talk about. And you're the worst of the lot. No matter where we are or what we're doing, you're constantly distracted, wondering whether some bloke's constipation has cleared up or whether some old codger you've treated is going to survive. A part of you is always there on that ward. You're obsessed, Dawn. I'm telling you, it's not normal.'

'Obsessed' was a bit strong, Dawn thought. But she tried to see his point of view. Medics were notorious for talking shop. It was why they often ended up marrying each other – because they bored outsiders to dribble with their endless hospital anecdotes: 'So I said to myself, what about putting it in the *left* nostril, and then . . .' But it was fair to say that Kevin didn't go on all the time about *his* job as a quantity surveyor. So she made an effort to tone things down, kept her work tales for work and stuck to other topics when she was with Kevin. Apart from that – and you could hardly call it an issue – things ran smoothly between them.

Once or twice, one tiny niggle occurred to her. Nothing she would have mentioned to anyone because it would have made her sound like one of those neurotic women who thinks that life should be like a fairy tale. It had come to her one evening as she was on her way home from watching some cheesy romantic blockbuster at Judy's. Sitting on the illuminated bus, she had seen her own serious, oval face gazing back at her from the window, and what she thought was: *Kevin never looks at me.*

Of course, he looked at her. He looked at her every time she spoke to him, brushed past him in the tiny flat, passed him something while he was eating, reading, watching TV. But he didn't *look* at her. Not the way the hero had looked at the heroine in the film.

Then her normal, sensible self intervened. Real life was not a cheesy film. Men did not – after the first few weeks, at least – spend their time gazing deeply into women's eyes. She and Kevin got on well, they were good friends, they cared about each other and looked out for each other. And in a proper, long-term relationship, those were the things that mattered.

The Friday she came home from work early to surprise him was a warm August afternoon. The temperature on the deep, crowded Northern Line had soared to over thirty-five degrees. Dawn's uniform had stuck to her back and legs, making her skin itch. It was a relief to get off at London Bridge and feel the cool breeze from the river. She had spent the journey planning the evening ahead. She would have Kevin's favourite dinner ready for him when he finished work.

He was right; these past few months she *had* been neglecting him. She'd been torn between him and Dora, and Dora had won because she was the one who needed Dawn more. Dawn had been spending most of her nights at Crocus Road, and even the nights she had stayed in London she'd had to get up early the next morning to leave for work. Kevin came home in the evenings to an empty flat, ate dinner on his own, sat by himself on Friday nights when everyone else was out in couples. No wonder he'd been out of sorts. But now, bit by bit, Dawn was going to start moving back. Dora was so much better these days. She got on brilliantly with her carers; she was able to manage in the house overnight with just Milly for company. The worst was over.

Light-hearted, she went down the steps past Southwark Cathedral into Borough Market. She joined the crowds filing past barrows piled with mangos and tomatoes, braces of pheasant hanging on pillars, wooden barrels filled with spices and powders. The high-roofed sheds smelled of fish and cheeses, grilling meats, warm, herby bread. Dawn went from stall to stall, gathering the ingredients for her Moroccan buffet: fresh mint and coriander, new-baked flatbreads, a pot of home-made hummus. It was ten past five. The cobbled streets beyond the market were packed with tourists and City workers with their ties off, perched on high stools, resting wine glasses on the tops of barrels. Moist patches appeared on Dawn's brown paper bag as she walked in the heat to her tall, narrow building, sandwiched in its crooked terrace. The hall was cool and dim. A pile of junk mail teetered on the shelf inside the door. Kevin's bicycle was chained to the banister. He was home early. Dawn climbed the stairs to the second floor and stuck her key in the lock of flat three.

Kevin was in the kitchen, sitting at the table with a girl she didn't recognize. In front of them stood two wine glasses and a takeaway pizza box.

Kevin leaped to his feet. 'Dawn. Hi!' He glanced from her to the girl and back again. 'I thought you'd be at your gran's. You said you'd be staying down there till tomorrow.'

'Well . . . since it was such a nice evening . . .' Dawn's hands were slippery. Something in the paper bag had leaked. The girl sat at the table, dabbing her finger at the crumbs in the pizza box.

'Sister of a mate, just passing,' Kevin explained.

The girl smiled. She gave Dawn a little wave. 'Hi.'

'Hi,' Dawn said.

The girl seemed nice. Friendly. She had streaked, blonde-brown hair to her shoulders. She was maybe five or six years younger than Dawn. Dawn stared at her smooth golden skin, her low-cut green dress with the tiny yellow shoulder straps. Beside her, Kevin was staring as well, gazing directly at the girl, the way men looked at women in films. And Dawn knew there and then, standing with the leaking brown bag in her arms, that she had lost him.

She moved all her stuff back to Silham Vale and busied herself full-time with Dora. She researched mobility programmes, speech therapy, new physio techniques and did all the exercises with Dora over and over. 'I've never seen such progress,' Dr Barnes, their GP, said in amazement. 'She'll be walking by Christmas.'

But then the second, bigger stroke happened, and she never did.

Looking back, Dawn did not regret one second of it. She had loved Dora, and Dora wouldn't have hesitated – had not hesitated – to do the same thing for her. But she was gone now, and for the first time in three years there was a gap in Dawn's life. A gap which she could fill with work – very easily, if she chose. Or she could take Francine's advice and fill it with something else. The question was – with what?

Back at number 59, Milly didn't come trotting to greet Dawn at the gate as she usually did. She made an attempt at wagging her tail as Dawn lifted the latch but stayed where she was, sitting outside the porch, her tongue out, her head drooping towards the step.

'What's wrong, Mill?' Dawn came up the path. 'Is it your arthritis again?' The recent rain had been hard on Milly's joints. Some mornings she was barely able to climb out of her basket. But today was far from damp. The small garden was a heat trap, the sun beaming directly over the front of the terrace. The only real shade came from the porch, which as Dawn discovered when she slid back the glass door, was even hotter than outside. Milly's breath smelled like a sewage plant. Her nose was pale and dry.

'You poor thing. You're thirsty, aren't you? Come and have some water.'

But the plastic bowl in the porch was upended, the terracotta tiles long dry. Milly must have stood on the edge of it and flipped it over.

'Oh no.' Dawn was horrified. 'Poor Milly.'

She took the bowl through to the kitchen and ran the tap until it was cold. She filled the bowl to the top. Milly planted herself in front of it and lapped noisily. Minutes later, the bowl was empty. Dawn refilled it and the dog drank again.

'Oh Milly.' Dawn crouched beside her. 'I feel so bad.' She stroked Milly's broad, furrowed head. In recent months, the fur had grown stiffer and coarser. 'What are we going to do? I can't leave you out there all summer by yourself.'

It was a worry. Milly was used to being with people. She hated being on her own. As a pup, she had been found starving and covered in sores in a garden shed, left there by her owner to die. She had been pathetically grateful to be rescued, crying with joy and clinging to the RSPCA girl, so desperate to be petted and spoken to that she had ignored even the food and drink they had tried to give her. For years, everywhere Dora had gone, to the shops, to church, to her friends' houses, Milly had stuck close behind her like her short, hairy shadow. Even when Dora had been ill and unable to go anywhere, she had been *there*, and there had been people in the house all day, coming and going. Now Dawn sensed that the long hours alone were a misery for Milly. What did she *do* all day, by herself in that tiny garden? It was no life for a sociable animal.

Milly continued to lap at the water. Her ear brushed off Dawn's arm. The softness of it reminded Dawn of something. That little boy's hair in the café, brushing over her skin as his mum pulled him away.

You saved that boy's life. You should be very proud.

Will . . .

Dawn stood up and went to her bag. The napkin was still there, tucked away in the side pocket. She took it out and unfolded it. Coombs. Will Coombs. *He* had offered to walk Milly.

A spur-of-the-moment suggestion? People often said, 'Call me,' and didn't really mean it. Will had seemed pleasant but a little odd, as if he wasn't quite used to humans. Dawn looked again at the squiggles on the napkin. Will might not be too good with people but he'd had a definite rapport with Boris. The two had seemed quite happy in each other's company. And the way he had offered to walk Milly – it had sounded as though *she'd* be doing *him* a favour. He had said how nice it would be to have a dog in London.

Aloud, she said, 'He can only say no.' For Milly, it was worth a try.

She dialled the number on the napkin. The phone purred. Then a click.

'Hello?' A slow, deep, cautious voice.

'Hello. Is that Will?'

'Ye-es?'

'This is Dawn. From the café on Saturday—'

'Dawn Torridge! I remember.'

Ah rememba. The misty fell-sides again, and the row of wellies by the back door.

Dawn said, 'It really was lovely to meet you again after all this time.'

'Yes. Yes, it was.'

Will's tone was still cautious, as if he was wondering what on earth she was doing phoning him up out of the blue like this. Dawn got to the point. 'The reason I'm calling is because you mentioned that you might like to walk my dog, Milly.'

'Yes. I did say that.'

Silence. Dawn waited for him to add something like 'I'd be delighted,' or 'When would you like me to start?' but nothing seemed to be forthcoming.

'Was it a genuine offer?' she asked, uncertain now. 'Because if so, I think Milly would really enjoy it. But if you've changed your mind, there's no—'

'No,' Will said. 'No, it was a genuine offer. If Milly would like it, then I'd be very happy to do it.'

From the formality of his speech, he might have been engaged in a professional job interview rather than a casual conversation about dog-walking.

'Well – great,' Dawn said. 'Great. If you're sure it's OK. She's not as young as she was. Sometimes she's up for a long walk but other times she's only able to go for a potter. Her hips bother her quite a bit.'

'I understand,' Will said. 'I won't push her.'

Dawn guessed he wouldn't. She remembered how he had been with Boris, the patient way he had stepped over the puddle to let the red setter sniff at the bin. More confidently, she said, 'What way would it work? I mean . . . how would you . . . ?'

'I work from home mostly,' Will said. 'With Boris, when I feel like a break, I just go round and collect him.'

'Oh, I see.' As simple as that. 'Yes, that would work. Milly's in the garden during the day so you'd just have to open the gate.' But she hesitated. Much as Milly would enjoy the company, would she be happy to leave her territory and go off with someone she didn't know?

'Should I meet you the first time?' she asked. 'Just

so Milly can see us together. The only thing is, I work most days during the day so evenings are the best times for me.' She paused. She had no idea what Will did with his evenings. Partners? Children? The priesthood? Their conversation in the café hadn't quite got around to that level. 'Or,' she remembered, 'I've got a half day tomorrow? If that would suit you better?'

Will said, 'Tomorrow would be fine.'

'Wonderful.' Dawn gave him her phone number and address. They arranged to meet outside her house the following afternoon.

'See you then,' she said.

She hung up and wiped her forehead. Criminy! Will was hard work, there was no doubt about it. He had a very odd habit of leaving a gap at the start of each sentence, as if he was pausing to consider what to say. It was like trying to communicate with someone by satellite millions of light years away instead of just up the road in Streatham. But he had relaxed a bit towards the end, and Milly had seemed to like him that time they'd met in the café. It was better than her having to spend the whole day on her own.

After her two bowls of water, Milly was looking much happier. Her nose was wetter, her eyes brighter and more alert. She stuck her tongue out and grinned her Labrador grin up at Dawn. Dawn gave her a pat. '*That's* sorted,' she said.

Chapter Eight

'What the hell is *he* doing here?' Mandy hissed.

Dawn looked up from her desk where she had been ploughing through the recurrent headache of compiling the following month's off-duty rota. The break was far from unwelcome.

'What's who doing here?' she asked.

'*Him.*' Mandy jerked her chin towards the doors.

Standing outside the stock room with his hands behind his back was Dr Coulton. His white coat folded in long creases down his shoulders, like the wings of a giant, pallid vulture.

'He's been hanging about here all morning,' Mandy complained. 'Just staring in at the feeding tubes or whatever. It's getting on my nerves. He's just waiting for us to go over there and ask him what he wants so he can be rude.'

Dawn remembered the last time she had seen Dr Coulton. In the canteen that day, when she had dumped her tray and rushed off in the middle of their conversation. She must have left a rather strange impression of herself. It would do no harm for her to try to reverse it. She put the cap back on her pen and stood up from the desk.

'I'll go and talk to him,' she said. 'See if he's all right.'

Dr Coulton had his back to her as she approached. He did seem to be unusually interested in something in the stock room, standing with his head tipped back, staring down his nose at all the cupboards and shelves. Dawn looked into the room herself but all she could see was the latest delivery of urinary catheters, sitting in a box in the middle of the floor. It was only when she had almost reached Dr Coulton that she realized it wasn't actually the stock room he was looking at but the new patient in the side room next door.

She came up beside him. 'Good morning.'

Dr Coulton turned, jerking his hands apart. The un-flattering overhead light cast deep shadows under his cheekbones and in his temples, giving his long head a skull-like appearance. *Like he lives underground*, Mandy had said unkindly. Dawn wouldn't have gone that far, but he did look as if he could do with a week on a beach somewhere.

'You look lost,' she said. 'Can I help?'

Dr Coulton's condescending expression had re-turned.

146

'Yes,' he said, 'as a matter of fact, you can. I was wondering what—'

He broke off. Dawn heard a footstep on the tiles behind her. Mandy, coming up to hear what was going on.

She said encouragingly to Dr Coulton, 'Yes? You were wondering?'

Dr Coulton looked again at the side room.

'I was just checking on the patient,' he said. 'He looks a bit behind on fluids. Your nurses really should keep an eye on his intake.'

The tail of his white coat whipped between the doors of the ward as he left.

'What did he say? What did he say?' Mandy had missed it.

Dawn looked thoughtfully at the doors. 'He said we need to keep an eye on the patient's fluids.'

'His *fluids*?' Mandy was indignant. 'I told you, didn't I? I said he'd have some rude comment to make. Implying we're not doing our jobs. I was just in there with Lewis a few minutes ago. Does he look to you like he's got a problem with fluids?'

Dawn looked through the glass pane in the door of the side room. The patient, eighteen-year-old Lewis Kerr, was sitting up in bed, swigging from a giant bottle of coke.

'No,' Dawn had to admit. 'He seems to be managing pretty well.'

'That patient's not even his,' Mandy said. 'Rude Ed covers general surgery. Lewis is orthopaedics. Why's he up here hanging around an orthopaedic patient's room?' She tutted and shook her head. 'I'm telling you, Dawn, there's something funny about that man. Sinister. Whenever I see him, I always expect to hear that creepy *duh duh duh* music, like in a horror film. He's always in the hospital, prowling around at night, even when he's not on call.'

'Prowling around *this* ward?'

'Well – prowling everywhere. Clive said yesterday he caught him staring at him in the canteen. Gave him the creeps, he said. He was queuing up for his lunch and he suddenly got this really weird feeling down his back, like he was being watched, so he turned around and there was Rude Ed, sitting at a table on his own, just staring over at him. And Daphne from Orthopaedics said she was fetching a chart from Records in the basement the other evening and she turned a corner and ran straight into him. Just loomed up out of nowhere, he did. When she asked him what he was doing there, he claimed he was doing after-hours work in the lab. Something to do with that research conference that was on here last week.' Mandy said darkly, 'I just hope he's being supervised. I wouldn't be surprised if he's developing some new disease to unleash on us all.'

She added, 'By the way, Dawn, I forgot to tell you: we're out of paracetamol.'

'Already? I only checked the stock yesterday.'

'Yes, but all the patients keep on asking for extra. Everyone's in pain lately for some reason. Must be something in the water. Shall I send the student down to Pharmacy?'

Dawn considered. 'No. I'll nip across and get some from ITU.'

The wards often did that: borrowed drugs or equipment from each other, then paid it back when they were re-stocked. Dawn hadn't seen Francine for a while. She'd take the chance to see if she was free for a quick cuppa.

Before she left, she looked again through the window of the side room. Why *had* Dr Coulton been up here, checking on a patient who wasn't even his? There was nothing remarkable about Lewis, aside from his badly smashed tibia. His right leg was propped up on a pillow, temporarily immobilized in a fixator, like a spiky metal cage around his calf. He was waiting to have major surgery to repair it, but apart from that he was perfectly healthy. He was able to mobilize and feed and wash himself; he needed minimal nursing care. The room was cluttered with his belongings: a pair of jeans with one leg cut off flung over a chair, the *Mirror* sports pages spread out on the bed, lurid get-well cards everywhere. The character of the room had been transformed, the essence of any previous patient well and truly exorcized. Dawn could go in there now.

She gave up wondering about Dr Coulton and pushed the door open to the corridor. The hall was filled with visitors and staff hurrying up and down between the various wards. Dr Coulton had disappeared. Dawn's shoes made a soft *snip snip* sound as she walked towards the ITU. The tiled floor was striped with sunlight from the windows all down one side. The sky was clear, the only clouds a few puffy wisps high in the blue. Milly and Will would be in luck for their walk this afternoon.

The ITU was filled with the odours Dawn always associated with these sicker patients: Chlorhexidine, Pseudomonas, Vitamin B. Most of the patients were unconscious in their high beds, their closed eyes protected by strips of gel across the lids. In the middle of the room, Francine was helping two other nurses to roll a man who must have weighed twenty stone so that they could change his sheets. One nurse's job was just to hold all his lines and drips and catheters, making sure nothing got pulled out as they moved him.

'Just stealing some paracetamol.' Dawn waved the box she'd taken at Francine. 'I'll put it back later.'

'OK.' Francine straightened, touching her arm to her forehead. She looked tired, less sleek and groomed than usual. Her chignon had come loose. A hank of blonde hair hung down over one ear.

'Coffee?' Dawn raised her eyebrows.

'Go on then. I'll be there in a minute.'

Dawn filled the kettle in the ITU kitchen. In the cupboard over the sink, she found Francine's purple mug with the slogan 'World's Best Mum' and a plain white mug for herself with a patient ID bracelet marked 'Visitor' looped around the handle. Francine appeared with a couple of hair-pins in her mouth, re-doing her chignon.

'Busy today?' Dawn asked.

'So-so,' Francine said through the pins. 'Three sick laparotomies arrived a couple of hours ago all at the same time, so we've been kept going.' She finished with her hair and took the purple mug from Dawn. 'Thanks.'

She sipped the coffee, leaning against the sink, gazing in a preoccupied way at the lino.

'Everything all right?' Dawn asked.

Francine looked up. Then she sighed. 'Not really. Vinnie's firm's in trouble again. The owners have been over-investing elsewhere and now they're threatening wholesale redundancies to save their own skins.'

'Oh no, Fran.'

'It's so corrupt.' Francine's fingers whitened on the handle of her mug. 'Vinnie and the others have been loyal to them for years and this is how they repay them. The shareholders'll be all right; they'll just declare themselves bankrupt and walk away and start up again under a different name. I saw one of them the other day, sailing down Streatham High Road in a brand new Mercedes. If looks could kill, I swear, the old fart would have driven into the Thames and sunk straight to the bottom.'

It was rare to see Francine so agitated. Normally she was the epitome of the serene ward sister, placid and unruffled amidst the chaos. It was a bad time to have a husband out of work. Vinnie, a builder, and Francine had a large mortgage and two expensive teenage boys to support. Dawn wasn't the only one, it seemed, with her own private troubles to worry about. Everyone had their problems.

'I feel better already,' Francine said after a while. 'Even just having a moan about it helps. Don't say it around, though, will you, Dawn? I wouldn't have told anyone but you.'

'Of course I won't.'

Francine grinned suddenly. 'Anyway, that's the thing about nursing, isn't it? We moan during the good times, when everyone else is earning more than us, but it is recession-proof. You can always do a few extra shifts if you're stuck.'

'That's true. And if there's anything I can do . . .'

'I know,' Francine said. 'Thanks, Dawn.'

*   *   *

It being early afternoon, the journey to Silham Vale took half its usual time. By three o'clock, Dawn was walking down Crocus Road. On the street outside number 59 was parked an unfamiliar red Honda with dried mud on the wheels. A man was waiting by the car, looking up and down the pavement, his arms hanging awkwardly by his sides as if he didn't quite know where to put them. The shambling posture was unmistakeable. The sun glinted on his glasses, turning the lenses opaque. All that could be seen of his eyes were two bright yellow squares. Dawn couldn't decide if it made him look mysterious or just slightly gormless.

'Hello.' She waved to attract his attention as she approached.

Will turned. The two yellow opacities turned with him. 'Hello.'

The bright squares made his face look like a microchip. Dawn wanted to laugh, but she kept the friendly smile on her face. 'Lovely day, isn't it?'

'Yes.'

Will's hands still dangled at his sides. Under his navy jacket today he wore a plain grey T-shirt. Dawn noticed again how tall he was. She was five feet eight but he stood a good head higher than her. Milly puffed and snuffled, struggling to push her nose through the bars of the gate.

'Where were you thinking of going?' Dawn asked.

'The North Downs. Or further. East Sussex, maybe.'

'Oh.' Dawn was surprised. She had assumed one of the local parks. Tooting Bec Common maybe, or Wandsworth. 'That sounds nice. I don't think Milly's been down there in years.'

Will jammed his hands into his pockets, so deep that his knuckles made a knobbly rim around the hem of his jacket.

'Come with us,' he said.

'Oh, no. No. It sounds lovely, but I've got too much to do.' Half days didn't come Dawn's way very often and she'd been planning this one for ages. The first thing she was going to do was make a large, hot mug of tea and have it in her kitchen with the salad roll she had bought specially in Waitrose, luxuriating in the fact that there would be no pagers going off, no managers flustering up to her and saying, 'Matron, when you have a moment . . .' Afterwards she would tackle the mound of paperwork that had been building up over the past few days. Off-duty rotas. An appraisal of the new portable cardiac Resus kit. Her Disaster Plan. There was enough to keep her going for a week.

The sun beat down on her head. The air shimmered above the tarmac. Francine's voice: *You need some perspective . . .*

'How long would we be?' she asked.

Will squinted at the sky. 'As long as you like. We could be back in three hours.'

Dawn thought.

'I'll just grab a sandwich and change out of my uniform.'

The red Honda had seen better days. Piles of papers lay everywhere, printed with rows of numbers and brackets and semicolons. The seats were matted with dog hairs.

'Sorry about this.' Will had his arms full of computer magazines, looking around for somewhere to put them. His glasses were slipping down his nose again. 'I'll put some newspaper on that seat for you.'

'No. Really. These are the clothes I usually walk Milly in.' It was fascinating, the way people's cars often fit with their personalities. Will's car, messy as it was, matched what she had seen of him so far. Not flashy or trendy but . . . useful. That sounded like an insult, as if she was saying he was boring, but she didn't mean it like that. There was nothing wrong with being useful. Dawn understood useful people. She felt at ease with them. They weren't as easy to find as you might think.

She patted the back seat. 'Come on, Milly.' Gently, she shoved at Milly's rear to give her stiff hip some leverage. Milly squeezed into the space between the seats and settled down with her muzzle on a magazine called *Linux Pro* which had a picture of some kind of microchip on the front.

Will drove around the edges of Croydon, skirting the giant new shopping centres and office blocks. At Purley they joined the A23, heading south to the motorway. Gradually, the towers and housing estates gave way to individual houses, then to fields on either side of the road.

'This is a great idea,' Dawn said. Now that they were leaving London behind, she had a feeling of relaxation, of letting go. The mounds of paperwork would still be there when she got back but in the meantime there was nothing she could do about them. Will was quiet, concentrating on the road. Having gone to the trouble of asking her to join them, he seemed to have retreated again into his usual tongue-tied silence. Well, that was OK. She was quite happy just to sit back and enjoy the journey. She had never got around to buying a car. Hardly anyone she knew in London owned one. There seemed little point in forking out for insurance and parking and congestion charges when the trains and buses could take you anywhere you wanted to go. But on a day like this it was lovely to be able to escape the noise and grime of the city.

At a junction, Will took a slip road that climbed to a roundabout surrounded by trees. Now they were definitely in the countryside. Green and yellow fields sloped between the gaps in the hedgerow. They took the second exit and came to a village, all timbered houses and high, red-bricked walls covered with creeper. The village seemed utterly deserted, yet it was beautifully kept and cared-for. The ancient church at one end, all leaded panes and steep roof, surrounded by crooked, lichen-covered headstones, looked like something from a fairy tale. Will turned right at a crossroads and the road climbed again, narrowing to a single lane with grass growing in the centre. Twigs and leaves brushed the sides of the car. Finally, little more than an hour after they had left London, Will steered the car into a lay-by and turned off the engine.

Silence pulsed through the windows. It was as if the wide, empty sky was trying to push its way right into the car with them. The only sound was the distant plaintive *oo-oo* of a wood pigeon.

'It's beautiful,' Dawn said. She opened her door. Below the car spread the long valley, thickly buttered with bright yellow oil-seed rape. A swarm of midges blurred the air under the hedgerow. Several feet away, a wooden stile led into a field.

Will said, 'If we follow the path through that stile, it'll bring us right around in a circuit and back to the car. About four miles or so. Will Milly manage that?'

Milly had leaped from the car and was in the field already, sniffing under the hedgerow with just her rear sticking out. At the sound of her name she came backing out, covered in twigs, one ear bent over her eye. Dawn laughed. 'I think she'll be OK.'

They followed the dirt track around the edge of the

field. The sun was hot on Dawn's face. She took her jumper off and tied it around her waist. Around them sloped more fields and low hills, criss-crossing into a haze. This was farming country, lush and fertile, the grass a dark blue-green. Milly trotted ahead of them, occasionally stopping to eat some grass or sniff at a tree. Beside Dawn, Will's heavy brown boots tramped along, flattening the grass. *Thud. Thud.*

'Did you say you lived in Streatham?' Dawn asked.

'Yes.'

'Whereabouts?'

'Telford Road.'

'Oh, I know it. Some lovely houses up there.'

'Yes.'

Thud. He really was hard to talk to. In the next field, a flock of lambs came crowding to check out their visitors. They shouldered each other out of the way, their woolly bodies splodged with bright red ink, some of them with soot-black faces and eyes like shiny buttons in the wool. Dawn clipped Milly's lead on to her collar. Her chasing days were long over but in the past half an hour she seemed to have dropped five years. The lambs' mothers kept their distance, lying down or chomping on the grass, but keeping an eye on what their offspring were up to; calling them in their bass voices to come away if they got too close to the strangers.

'They sound so funny,' Dawn said. 'Like Pavarotti.'

Forest Ward and St Iberius seemed a million miles away. Dawn said, 'I remember years ago, on our farm in Cumbria, seeing two sets of twin lambs playing in a hollow tree. They were pushing and shoving each other, fighting for the best spot. The twins who got pushed out ran back across the field to their mum, bawling all the way, as if they were telling tales. It was so sweet. Exactly as if they were children.'

Will's feet continued to thud on the grass. Dawn sighed to herself. This had been a mistake. Will was making no effort at all; hadn't, in fact, since they had climbed into the car and begun their journey here. He didn't seem the least bit interested in her or Milly. Probably he had never expected her to take him up on his offer and had only come to meet her today out of politeness. Well, at least she had tried. It was so lovely here, she didn't regret coming, but once today was over she would find some other way of keeping Milly entertained.

They had reached the road again. Two little girls ran giggling along the path towards a group of cars parked under some trees. Behind them puffed a smaller child, struggling to keep up.

'Wait,' the child shouted. 'Wait for me.'

His chubby face was red and cross and anxious. His cheeks turned purple with the effort not to be left behind. The girls glanced behind them, giggled again, ran faster.

'Wait! Wait!' The child's voice rose in a wail.

Will's voice, somewhere over Dawn's left ear. 'About the same age, aren't they?'

'Sorry?' Dawn looked at him. 'As who?'

'The boy on Saturday. In the café.'

'Oh. Yes, so they are.'

The cross little boy tripped and plopped forward to the ground. He didn't bother to get up but lay face down in the mud and howled. A woman appeared from somewhere between the parked cars and came to pick him up. He clung to her, still howling, pointing at the two girls. The woman stroked his hair and murmured to him. Then she took all three children away with her. The child's wails faded behind the trees until there was silence.

'Look,' Dawn said, 'it's getting late. I think maybe we'd better—'

'That was so incredible,' Will said. 'What you did that day.'

He had stopped walking and turned to look at her. The sun had moved off his glasses; for the first time she could see his face clearly. The frank admiration in his eyes was unmistakable. Dawn realized suddenly that it wasn't lack of interest that was making him so quiet. It was shyness.

'You were so calm,' he said. 'Everyone else froze or panicked. But you . . . you just got on with it.'

The awe in his tone. Such openness and earnestness in such a large man made him seem vulnerable. It struck Dawn suddenly that he fancied her. Will was exactly the sort of man who would have a thing about nurses. Her nursing friends had often joked about men like him. Men who liked being looked after and had a fixation about mothers and breasts and thermometers. Not her type at all. Not anyone's type, surely! Despite that, his shyness touched her. She always felt a sympathy, a protectiveness, towards people who were in some way vulnerable, especially if they weren't shrewd or streetwise enough to have learned how to hide it.

She said, 'Well, you could always do a first aid course. What I did was much more to do with that really than with nursing.'

'I'd like that,' Will said eagerly. 'It's only when something like this happens that you realize how much you don't know.'

'I could look up the details of a good course in your area if you'd like.'

'Would you? That would be great.'

They had started walking again, a little easier now with each other. Ahead of them was a pub, low and white, with a beamed doorway and black-painted shutters. The garden to the side was scattered with wooden trestle tables and barrels filled with flowers. Above the door was an iron bracket holding a sign with a painting of a stag. The words underneath the painting read, *The Black Hart*.

'Would you mind if we stopped here for a minute?' Dawn asked. 'I want to get Milly a drink.'

The doorway of the pub was so low that Will had to bend his head to go through. Inside, the room was all dark wood and black beams, the only illumination a sharp slash of sunlight on the patterned carpet. Behind the bar, a teenage girl was reading a magazine.

'Excuse me,' Dawn said. 'Could we have some water for my dog?'

'Sure.' The girl slid off her high stool. 'Anything else?'

Will looked at Dawn.

'I'll have a glass of white wine,' she said. Why not? She *had* just done a four mile walk. Will ordered a shandy for himself. They took the drinks outside to one of the wooden tables under the trees. They were the only people there. Milly stood in the shade and slurped from her bowl of water. Will sat across the table from Dawn. He had taken off his jacket. His legs were stretched out, his fine, straight hair messy from the breeze. He looked much more relaxed and at home than he had in the cramped café in Tooting.

'Can I ask you something?' Dawn leaned forward on her elbows. 'What exactly do IT people do?'

The reflection of the trees moved over Will's glasses as he turned his head. He grinned. 'Do you really want to know? I'm a systems engineer.'

Dawn said knowledgeably, 'You design websites.'

'No. That's the trendy end of things. I'm more of a back-room person. People hire me, say, when their company has just installed a new type of program and it doesn't work or crashes their system.'

'Do you enjoy it?'

'Yes, I do. I like being able to choose where I go, what pace to work at.'

He liked not having to talk too much to people was what he meant. Dawn could see now that a career in IT probably suited him very well. It was like farming in that way – good for loners.

'How long have you lived in London?' she asked.

'Two years.'

'But you'd like to go back.'

'Yes.' The corner of Will's mouth twisted. 'I'm not really a city person, as you can probably tell. I applied for a job up there recently.'

'Only recently?'

'Yes.' He hesitated. 'Well,' he went on, 'I couldn't before. Because of my girlfriend.'

'Oh.' A girlfriend. There was a surprise! Dawn would have sworn that he was on his own.

'Well,' Will said, 'my fiancée, really. She was from Keswick, and . . . I had to leave for a while. I couldn't stay. It's just that she . . . well, she . . .'

Dawn, understanding, said, 'She finished things.'

A stab of sympathy. She pictured a brisk, efficient young woman, finally reaching the end of her patience with this shy, bespectacled, lumbering man.

'No. Actually, she died.'

Dawn recoiled, pulling her elbows off the table. 'How? Oh God, I'm sorry. It's none of my business.'

'That's all right,' Will said. 'It was three years ago. She had . . . breast cancer.' The hesitancy before he said the words told her it was still difficult for him to talk about.

'I'm sorry.' Dawn was still horrified at her crassness. And to think she'd wondered if he fancied her!

'It's all right. Like I said, I'm ready to move back there now.' Will took a mouthful of his shandy. Then he planted the glass firmly back on the table and looked up. 'So,' he said, 'what about you? What kind of nursing do you do?'

Dawn took the hint.

'I'm the Surgical Matron,' she said, 'at St Iberius Hospital in Battersea.'

'The Matron!' Will made a whistle shape with his mouth to show that he was impressed. 'So you don't deal with actual patients any more?'

'Oh no, I do. That's the most important part of it for me.'

'What does it involve? What's a typical day for you?'

'Well . . .' Clearly he was determined to move on from talk about his fiancée. Dawn thought for a moment. She had plenty of stories from the ward; every nurse did. She began to sketch out an average day for Will, making sure to steer clear of any deaths and tragedies, concentrating instead on the stories that were funny, brave, tender. Conscious of not wanting to bore him, she kept an eye out for the ballooning double chin that had always signified that Kevin was stifling a yawn. But no yawn came. Will seemed genuinely interested, watching her as she spoke, nodding and crinkling his eyes up at all the funny bits. Unlike with most lay people, Dawn noticed, she didn't keep having to stop and explain things to him. Even though he mightn't initially know what she meant by terms like TPN or infusion pump, he seemed to work out what she meant soon enough from the context. His technical background, she supposed. This quickness was a new side of him she hadn't seen before. Will, she was beginning to suspect, was one of those people who knew things, but unless you asked him directly you would never find out. There was a core of intelligence to him, hidden but definitely there. The light moved off his glasses. For the first time she noticed how grey his eyes were. Like hers.

'Northern eyes,' her Cumbrian grandfather had once said. 'Adapted to our long, dark winters. We can see further in the mountains than other people.'

'You really love it, don't you?' Will was watching her. 'What you do.'

'Most of the time.' Dawn picked up her wineglass

and took a sip. 'There can be bad days, some difficult decisions. You don't always get it right.'

'But the way you feel about it.' Will was leaning forward, the most animated she had ever seen him. 'So many people are bored with their jobs, just doing it for the money. But you . . . You must never wake up at night and think, *What have I done with my life? What is the point of me?*'

'That's true,' Dawn said, surprised.

If a touch idealistic. The public could be funny about nurses. Some thought that all nurses did was make beds and clean up vomit. Others, just as unrealistically, viewed them as martyred beings, one wing's-breadth below the angels, devoting themselves to the care of others for the sheer love of humankind. 'Don't you find it very *sad*?' these people would say. Or: 'I couldn't do nursing myself. I'm very sensitive about blood.' As if they lived on some higher plane. What did they think would happen if they were ill or injured and everyone was too sensitive to deal with *their* blood?

The truth was that nursing was like any other job. It had its dramatic moments but most of it was routine. Common sense. Still, it was nice to see herself through Will's eyes. Who could resist being thought of as a heroine?

'The nurses at the hospital were excellent with Kate,' Will said. 'I always remember that. So kind to her, even though they were so busy. They always seemed to be under-staffed. It's such a worthwhile job. I don't know why more people don't do it.'

'Well, it's not for those who like a luxury lifestyle,' Dawn said lightly. 'Try living in London on a nurse's salary.'

'The lack of money doesn't bother you though, does it?' He was still looking at her. 'Why did you decide to do it?'

People often asked her that. Usually she said something like, 'I wanted to help people,' or, 'I enjoy the variety.'

She heard the words come out of her mouth. 'My parents were killed. In a car accident, the day after Boxing Day. A drunk driver slammed into them on the Honister Pass.'

Will looked away. 'I heard about that.'

So he did know. 'My father,' she said, 'died there and then but my mother lasted a week. I saw her in the hospital every day.'

Will said quietly, 'And you were inspired by her care.'

'Well, in a way. The ward she was on was terrible. Absolutely filthy. And the noise. Like a tube station at rush hour.' She'd been ten years old but she could see it. The bloodstains on the floor beside her mum's bed that weren't cleaned for days. The constant banging and clatter of trolleys, the shrill of unanswered phones, the cackles of laughter from the nurse's desk. And when she had gone to beg them to do something to help her mother because the pain was literally preventing her from breathing, the endless litany of excuses: 'I'm busy at the moment', 'I'm on my break', 'I've just come back from my leave'.

'On my mother's last day,' she said, 'a new ward sister started who I hadn't seen before. The ward was a different place with her there. Quieter. Cleaner. And she found the time to come and sit with me and my mum. She was with me when . . . I was only a child but I saw it: the difference proper nursing could make.'

She shut herself up. Why on earth was she saying all this? She didn't normally talk about herself in this way. The Importance of Not Being Earnest. The situation had flipped like a coin from Will being too open and intense to her sitting here blabbing like a child. He had sat across from her and listened and she had blurted it all out. Probably he had revealed more than he'd meant to as well.

She stood up from the bench.

'We should go,' she said. 'It's getting late.'

She covered her confusion by walking around the table, looking underneath. 'Milly,' she called. 'Milly, it's time to go.' As she reached Will's side of the table, he stood up too. His large, solid frame brought her to a halt.

'You saved a life,' he said. 'The other day. Most people will never do that.'

Dawn heard her own breathing in her ears. This was the closest she had ever been to him. In the light from the sky Will's face was gold-pink. The air was filled with the smell of frying onions and the heavy scent from the trees. Maybe it was the wine – it was a large glass and she'd had nothing to eat since lunch – but Dawn became suddenly aware that she was standing inches from, not just a person but a man. Not, perhaps, a man who would turn heads in the street, with his hunched posture and square face and too-serious expression. But with eyes that were keen and grey, and with a quiet intelligence like the rocky bed of a river, deep and unshowy but there. Distracted, she gazed down at his heavy brown boots. She said the first thing that came into her head. 'Your limp is gone.'

'My limp?'

'The one you had that day. In the café.'

Will maintained a puzzled silence. It was only when Dawn looked up at him again that the frown cleared from his face.

'My ankle,' he said. 'Boris crashed into me on the common that morning. It's an old injury that keeps coming back. But it was so slight . . . I'd forgotten all about it . . . the pain was gone by the next day. How on earth did you—?'

She'd been showing off, of course. Showcasing her nursing skills, playing up to his idealism. And it had worked; that look of admiration was back in his eyes which, she had to admit to herself now, was the reason she'd made the observation in the first place. But the look was different this time. More intent. For the first time, more . . . male. Dawn felt powerful. Reckless. Not lumpy and sensible and navy-clad, but floating from her clumpy shoes. Her body was moving, leaning into him of its own accord, as if drawn by some strange magnetic field.

Then, abruptly, the field switched itself off. *What are you doing?* Too much sun, too much wine. This was all wrong. She didn't fancy him. He was too shy for her, too odd. She hardly knew him.

She stepped back.

'We'd best call it a day,' she said. 'I've got an early start tomorrow.'

She didn't look at Will again but walked ahead of him, calling to Milly to join her. 'Did you have a nice time? You did, didn't you?' By the time they had reached the car, her pulse and breathing were almost back to normal. She was even able to make some light-hearted comment to Will about the brighter evenings these days making it difficult to keep track of the time. He made some reply in return but the earlier easiness between them was gone.

Chapter Nine

'Have you done something to yourself?' Mandy stood in front of Dawn with her hands on her hips.

'What do you mean?' Dawn looked up from the sterile dressing packs she had been checking. 'Why?'

'I don't know.' Mandy was still studying her, her eyes narrowed. 'Maybe it's your hair. It seems longer. More natural. Or maybe it's not your hair but you do look different in some way. Healthier or something.'

The clock over the desk read five to five. Almost time for the ward round. Dawn began to stack the remaining dressing packs back in their boxes.

'How's Jason?' she asked.

'Doing really well,' Mandy said proudly. 'Got another medal for football the other day. But he's just told me this morning they've got another school trip coming up.'

'More money?'

'They must think I'm made of it.' Mandy rolled her eyes. She had returned to nursing three years ago after her husband, Claud, had scarpered with the receptionist at his garage, leaving Mandy as the single mother to nine-year-old Jason.

'Oh look,' Mandy added, 'Prof's arrived. We'd best get our skates on.'

Professor Kneebone was at the chart trolley, his team gathered concentrically around him; registrars in the inner ring, house officers around them, medical students orbiting in the outer reaches. He was like the planet Saturn, or a stone that had been dropped in a pond.

Walking up the ward with Dawn, Mandy looked at her again and clicked her fingers. 'No,' she said. 'No, I've got it. It's not your hair. It's your face in general. You've got a sort of glow about you. Healthy-looking.'

Dawn glanced into the mirror over a sink they were passing. Then she stopped. Mandy was right – she did look better. Was it just the light in here? Or what had happened to that woman of a couple of weeks ago with the pallor and the purple bags under her eyes? This woman looked younger, plumper, her nose and cheeks flushed from the sun.

'I was in the countryside,' she said. 'A couple of days ago. In Sussex with . . . with a friend.'

'Well, you should go more often. It suits you.'

'Maybe I will.' Somewhat self-consciously, Dawn touched her face. 'You're right, it does seem to have done some good. I do feel a lot healthier these days.'

'No more trouble with that headache, then?' Mandy asked as they approached the medical team.

'Headache?'

'The one you had that afternoon,' Mandy said. 'When you took the rest of the day off?'

'Oh, no. No more trouble with that.'

Mandy smiled. 'Good.'

Jack Benson, the thyroid patient, was out of ITU. After the ward round, Dawn returned to check on him. He was sitting up in bed, dressed in a new pair of paisley pyjamas, tucking into his tea. The wound in his neck was closed, the silver necklace of Frankenstein staples back in place. His neck was back to its normal size, tucked well in under his chin where a neck should be. His breathing was effortless and relaxed.

'How are you feeling?' Dawn asked.

'Very well, Sister. I've got to say, though, I don't know why so many people complain about hospital food. Tastes pretty bloody good to me.'

His wife, sitting by his bed, said, 'But, Jack, you've been fed through a drip for the last few days. That's why you've got such an appetite now. It's a good sign, Sister, isn't it?'

'Yes, it is,' Dawn said. 'A very good sign.'

'They don't give you much, though,' Mr Benson said through a mouthful of gammon and mashed potato. He tried to reach under the wheeled tray-table to pat his belly but there wasn't much space between the two. He leaned towards Dawn in a furtive way. 'Any chance of an extra slice of toast?'

Dawn murmured, mimicking his conspiratorial air, 'I'll take a look.'

In the fridge in the kitchen, between the yogurts and boxes of nasogastric feed, she found a loaf of bread. She took two slices and put them in the toaster. The sun came through the window, sparkling on the taps, the fridge door, the steel racks of patient trays. Once again, the day in Sussex was with her. Even with the slight awkwardness over what had happened with Will at the end, the memory of the afternoon – the fields, the lambs, the bluebells like purple smoke under the trees – still lay like a sweet in her pocket waiting to be unwrapped.

Since the outing a week ago, she had heard nothing from Will. What had happened between them had been so subtle, so indefinite. Had he even realized what was going on? She hoped she hadn't hurt his feelings. But pulling back had been the right decision; she was quite clear about that now. Looking back, it was obvious how it had almost happened. The day had been so lovely – the sun, the countryside, the pink sky – and all of those things she had ended up confusing with Will himself. He was such a nice man, but he was so odd. Those peculiar pauses before he spoke, as if he needed time to work out what to say; the way it always took so long for him to unstiffen enough to have a normal conversation. How could you possibly have a relationship with someone as awkward and intense as that? Anyway, what was to say he even liked *her* in that way? He was so guarded and reserved, so difficult to get to know. Now and again she had caught glimpses of something underneath, something more complex than the simple, rather dull man he chose to reveal, but every time she thought she might be getting somewhere with him, down slammed the shutters again with her firmly on the other side. Either he was choosing, for some reason, not to open up to her – or there really was nothing else there.

Dawn thought she knew what the problem was. Will was still grieving over his fiancée. He might think he was over her, but he wasn't. The moment outside the Black Hart had been an impulse for him as much as for Dawn. Walking together through the fields had reminded them of their childhoods. Meeting each other out of the blue like that – Dora having died recently and Will's fiancée – it was only natural that they should have turned to each other for comfort. Will was lonely here in London. He had come to idealize nurses a little, and who could blame him for that? Dawn's rescue of the child in the café had made her seem heroic and glamorous in his eyes. But if he got to know the real her, with her nylon uniform and sensible shoes and piles of paperwork, it would be a different story.

If he got to know her. He had no intention of staying in London. He had applied for that job in Cumbria, 300 miles away. So there was no sense in her wondering about what some vague moment outside a country pub might or might not have meant, or developing a guilt complex about Will's feelings, because in a very short time he wasn't even going to be here any more.

Mr Benson's toast popped up. Dawn took the slices and put them on a plate. Searching in the fridge for some butter, she found herself remembering something. Once, years ago, at the school in Buttermere, a hedgehog had wandered into the playground, blinded by a plastic fast-food cup which had become wedged over its face. Several of the girls had screamed; one of the boys had tried to kick it under the climbing frame. Then an older, taller, fair-haired boy had appeared from nowhere and shoved the other boy out of the way. He had reached down and eased the cup from the hedgehog's nose, then gently lifted him back over the wall into the field. Afterwards he had walked away without a word so that some of the girls had giggled and whispered how strange he was. 'That's Will Coombs,' Jill Arscott from Year Six had said. 'Total oddball. Only ever talks to his dog.' Shortly after that, Dawn's parents had died and she had moved away from Cumbria and never seen any of those people in the playground again.

She took the toast out to Mr Benson.

'There you are.' She placed the plate on his tray. 'Hope that does the trick.'

'Thank you, Sister.' Mr Benson rubbed his hands together.

When Dawn went to leave them, his wife got up and came a little way down the ward with her.

'Sister, may I talk to you for a moment?'

'Of course.' Dawn stopped. She led her in behind a nearby curtain for some privacy.

'I just wanted to say . . .' Mrs Benson was twisting the thin gold chain on her glasses between her fingers. 'My husband is being very casual about all of this, but we both know what . . . what could have happened that day.'

'Well, that's all in the past,' Dawn reassured her. 'He's doing very well now. We're very pleased with his progress.'

'Professor Kneebone said . . . he said if it wasn't for you—' Mrs Benson looked down, fiddling harder with her glasses.

'It's all part of the job,' Dawn said. 'Really. I was happy to be able to help.'

'But you . . . I'm sorry.' Mrs Benson dropped the

glasses and took a deep breath. She touched her finger to her eyes. 'I'm sorry. This is very silly of me. I'll let you get back to your work.'

She turned to leave but Dawn reached to touch her arm.

'Mrs Benson,' she said, 'as I say, it was a privilege to be able to help. I was very proud and happy to do it.'

Mrs Benson nodded, unable to speak. Dawn squeezed her hand. She smiled at her and watched as she returned to her husband.

Before her shift ended, she toured the ward, checking that the stock room was filled, the defibrillator plugged in, all patients comfortable and stable. She passed down between the rows of beds, her keen eye missing nothing: the empty hand-wash dispenser over the sink, the bag of saline that would soon need changing. All the little things that kept a ward ticking over. It was when she heard herself humming aloud that she realized. She *was* happy. She loved this, all of it. The soft, steady *bip-bip* of the monitors, the lemon smell of the polished floor. Over the past few months, for some reason, the work had lost some of its joy. She had gone about the job as efficiently as ever, but abruptly, *bam bam bam*, head down, not pausing to pass the time of day with anyone or gain any enjoyment from it. In the mornings she had walked up to her staff and said, 'What was bed ten's temperature last night?', not even bothering to preface the query with a simple 'Hello,' or

'How are you?' She had become disillusioned with the patients, begun fighting with people like Clive.

And now. One day in the sun and everything seemed different and possible again.

Over the past few days, an idea had been building in her mind. Why not go to Cumbria for her holiday? When Priya came back from her maternity leave, she would take a proper break – a full fortnight, even – and spend it at the Lakes. Talking about them with Will had given her a longing to see them again. She had never been back there, not once, since she had moved away. There had been school, and then her nursing training, and when she had gone on holidays with Kevin or her friends they had hopped on a plane and flown abroad. And in the last couple of years, because of Dora, she hadn't been able to leave London at all. But now . . . now she felt an urge to see all her childhood haunts again. The farm, the school, the broad, Canadian sweeps of water. Milly would enjoy it too. The day in Sussex had shown that she still had plenty of pep left in her. It was so simple and easy; she couldn't believe it had all seemed so difficult before.

'It's like toads,' Francine had once said. 'If you put a toad in a pot of water and heat it up slowly enough, it'll keep on sitting there until it boils to death. If it happens gradually enough, the toad never realizes how bad things have become.'

Toads indeed!

Still humming, Dawn went to collect her bag from her office. The sun through the blinds cast stripy shadows like bars across the thank-you cards and the Disaster Plan guidelines on the walls. These past few days she'd hardly done any work on her Disaster Plan. Tomorrow she would take the red folder out and give the contents a good going-over. For now, she would just run a final check of her work e-mails before she left.

She keyed her password into the computer and clicked on the icon marked, 'Internal mail'. The screen lit up with her account. One new message.

Important, the subject line read. *For the attention of Matron Torridge, Forest Ward.*

Dawn clicked on the e-mail, searching at the same time in her bag for a pen. The message flashed up on the screen. She glanced at it, still half-concentrating on her bag.

Then she lowered the bag and looked at the message again.

She sank on to the chair. Her bag slid sideways off her knee. She barely noticed. Her entire field of vision was taken up by the screen. For the third time, she took in the opening lines of the e-mail.

Dear Matron,
Well done. You killed Ivy Walker so discreetly.
If it wasn't for me, no one would ever have
known.

Chapter Ten

Dawn's first instinct was to shove the computer away from her as if the keys were contaminated. Dear God! This was a joke. Some kind of sick, tasteless joke. Any second now, someone was going to leap up from behind the filing cabinet and shout, 'Gotcha!' She spun in her chair, searching for the swivelling cameras, the sniggering faces at the window.

The office door was open. Instinctively, Dawn leaped up to close it. 'Custard with that, love?' Becky from Catering was shouting somewhere out on the ward. In the nearest bed, a pair of feet wiggled from behind the curtains. A woman's voice was saying, 'Yes. No. They said I'd get done tomorrow.' Dawn shut the door, blocking out the sounds, and turned the key. As a final precaution, she yanked the blind down over the glass.

Then she sat at the desk again, her heart hammering.

Calm. Stay calm. Read this through properly.

She went through the e-mail again, her shoulders hunched, her eyes narrowed so as not to miss a single word.

Dear Matron,
Well done. You killed Ivy Walker so discreetly.
If it wasn't for me, no one would ever have
known.
    Plenty of people would say I should go to
the police. But I've said to myself, you're the
Matron. You must have had your reasons,
and I respect that. So here's what we'll do.
I'll mind my own business and say nothing.
And in return, you will send me something to
ease my conscience. Shall we say £5,000 in
cash? By the 17th, or I'll assume you're not
interested.

The e-mail went on to give a postal address in Essex.

This is an accommodation address. Even the
police would have trouble tracing it, though
I suppose they could if they tried. But I don't
think either of us would want that.
    I would prefer not to communicate by e-mail.

*I look forward to hearing from you by post very
soon.*
   Sincerely,
   A well-wisher

Dawn's lips were numb. Five thousand pounds!
Accommodation address! It took her several attempts
to read the message all the way to the end because the
words kept blurring into each other. She had to keep
taking extra breaths; there wasn't enough air in the
normal ones to fill her chest. *You killed Ivy Walker so
discreetly.* Her lungs emptied again. What was going
on here? Who had written this?

   It came to her a second later.

   The post-mortem! The lab had found the potassium
in Mrs Walker's body. The pathologists had come up
to the ward to ask some questions and . . . The syringe!
They had searched the stock room and found the
empty potassium syringe in the sharps bin. With her
fingerprints all over it! What had she been *thinking*?
Had she left her brain at home that morning?

   As she had today, it seemed. Because it was another
few seconds before she remembered. There hadn't
been a post-mortem. Whoever had written this, it
couldn't be someone from the lab. Mrs Walker had
gone straight from the ward to the mortuary. She
had been cremated two days after her death; Dawn

had seen with her own eyes the coffin go through the curtains.

But if not the lab, then who? Who the hell had sent this? Dawn scrolled the screen back up to see the sender address. *Well-wisher*. The same name as the signature on the message. She didn't know anyone who used that as their e-mail address. Almost certainly it was a fake, specially created to send this toxic little memo.

Her chest was sucking at nothing again. Blackmail letters. Fake e-mail addresses. Here she was, sitting in her office on a perfectly normal Thursday afternoon, surrounded by her filing cabinet and her shelves and the poster on the back of her door advertising the International Research Conference, everything so ordinary and everyday, and yet this . . . this unspeakable message sitting on the screen in front of her. From outside the door of the office came a shuffling sound. Then a woman's voice.

'That's right, Mrs Potterton.' It was Trish, the ward physiotherapist. 'Just a few more steps. Doing really, really well. Your niece will be delighted.'

The voices and the shuffling passed on. But Dawn sat as if glued into place.

Your niece.

Mrs Walker's niece! That was it. All along Dawn had thought there was something funny about her. She had wanted to speak to her at the funeral but at the last minute Heather Warmington hadn't turned up. It had left Dawn feeling uneasy, and now, at last, she knew why. That time they had spoken on the phone . . . Dawn couldn't remember exactly what had been said but . . . there'd been something, hadn't there, about Mrs Walker being better off dead? And then afterwards, when Mrs Walker had died, Heather Warmington must have remembered the conversation and concluded there was something suspicious going on. She had gone to her lawyer who had said . . . Dawn leaned in again to read the e-mail. Why did she keep forgetting what was in it?

But as she read the words again, her stomach settled in her like a stone. This was no lawyer's letter. *You killed Ivy Walker so discreetly.* The implication was there right under her nose. Whoever had written this was telling her something: telling her that they had been there.

Had been there and seen her kill Mrs Walker.

The room went blotchy. Dawn put her forehead on her hands. *God. Oh God.* Her breathing echoed harshly from her palms. The blind. That stupid, broken blind. What was the point in her checking before she went in to the room that no one was about if anyone walking past afterwards could have looked through the window and got a ring-side view? How had she been so *stupid*? How could she ever have thought she could do something like that on a busy ward in the middle of the day and not be seen?

She took her hands from her face and folded her arms around herself, rocking on her chair. Something was wrong. Something didn't fit with that scenario. Even if someone *had* happened to look in, what would they have seen? A nurse tending to a patient. Fiddling with her drip, which nurses did with patients a hundred times a day. Mrs Walker's body had not been discovered for almost an hour after her death; Dawn had been long gone from the room by then. Why would anyone jump to the conclusion that the death of a frail, elderly, terminally ill lady was due to *her*?

Another sound from outside the office. A faint scratching noise, close to the bottom of the door. Dawn stopped rocking to listen.

Scrttch. There it was again.

Someone was out there. Listening.

Dawn sat frozen, hunched over her desk, her gaze fixed on the door. Through the blind, a dark shape moved. The scratching noise had stopped now; there was silence on the other side, but the person, whoever it was, was still there. The dark shape moved again. Then someone gave a cough.

'Nearly there, Mrs Potterton.' Trish's voice again. 'Soon have you back in bed.'

Another *scrttch* on the tiles as Mrs Potterton's walking frame scraped past.

Dawn waited for the blotchiness around her to settle. She had to get out of here, think about this properly. There was an explanation for this; she was missing something, she just couldn't think clearly enough at the moment to work out what. Her computer screen glowed on her desk. She felt a sudden lurch of dread. How long had that e-mail been open? E-mails could be read by the hospital. Every time you logged on there was a warning. She almost lunged to press Delete. Then she stopped. She was going to need to read this again. She stabbed instead on the Print button. The page with Well-wisher's message on it came spooling out from the machine under the desk.

Plenty of people would say I should go to the police . . .

The words wobbled. The computer enquired, 'Are you sure you want to permanently delete this message?' Dawn stamped her finger on the Return key. *Yes*.

She folded the paper up into a square small enough to fit in her hand. Then she picked her bag up from where she'd dropped it on the floor. To reach the main entrance of the ward she was going to have to walk all the way up between the beds, past all the staff and the patients and whatever visitors happened to be around. *Act normal*, she told herself. *Just leave the ward in a normal, unremarkable way, and go some-where quiet and sort this out*. She swung her bag over her shoulder. She had to fold her arms because of the way her hands were shaking.

The normal working day was coming to a close. Paradoxically, this was one of the ward's busiest times, when the doctors and other staff crowded in to finish their rounds and finalize their management plans for the night. Dieticians and pharmacists scribbled in charts. At the nurses' desk, a group of junior doctors was clustered around a CT scan, arguing about the contents. 'Look. That's definitely fluid, you can see it right there.' 'I don't agree. I think it looks more solid.' Dawn was almost at the doors to the hall when Mandy appeared from nowhere.

'Off now, Matron?' she shouted in her cheerful, fog-horn voice. Everyone within a radius of ten feet promptly turned to look at the two of them.

'Yes.' Dawn tried to stretch her lips in a smile. 'Thought I'd try to beat the traffic today.'

'Any final instructions for the evening?' Mandy was covering the late shift.

'Final instructions . . . let's see . . .' The corners of the folded paper were digging into her palm. 'Mr Hughes can move on to solids this evening. If he's up to it.'

'Righty-ho.'

'And if Micro phones with his results, just let the medics know.'

'Ooh, let me get that down.' Mandy unfolded

her ward list. She spread the sheet of paper over her thigh and bent to scribble the details. 'Oh hell,' she said, standing up again and shaking her pen. 'Bloody thing's stopped working.'

Hurry, Dawn thought. *Please hurry.* Her face was pounding in time with her pulse. Already she had an almost uncontrollable urge to open the note up and read it again. Check she hadn't missed something, that there wasn't some bit at the end she hadn't registered that would explain everything. Waiting for Mandy to fix her pen, she felt an odd sensation: a hollowness at the back of her neck, as if the space behind it was too open and exposed. She swung around. Trish the physio was helping Mrs Potterton back to bed. At bed six, Elspeth was hanging a bag of antibiotic. The doctors were still at the desk, squabbling over their CT scan. Everyone was busy, absorbed in what they were doing. No one was looking at Dawn at all. All the same, she knew beyond a shadow of a doubt. Before she had turned, someone had been watching her. Somebody on the ward, right here, right now, had sent that e-mail! The faces tilted and curved. Suddenly there were eyes everywhere, swivelling to follow her as she moved. She had to get out. She had to get out now!

Mandy gave her pen a final, vigorous shake. Ink spattered over the nearest curtain.

'*There* we go,' she said. She wrote on her page with

her tongue sticking out. 'Micro . . . Hughes. Got it. Anything else?'

'No, that's it. Thanks, Mandy.' Dawn was already moving away, heading for the doors. Not quite running, but very nearly. The hall was as busy as the ward. At the lift, a long queue waited. Dawn hurried past it to the fire escape and shouldered through the door. The cement stairwell was cool, blessedly empty. The heavy door clanged shut behind her. She leaned against it, resting her head back on the metal. Now she knew what some of her patients meant when they described a panic attack as feeling like something alive was trapped in their chests, fighting to escape. She closed her eyes and put her hand to her ribs, waiting for the sensation to pass, feeling the breeze on her face from the steep, snail-shell drop of the stairwell.

Then she opened her eyes again and started down the steps. Down she went, around and around, the stairwell turning and circling on itself like her thoughts, the same questions repeating in her head over and over. Who had sent that message? *Who?* Once more her breaths were coming too fast. She stopped again, holding on to the wall, making herself breathe more slowly. *Count*, she told herself. *Count between breaths.* No point blacking out on the fire escape and being found here with this letter in her hand.

*   *   *

By the time she reached Café Pio on Lavender Hill she had started to calm down. The café was a place she sometimes came to if the traffic was too heavy to catch the bus straight home. The warm, familiar smells of fresh-baked muffins and flapjacks enveloped her as soon as she opened the door.

'Large cappuccino, please,' she said to the waitress.

She leaned on the top of the counter, still feeling as if her legs could do with the help. Next to her elbow were rows of plates piled with scones, biscuits and slices of cake. A cast-iron cauldron filled with soup bubbled on a tripod. Two women at a nearby table chatted over a pot of tea. It was all so cosy and peaceful and normal here. She had read that e-mail all wrong. She *must* have done. Things like this did not happen to people like her. Her, the Matron, at one of London's top teaching hospitals! The sharp corners of the note had softened in her sweaty palm. She had completely overreacted just now on the ward. She'd get some coffee into her, sit at one of the quiet tables under the bookshelves and read the note through again. Properly this time.

She took her cappuccino to a table at the back. At the next table, a woman sat by herself, reading a magazine. Dawn hung her bag from the back of the chair and sat down, feeling much more settled and in control.

She was just opening the note out again when a high-pitched screech erupted from somewhere around her: *BLEEE-BLEEE-BLEEEEE*—

Her nerves already operating at maximum voltage, Dawn almost knocked over her cappuccino. The noise sounded so exactly like a cardiac arrest alarm. The woman at the next table had jumped as well. She dragged her bag up from the floor and began to scrabble around in it. Keys and tissues and pens flew out all over her table. *Sorry, sorry*, the woman mouthed at Dawn. She pulled a phone from the bag and flipped it open. *BLEEEEE* – the high-pitched screeching stopped.

'Hello?' the woman said into her phone.

Dawn sat, dry-lipped, in her chair.

The high-pitched shriek of the phone. Like the high-pitched shriek of an ECG alarm.

Mrs Walker's ECG alarm.

She leaned forward, putting her hands to her face. Now she saw it! Now she understood how this Well-wisher person knew what had happened. On the day Dawn had killed Mrs Walker, she had turned the ECG alarm in the side room to Silent and then forgotten all about it. And so, all the while she stood injecting the potassium into Mrs Walker's drip, no alarm had gone off to remind her that the ECG above her head was changing – changing from a normal to a lethal rhythm. On the screen above

Mrs Walker's bed, in full view of the [   ]
the door.

Dawn wanted to lie down on the floor. To pull her
knees up, cover her face, curl up into a ball. *Stop this.
Stop this. It's too late now. You can think about this
calmly, work out what to do. Or you can end up in
prison. Lose your job. Be banned for ever from working in a hospital. It's up to you.*

She made herself drink some of her coffee. The mug
shook so violently that it banged off her tooth. Beside
her, the woman was still talking into her phone.
The waitress was at the counter, mopping the floor.
Everything was fine. Everything was going on just
as normal. No one had noticed that anything was
wrong.

Dawn rattled the mug back on to its saucer. Then
she took the crumpled page with the e-mail on it and
opened it out on the table.

OK. She flattened the creases out with her fist.
OK. This had happened. She'd been seen. She'd been
caught. And now she had to deal with the consequences. The first thing, the most important thing,
was to work out who this person was. Then at least
she would know who she was dealing with. Just now
on the ward she'd had the sensation that someone
was watching her while her back was turned. One of
those people there had written this note. But who?
There'd been dozens of people about. She'd been in

t she'd run out of the ward without
...ore than half of them.

Well, whoever it was, they had also been on the
ward the day Dawn had . . . the day Mrs Walker
had died. If she could find out who had been there
on both days, she might have a chance of narrowing
things down. Her mind was clearer now. She was
thinking better. The day of Mrs Walker's death
had been the day of the International Research
Conference. Dawn remembered because it had
struck her how very quiet the ward was. In fact – her
hands tightened on the page – the only staff present
had been the nurses on duty that afternoon. And she
could find out quite easily who they were. She was
the one who drew up all the rotas. It would take her
less than a minute to check the off-duty folder in
her office.

But even as she thought this, she realized something
else. She already knew which nurses had been there,
because before going in to Mrs Walker's room she
remembered pausing to check on the whereabouts of
each of them.

Suddenly she was reaching behind her, rummaging
in her bag for a pen.

Mandy. Elspeth. And Trudy Dawes, the new
student.

Those three. She could swear to it.

Dawn hauled the pen from her bag. On the back of

the crumpled page, she printed the initials, one below the other: M, E, T.

Then she sat back.

All right. Which of them?

The truth was, she couldn't see *any* of them doing it. These were her colleagues, her team. They had worked some tough shifts together, had helped and supported each other through some difficult cases. The thought of one of them betraying her in this way was horrible. But like it or not, the facts were there. *Someone* had sent this e-mail. Someone who had been on the ward that day – someone who, it now occurred to her, knew her work e-mail address, the one she used to circulate rotas and memos to the nursing staff.

She wiped the sweat from her pen.

Right then. Trudy first. She knew next to nothing about the girl. She had only started on the ward a few weeks ago. But surely she could discount Trudy? Nervous, rabbit-in-headlights Trudy who had almost passed out the other day while changing a dressing and had to be helped to the staff room to put her head between her knees. Would she have the guts to do something like this? And more to the point, how well could she read an ECG?

Of the three of them, Mandy, the most senior, was the most likely to have spotted the changes in the ECG and to have put two and two together. She had been covering the Day Ward that day, directly across the floor from the side room. She'd had her back to Dawn, but Dawn hadn't been watching her all the time. Mandy could have turned her head at any minute without her noticing. And this sort of scandal would be right up her street. Mandy loved gossip, the juicier the better. And she wasn't above a touch of maliciousness if she thought it would add to the excitement.

But Mandy had been on Forest Ward for nearly three years. She was good with the patients, friendly and interested, if occasionally sloppy with details. She and Dawn had always worked well together. Hadn't they? A memory surfaced: Dawn, a couple of months ago, asking Mandy not to sit on a patient's bed while she took her blood pressure. Mandy, normally easygoing, had blown up in a burst of unexpected temper.

'Don't patronize me, Dawn. If I didn't have a child to take care of, I could be in charge of my own ward by now. So keep your superior tone to yourself and don't treat me like a half-wit.'

Dawn had been astonished by the outburst. She hadn't meant to sound patronizing. As the Matron, it was her job to make sure that infections didn't spread from one bed to another. Surely Mandy understood that? As it happened, Mandy's anger had seemed to fade quickly enough. The following day she had be-haved towards Dawn in her usual cheery way. But

had the resentment still been there, festering underneath? Was there enough dislike there to make her
want to do something like this?

Dawn left Mandy for the moment and moved on
to the E on her piece of paper. She had left Elspeth to
last because, in fact, she was a bit unsure about her.
Elspeth was a junior nurse, a couple of years out of
her nursing degree. There had never been any overt
row or confrontation that Dawn could recall; Elspeth
was a competent enough nurse, if not the type to do
more than she had to. It was more a series of little
things – like the time Dawn had asked her to help
clean up a patient who had vomited and had heard
her grumble to Mandy, 'Who does she think she is?
I didn't do a degree to end up as a skivvy.' Elspeth
had a habit of calling in sick, often on a Monday or
a Friday, leaving her colleagues to pick up the slack
at the last minute. Recently Dawn had been forced to
pull her up on it, warning her that the next time she
called in sick she would have to produce a doctor's
cert. Later she had overheard Elspeth in the canteen,
discussing her with another nurse.

'She's got no life,' Elspeth had complained. 'It's
pathetic. She's in here at all hours, sneaking up on
people long after her shift's supposed to be finished.'

'One of those spinster types, do you reckon?' the
other nurse had said. 'Became a Matron so she could
feel needed.'

'Probably. Promise me one thing, though: if I'm still working here when I'm her age, shoot me.'

Dawn's lips tightened. Well, Elspeth needn't worry. She was not Matron material. For a start, she was not reliable. She'd been on the ward with Clive, both of them sitting around in the coffee room, the day Jack Benson had almost died. And, Dawn remembered, Elspeth might have a degree but she was not good at ECGs. Only the other morning she'd had to call Clive over to explain to her what a funny rhythm on one of the monitors meant.

Dawn stared at the crinkled page on the table.

Clive.

Of all the nurses on Forest, he was by far the most likely to do something like this. He was excellent at ECGs. He was good, in fact, at all the technical aspects of nursing, she had to give him that. Just unpleasant when it came to dealing with the actual patients. He would have spotted straight away that the ECG wasn't right, would have found it strange that Dawn had continued to stand beside Mrs Walker and not pressed the emergency button over her bed or seemed to notice that anything was amiss. And there was no question that he disliked her. Particularly after their confrontation the other day in front of the ward. What a perfect, juicy revenge this would be for him.

But he hadn't been there. His shift had ended at lunchtime; he'd been gone from the ward half an hour before Dawn had given Mrs Walker the potassium. She had seen him herself, barging through the doors on his way out. Clive was not the sort to hang around the workplace on his afternoon off for a second longer than he had to. He might be the most likely person to do this. But it was not him.

Dawn threw the pen down. This was useless. She was getting nowhere, sitting here scribbling things on bits of paper. Who was even to say that someone *had* seen her that day? She could be on completely the wrong track; the blackmailer could have found out about Mrs Walker some other way; it could be *anything*, something she hadn't even begun to think of.

The sweat-dampened paper had torn; the pen, in places, had poked right through. Dawn made a couple of half-hearted attempts to piece the writing back together. Then she took the page and ripped it in half. She folded the pieces over, tore them again. She stuffed the scraps into her cappuccino mug. Stirred them with the spoon, soaking them in the brown, creamy froth so that no one would ever be able to read them.

At home, Milly flew to meet her, licking her hands, panting and yelping with excitement. Her ropy tail whacked off Dawn's calves. Dawn patted the warm, stubby flanks. The dog's simple, open pleasure brought a lump to her throat. She thought, *She doesn't know what I've done.*

In the kitchen, she prised open a tin of Milly's favourite rabbit in gravy. But even as she spooned the chunks into Milly's plastic bowl, her mind was still working.

She had moved on for now from the question of 'Who'. Even if the blackmailer *was* Elspeth or Trudy or Mandy, she had no way of knowing which. Ultimately, the question now was, 'What was she going to do?'

On the bus home, she had passed a police station with its familiar blue and white lantern on a pole outside. It had occurred to her that she could get off the bus and just march on in there. Blackmail was a crime. The police could track the person through that address they had given in Essex. Dawn had looked up the term 'accommodation address' on her laptop. An accommodation address, it turned out, was a place to where people could have their mail sent, from where it would be forwarded to their real address. All sorts of people used them: businesses who wanted to pretend that their firm was in a posher area, women who didn't want an abusive ex to know where they lived. And now, it seemed, blackmailers. The companies who handled the mail promised security and discretion. Even the police, they claimed, would never be able to discover the client's real address. But surely when a crime was involved they would be forced to hand over the details?

Yes – and then what? Blackmail was a crime. But murder was worse. One look at the contents of that e-mail and the police would be far more interested in her than in any blackmailer.

No. The police were not an option.

While Milly gobbled up her rabbit chunks, Dawn went around and around the kitchen with a cloth, restlessly wiping the already spotless taps, surfaces and doors.

So then, what should she do? Ignore the note?

Of all the alternatives, this was the one she kept returning to. It seemed by far the most sensible. Blackmailers should not be given in to. Everyone knew that. Once this person had her in their power, what else might they want from her? On the other hand, if she refused to pay up, what could they do? What proof did they have to back up their ridiculous accusations? Mrs Walker had been cremated. There were no remains on which a drug test could be performed. No matter what the blackmailer thought they might know or have seen, it would end up being their word against hers.

As the evening wore on, she became more and more convinced that this was the right thing to do. Ignoring the message might give her a few sleepless nights, but in the end the blackmailer would have to back off.

They might even start to assume they'd been mistaken. It was a big jump, from seeing a nurse happening to stand near a patient to assuming that she had actually murdered her. This person was testing her, sizing her up to see how she would respond. Well, if that was the case, they weren't going to get very far.

For almost the first time since she had received the message, the tight band constricting Dawn's chest seemed to loosen. She even brewed herself some coffee and drank it on the couch in front of the television – although afterwards, to save her life, she couldn't have told anyone which programme had been on. At bedtime, however, her confidence collapsed all over again.

Why couldn't she get it into her head? The e-mail was not a guess. *You killed Ivy Walker so discreetly.* This person had *seen*! Otherwise how would they have known to write to her in the first place? And something else had occurred to her. Even if Well-wisher had no proof, the suddenness of Mrs Walker's death had not gone unnoticed. Professor Kneebone had commented on how unexpected it was. Dr Coulton, that day in the canteen, had seemed astonished to hear that she had died. Who else might think it was odd if anyone asked them to look back? People would ask, 'Why didn't she have a post-mortem?' Geoffrey Kneebone would recall how Dawn had talked him out of doing one. And she had gone to that funeral, even though she had admitted to Celia Dartson that she hadn't known Mrs Walker at all. Not that there was anything wrong with going to a patient's funeral. But when you added it in with everything else . . .

The tight band was back around her chest. Hospitals loathed publicity. Particularly with St Iberius currently attempting to stamp itself on the map as an international Centre of Excellence. But a matter like this . . . no matter how vague the evidence was, they would have to investigate it thoroughly. The public would have to be assured that St Iberius considered patient safety to be of paramount importance.

A Matron accused of killing a patient. Dawn's stomach retracted.

In bed, she lay twisting her fingers around each other. The light from the street stained the walls with a grim, orange glow.

The bottom line here was that she could lose her job. Whether there was enough evidence actually to send her to prison was another matter. But one thing she knew for certain. If there was a shadow of doubt as to whether the patients were safe in her care, the hospital would not keep her working there.

She dug her nails into her fingers.

Could she pay the blackmailer? Supposing she had to? Five thousand pounds! Dawn was far from rich. Three years of home care for Dora, alterations to the downstairs bathroom and a wheelchair ramp for the front porch had not come cheap. Dora and Dawn had not been entitled to any help. Everything had come out of their own pockets and in the end they'd had to remortgage the house. Dawn was paying back the mortgage now but there was very little of her salary left at the end of each month. But she did have the money. It would be a huge chunk from her savings, but if it came right down to it, she could pay it.

Out of the corner of her eye, she saw a movement. A stirring near the wall, a darkness gathering from the shadows behind. Then the shape detached itself; rose up into the room.

Dawn's heart began to pound. Something told her to stay lying on her back, to keep staring ahead, not to turn and look at it directly. The feeling was very strong, that she wasn't alone, that someone else was here in the room with her. The shape coalesced. Now it was a person. A tall woman in a dark dress, floating above the floor. The figure moved closer. Now it was beside her locker. Beside her bed. *Jesus!* Dawn jerked her head off the pillow. The shape fled at once, shrinking back to the shadows. When Dawn, her fingers shaking, managed to turn her lamp on and looked to where it had vanished, all she saw was her navy uniform, hanging from its hanger on the wardrobe door.

Her head fell back on to the pillow.

It's only me, she had said when she had entered Mrs

Walker's room. And Mrs Walker had relaxed again, knowing that everything was all right. The Matron was here. The one person above all others that she could trust with her life, to guard her and protect her and keep her safe.

Dawn lay rigid under the grim orange light.

She thought to herself, *You deserve this.*

'Bed six didn't sleep until two,' Pam, the night nurse, reported. 'So I gave her a Temazepam and she settled in twenty minutes.'

The day staff scribbled down the information. Dawn sat with her chair pushed back so that she could watch the semicircle of staff around the desk without being observed. Was Elspeth glancing towards her more often? Did Trudy seem more jumpy and anxious?

She hadn't slept at all. She had seriously considered calling in sick this morning. The thought of having to face this person, whoever they were, knowing that they would be watching her behind her back, hugging their nasty little secret to themselves, was intolerable. But by the time her alarm went off, even the thought of that was better than having to endure more sleepless hours in her silent house. She'd be better off at work. She could distract herself there, tire herself out. She didn't have to face anyone she didn't want to; she could keep her head down, avoid interacting with anyone unless it was absolutely necessary.

After the handover, she went straight to her office and shut the door. She spread some papers out on her desk, but sat without reading them, staring at the ward through the little pane of glass, watching the staff as they went about their work.

Something had occurred to her during the handover. It was a risk, the blackmailer sending her a message like this. If Dawn did decide to go to the police and the person was caught, the least that would happen to them was that they would lose their job. Five thousand pounds was a lot of money but it wouldn't get you very far if you were out of work. Either the blackmailer was very confident of not getting caught or they needed the money urgently enough for it to be worth the risk. Which of her three suspects might need five thousand pounds that badly?

A few feet from the office, Mandy was busy admitting a woman with varicose veins. She was showing something to the patient – from the look of it, a photo of Jason, her nine-year-old, covered in mud and holding up his football medal. Mandy showed that picture to everyone. She was the sort of person who was happy to share the details of her private life with any stranger who walked through the door. A mother like Mandy would do a lot for her child. Five thousand pounds would pay for a lot of school trips and football lessons and new boots. Dawn watched her sitting on the patient's bed – again! – the two of them chatting as if they had known each other for years. How did Mandy do that? Become so friendly with someone in such a short space of time? Dawn had had many conversations with patients over the years, some of them very intimate and profound, but never this easy banter with a total stranger after only a few minutes. Would Mandy be able to chatter on like that if she was blackmailing her own boss, sitting just a few feet away from her?

Elspeth hove into view, pushing the drugs trolley. She wore her usual impassive expression; impossible to tell whether she was thinking anything out of the ordinary. Elspeth was by far the most attractive nurse on Forest, dark and graceful, with high cheekbones and very small teeth, like a cat's. The one thing that Dawn thought detracted from her looks was that she always looked completely bored. She handed each patient their little container of pills and moved on to the next bed without a word. Not for Elspeth the easy Mandy banter. Nothing wrong with that, necessarily; gregariousness was not for everyone. Part of the job of a ward sister was to match the staff with the type of patient that suited them best. Elspeth was good at quick, technical tasks: preparing a run of young, fit patients for theatre, getting each one promptly through the doors. Mandy was better with the slower, frailer patients who needed someone to chat to. But capable though Elspeth was, it was clear that her main interest and preoccupation lay elsewhere. She did the work in a mechanical, emotionless way, utterly lacking in warmth or empathy, that Dawn knew the patients found off-putting. Many of them were too intimidated to ask Elspeth for help with things like washing or the commode and would wait instead until Dawn or Mandy came around. If Elspeth had no plans to stay on long-term at St Iberius, did that mean she wanted to leave nursing altogether? How much would five thousand pounds help with that?

Trudy, the student, crouched by bed eighteen, fumbling to change a urine bag. She seemed to be having difficulty separating the stiff catheter tubing from the bag. All that could be seen of the patient was his grey, curly hair sticking up over the top of his *Telegraph*. Trudy gave the bag a couple of tentative tugs, then pulled again, more forcefully. The *Telegraph* gave a convulsive jerk. The patient's face, lavender in colour, shot out from behind it. He clutched at his groin, glaring at Trudy, his lips moving at speed. Trudy flushed dark red, fumbling even more. Dawn didn't need to hear her to know that she was babbling, almost in tears. *Sorry. Sorry. I'm so sorry.*

Student nurses were paid very little. Who knew what Trudy might need with five thousand pounds? A holiday? Loan repayment? Food? But she was so diffident, so terrified of everything. Daphne from Orthopaedics had reported that when Trudy was doing her placement there she had upset the relatives of one patient, a teenage girl with a spinal tumour, by bursting into tears every time she treated her.

'She won't last,' Daphne had scoffed. 'Much too soft to be a nurse.'

Being soft, in Dawn's opinion, didn't make you a bad nurse. But you did need to be able to hold it together enough to get on with things and give the patient the treatment they needed. Trudy seemed to go to pieces in any situation where a patient deteriorated. Surely if she had witnessed what Dawn had done, she would have spoken to someone about it? Mandy perhaps, or one of her student friends – or even the police? Or said nothing at all, out of fear? But this ruthless, hard-nosed cunning – setting up a fake address, demanding thousands of pounds. No. Dawn could not see it in her.

The office door opened, banging off the edge of the desk.

'Coffee?' Mandy stood planted in the middle of the doorway.

'No. No, thanks. I'm all right.'

Mandy stayed where she was.

'*You're* up to something,' she said.

'Am I?'

'Yes. You've been hiding in here all morning. Spying on us through your little window. Not like you.'

'Oh. No, it's just . . . I've got a lot to catch up on.'

'Oh, right.' Mandy came on into the office. 'Thought there might be something on your mind.' She settled her bottom on the desk, shoving the keyboard and a container of paperclips to one side. 'Warm today, isn't it?' she said, fanning herself with her ward sheet. 'Muggy.' She was very chatty, even for her. 'Hope the new ward's got air-con when we move to it. I've been thinking where to bring Jace on his holidays when his school breaks up.'

Dawn wanted nothing more than for Mandy to go away and leave her alone. But she kept the smile on her face, listening to Mandy bang on about her plans for a week-long trip to Euro Disney in July. She thought with a shiver, *I can't antagonize anyone now.*

It was when Mandy finally left the office that it hit her.

She could not stay on Forest Ward. Even if she sorted things out with the blackmailer, even if they agreed never to tell anyone, how could she go on working here, knowing that one of her nurses knew something like this about her? She couldn't do her job properly, be a proper ward sister if she was always wondering and fearful, walking on eggshells, afraid to antagonize anyone. No matter what happened, she would have to leave St Iberius.

That's if she was still allowed to work as a nurse at all.

A peremptory *tat-tat* on the door stopped the rush of nausea, brought the room back into focus.

'Come in,' she managed.

Elspeth's sly, feline face appeared around the door.

'Sister,' she said, 'I'm sorry to have to ask you this, but I need to take Monday afternoon off for the dentist.'

Even in the state she was in, Dawn's instinct was to glance at the off-duty rota. 'But you're down for the late shift on Monday.'

'Yes, I know – but you see, the thing is, I'd agreed to the appointment before I realized.'

'Is it an emergency?'

'Well – not an *emergency*,' Elspeth said. 'Not as such. But I'm booked in now, and it's so hard to get an appointment there. The next one mightn't be for weeks.'

Elspeth stood with her hands clasped in front of her, looking up through her lashes in a guileless, Princess Diana way. She knew the policy every bit as well as Dawn did. If she took Monday off, the ward would be left short-staffed and at this stage it was going to be very difficult to find someone else. Unless Elspeth could produce a cert to say it was an emergency, she could not have the time off.

Dawn could not look at her. She kept her eyes on the off-duty rota.

'Go to your appointment,' she said. 'We'll manage.'

211

She heard the satisfied smile in Elspeth's tone.

'Thank you, Matron.'

By the end of her shift, every last drop of adrenaline had been sucked from Dawn's nerve endings. Her legs barely had the strength left to carry her to the door. There was no way she could go through another day like that.

Walking to her bus stop, she passed the bank near the hospital and stopped. In the e-mail, the blackmailer had said that the money had to arrive by the seventeenth of May. Today was Friday, the twelfth. If the cash was to get there in time, the latest she could wait before posting it would be Monday. But there was no guarantee that on Monday she would get out of work in time to reach the bank.

That meant, if she was to have the cash ready to post in time, she would have to withdraw it today.

She debated with herself, standing on the corner of Lavender Hill and St John's Road. What was the rush? She hadn't even decided yet whether she was going to pay it, had she?

No, she hadn't. But how many more days like today was she prepared to go through? Hiding away all day in her office. Smiling ghastly smiles at people through stiff, corpse-like lips.

On the bus, she stared out, unseeing, over the cafés and galleries and coloured canopies of Northcote

Road. What if she did withdraw the money? Not to post straight away – just to have in the house. Then, if she did make the decision over the weekend to post it – and she wasn't saying she would – the money would be there. If she *didn't* have it, the option would no longer be available.

She checked her watch. Half past four. Thirty minutes before the banks closed. Suddenly it was vital that she reached her bank in time. She leaned forward on her seat, willing the bus to hurry. They reached Silham Vale at a quarter to five. Dawn stepped out on to the green and almost ran towards the bank beside the Somerfield. Then she stopped. To take out that amount of money, wouldn't she need her passport or some kind of ID? Swearing softly, she ran back across the green. She turned down Crocus Road and flew past Milly into the house. She hurried upstairs, grabbed her passport from the drawer in her bedside table and raced back up the road before she could change her mind. She made it through the doors of the bank with three minutes to spare.

Just one cashier was still operating. Only one customer was ahead of Dawn in the queue: an old man in a long white robe, clutching a cheque. Dawn stood behind him, flipping her passport in and out of its plastic cover. Five thousand pounds! She'd never taken that much out before in one go. What if the bank said she couldn't have it? The girl behind the cash desk with the knife-edge creases down the arms of her blouse looked the type to do everything by the book. What if she said that the bank didn't keep that much cash on the premises and Dawn should have booked it in advance? Dawn's foot tapped like a rabbit's on the floor. She was being ridiculous. Of course a bank would have that much cash available. And it was her money. She had a perfect right to take every penny of it if she chose; she didn't have to explain herself to anyone. But her agitation grew. She imagined herself arguing with the cashier: 'I can't come back on Monday. I'm telling you, I have to have it today,' and the girl in her stiff white blouse, monotonously repeating, 'I'm sorry, Madam, but there's nothing I can do.' By the time she got to the desk, Dawn's jaw muscles were tense with rage.

She pushed her bank card under the barrier.

'I need five thousand pounds, please. In cash.'

The girl glanced at the card. 'Of course, Ms Torridge,' she said. 'Are you sure about the cash? You wouldn't prefer a cheque or transfer?'

'No. It has to be cash.'

'Certainly.'

Dawn held the ledge, her heart slowing. It was all right. She was going to get it.

And then? Hand it all over to the blackmailer? What if the next time they e-mailed her it was to demand ten thousand?

The girl behind the cash desk was saying something. 'Have you got some ID?'

'Oh, yes.' Dawn slid her passport under the barrier.

'I'll need to photocopy this.' The girl rose to her feet.

Dawn flexed her fingers, opening and closing her sweaty hands. This was fine. It was fine. Photocopying the passport was standard for such large sums. That was the reason she'd brought it in the first place. But she couldn't keep her eyes off the door the girl had gone through. Was that whispering she could hear from the room at the back?

Keith, if I could just run this by you. There's a woman here wants to take out five thousand pounds in cash.

In cash? What on earth for?

She didn't say. Do you think we should inform Mr Braintree?

The door opened. The girl returned to the desk.

'That's all fine.' She was flicking through something in her hands. 'Here we are.'

She counted the notes out in front of Dawn. Then she slid them into an envelope and pushed it under the barrier. Dawn took the envelope. Smaller and slimmer than she had expected. She had envisaged a large parcel.

'Tuck that somewhere safe before you leave,' the

girl advised. She beamed at Dawn. 'Have a lovely weekend.'

Dawn sat on the gold-coloured couch in the sitting-room. In front of her, on the coffee table, the coloured bank notes lay fanned out like a rainbow. The outer curve of red fifties, the blue and purple twenties in the middle, the orange inner arc of ten-pound notes. Beneath them, compressed under the glass table-top, the selection of lace doilies that Dora had always used for visitors.

Dawn got up off the couch. With her hands on her head, she walked up and down the room, from the cabinet by the window to the double doors leading to the dining-room and back again. She couldn't do this. She couldn't do this on her own. If only there was someone she could *talk* to. Someone she could bounce ideas off instead of just going around in circles here on her own. Crazy, of course. This was not the sort of thing you could tell anyone about.

But some people did. Her friend Judy had told her that there was nothing she wouldn't tell Andy, her husband; that even if she committed the most terrible, awful crime, Andy would still be on her side.

'He'd spring me from the clink somehow,' Judy had said. 'I'd just have to do my nails and wait.'

Could she talk about this to Judy?

They'd been very close once, as close as sisters. And

Judy was a nurse. She would know what Mrs Walker had been going through. What Dawn had done wouldn't seem so awful to a person who had witnessed that sort of suffering many times for herself.

But Judy had left nursing years ago. She and Andy had moved abroad for Andy's work. Even though they were back in London now, Judy never had returned to nursing. And apart from Dora's funeral, when was the last time Dawn and Judy had seen each other? Both had been busy with their own lives; Dawn with work and Dora, and Judy pregnant with her fourth child. How would Dawn even begin to raise the subject? 'Hi, Judy. How are you? Morning sickness and bloating? Poor you. Me? I'm fine. Well, perhaps a *teeny* bit stressed. I recently murdered someone at work and now, would you believe it, I'm being blackmailed.'

Judy would be very shocked. She would pretend not to be. She would do her best to see things from Dawn's point of view. But she would not understand.

In the hall, the phone rang.

Dawn stopped her pacing at once.

The blackmailer!

Her legs had gone flubbery again. No. No, it couldn't be. Whoever Well-wisher was, they had made it very clear that they only wanted to communicate by post. Why on earth would they do something so stupid now as to phone up and let her hear their voice?

Brrrr.

Maybe they wanted to check that she'd got their message. Maybe this was some friend or accomplice they'd got to phone her up on their behalf.

Brrrr.

Well, if she didn't hurry up and answer it, the person, whoever it was, would hang up. That would be one way of solving the problem. Then, as soon as she thought that, she realized she had to know. She flew out into the hall, snatched the receiver up before the ringing stopped.

'Hello?'

'Dawn?' A deep, cautious voice.

'Yes?'

'It's Will.'

Will! It took a couple of seconds for her to remember who he was. In the past couple of days she hadn't so much as given him a single thought.

Will spoke hesitantly into the silence. 'Is this a bad time?'

'No. No, I'm fine.' But she wasn't. At the sound of his accent she had felt a kind of panic, looking through the doorway to the sitting-room, seeing the money there lying all over the table.

'How are you?' she said inanely. 'Have you been well?'

'Very well,' Will said. 'I got that job.'

'Job?'

'The one I applied for. In Cumbria.'

Dawn had no idea what he was talking about. She had to think back before it finally came to her.

'The IT job. Of course.' It took an enormous effort to make herself sound enthusiastic. 'Congratulations! That's wonderful. You must be delighted.'

'Yes, I am.' There seemed something different about Will this evening. He was speaking much more animatedly than usual, as if the words were vying to burst out of his mouth. He blurted, 'I was wondering whether . . . if you'd like to meet? During the week, maybe? Or even this weekend?'

'Meet? To walk Milly, you mean?'

'Well. I was thinking . . .' Will cleared his throat. 'More for dinner.'

When she didn't answer, he added quickly, 'Or whatever. I understand if . . . I mean, we could go out just as friends. Just to celebrate.'

Dawn was gazing into the sitting-room, at the red and purple and orange rainbow spread out over the glass. The last time she had met Will she had sat across from him under the trees and the pink sky, seen the admiration in his eyes as she told him all about what a wonderful nurse she was.

'I'm sorry.' She stretched the phone cord taut between her fingers. 'But this is a really busy . . . this really isn't a good week for me.'

'Some other time, then.' Will's eager tone dipped a little.

'Maybe. But if not, the very best of luck with your new job.'

'Oh—'

'I've got to go now,' Dawn said. 'Goodbye.'

She put the phone down, cutting him off. The day in Sussex was with her again, filling her chest with a dull pain. There was no doubt now about how Will felt about her. The disappointment and confusion in his voice had been hard to hear. She had hurt him and she was sorry. But it was the best way. Even if there had been any kind of future for them, there was no way she could involve someone else in this mess. And by the time it was all over, Will would be gone, back to his old life in Cumbria. She had never really known him, and now she never would.

The fight had gone out of her. She had no stomach for it any more. Time to get this over with.

On the table in front of her was a package. She had put all the banknotes back into their envelope, then placed that into a larger envelope with the address printed on the front. Well-wisher's address in Essex. She remembered all the details from the e-mail.

She had written a letter, too, and tucked it in with the cash.

This is all the money I have, she had written. *There's no point asking for any more.*

The blackmailer could ask to see her bank statement if they liked. If they thought they were on to a
good thing and their plan was to bleed her dry, they
would have to think again. She just had to pray that
whoever the person was, they would accept that she
had done what she could to stick to their 'agreement'.
And that they would return the favour by honouring
their side in their turn.

She took Milly with her when she went up to the
green. Milly was thrilled to be out. She trotted over
the grass, sniffing at the empty burger cartons and
crisp packets under the bushes. The post box by the
railings was a blurry red oblong in the dusk. Before
posting her letter, Dawn glanced about her at the other
people on the green: a woman in a blue dress coming
out of the Somerfield, a boy kicking a ball against the
railings, two men holding beer cans, sitting side by
side on a bench. None of them were paying Dawn any
attention. And why should they? There was nothing
so unusual about her. She was just a woman, not old,
not young, posting an envelope. She dropped the
package into the post box and walked away.

Chapter Eleven

That weekend was one of the longest she could re-member.

Dawn did her best to get on with all her usual pastimes – walking Milly, cooking dinner, sitting on the couch staring at the television. But the parcel of money was all she could think about. How long until she heard back from the Well-wisher? The package should reach the address by Tuesday at the latest. Maybe even Monday. But Well-wisher probably wouldn't receive it then. It would still have to be forwarded to the real address.

As the weekend dragged by, Dawn began to develop a fixation that she had put the wrong address on the envelope. She'd been so certain she had remembered the right one from the e-mail, but now that the parcel was posted she wasn't so sure. She wrote the address down again on a piece of paper, trying to gauge from the shape of how it fitted together, whether it matched her memory of the e-mail. Had she got the house number right? The postcode? The last thing she needed was for Well-wisher to go ahead and report her to the police because the deadline had passed and they had assumed she wasn't interested.

By Sunday, she could stand it no longer. The blackmailer had insisted on only communicating by post, but surely if Dawn actually sent an e-mail they wouldn't delete it without reading it? This Well-wisher person must be as on edge as she, as curious to know what her response would be, what she would do. She sat at the dining-room table and opened up her laptop.

I have posted the money, she wrote. *This is where I sent it to.*

She typed the address in bold, block capitals. Now if she'd got it wrong, Well-wisher could get back to her and they could sort something out. But although she checked her laptop obsessively for the rest of the day she received no reply.

On Monday morning, the familiar crackle in her hair as her uniform slid over her head sparked a fizz of dread in her stomach. Another day of having to face the ward, pretending everything was normal. Once again she had hardly slept. What if the parcel got lost and the blackmailer went ahead and reported her? What if the parcel *did* arrive and the person took the money, then reported her anyway? There wouldn't be a single thing she could do about it.

She was a few minutes late for the ward round. Professor Kneebone was already listening to the first patient's chest. Mandy and Trudy were there amongst the crowd of white coats, jotting down notes on their ward sheets. Elspeth was off today. At least that meant Dawn only had two people to avoid.

If it *was* one of those three.

If only she *knew*! That was the worst part – this endless waiting, this not knowing who or when or what. She could cope with anything that was thrown at her; it was only when you didn't know what you were dealing with, when you couldn't plan or prepare or do anything because you didn't know what to expect that things became so intolerable. Last night she'd had a dream that the Nursing Council had somehow discovered what had happened. Dawn had been ordered to appear in front of the Fitness to Practice Committee at their offices in Holborn. Dressed in the dark skirt and jacket she had worn to Dora's funeral, she had walked up the aisle past the public seating area, hearing the murmurs and whispers grow louder as she reached the top of the room. She took her seat facing the long table where the nine stern-faced Committee members were sitting. The members stared down at the papers in front of them, refusing to meet her eye. Then a voice said, *Make way for the Chief Witness*, and there was a flurry of activity to the right. Dawn turned. Someone was being led to the witness stand. She fixed her gaze on the back of the brawny Council clerk's head, waiting for him to move out of the way so that she could see. Any minute now she would know who Well-wisher was. Any minute now the blackmailer would have to look her in the eye and tell her what they knew and what they had seen instead of sneaking about behind her back, hiding behind fake names and made-up e-mail addresses. But when the clerk finally stood back and the Chief Witness came into view, Dawn saw that she was looking into the icy, vengeful face of Ivy Walker.

'Matron? *Matron!*'

Dawn started and blinked. The white coats rematerialized around her. Professor Kneebone was in front of her, his eyebrows pleated into a line.

'*Welcome* back, Matron. I was just asking if you thought it would be all right for Mr Cantwell to go home today?'

Mr Cantwell, bearded and bright-eyed in his polkadot pyjamas, watched Dawn eagerly from his bed.

'Yes,' she said. 'Yes, of course he can.'

Geoffrey Kneebone was still eyeing her. She bent her head to write in the Rounds book. That was all she needed! To draw even more attention to herself than she had already. She forced herself to concentrate on the rest of the round.

Afterwards, however, she was glad to return to her office and shut the door on the lot of them. She sat in her chair, facing the blank screen of her computer. This was ridiculous. Here she was again, scuttling off to hide in here like a beetle in a crack. How long was this going to go on? Angrily, she pulled the computer towards her and switched it on. For possibly the hundredth time since she had posted the money, she logged on to check her e-mails. But still there was no reply.

Her desk phone purred. She picked up the receiver. 'Good morning. Matron's office.'

'Dawn!' A deep, penetrating voice in her ear. 'Claudia here!'

Claudia Lynch! Dawn had the distinct sensation of being in a lift whose cable had just snapped. The Director of Nursing. What did *she* want?

'Got a minute for a quick word?'

'Well—'

'Excellent! I'll be right there.' The line went dead.

Dawn sat holding the receiver for a further couple of seconds before slowly putting it down. Claudia never just dropped in for a 'quick word'. She was far too busy to pay unscheduled visits to people's offices. Claudia sent memos, communicated by post, pencilled in meetings months in advance. That was it then. She knew! Dawn had no idea how, but she did. Her desk grew fuzzy at the edges. It was strewn with pens, folders, crumpled sheets of paper. She hadn't bothered to clear it before she left on Friday. She might as well do it now, while she was waiting. While she still had the right to be here. Her fingers felt like pieces of carpet as she dropped stray pens back into their jar, threw used Post-its into the bin, filed away documents it looked as if she wasn't going to be needing any more.

'*Good* morning!' Claudia came barrelling through the door, bringing a breeze with her from somewhere even though they were not outdoors. 'How are you today?'

Her voice could have been heard two floors away. Even when she was just having a normal conversation with someone, Claudia always sounded as if she was shouting from a boat at sea. Probably this had been no barrier to her having risen so high in management. It was years since she had laid a hand on an actual patient, but she was well used to defending them at meetings, fighting their corner, steamrollering over everyone else's arguments to make sure her point was heard. Her tight maroon skirt suit was more or less exactly the same colour as her cheeks.

From the wide, stretched feeling around her eyes, Dawn guessed she must look pleading and desperate but she rose from her chair and said in as normal a voice as she could manage, 'Good morning, Claudia.'

'I'll make this quick,' Claudia said. 'I know you're busy. I just wanted a word about these burglaries.'

'Burglaries?'

'Yes. The ones we've been having lately. Jim Evans tells me your locker was broken into recently.'

Dawn had to think back. The burglary in the locker room, when her coat had been ripped. It might have happened months ago rather than a couple of weeks. 'Yes,' she said. 'Yes, that's right.'

'Well, now we've had a further run,' Claudia said. 'Three of the A&E staff have had money taken. There've been complaints from several of the patients. Jim Evans wants CCTV cameras installed on every floor. I agree with him, and I think the time has come to push the issue at the next budget meeting. The problem is, I've got a seminar in Birmingham that week. That's what I wanted to ask you, Dawn. Will you stand in for me at the meeting? You'll be the ideal person, since you've been personally affected by the issue.'

Dawn's brain was struggling to adjust to the swerve in proceedings. *This* was what Claudia had wanted?

'Of course,' she said. 'Of course I will.'

'Excellent. They'll have to listen to you. The Matron being a victim is bound to have an impact.' Claudia frowned. 'You know, Dawn, I'm surprised you never mentioned it to me. I would have taken something like that very seriously.'

'I know, I know.' Dawn was still floating, high with relief. 'I just never seemed to get around to it.'

'You work too hard,' Claudia said. 'You should come sailing some time. Only worry on a boat is which way the wind's blowing.' She looked at her watch. 'Right. I'd best be on my way. I've got three meetings this morning and I'm already late.'

She was off, sweeping out of the office before Dawn even had time to register that the conversation was over. Claudia didn't know! She knew nothing about Mrs Walker, she didn't have a clue about anything that had happened. Light-headed, Dawn lowered herself back on to her chair. Her cheeks ached as the fake rictus grin she hadn't even realized was there faded from her face.

For the first time, the fuzzy ball of fear inside her hardened into a tight knot of anger. This was *her* office. *Her* ward. She should not have to be like this. Forcing a smile at every Tom, Dick and Harry who barged in on top of her. Creeping around like a scared little mouse, keeping to the corners, while all the time the blackmailer strutted about outside, thinking they were in control. Well, she'd had enough. Whether Well-wisher liked it or not, she was still the Matron here. There were *some* things she could do.

She sat up, yanked open the drawer of her desk and hauled out the off-duty ledger. If this person, whoever they were, was getting some sort of sick enjoyment out of watching her squirm, they weren't going to get it for much longer. She would go on leave. Next week, if possible. She could communicate with the blackmailer from home just as easily as she could from here, and it would be a lot easier to get through all of this away from the sensation of being constantly watched by sly, gloating eyes. She'd been going to wait until Priya was back before taking her holiday but it couldn't be helped. Mandy could act up as ward sister, and she would ask Francine to cover for any Matron-related emergencies. Francine had prepared for the Matron interview at the same time as Dawn had so she knew the ropes.

Dawn printed her initials into the Leave column for next week. There. That just left the rest of this week to get through. But now she had an idea for that, too. She flipped further through the ledger until she came to the section marked Night Shifts.

Normally, ward managers and Matrons did not do night shifts. But Dawn had stayed in the habit of doing them every now and again, just to keep in touch with what went on in the hospital after hours. And she was glad now that she had, because no one would think twice about her swapping into one. There were fewer staff about at night; fewer people to have to face. She studied the rota. Two night shifts still to be covered this week; one on Friday, one on Saturday.

The hospital had been going to book an agency nurse to fill them but now Dawn would do them herself. Let the agency nurse cover her day shifts instead. Perfect! She wrote in her initials. As a bonus, she noted that the other nurse covering the Friday and Saturday night shifts was Clive. Normally the last person she would want to work with, but now, ironically, out of all of her staff, probably the one person with whom she would feel at ease.

She closed the ledger and sank back in her chair, feeling as weary as if she had single-handedly lifted every patient on the ward. But it felt good to have done something, however small, to claw back some degree of control. From outside, sixty feet below, came the familiar clanking howl as a train roared over the railway bridge. One of the more than two thousand trains a day to pass through Clapham Junction. The howling was as much a part of the background here as the hum of the patients' voices, the rattle of the meal trolleys, the steady *blip-blip-blips* of the monitors and infusion pumps.

This is my ward, Dawn thought, banging shut the drawer of her desk. *My hospital. I am in charge here.*

Well-wisher's e-mail came the next day.

It arrived just before lunch. When Dawn switched on her computer and found the words, *Attention.*

Matron Torridge, Forest Ward, in her inbox, she almost lay across her keyboard with relief. The long wait was over. No matter what was in the e-mail, she could get on now and deal with it.

She was about to open the message when the screen blinked up a warning: *This is a public network. All e-mails may be read*. Dawn's finger froze over the keyboard. Did the IT department really bother trawling through other people's work e-mails? But she couldn't take the chance. It would be risky, beyond reckless, to open the message here. She took her hand away from the keyboard and placed it with her other hand between her knees, squeezing the knuckles together. How was she going to last until the evening? Her pager buzzed at her belt. She looked down. Mrs Ford in bed four was waiting for her tracheostomy change. There was nothing for it now anyway but to shut down the computer and go out.

At bed four, Elspeth was waiting with the tracheostomy trolley all set up. Trudy stood beside her, her gloved hands held in front of her in the correct, sterile, above-the-waist position. She was there as an observer only, never having seen the procedure before. Dawn couldn't look at either of them. She went straight to the patient.

'Hello, Mrs Ford. How are you feeling?'

Mrs Ford, a thin, tough-looking woman in her

fifties, wiggled her hand in the air in an apprehensive way. She couldn't speak because of the plastic tube in her throat.

'This shouldn't take long,' Dawn promised. 'That tube you've got in at the moment keeps blocking but the new one should feel a lot more comfortable. The change might make you cough but you can squeeze my hand whenever you need to.'

She was casting an eye over the trolley Elspeth had prepared. Sterile drapes, a fresh tracheostomy set, clean ties.

'What about the suction?' she asked.

'Oops, sorry.' Elspeth unrolled a length of tubing and attached it to the sterile, plastic suction catheter on the trolley.

'OK,' Dawn said. 'Let's start.'

She still found it hard to look directly at Elspeth or Trudy. Instead, she addressed all her conversation to Mrs Ford.

'Now we're going to open the ties on your old tracheostomy. Then, just before we take the tube out, we'll give your airway a good clean with the suction.'

In this way, she was able to lead Elspeth through the procedure while concentrating all her attention on the patient. She watched Sheila Ford's face, alert for any grimace or narrowing of the eyes which might indicate discomfort.

'Tube's coming out now,' she said. 'This might make you cough a bit.'

It did. As the tube slid from the hole in her neck, trailing a slick of yellow mucus, Mrs Ford coughed with such violence that the force of it propelled her head right off her pillow. Her face turned purple; a tear spilled from her left eye. The harsh, hacking sounds came from two places at once: her mouth and the hole in the front of her throat. The cough was a natural, healthy reflex but it was uncomfortable for the patient and distressing to watch. Dawn glanced towards Trudy. Judging from past performances, she expected to see her turning every shade of green, perhaps even starting to sway. To her surprise, however, Trudy appeared perfectly relaxed. She stood by the trolley, still with her hands clasped, watching everything with calm interest.

Dawn said to Mrs Ford, 'Now the new tube is going in. You might feel some pressure. A slight pop as it goes into place – there! That's it.'

Mrs Ford was coughing again. Her eyes were squeezed shut. Tears rolled from under the lids. Dawn touched her hand. 'Just tying the new tube in place. When you've recovered, I think you deserve a cup of tea.'

Mrs Ford, still purple, managed to stick her thumb in the air.

Dawn said in a professional way to Elspeth, 'That was very smooth. Well done.'

Elspeth said nothing but she looked pleased. She peeled off her sterile gown and gloves and began to clear the trolley. Trudy helped her, gathering up the used ties and packaging and popping them into the yellow plastic bin. She was still very composed; Mrs Ford's coughing and discomfort appeared to have had no effect on her whatsoever. Dawn watched her as she wheeled the trolley down the ward but already her mind was beginning to wander. Now that the worst was over for Mrs Ford, all her anxiety was back. She couldn't wait until this evening to find out what was in that e-mail. She had to read it now.

Dawn went to the locker room and pulled her jacket on over her uniform. Down in the main hall, the queues for the WRVS shop almost reached the door. People in dressing gowns sat on the benches around the fountain, chatting to relatives or reading the papers. On the steps outside the entrance, a cluster of patients sucked frantically on cigarettes, clutching their drip poles. Dawn continued past them down the hill. Somewhere near the bus stop on St John's Road was an internet café. She had often noticed it as she passed, though never paid it too much attention. Now that she was trying to find it, of course, she couldn't see it anywhere. She walked up and down the pavement, studying the shop signs over the doors. Finally she found it, further from the bus stop than she had thought. The café was down a set of steps, in a windowless basement lined with computer terminals. Half of them were in use, mostly by tourists with backpacks or teenage boys busy blowing up tanks.

'Number five,' said the listless-looking youth at the counter.

Sitting at the table, waiting for the screen to load, Dawn had the oppressive sensation that her abdominal organs were crushing right up against her diaphragm. It was hard to take a deep breath. Any second now. Any second . . . The possibilities flew again through her mind. The money had not arrived. The money *had* arrived, but the blackmailer wanted more. Well, at least she would know. At least the wait would be over and . . . Oh God! Oh God! Here it came. The e-mail was there on the screen. She gripped the edge of the table.

> *Dear Matron,*
> *Thank you for your gift. I am glad we have*
> *come to an agreement.*

The money had arrived. *Oh, thank God. Thank God.* The letters swam about on the screen. Dawn blinked to still them, took a deep breath, read on.

*You mention in your letter that you don't
have any more money. I can understand that.
However, this is such a delicate matter, I'm sure
you would feel better if you thought my silence
was properly guaranteed. So I have thought of
something else you can do. I would like you to
send me ten ampoules of Morphine Sulphate.
The postal arrangement will be the same as
before. The Morphine should arrive within one
week. How you obtain it is up to you. It will
be tricky but I know you will find a way. You
are a powerful ward sister with lives in your
hands.*
   Sincerely,
   A well-wisher

All right. All right. So it wasn't over. She'd known it wouldn't be. But her overwhelming sensation was one of relief. The money had arrived. Well-wisher was not going to report her. Not yet anyway.

Walking back to the hospital she had a light, insubstantial feeling, as if her feet weren't quite touching the cement. OK. So, not money. Morphine instead. To sell for money, presumably. She should be anxious; she was right back to where she'd started. Yet her head felt too flimsy and porous to grasp anything apart from the reprieve. Some idea, some notion, was hovering at the edge of her mind. There had been something odd about that e-mail. But just at the moment, Dawn was far too distracted to think what it was.

Trudy greeted her at the doors of Forest Ward.

'Sister! Oh, Sister, I'm so glad you're back!'

The insubstantial sensation in Dawn's feet vanished abruptly. Now what?

'What is it?' she asked.

'It's the new girl in bed eight, Sister. She took her steroids at lunchtime but she's just vomited them all up.'

Dawn breathed again. Trust Trudy to make a drama out of something simple.

'Not to worry,' she said. 'We can put in an IV.' Her mind was back on the e-mail. In the lift on the way up she had realized what was odd about it. Ten ampoules of morphine. It was so little. A single ampoule cost the hospital, at most, about fifty pence. If the blackmailer was hoping to make money by selling it, they were in for a shock. Clearly whoever had written the message didn't know very much about morphine. But if that was the case, why ask for it?

Trudy was still there, trotting beside her.

'I tried to tell her that, Sister. About the IV. But she's very upset. Dr Coulton was here and said she had to have an operation tomorrow. And when she said she didn't want one, he told her she was wasting his time—'

Dawn paused. 'He told her what?'

'That she was wasting his time. He said if she didn't want to listen to him, there were plenty of other patients who would love to have her bed.'

'I see.'

'She's gone to the bathroom,' Trudy said. 'I tried to go after her but she shouted at me to go away. But I think she's really sick, Sister. I didn't know what to do . . . I . . .'

Dawn said, 'It's all right. I'll see her.'

She put her jacket and bag away in her office. She knew the patient, twenty-six-year-old Danielle Jones, a lawyer who had very early on managed to acquire the label of Difficult Patient. Danielle was tall, slim and attractive with a posh, confident accent. A girl who was used to being in charge. Which was probably why, when her Crohn's disease had started up last year, shredding the lining from her bowels and the control from her life, she had found it very difficult to cope. She had refused surgery, saying she couldn't afford the time off work and she didn't want a scar. But the steroids she'd been put on had made her look fat so she had stopped taking those as well. Now her condition was getting worse. This was her fourth hospital admission in six months and she was growing more and more angry. She was abusive to the staff, snapping at them that they were useless and a waste of her taxes. Most of them did their best to avoid her.

Dawn tapped on the bathroom door.

'Danielle?'

No reply. She pushed the door open. The room was high-ceilinged and strip-lit, with four grey marble cubicles at one end and four discoloured china sinks along the other. The walls and floor were covered with tiny tiles, the grouting grimy from the years.

'Danielle?' Dawn's voice bounced off the tiles. There was a strong odour of vomit and faeces. On the floor outside the furthest cubicle was a puddle of greenish liquid. A bare foot stuck out from under the half-closed door.

'Go away,' a shaky voice called from the cubicle.

'It's Dawn. The Matron.'

'I said, go away.'

Dawn picked her way across the tiles. The smell grew stronger. The greenish puddle had blood mixed in with it. In the end cubicle, Danielle sat slumped on the floor, her arms resting on the seat of the toilet. The hem of her dressing gown was spattered with the foul-smelling liquid.

'I didn't make it.' Her eyes were red and swollen. 'I'm sorry.'

Dawn touched her shoulder. 'It's OK. Just rest for a moment.' She was horrified at the state the girl was in. She would have to get her up from there but not just yet. She was exhausted, too weak right now to stand.

Danielle began to sob. 'Look at me. I'm disgusting.'

'No, you're not.'

'Yes, I *am*.'

Dawn said nothing. Danielle put her head on her arms and wept. 'What's happening to me? What's happening? I hate this.'

'Shh. We'll sort it out.' Dawn stroked the hair that hung in sticky ropes around Danielle's face.

'How? How can you sort it out? No one can. That horrible doctor – the weird one . . .'

'Dr Coulton?'

'Whatever.' Danielle flicked a hand. 'Dr Death, *I* call him. All he needs is a black hood and one of those sickle things. He said it was all my fault for not taking the steroids. I told him I *would* take them now, if only they'd help, but they won't stay down. I tried to tell him but he wouldn't believe me . . . he said I wasn't trying, but I am, they won't work, they won't stay down—'

The words degenerated into another storm of sobbing. Dawn waited for it to pass.

'What did Dr . . . er . . . Dr Coulton say about the operation?'

'He said it was my only chance. But I don't want an operation.'

'Why not?'

'Because . . . because . . . I haven't got the time. I've got work to do . . . exams I've got to pass . . .'

'Is that the only reason?'

A tap dripped, the sound echoing around the bathroom.

Dawn said gently, 'Is it?'

Danielle cried. 'I'm scared, Sister. I'm scared I might die.'

The anger had burned itself out. All that was left was despair. Danielle's defences were flattened, her arrogance crushed. She was a frightened child, as all truly sick people were. Dawn crouched down in the brownish mess and took Danielle in her arms.

'You won't die,' she said.

Danielle clung to her, as she probably hadn't clung to anyone since she had been very young. She was used to being in control of her life, but here she was not. She was learning a hard lesson: no matter what you had, if your health went, it was worth nothing. Dawn held her and stroked the sticky ropes of hair.

After a while, Danielle sniffled.

'If I did have the operation,' she said. 'And I'm not,' she added angrily, 'saying I will.'

'Of course not.'

Danielle sniffled again. 'You'd look after me? You'd be there?'

'I'll be there.'

This privilege, not lightly won. The distraught girl on her arm, the sense of a crisis passed. Even the smells of vomit and faeces, so redolent and familiar. Dawn's jaw hardened. This hospital needed her. And she needed it. Why should she lose everything? She might have badly misjudged things but she had acted out of mercy and compassion. The only things this Well-wisher person was acting out of were spite and selfishness and greed.

She tore a sheet of loo roll from the dispenser and handed it to Danielle. The girl blew her nose.

'Feeling better?' Dawn asked.

Danielle nodded. She looked very tired. Her arms were like pale strips of ribbon, much too thin and flimsy for her height.

'Come on, then.' Dawn helped her to her feet. 'Let's get you back to bed.'

Behind the curtains of her cubicle, Dawn helped Danielle to remove her soiled clothes and put on a clean gown. She cleaned her hair as best she could with a towel and got her in to bed.

'I'll call the doctor to put a drip in,' she said. 'We'll give you some fluids. You'll feel better with some hydration on board.'

She put a sign on the door of the toilets saying *Out of Order* and phoned Housekeeping to let them know. Then she headed to the locker room to change out of her ruined uniform. Ahead of her, she spotted Dr Coulton about to leave the ward.

'Excuse me,' she called. 'Dr Coulton!'

Dr Coulton paused but he continued to look at the doors for a moment in a way that made it clear he wasn't happy to be interrupted. 'Yes?'

Dawn caught up with him. 'It's about Danielle Jones. Before you go, would you mind putting in a drip?'

'I haven't got time,' Dr Coulton said. 'I've got somewhere I need to be.'

He began to walk again. Dawn walked right after him. 'If you could do it now,' she said firmly, 'it would be extremely helpful. She really needs the fluid.'

Dr Coulton stopped again, his eyebrows dipped into a V of irritation. 'Perhaps when I was with her a few minutes ago,' he said, 'she should have been more cooperative.' Clearly he wasn't the slightest bit pleased to have been called Dr Death by one of his patients.

Dawn said, 'Well, perhaps if you had been more understanding—'

'About what? If she's not interested in taking my advice, there are plenty of other patients who are. Now, if you'll excuse me, I've got work to do.'

He put his hand on the door. Dawn said sharply, remembering the weeping girl, 'Don't you think *she* wouldn't rather be at work right now?'

Dr Coulton paused again. His gaze travelled down the length of Dawn's uniform. Near the hem of the dress, was a large brownish stain. She thought he was going to comment on it but instead he looked over at the side room.

Seemingly for no reason at all, he said, 'I see you got that blind fixed.'

'I beg your pardon?'

'I said, I see you got that blind fixed.'

'Of course I got it fixed.' What was he on about? 'Blinds provide privacy for the patients.'

'Privacy for the staff, too,' Dr Coulton said.

'Excuse me?'

Dr Coulton didn't reply. He pushed the doors open and strode off down the hall. Dawn stared after him, baffled. What had *that* been about? What did the side room blind have to do with anything? She looked at the little window. The blind was drawn all the way up to the top. Through the glass, facing the door, she could see Lewis's ECG monitor, blipping away above his bed.

Suddenly her throat was dry.

That day in the canteen. Dr Coulton coming up behind her in the queue. *I admire what you did* . . .

She needed to hold on to something. The wall or a table or even the floor. The stock room was empty. She went in and leaned on her arms on the counter. *Easy*, she told herself. *Easy*. She was overreacting here. She was as jumpy as a nerve because of that morphine e-mail. Dr Coulton hadn't meant anything by his comment. How could he have seen her with Mrs Walker? He hadn't even been on the ward that day.

The feeling returned to her legs. She stood up again. From this angle, she had a perfect view of Lewis's side room. The brown plywood door; the rectangular window in the centre. And then, as abruptly as if she had climbed a hill and gained a panoramic view of the landscape, she noticed something else. Right next to the side room were the main doors to the ward. If anyone happened to walk through those doors, the ECG screen over Lewis's bed would be almost the first thing they saw.

Dawn recoiled as sharply as if a snake had just slid out from under the gauze packs. *I admire what you did.* Dr Coulton's air of astonishment when she had told him that Mrs Walker was dead. But he was on Mrs Walker's surgical team. How could he not have missed her on the ward round that morning? How could he not have known? And surely – surely if Dr Coulton *had* come through the doors that day, if he had seen what Dawn had done, he would have confronted her. Reported her. A senior doctor like him! He'd have to be crazy to jeopardize his career over something like this. Anyway, he of all people would know how much an ampoule of morphine cost.

Dawn leaned on her elbows again and pushed

her hair back with her hands. It just showed how unsettled she was, jumping to conclusions over a simple comment about a blind. The best thing to do, if she was going to start obsessing about this, was to confront Dr Coulton. Go after him right now; ask him what he had meant.

But almost immediately, she backed off. If Dr Coulton wasn't the blackmailer, her marching up and asking questions might make him wonder why she was so concerned. The last thing she needed was for people to start making connections between her and the side room.

From behind her came a soft, scraping sound. Dawn turned. In the darkness of the stock room, something was moving towards her. A grey, wraithlike shape, creeping over the floor. Dawn sprang backwards, knocking her elbow hard off the corner of the counter.

'Aah!'

The grey shape cried out too. Then the overhead light came blinking on. The wraithlike figure assembled itself into the solid, everyday figure of a nurse in a white ITU uniform.

'Crikey, Dawn.' Francine stood with one hand on the light switch, the other to her throat. 'I didn't mean to startle you. I just came in to borrow some Labetolol. I didn't expect to find anyone hiding in here in the dark.'

'No, I . . . I was just looking for something.'

Francine gave a rather high-pitched laugh. 'Look at the pair of us. We're turning into a right couple of mad old bats.' Her smiling gaze, moving over Dawn, hesitated at the brown stains on her dress. The smile faded. Dawn remembered suddenly what she had been going to ask her.

'I was thinking, Fran,' she said. 'I was wondering about taking next week off. For a holiday.'

Francine's smile reappeared. 'That's brilliant, Dawn. I've said it to you before, I really think you could do with the break.'

'The only thing is,' Dawn said, 'I'll need someone to cover. There won't be much to do, but just in case. I know it's short notice, but—'

'Ah, ah.' Francine had her hand in the air. 'Don't say another word. You just go ahead and plan your break and have a lovely time. Are you going somewhere nice?'

'Well . . . maybe . . .' The original plan had been to spend her holidays at the Lakes. She couldn't now, of course. Not while all of this was going on.

'I haven't decided yet,' she said. The relief was enormous. One more hurdle dealt with. Francine didn't seem to mind in the least helping her out. Only one more day shift to go. Then the two night shifts, which would be easier, and after that she would be free; out of here until all of this was over.

'Thanks, Francine,' she said.

*   *   *

On the bus home, Dawn sat with her jacket on over a set of theatre scrubs, her soiled uniform in a plastic bag on her knee. Every time the bus jolted, a sour smell of vomit wafted from the bag. Danielle had finally settled on the IV steroids. She had been asleep by the time Dawn had left, lying on her back with her mouth open, her tear-blotched face like a child's. Dawn's neck and arms and shoulders ached. She had been standing to attention all day, like a bird in the winter, watching its back every time it snatched at a crumb.

The realization had finally dawned on her. If Dr Coulton could have come through those doors that day on to the ward, then so could anyone. Any one of the pharmacists, bed managers, dieticians. Trish the physio. Professor Kneebone himself. Anyone at all. How naive had she been, to think she could narrow her list of suspects down to just three people. Dawn pressed her forehead on the window, feeling her head bump hard on the glass. The vibration numbed her lips and nose. In spite of all the possibilities, her mind kept returning to Dr Coulton. Standing there with that contemptuous expression on his face, looking over at the blinds. *Privacy for the staff too*. Why would he have said that unless it meant something? And now that she thought about it, the morphine e-mail wasn't so hard to explain. Doctors were notoriously naive. Despite the fact that they met patients from all sorts of backgrounds every day, they tended to just treat the disease, then scurry back to their journals and their rugby clubs and their circles of all-medical friends. She and Francine had often commented on how easy it would be to fleece them. Dr Coulton might well be under the impression that ten ampoules of morphine would net him a fortune down the side streets of Brixton.

She had no way, for now, of knowing. But lifting her forehead from the window, she was buoyed by a sudden feeling of determination. Whoever Well-wisher was, she had no intention of going along any further with his nasty little games. Stealing the morphine – yes, it would be tricky. But he was right: she could think of a way. It was such a small amount; stealing it would not compromise patient care in any way. But it would compromise *him*. His demanding cash was one thing. If she ended up being charged with murder, the police may or may not care so much about that. But stealing drugs from the hospital . . . The hospital authorities would be extremely anxious to know who was involved. And she had plenty of evidence to hand to the police: the morphine e-mail, the accommodation address in Essex, which the police could use to track the person down.

Another waft of vomit rose from the plastic bag. Dawn's nostrils constricted. She had been working at St Iberius for almost twenty years. Dr Coulton – if it *was* him – had been there for a matter of weeks. How dare he think he could push her around like this, turning her into his cash cow, his petty thief! She twisted the neck of the plastic bag, trapping the foul air inside so tightly that no more of it could possibly escape.

'If I go down,' she said grimly, aloud, 'so will you.'

Chapter Twelve

By the following day, however, despite having been awake worrying about it for most of the night, Dawn still hadn't figured out a way to steal the morphine.

On the face of it, it seemed easy enough. There was plenty of morphine on the ward, sitting right there in the stock room. The difficulty, however, was getting her hands on it. Two nurses had to be present to act as witnesses every time the safe was opened. It had occurred to Dawn that she could take charge of the keys herself. Sneak in to the stock room when no one was around and whip a box from the shelf. But ward sisters very rarely held the safe keys. And it would seem doubly suspicious for her to have insisted on taking them on the very day the morphine was found to have disappeared.

She hadn't reached the stage yet of panicking. Given time, she was sure she would come up with something. The problem was, she didn't *have* that much time. Today was Wednesday, her last day shift before she went on leave. Perhaps the night shifts would provide more of an opportunity. Nights were when most emergencies happened in a hospital. Some incident or other might occur that would give Dawn a chance to grab the keys and nip in to the safe while the other staff were distracted. But it wasn't much to pin her hopes on.

One thing that struck her was how easy it was to focus on the problem now that she no longer had to watch her back all the time. She had her ward back to herself, and that was a very good feeling. Not that she knew for sure that the blackmailer *wasn't* one of her nurses – but somehow none of them had ever fitted the profile, and now that there were so many other possibilities it felt natural to exclude them. The thing was, Dawn *knew* people. You didn't spend eight years as a ward sister without learning to read people. Dawn was long used to judging within minutes of working with them which nurses would be good and which mediocre, to gauging from a patient's body language and expression what they needed when they were too ill or frightened to speak. And time and again, her assessment had proven to be accurate. She stood at the nurse's desk, looking around the ward. Down at bed six, Mandy was washing the hair of an elderly woman with a liver abscess. The patient lay with her eyes closed, clearly enjoying the feel of the warm water sluicing over her head. Mandy sang softly to her as she rinsed out the shampoo. Watching her, Dawn thought: *I always knew it wasn't you.*

Mandy was just too soft-hearted for blackmail. Plus she would never have been organized enough to go about setting up the fake postal and e-mail addresses, all the while having to keep her mouth shut about what she'd seen. Anyway, unless she had exceptional eyesight, the day ward was too far from the side room for her to have been able to read the ECG. Further up the ward, in the stock room, Trudy was unpacking a new delivery of central lines. Her small, pointed face was serious as she cleared a space on the shelf. Trudy, too, Dawn had never seen as a significant candidate. In fact, recently Trudy had started to come on really well as a nurse. A lot of her earlier wobbliness seemed to have evaporated; she was developing more confidence and initiative. Look how good she had been with Danielle the previous day, showing compassion in the way she had stood up for a patient who had been so difficult and hostile towards her.

No – the one person in all of this who ticked all the boxes was Dr Coulton. Despite having no proof, Dawn couldn't help thinking of him as the blackmailer. His personality fit. He was cold and calculating enough to go through with it and to take whatever precautions were needed not to be caught. And he was just patronizing and arrogant enough to have dropped that comment about the blind – probably thinking it was too subtle for Dawn to know what he was talking about. And if she did, so what? He was so sure he had her in his power. And just because he was a doctor didn't mean he didn't need the money. Hadn't Mandy mentioned something about him doing research? Research posts at St Iberius, despite being highly sought-after, paid very little. Dr Coulton could have debts that Dawn didn't know about. He could be into all sorts of things she didn't know about. She knew next to nothing about the man. No one did. The only topics of conversation he ever engaged in with any of the staff were to do with lab results and fluid drainage and blood counts. Any attempts at small talk were met with a blank stare. Even his age was hard to gauge. He was a registrar, which normally would make him at least a couple of years younger than Dawn, but his dour face and receding hairline made him seem older. Dawn pictured him trudging home in the evenings to a bare basement flat, lit by a single bulb, with sterile books and piles of papers everywhere instead of furniture. And, she remembered, he had been on the ward the other day, the day she had felt she was being watched. He had been one of the doctors gathered around the nurse's desk, examining the CT scan.

Almost lunchtime. She still had to do a quick check

on all her patients before the dinner trolleys came round. She started with Lewis in the side room.

'Good news, I hear,' she said as cheerfully as she could. 'You've been given a date for your operation.'

'Yeah. Friday.'

Dawn nodded at the spiky metal cage on his calf. 'I'm sure you can't wait to be rid of that.'

'Yeah, it'll be great.' Lewis was saying all the right things, but to Dawn's mind there was something forced about his enthusiasm.

'Nervous?' she asked.

Lewis picked at his blanket. 'Not really. Just – you know. Worrying about what could go wrong.'

'Wrong, like what?' Dawn sat down on the chair beside his bed.

Lewis shrugged, still picking at the blanket. 'I don't know. Complications. Reactions. You hear things.'

'But you've already had one operation. To put the fixator on in the first place. And that went very well, didn't it?'

'Yeah, but this one's going to be much bigger. I don't know. I just keep thinking about it. If something happened . . . if I lost my leg . . . I don't know what I'd do.'

Dawn gave the fixator a light tap. 'Don't think like that,' she said. 'The surgeons here are very experienced. The chances of anything bad happening are very small.'

'I know, I know. That's what the docs said. But I can't help it. I've just got this feeling.' Lewis put his hands behind his head and puffed out his cheeks. 'Stupid, I know.'

'It's not stupid at all,' Dawn said. 'It's perfectly normal to worry. But think of it this way, by Friday afternoon, it'll be all over. And I'll be working here on Friday night so I'll come in to check on you. You'll be sitting here, listening to your earphones, wondering what on earth you were so worried about.' She bent her head to catch his eye. 'OK?'

'Yeah, OK.'

She left him looking a bit happier, fiddling with the buttons on his mobile phone.

Danielle Jones was next. That morning she had gone ahead with the surgery for her Crohn's Disease. She had been very drowsy when she had returned from theatre but was now awake.

Dawn asked her softly, 'How are you feeling?'

'Very sore.' Danielle lay in a weary, flattened-looking way, her hair spread around her on the pillow. Fluid dripped from a bag into her arm. More tubes drained blood and other body fluids into various containers under the bed. Between the buttons of her pyjamas, a long white bandage was visible all the way down her middle.

'Do you need something for pain?' Dawn asked.

'Oh, yes. Please.'

The jingling of keys announced Mandy's arrival. 'Already sorted, Dawn. I just gave her some morphine.'

'It's not working.' Danielle gave a weak shake of her head. 'I would have felt it by now.'

'Just give it a chance,' Mandy advised. 'You've only had it a few minutes.'

'There's no point. It won't work. I'm telling you it won't.' Danielle gave a little sob and put her arm over her face.

Mandy rolled her eyes at Dawn. She showed her Danielle's drug chart. 'Ten milligrams, see?' she whispered. 'She couldn't possibly need any more than that.'

Dawn's gaze was fixed a couple of inches below the chart, at the morphine keys on Mandy's belt, clinking a little every time she moved.

Slowly, she said, 'Let's give her the benefit of the doubt. She's awake, she's clearly uncomfortable, her pulse and BP are up. She'll take another dose. I'll come with you and sign it out.'

Mandy sighed. 'OK, Dawn. You're the boss.'

Dawn followed Mandy to the stock room. She couldn't take her eyes off the keys. Her heart was beating faster. Had she really thought that Danielle was uncomfortable enough to need an extra dose? Or was it just an excuse for her to get near the morphine cupboard? If so, what did she think it was going to achieve? It wasn't as if she could do anything with Mandy there watching. But just seeing the morphine, she thought, might spark an idea in her mind, help her to come up with some sort of plan.

Mandy unclipped her keys and opened the padlock on the safe. Dawn found herself scrutinizing every inch of the interior in a way she never had before. On the metal shelf was a stack of cardboard boxes filled with morphine ampoules. The flap on the top box was open. Still grumbling, Mandy lifted it out.

'Mark my words, Dawn, we'll be pandering to Miss Drama Queen for the rest of the week. I know she's just had surgery, but you see if I'm—'

She stopped. She had taken an ampoule from the box and snapped it open without paying attention to what she was doing. A long sliver of glass had driven into her finger.

'Shit,' Mandy said. Already, a shiny red bead was starting to swell on her fingertip.

'Here, quick.' Dawn yanked a sheet of tissue paper from the roll on the wall. Mandy pressed the paper to her finger but the blood still came soaking through.

'Try holding it under the tap,' Dawn said. 'The cold might stop the bleeding.'

Mandy went to the sink and turned the tap on full force. She sloshed her finger about under the water. Crimson streaks ran down the sides of the basin. Dawn, watching from a few feet away, turned her head a couple of degrees and found herself looking straight at the boxes of morphine. The sink was directly behind the door of the safe. With Mandy standing where she was, the open door blocked her view of the shelf.

Dawn's heart rate sped up further.

'Still haemorrhaging,' Mandy called from the sink.

'Just give it a minute,' Dawn called back. Her eyes were still glued to the boxes. *Ten ampoules*, the e-mail had said. The exact number of ampoules in each box.

Before she could think any more about it, she snatched one of the lower boxes out from under the stack. Under the sound of the running water, she ripped the cardboard flap open. In almost the same movement, she tipped the ampoules into her hand and crammed them into the pocket of her dress. The glass containers clinked off each other. Dawn gripped her pocket, whipping her head towards the sink. Mandy was still rinsing her finger. Dawn shoved the empty box back at the bottom of the stack.

'Any chance of a band-aid?' Mandy called.

'Coming up.'

How normal her voice sounded! She wiped her hands on her uniform and took a band-aid from a box on the shelf. She couldn't quite believe what had just happened. All that plotting and planning and worrying, and now here she was with the morphine in her pocket, just like that. But it wasn't over yet. The thing now was to get out of here as soon as possible, before Mandy had a chance to start poking around. She passed the band-aid around the door. While Mandy was occupied with peeling the back off the sticky part, Dawn threw the bloodstained morphine ampoule into the bin and took a fresh one from the top box. By the time Mandy appeared, smoothing the band-aid around her finger, Dawn had broken open the new ampoule and drawn the morphine into a syringe.

'Oh, thanks,' Mandy said. 'Save me chopping another one of my fingers off. How many's that left now?'

'We've taken two,' Dawn said. 'This one and the one you bled on. That leaves four in the top box.' She paused.

Mandy said, 'And ten in each of the others.'

Dawn said nothing. Staff were supposed to check all the boxes, not just the one on top. If Mandy opened the other boxes . . . But she didn't. She clicked the top of her pen and wrote the numbers into the pink-paged ledger.

'Forty-four left in total,' she said.

Dawn could have thrown her arms around her. Sloppy, careless, wonderful Mandy. Mandy slammed the ledger shut and tossed it into the safe. Then she closed the door and snapped on the padlock.

'Here's the syringe for Danielle.' Dawn held it out, praying that Mandy's finger wasn't too sore to prevent her from taking it. She had to get her out of the stock room. She couldn't move properly until Mandy had left; she was trying to keep as still as she could, one hand clamped over her bulging pocket. All she needed now was for the ampoules to clink against each other – or worse, for some of them to fall out and smash on the floor.

Thankfully, Mandy took the syringe.

'I'll give this to Miss Lawyer,' she said. 'Get her off our backs.'

She went out, still fiddling with her bandage. Dawn stayed where she was, locked in the same stiff, clenched position, clasping the knobbly heap in her pocket until well after Mandy's footsteps and the jangle of her keys had faded.

The morphine ampoules were bulkier than the cash had been. Dawn was going to need a larger envelope to post them. With some kind of padding to protect the glass. At the post-office in the Georgian terrace of shops at Silham Vale, she bought an A3-sized envelope with bubble wrap on the inside. Also plenty of stamps – far more than she probably needed, but she wasn't taking any chances.

Walking down the patchwork pavement of Crocus Road, past the parked cars with their windscreens shimmering in the sun, she felt herself lifted by a sense of control. She'd done it. She'd got the morphine! Once she had posted it, the blackmailer would be in her power. For the twentieth time, she thought it: *Thank God Mandy had been so careless*. A more thorough nurse might have insisted on opening each and every box. How long, Dawn wondered, before the missing morphine was discovered? Anything from a day to a couple of weeks, depending on whether anyone ever actually did check all the boxes or whether the theft only came to light when the upper boxes were empty and the bottom one was reached.

And that was when it hit her. She stopped.

If whoever took the keys from Mandy this evening did a proper count and discovered the empty box, Mandy would be blamed. She would have been the last one to hold the keys. Pharmacy would go into meltdown. Even one ampoule going accidentally astray was a matter for all kinds of meetings, explanations, overhaul of policy. But ten! And the empty box still in the safe, carefully closed over and placed at the bottom. A deliberate attempt to mislead. Mandy would find herself at the centre of a massive investigation, surrounded by pointing fingers. *When did this happen? When did you last check all the boxes?* At the very least, she would be hauled before a disciplinary panel for negligence. At worst, accused outright of the theft.

Dawn sank on to a nearby wall. *Shit, shit, shit. Now what?*

Mandy might not be the best nurse Dawn had ever worked with. But she was a long way from being the worst either. The patients liked and trusted her, and her interest was warm and genuine. Mandy might forget to chart a patient's temperature, but she would happily spend twenty minutes nattering with them about their womanizing husbands or the latest episode of *Coronation Street* – a practice which, in Dawn's opinion, could often reveal at least as much about a person's condition as taking their temperature ever could. She pictured Mandy sitting white-faced in the HR office, worried sick about what might happen to her son if she lost her job. Mandy was part of Dawn's team. Her responsibility. She could not let that happen.

Dawn sighed, slumping her shoulders. No sooner had she solved one problem than another took its place. Was this ever going to end?

'It's the padlock on my shed,' Dawn told the cashier. 'I seem to have lost the key.'

The hardware shop smelled of paint and cardboard and oil. Along the counter was a row of plastic containers filled with screws, bolts and various other small, unidentifiable metal objects. The teenage cashier wore a set of overalls with the name 'Alan' stitched in red over the pocket.

'What you need,' he said, 'is a pair of bolt-cutters.'

He led Dawn down an aisle, between shelves stacked with paint brushes and pots of turpentine. At a stand hung with long plastic packages, he stopped.

'Here we are.' He flipped the edges of the packages. 'What kind do you need? Angled? Clipper cut?'

'I don't know.' Dawn stared at the profusion of blades and handles. 'It's just an ordinary padlock.'

'What size?'

'Well . . . around so . . . ?' She held up her finger and thumb an inch apart.

Alan pulled a package off the stand. 'This one's quite good,' he said. Through the plastic Dawn saw a pair of shiny red handles. 'It's our most popular brand.'

'How does it work?'

The teenager explained. 'You put the shackle of the lock – the thin part – between the blades. Then you squeeze the handles and . . .' He brought his knuckles together and made a regurgitative noise in his throat, presumably to indicate the shattering of solid metal.

Dawn studied the curved blades. A bit like a clip-cutter, then. Breaking a padlock didn't seem a million miles away from removing a stitch.

'And this is a popular brand?' she said. 'You could buy it just about anywhere? In any shop?'

Alan shrugged. 'Pretty much.'

'OK then. I'll take it.'

On her way home, Dawn went through her plan again. It was very straightforward. Tonight she was going to sneak back to the ward and break open the padlock on the morphine safe. That way, the missing morphine would look like an outside job and Mandy would not be blamed. It was as simple as that.

The plan, when she had first thought of it, had seemed preposterous, but the more she thought about it, the more she saw that with a few basic precautions there was no reason why it shouldn't work. It was the recent break-ins at the hospital that had given her the idea. If anyone saw her in the hospital tonight, all she'd have to say was that she had returned to fetch something she had forgotten. Of course, if that happened she would have to turn around and leave again and think of something else. But it was worth a try.

At home, in her kitchen, she cut the plastic packaging away from the bolt-cutters. The blades were slate-grey, heavy and greasy-looking. Dawn avoided touching any part of the cutters with her fingers. She wrapped them in a sheet of newspaper and stashed them in her navy bag. They just about fit.

The trickiest part of the plan was the timing. The most obvious thing would be to wait until after nine when the night shift started and there would be fewer people about to see her. But if she waited too long, the new shift might discover the empty morphine box. Dawn checked the rota to see who was on. Elspeth and an agency nurse called Lucy whom Dawn had never met. Elspeth, being the 'home' nurse, would probably be the one to take the morphine keys. Dawn seriously doubted that Elspeth would bother to check all the boxes. So unless the agency nurse turned out to be exceptionally conscientious, the missing morphine was unlikely to be discovered tonight. On balance, it was a chance worth taking.

Dawn forced down some food: a banana and a slice of toast. Then she packed her stolen morphine ampoules carefully into the A3-sized envelope. She wrote another letter to the blackmailer and added it in with the ampoules:

> *This is the last 'favour' I will do for you. I think we both have enough information about each other now to call it quits.*

At ten o'clock she went upstairs and changed into a pair of jeans and a dark top.

'Sorry, Milly,' she said to the dog, faithfully plodding behind her to the front door. 'No walk for you this evening, I'm afraid. But wish me luck.'

She took the envelope with her up to the green. The night was fresh, with a brisk, rising breeze. To fit the parcel through the post box she had to squeeze it and compress it right down. There was a muffled thud as it landed on the pile of letters inside. There. Everything Well-wisher had asked, she had done to the best of her ability. Now, no more. No more.

It was almost eleven when she reached St Iberius. The tower block was patched with lights, pocked by tiny black shapes moving about inside. The air was cool; the sounds of the breeze in the trees and the bus as it pulled away were very close and clear. Dawn felt alert, energized, ready for anything. Through the glass sliding doors she saw the empty main hall, the WRVS shop closed and shuttered, the fountain switched off. Arnold, the night porter was sitting in his cubicle just inside the entrance. From her position in a dark corner of the car park, Dawn watched him talking on the phone, pushing his hand up under his navy-brimmed cap to scratch his head.

Then, carrying her bag with the bolt-cutters, she went around the side of the tower block. In a high, concrete wall, a door led to a yard filled with large, plastic bins. The yard was filled with the sweetish smell of rotting food. At the far end, a heavy metal door led directly into the building. There was no handle on the door, just a keypad set into the wall beside it. Dawn tapped in the code. Inside was a narrow, unlit hallway. Through a set of grey, floppy doors were the kitchens, mopped and silent, ready for the next day. Beside the kitchens was the service lift.

This also required a code but Dawn knew this as well. There was nothing about this hospital that she didn't know. Every doorway, every crevice, every pipe and leak and gurgle – all were as familiar to her as the body of any long-term patient she had ever cared for and watched over.

The lift took her to the second floor of the tower block. From there, a glass-walled link tunnel led to the old Victorian wing. At this time of night, the link was empty. At the far end, Dawn used the fire escape to climb the remaining flights to the fifth floor. The corridor leading to Forest Ward was deserted as well. There was only Dawn, her soft-soled trainers squeaking on the moonlit floor. How many nights had she walked this corridor, floating with the euphoria that always hit in the earliest part of the morning, after twenty hours with no sleep? How often had she stood at this window, looking out at the rows of darkened houses, calm in the knowledge that the hospital was here for them if they needed it, guarding them while they slept?

The hall directly outside Forest Ward was silent. No sound of any voices or activity. Dawn swung the door open an inch. In the centre of the floor was the nurses' desk with its computer and phones, sitting in the pool of light from the bendy lamp. Beyond the desk, the rows of beds faded into the dimness. There was no sign of Elspeth or the agency nurse. They were probably in the staff room at the far end. From there, they wouldn't hear Dawn moving about. And if one of them did happen to come up the ward, she would hear them long before they reached her.

She slipped through the doors and went straight to the stock room. There was no need to turn on the light. The glow from the nurses' desk was more than enough to make out the counters and shelves, the metallic gleam of the safe on the wall. Dawn pulled a pair of latex gloves from the dispenser and put them on. Then she eased the bolt-cutters from her bag. Just as she was unwrapping them from their newspaper, a man's voice shouted from somewhere outside the door, 'Oi! What the hell do you think you're doing?'

Dawn just managed to catch the cutters before they crashed to the ground. The man's voice came again. 'Get off me, you bastards! I'll kill you.'

Dawn breathed again in relief. Mr Otway, in bed sixteen. By day, the sweetest-natured elderly man, but at night when the lights went off he had a tendency to become confused. One of his recurrent beliefs was that he was in an experimental institute run by MI5. She listened for a moment but there was no sound of anyone coming to see to him. His shouts were beginning to subside. *Get on with it*. Quickly, Dawn positioned the metal blades one on either side of the padlock. The shackle looked very light and frail between the cutters. This was going to be easy. At the last minute, she lifted the corner of her jacket and stuffed it between the shackle and the blades to muffle the noise. Then she brought the handles together.

She had expected it to be easy, but she was surprised at just how easy it was. The lock gave immediately with a soft crack. The sound of Dawn's shoe touching the floor would have been louder. St Iberius really did need to spend more on security. She opened the safe, removed the morphine boxes and shook them to empty the ampoules out over the counter. Ideally, if she was staging a drug theft, she should take the ampoules with her, but if she met someone on the way out she didn't want to have them on her. Hopefully the general assumption would be that the burglar had been interrupted and fled. For effect, she slid open a couple of drawers and scattered the contents – needles, syringes, cannulas – over the floor. Also a few dressing packs from a shelf. There. That should be enough to suggest that someone had had a quick rummage around before finding their main target.

The minutes were ticking by. *Time to get out of here.* She placed the bolt cutters on the counter, peeled her latex gloves off and stuffed them into her bag. Before going back out to the ward, she paused again to listen. Now would definitely not be a good time to get caught. The main doors were mere feet away. Five, six steps and she was there. Mr Otway seemed to have settled down. The only sound from the ward was a soft snore. *Go for it!* Dawn flew across the floor. She was almost at the doors when she heard something behind her: a soft, rubbing squeak, like a footstep. In another second she was out in the hall. She did not slow but headed straight for the fire escape and flung herself through the door. At the last second, just before the door clunked shut, she looked back. The corridor was empty. No one was following her. The double doors to Forest Ward were closed.

She was much more cautious leaving the hospital even than she had been on her way in. Before every door and corner she paused to check that the way ahead was clear. But all she saw were locked departments, shadowy, deserted seating areas, the eerie green reflections of the Exit signs on the floor. At the other end of the link tunnel she took the lift to the kitchen entrance and opened the door to the bin-smelling yard. In seconds, she was through the door in the wall and out into the fresh night. The door clicked shut behind her. She'd done it! She'd made it! Mandy could not be blamed. No one could be blamed. In the distance, the eerie, up-and-down wail of an ambulance. The lights twinkling across the city, the breeze on her face. Exultation.

Chapter Thirteen

Brrrrr.

Dawn, woken by the noise, became aware that she was lying, fully-dressed, face-down on her duvet. Her mouth was stuck to the pillow. Why on earth had she set the alarm? She wasn't working today. Her night shifts didn't start until tomorrow. She stuck her hand out and hit the top of the alarm clock but the shrill noise continued. It was a couple of seconds before she realized that the sound was coming from her phone.

She felt about on her bedside table for the receiver.

'Hello?'

'Sister Torridge?'

'Elspeth!' Still groggy, Dawn pulled herself up on her elbows. The daisy-patterned wallpaper by the window was lit by a greyish glow. The red digits on her clock read seven fifteen.

'I'm sorry to disturb you, Sister.' Elspeth sounded

agitated, for her. 'I know you're not working today, but there's been a problem.'

Dawn, alert now, pulled herself up further in the bed.

'What's happened?' she asked, though of course she already knew. The phone call had come earlier than expected but she was ready for it.

Elspeth said, 'We've had a break-in.'

'A break-in?' *Easy. Easy. Surprise . . . concern . . . don't overdo it.*

'Last night,' Elspeth said. 'Someone smashed open the stock-room safe and took some of the morphine.'

'Good Lord!'

'Yes, Sister. Security's been up, and Sister Clark, the night manager. She called the police. She said I should let you know, but to wait till this morning. Not to phone you in the middle of the night.'

'No, of course. I mean, it's fine to call me whenever you need to.' Dawn remembered to ask, 'Was anyone hurt?'

'No,' Elspeth said. 'At least – the agency nurse had to go to A&E.'

'To A&E? Whatever for?'

'To be treated for shock.'

'Shock? From the break-in?'

'Well, I suppose,' Elspeth said. 'And also because she actually saw the person.'

Dawn sat up in bed.

'She *saw* the person?'

'Yes. She thought she heard something up at the top of the ward so she went to check and she saw someone just leaving through the doors. Then she saw the mess in the stock room and realized that the person she'd just seen was the burglar.'

Dawn was sitting out on the edge of the bed, staring sightlessly at the wardrobe. That squeaking sound behind her, like a footstep, as she'd been leaving the ward. But she'd seen no one . . . nobody had followed her out . . .

Elspeth said, 'She's given a description to the police.'

'The police. I see.'

'Just a moment, Sister.' Elspeth's voice faded. A second later she was back. 'It's chaos here. All the patients' bells keep ringing. They've all heard what's happened and some of them are a bit upset.'

Dawn hardly heard her. A description to the police! Elspeth hadn't sounded funny when she'd said it so obviously she hadn't connected the burglar with Dawn. What sort of description had the agency nurse given? Tall woman? Jeans? Fair hair? How many people out there would fit those criteria?

'Sister Torridge?' Elspeth sounded agitated again. 'Could you come in? Just for a while. I know it's your day off, but I'm on my own here and the agency nurse is useless. She's been sitting with her head between her knees ever since she came back from A&E, saying she thinks she's going to black out.'

The agency nurse! Dawn had never met her before, but if she went in there now, as sure as eggs were eggs, the nurse would recognize her immediately as the person she'd seen last night.

She said sharply, 'I'm sorry, Elspeth. I can't possibly come in this morning.'

'But, Sister,' Elspeth's voice rose. 'I can't cope here on my own. I've got none of the obs done and no one's had their morning meds. I can't handle the patients and her having hysterics all over the place as well. Could you speak to her? She might listen to you.'

Dawn hesitated. But what harm could it do? The agency nurse hadn't heard her voice last night, had she?

'All right,' she said. 'Put her on.'

'I'll see if I can get her to come to the phone. Last time she stood up she said she nearly . . .' Elspeth's voice disappeared again. Then she returned and said with relief, 'Here she is.'

The sound of heavy breathing came down the line. Dawn said, 'Hello?'

'M-matron?'

'Yes, this is Sister Torridge speaking,' Dawn said kindly. 'I'm sorry you had such a bad experience last night.'

'Oh, Sister.' A long, jerky intake of breath. 'It was

awful. When you can't even feel safe in your own workspace . . .'

Dawn said carefully, 'But I hear you've been a wonderful help to the police. I believe you gave them a full description of the burglar?'

'Yes, I did. But when you think of it . . . What could have happened . . .'

'I know.'

'I mean,' another shuddery gasp, 'a minute sooner and I'd have walked straight in on top of him.'

'Him?'

'Yes. The burglar.'

Dawn paused.

'The burglar was a man?'

Another long, stuttery inhalation. 'Oh, Sister. When you just think about what—'

Dawn interrupted her. 'Sorry – I'm sorry to ask you this, but . . . are you quite sure it was the burglar you saw? It couldn't have been one of the patients? Or a doctor?'

'No, definitely not. He was wearing outdoor clothes. Jeans.'

Dawn looked down at her blue Gap denims.

'And anyway,' the nurse added, 'he was armed.'

'*Armed?*'

'Yes. He had a huge, bulky bag. The exact sort you'd put a gun in.'

For a moment, Dawn was speechless.

'Did you actually *see* the gun?' she asked. 'Did he actually threaten you with it?'

'No. But the way he looked. I know he would have. I always know. Once I had a feeling about my gran and I called her to see if she was all right, and the next day she rang back to say her neighbour had been broken into just at the exact moment I'd phoned . . .' The agency nurse began to sob. 'I'm never working at this hospital again! Never. I'm going to sue—'

There was a muffled clattering at the end of the phone. A second voice said, 'All right. All right now. You just sit down there and have a little rest.'

Claudia's brisk tones came booming down the line. 'Good morning, Dawn. You've heard our news.'

'Yes, I have.'

'Everyone's rather shocked here, as you can tell. But the day staff will be in shortly. No need for you to come in on your day off.'

'Thanks, Claudia. Did she . . . did she really see an armed man?'

'Well,' Claudia lowered her voice, 'you know. The police were very sympathetic. Nice to have that sort of attention, if you're with me. But the main thing is, no one was hurt. And the other thing . . .' Her voice rose again. 'I don't think we'll need to wait now until that budget meeting to get our CCTV cameras. Armed burglars, Dawn! I've called an emergency meeting this morning with the CEO. I think we'll find that by next week there'll be a camera on every floor of the hospital.' Triumph filled Claudia's tone.

Dawn had to lie down again when she had hung up. The daisies on the wallpaper leaped and jittered in front of her eyes. But once she had recovered she began to see the episode for what it was. This was all *good*. It was very, very good. They were looking for a man now. In a million years, no one could connect any of this with her. Her plan had been more successful than she could ever have imagined. A classic example of two birds being killed with one stone. She had completely eliminated any possibility of Mandy or any of her other nurses being blamed for the disappearance of the morphine. And now that Claudia was on the case, the increased security that would result from the incident would make it next to impossible for anyone to steal anything else from the hospital. Once Dr Coulton heard about this, he would have to realize once and for all that no matter what his feelings were on the matter, there really was nothing more she could do for him.

By the afternoon, Dawn's euphoria had swung back to agitation. This whole situation was by no means over. She still had to wait for Well-wisher to receive the morphine and to hear what he had to say about it. And even if she had got the better of him for now, the truth was that he would always know what had happened to Mrs Walker. For as long as he was out there, she would never truly be safe.

She was too restless to stay in the house. Milly seemed off form as well, creeping around the kitchen with her tail down. Dawn thought that a walk might perk both of them up. Milly, at first, seemed happy enough to be out, waving her tail and sniffing at next door's wall where another dog had left an unpleasant-looking stain. But by the time they reached the green her pace had slowed to a crawl. Her hind legs were so stiff that she was moving almost in a waddle.

'Come on, Mill.' Dawn gave her a gentle nudge with her knee. 'Look – what's that over there? In the flower bed? I bet that smells nice.'

Milly gazed listlessly at the half-eaten hot dog. Then she looked up at Dawn, her dark eyes miserable, her tail curled right in between her legs.

'Not in the mood, eh?' Dawn crouched beside her and stroked the tense, shivery body. 'OK. Let's get you back home.'

Milly trotted faster on the way back, glancing up at Dawn every few feet as if to apologize for having ruined the outing. But once in the house it was clear that she wasn't well. She lay on her side on the sheepskin rug in the sitting-room, breathing in rapid, whimpery little gasps. Dawn found one of Dora's old anti-inflammatory tablets in the odds-and-ends drawer in the kitchen and crushed it up with the back of a spoon. She fed it to Milly mixed with a lump of bread and butter.

'Poor girl.' She ran her hand down Milly's side, careful not to put pressure on the inflamed hip. 'Poor old girl. You've been doing so well recently.'

It was unfortunate that today was one of Milly's bad days. Not just for the sake of the poor dog herself, but also because Dawn was desperate to get out of the house. A long walk would have been ideal, to Tooting Bec Common, perhaps, or even Wandsworth. She didn't feel like going on her own.

For something to do, she went upstairs, stripped the sheets and duvet from her bed and piled them along with a heap of towels into the washing-machine. Then she filled a bucket with hot water and started to mop the kitchen floor.

'Coo-ee! Dawn!'

A tapping noise from the hall. Dawn looked out. Peering through the sidelight beside the front door, hands cupped to the glass, was a stick-like figure with a permed, frizzy head. Eileen Warren, Dawn's neighbour from across the road.

'Daa-awn,' Eileen called, tapping her nails on the window. 'Open up. I can see you in there.'

Dawn went out and opened the door.

'Hello, Eileen. How are you?'

'Just on my way back from the Somerfield.' Eileen

jiggled her tartan shopping trolley. 'Thought I'd pop in and say hello. Lovely evening, isn't it?'

It *was* a lovely evening; the grass golden, the traffic sounds distant and muffled in the heat.

'Doing anything later?' Eileen asked.

'I've no plans yet.'

'Well, call over for a cup of tea any time you want to. You know where I am.'

'Thanks very much, Eileen. I'm not sure yet what I'm doing, but I'll bear it in mind.'

Dawn watched her elderly neighbour hobble back across the road, pushing her shopping trolley in front of her. Eileen was a nice lady, if garrulous; she and Dora had been close friends. With Dora gone, Eileen was often lonely. She was constantly calling at number 59 with various excuses: did Dawn need anything? Would she fancy coming across for tea? Often Dawn did go to Eileen's for a meal, or even just for a cuppa and a chat. But tonight she wasn't in the mood. She wanted to be out somewhere, away from all of this. Be someone else for a while. The sun shone down on a car parked in the street. The side windows were two bright yellow squares, like the lenses of a pair of glasses. Out of nowhere, Dawn found herself wondering: what was Will doing this evening? She had not thought of him – or not for more than a moment – since he had phoned the other day to invite her out to dinner and she had cut him off so abruptly. But one thing she knew from the way he had sounded: if she called him, he would come at once to meet her. She only had to say.

Guilt filled her. *You can't use him like this. You might not feel that way about him but you respect him too much to treat him badly.* Still, though. How wonderful would it be to have someone to go out with this evening, to have somewhere to go and something to do. She yearned to be normal. Not to be a Matron or a manager or a ward sister – just an ordinary person with no responsibilities, sitting in a crowd with nothing more pressing on her mind than what to order for a drink. Will was kind and down-to-earth and that was what she needed right now. It would be a simple, friendly night out; they could chat about farming, computers, dogs, holidays. She would make it clear that she wasn't promising anything else. Will was a grown man, wasn't he? He could take care of himself.

She picked up the phone.

'Will? It's Dawn.'

'Dawn!' The eager pleasure in his voice was unmistakable. Grimly, Dawn ploughed on.

'I was wondering – is that dinner you mentioned still on?'

'Dinner?' Will sounded surprised. 'But I thought this was a bad week for you.'

'Well, things are quieter now than I thought.' She

tried to keep the edge from her voice. What was the matter with him? Did he want to meet her or didn't he?

Will said, 'No, no – dinner sounds great.' He was smiling now; she could hear it. She pictured him like a *Sesame Street* puppet with a grin that split his face from ear to ear. 'When would you like?'

'How about tonight?'

'Tonight?' He sounded surprised again. 'I'd love to, but unfortunately I'm working this evening – doing a contract for a company in town. I'll be here until at least nine.'

'Oh.' Dawn rubbed at a scratch on the phone table. 'That's a pity. Tonight just happens to be a good night for me. I honestly don't know when I'll next be free.'

The sound of her own words disgusted her. The threat was a squalid little one, way beneath both of them. But Will was all over it at once. 'No, no, I didn't mean . . . Of course I can meet you. I just meant it might be late. I can get the train down as soon as I've finished.'

'Or I could go up there?' Dawn said. 'That would save us both some time.'

'Well, yes. Yes! If you're sure. It wouldn't be too much trouble?'

'No.' She was filled with relief. 'No trouble at all.'

*　　*　　*

She rarely got dressed up. But tonight, whatever tiny, feverish creature was flying and fluttering about inside her drove her to scrabble in the back of her wardrobe for the black glittery skirt and top she had bought at the Whitgift Centre last year for the ward's Christmas do. The skirt was too small; she'd been shopping in a hurry because of Dora and hadn't had much time to try things on. Now, however, pulling it up over her hips, she saw that she had lost weight. The skirt settled easily, slithering to just above her knees. She brushed out her hair. Mandy was right: it *had* grown. The practical, handy-for-work bob now seemed too long and thin and girlish for the sophisticated outfit. She tried holding it up, turning her head from side to side to gauge the effect in the mirror. She twisted it into a chignon like Francine's. It took a few attempts as she wasn't used to it but finally she managed to pin it in place.

She studied herself. She was too large and big-boned to have anything like Francine's willowy figure, but tonight she looked tall and slender, her legs long and slim in a pair of black, high-heeled sandals. After the past few days the last thing she would have expected was to look anything approaching normal, much less quite presentable, but there you were. No accounting for the way things went.

Milly, curled up in her basket in the kitchen, seemed more comfortable after her anti-inflammatory. Her tail banged against the washing-machine when Dawn went to say goodbye.

'Back later.' Dawn gave her a pat. She left a bowl of water and some dog biscuits within reach on the floor.

The warm breeze coaxed wispy strands from her chignon. The bus to Croydon was full of teenagers heading out for the night. The air smelled of burgers and aftershave. East Croydon station was jammed, but since it was the first stop for the London train Dawn managed to get a seat. At each stop, more people got on until the aisles were packed. Most of the travellers were young, dressed in jeans and trainers. Dawn caught sight of herself in the window, all dolled-up and shiny in her black skirt and heels. Abruptly, her mood plummeted again. Didn't anyone dress up in London any more? What was she doing, heading all this way to meet a nice but rather dull man for an evening that was bound to be awkward and filled with misunderstanding? The best thing would be to get out at the next station and turn back. Then the train flew across the Thames, and to the left, the Albert Bridge, lit up in the dusk, its necklace of lights like beads on a pink birthday cake, sparked in Dawn the familiar excitement that years of living in the City had never fully managed to diminish: *London. I'm in London.*

Will's contract was somewhere off Ludgate Hill.

He had said that he would wait for her near the Millennium Bridge, at the Tate Modern end. Dawn took the tube to Embankment, then walked across Blackfriars Bridge. Along the South Bank, the trees were strung with thousands of tiny blue lights, reflected in the black, choppy water. She reached the Tate Modern a few minutes early but Will was there, unfamiliar in a dark suit and tie, standing beneath the spindly, sculptured legs of a giant metal spider. The blue lights from the trees flashed in his glasses as he looked about him, presumably searching for her.

'Hello.' That crinkling up of his eyes again as he caught sight of her. Dawn saw him taking in her high heels and skirt and chignon as she approached and regretted all over again the impulse she'd had to call him.

'Where would you like to go?' Will asked when she was standing beside him.

'I don't mind.'

'Would you like a drink somewhere before dinner?'

Dawn hesitated. 'Maybe we should just find a restaurant. It's after nine now.' No sense in overly prolonging the evening.

'OK.' Will nodded. 'I know a nice place near here.'

The bank was thronged with tourists, most of whom seemed to be carrying cameras. A few yards from the bridge, a man lay on his front on the ground, photographing the floodlit dome of St Paul's across the river through the spokes of a bicycle wheel.

'So,' Will said as they walked, 'your week became quieter in the end?'

'Yes, it did.'

'Always nice when that happens.'

'Yes.'

It was the reverse of the day in Sussex, when Will had been silent and Dawn had been the one straining to keep the conversation going. The blue flash of Will's glasses again as he looked at her – as if he sensed that something was wrong but didn't want to ask.

They went to an Italian restaurant down a narrow lane. Inside, the walls were whitewashed, painted with murals of Venice and the Colosseum. Candles flickered in tiny blue glasses on the tables. Accordion music seesawed in the background. It was all very mellow and romantic. Dawn would have preferred a noisier, jollier place, with diners in large groups instead of couples tucked away in cosy little corners. A waiter showed them to a table.

'Something to drink?' he asked.

'I'll have a glass of white wine,' Dawn said.

'And for you, Sir?'

'A lager, please.'

Will looked at Dawn over the candle flame in a

smiley sort of way. Too late, she remembered what had happened the last time she had ordered a glass of white wine. She wondered if he was thinking it as well. She opened out her menu and concentrated on the list of main courses. There were only five of them.

'Everything looks very nice,' Dawn felt she should say after a minute of silence.

'What do you think you'll have?'

'Oh . . .' She hadn't actually managed to take in any of it. 'Maybe the chicken?'

The waiter returned with the drinks. 'Ready to order?'

Will looked at Dawn.

'The garlic chicken, please,' she said.

'No starter?' Will asked.

'Not for me, thanks. But you go ahead.'

As she had expected, he didn't. 'Just the steak for me. Medium.'

When the waiter had left, there was another silence. Dawn busied herself by opening out her napkin and spreading it over her knee. She took a sip of her wine. The tartness of it squeezed her salivary glands, shooting a sharp pain through her jaw.

'You're quiet tonight.' Will was watching her.

Dawn put down her glass. She was being rude. It had been her idea to drag Will here and she owed it to him not to make him feel uncomfortable. She searched for something to say and blurted out the first thing that came into her head: 'A patient of mine died.'

'Oh, I'm sorry.'

'A few days ago.' Now she felt guilty. No good could come of using Mrs Walker's death as an excuse for not having to make small talk with her date. But it had worked. Will drew back immediately, the puppyish, eager-to-please look in his eyes replaced by a respectful concern.

'Busy here, isn't it?' Dawn looked around her at the murmuring, cosy-couple tables, the waiters swerving between them, plates and glasses aloft.

'It always is,' Will said. 'The food is excellent.'

By the time their meals arrived, Dawn had begun to relax. She was hungry now. The wine had set her stomach rumbling.

'Another glass?' the waiter asked.

'Yes please.'

Her mood was climbing again; she was starting to feel glad she had come out. This was what she had wanted: a friendly dinner in a buzzy, cheerful setting. *Just enjoy it*, she told herself. What was the point in worrying? She could do nothing now except wait and see. For tonight, she was having dinner with a nice man who was glad she was here. She should make the most of it. When the waiter came past again, she ordered a third glass of wine.

'Good vintage?' Will asked.

'No idea.' She smiled at him. 'I just like the taste. Can't be sensible all the time, can I?'

'No indeed.' Will smiled back at her. He had taken off his suit jacket. Under the thin white material of his shirt, his shoulders looked enormous. How did he keep them like that – living in the city and spending his days sitting in front of a computer?

'Do you go to a gym?' Dawn asked.

'No.'

She slugged down another mouthful of wine. 'Could have fooled me.'

Will laughed, looking at her over the candle in a slightly puzzled way. He was playing with his water glass, turning it around and around on the cloth. His fingernails were cut very short. Dawn remembered how broad his arms had looked that day in Sussex. The solid, muscular frame of him as they had stood close together outside the pub. From nowhere, she thought: *I wonder what it would have been like to have kissed him?*

'What about a nightcap?' she said when they had finished eating. 'My treat.' The long trek back to her empty house did not appeal just yet. Anyway, Will had taken care of dinner so she owed him a favour.

'Why not? Lead the way.'

They walked westwards along the river, looking for somewhere to go. The bank was empty now, the painted human statues and second-hand book stalls

291

packed away, the camera-toting tourists dispersed. The blue lights from the trees gave the empty benches beneath a melancholy appearance, like the closing scenes of a French film after the heroine has met her tragic end. At Westminster Bridge, the reflection of the Houses of Parliament in the Thames made the buildings look like an open book, one page upright, the other lying in a Gothic, shimmering sheet on the water. But they still hadn't found anywhere they could go for a drink.

'Eleven fifteen,' Will said, looking up at the spider-web face of Big Ben. 'Last orders will be over now anyway.'

Dawn was disappointed. 'At least we'll make our last trains.'

'Train,' Will said. 'I'm on the same one as you as far as Streatham.'

The carriage was brightly lit, full and noisy. Will sat next to Dawn, his jacket over his arm. Across the aisle, a boy in a tracksuit slept with his mouth open, his head on the shoulder of the girl beside him. As the train swayed around a curve, Dawn's arm brushed off Will's. The warmth of it made her jump but Will didn't appear to have noticed. He was concentrating on reading the digital station announcements over the door. At Streatham Common station, the doors slammed open. Will didn't get up to leave. Dawn looked at him but he was now absorbed in a poster about safety procedures on the wall opposite. He didn't seem to have realized that the train had reached his stop. If he wasn't to miss it, she should say something. Let him know they were here. But she said nothing. The doors slammed shut again and the train continued on its way.

Back at Crocus Road, Dawn struggled to unlock her front door.

'Whoops,' she said. 'Key's a bit stiff.'

A scrabbling noise from the kitchen. Milly came whiffling into the hall to see what was happening. She headed straight for Will and began to sniff busily: *Who's this, who's this?* at his shoes.

'Hey.' Dawn knelt to pat her. 'You're looking much better. Her arthritis was very bad earlier,' she explained to Will.

'Poor thing.' Will reached down to scratch between Milly's ears. She tipped her head back and hung her tongue out, her tail spinning clockwise in circles around her rump.

'Coffee?' Dawn asked. 'I've got some really nice fresh stuff here. Guatemalan or Paraguayan?'

'I wouldn't know the difference,' Will said. 'I've only ever drunk instant.'

'What? Really?'

'Yes. I do like the smell of the fresh stuff, but it always seems too much trouble to make.'

'Well!' Dawn put her hands on her hips. The phone

table and stairs were spinning in time with Milly's tail. 'You *have* been missing out. Come on through. My Guatemalan blend will be an excellent introduction.'

In the kitchen, she rummaged in the cupboards for the coffee-machine and grounds. Where were the filters? Oh yes – in the odds-and-ends drawer by the sink. There they were, tucked in beside a knobbly green canvas package with a cross printed on the front. The sight of the package threw her for a moment before she realized what it was: the new portable cardiac Resus kit she was meant to be reviewing for the hospital. She had forgotten all about it. Things had been so strange and off-kilter lately, a lot of her work had fallen by the wayside.

She shut the drawer and tried to open out the coffee filter.

'I'm having some trouble with this,' she said after a minute. 'The filter doesn't seem to want to open.'

'Can I help?' Will came to stand beside her.

'It's the paper.' Dawn pulled at it. 'It's so flimsy, it falls apart when you . . .' She fiddled with it for another couple of seconds. Will was beside her, his head inches over hers.

'Would you like me to try?' he asked.

He was standing so close. She could smell his after-shave, the faint hint of wine and garlic from his breath. She fumbled again at the paper but her hands felt as if they were wearing mittens. She put the filter down.

'Actually,' she said, 'I don't know if I'm all that thirsty.'

Will said softly, 'Me neither.'

He was standing there, right there, just behind her. Dawn turned. Her eyes met his. That magnet feeling again; it was as if her face was a leaf, curving and lifting itself to the sun. She let it rise and their lips touched. Dawn closed her eyes. Will was so tall. She loved that; the way he was so solid. Like someone she could lean on. She brought her arms up around his neck, pulling herself in against him. His hands came up; there was a brief pressure as they encircled her waist. Then a give, an emptiness again as he pulled away.

Confused, Dawn opened her eyes. Will was looking down at her with a bemused expression, similar to the one he had worn in the restaurant earlier.

'What's wrong?' she asked.

'I'm not sure.'

Well, then. She went to kiss him again but he took the tops of her arms, very gently, as if to hold her away.

'I need to tell you something,' he said.

'What's that?'

Will looked away to the side. 'For a long time,' he said, 'I couldn't have done this. Not in a way that meant anything. I was . . . numb.'

'Because of Kate.'

'Yes. But recently – now – I don't seem to feel that way any more.'

It made her pause. She didn't know what to say. Then they were kissing again. Softer this time, less frantic – and yet deeper. She could hear her own breathing in the space between them. There was something she should say, pricking like a needle at the back of her mind. But all she could feel was the dropping sensation in her belly, as if she was in a car driving too fast down a hill.

She whispered, 'Come upstairs.'

They didn't bother with the lamp. On the bed, Will pulled her glittery top off over her head. Now she was vulnerable, exposed – no longer in charge, the responsible manager in her uniform, telling people what to do. The sensation took her breath away. Yet it also made her nervous. The last person she had undressed in front of was Kevin, and that was three years ago. She might have lost a couple of pounds recently, but overall she knew she had changed since then, and not for the better.

'You're beautiful.' Will was staring at her.

'No, I'm not.' She laughed. 'I'm too big. Too . . . sensible.'

'You're beautiful,' Will repeated. He brushed his hand down her shoulder, barely touching the skin. 'When I see you, I think of . . . I think of a tall, statuesque woman in a long robe. Holding a lamp to light the way.'

Then they were kissing again, lying together on

the bed. But even as Dawn floated away, something in her was struggling to pull back again. A woman with a lamp. The significance of the image wasn't lost on her. Will might as well have said straight out that she reminded him of Florence Nightingale. The idealized way he saw her, the altruistic heroine he clearly thought she was. And suddenly the mood was gone. She couldn't do this. Not to her. Not to him. She turned her head away.

'I'm sorry.'

'What's wrong?'

'I can't do this.' She was stiffening, pulling herself out from under him. 'I'm sorry.'

'It's OK—'

'No, it's not. It's not OK. And you haven't done anything wrong, don't think that. It's just . . .' She didn't know what to say. There was no way to explain.

'It's OK,' Will repeated. He had rolled off her and was lying on his side, facing away. His breathing was faster than normal. His hand lay beside him, exposed on the sheet. Dawn took it in hers. Will squeezed her fingers, once, still facing away. Then he let her hand go. Dawn lay there, hating herself for doing this to him. Their whole lovely evening, twisted and poisoned and contaminated and there was no way to tell him why.

She lay in silence, as still as she could, not wanting to make him feel worse. Will didn't speak either. Outside, below the window, a car engine revved. A door slammed. Voices called and laughed.

'See you in the morning.'

'Make that the afternoon, more like.'

More laughter. The engine revved again as the car pulled away. Then silence. Will's breathing had slowed to a quiet, steady pace. At last, when Dawn thought he must have fallen asleep, she dared to move. She pulled her arm out from under her hip and tried to settle herself without disturbing him. Then Will shifted in the bed. He turned back to face her. His nose and cheek were a fuzzy outline in the glow from the street. Dawn thought he might be about to kiss her again and went to speak. But he didn't try to kiss her. Instead, he reached up with his hands, took her head between them, very gently, and just held it, just like that.

It was the strangest feeling. So tender. No one, not even Kevin, had ever done that to her. She was normally the carer, the one who protected others. No person that she could remember, since she had been very small, had ever held her like this.

From the darkness, Will spoke.

'There's something wrong. Isn't there?'

She couldn't answer.

'Are you in some kind of trouble?' he asked. 'Can't you tell me what it is?'

The kindness in his voice. More than anything, she yearned to tell him. And not just because of the compassion, the tender cradling of her face. Will was intelligent. Probably one of the most intelligent people she knew. He had a logical, practical mind. If anyone could help her to find a way out of this, it would be him.

But she couldn't. She couldn't tell him. If he knew what she had done . . . He admired her so much. There was no question that it would change the way he saw her. Even if he did help, even if he found a way to resolve this, he would never want anything to do with her again. Lying there with her head in his hands, she suddenly knew that she could not bear for that look to leave his eyes.

'Nothing,' she said. 'There's nothing wrong.'

Later, when he was asleep, she lay beside him, wide eyed and determined in the dark. Will must not know. At all costs, no one could know.

Something had occurred to her. Very soon, Dr Coulton would be leaving St Iberius. Registrars worked on temporary contracts, rarely for more than a few months. In another few weeks he would be gone. There was nothing more he could ask of her. Once he had left and started again in a new environment, surely he would have to forget about all of this and move on? The end was in sight. It was. She just had to be patient.

Her temples still tingled from the pressure where Will had held her. She should have told him. Should have brought it out into the open. But you never know these things until it is too late.

Chapter Fourteen

She was woken by a persistent, clanking whine droning from somewhere outside her window. The lawnmower at number 62. Eileen Warren's nephew must have dropped by to do her grass. Dawn peeled a long strand of hair back from her eyes. The daisies were bright on her wallpaper. The clock on her table read twenty past ten. Dawn sat up. Poor Milly would be crossing her legs by the back door.

Halfway down the empty side of her bed, Will's pillow lay rumpled and abandoned. Earlier, Dawn had woken to see him standing in the dark, buttoning up his shirt. He had been tiptoeing about, trying not to wake her, but his bulky frame wasn't designed for stealth. When he had sat on the chair to pull on his socks, the wicker had cracked and squeaked under his weight. Dawn had lain still, enjoying the drowsy feel of watching him through half-closed eyes, putting his glasses on, fixing his tie. But when he had finished and stood up from the chair, she opened her eyes properly and said, 'Good morning.'

Will came over to her at once. 'I was going to leave you a note,' he said. 'Like they do in films.'

Dawn was sitting up, reaching for her dressing gown. 'Let me get you some breakfast.'

'No. Please. Stay in bed. I'll get something in town.' Will hesitated, concentrating on cleaning his glasses with his sleeve. 'I'll call you later.'

'I'm doing a night shift tonight,' Dawn reminded him. 'Tomorrow as well.'

'Then I'll call when your shifts are finished. We'll arrange something then.'

'I'd like that.' She smiled at him. Will's eyes crinkled in return. He leaned down, dropped a soft kiss on her forehead. Then he took his jacket and left. The sound of the front door closing downstairs made Dawn feel temporarily bereft. But almost before his footsteps had faded on the pavement she was asleep again, the deep, dreamless sleep of a person who hasn't slept properly in a long time.

Now, awake again and more alert, she had a mild headache and a feeling of distant floatiness she put down to the wine. Her mouth was dry, but overall she felt rested and well. The edginess of the previous day had receded, replaced by a sanguine sensation of *que sera, sera*. Whatever might happen now, she would face up to it and deal with it. She would cope.

In the back garden, Milly snapped at a wasp and barked at a magpie to move him off the lawn. She seemed much better than yesterday but her movements were still cautious; she was careful not to do anything that might bring back the pain. Dawn tied the belt of her dressing gown and put the kettle on. The crumpled coffee filter from last night still lay on the draining-board.

Will. She paused. Will Coombs! Here, last night, in her bed! It was still so hard to take in. Will, standing beside her in the early half-light, saying, 'I'll call you . . .' She knew that he meant it. And the difference was, this time she was looking forward to it. Once again, she touched the sides of her face. The subject of when Will was moving back to Cumbria had not come up during the evening. Now she knew she was going to be afraid to ask. Would they stay in touch when he went back? Cumbria was a long way away. It was still so early; they hardly knew each other. If they had met sooner, when he had first moved to London . . . But that wouldn't have worked. He wouldn't have been ready to get over Kate then, nor she over Kevin. She wondered what would have happened if they had met each other properly all those years ago in Cumbria. If she had lived there for longer. If her parents hadn't been killed . . .

Steam swirled around the kitchen. Pointless thinking like this. Dawn poured the boiling water into the coffee-maker. She had plenty to do before her shift started this evening. Walk Milly, iron a clean uniform, catch up on some paperwork before she took her holidays. She didn't want to leave too many loose ends for Francine. In fact, if she put a spurt on, she could get some of the admin out of the way right now.

She took her coffee through to the dining room. Next to a pile of papers on the table was her laptop. The sight of it caused a small, quick frog-leap in her throat. Computers did that to her now. She was like one of those dogs who salivated whenever a bell rang. It wasn't even as if she could expect anything from Well-wisher this morning; the morphine package would have just about reached him, if at all. And her letter telling him that they were quits would knock him off balance. It might take him a while to think of a reply. If he ever did. There was a possibility she might never hear from him again. So she would have to get over hyperventilating every time she saw a computer.

She turned on the laptop and sipped her coffee, waiting for it to boot up. The sun poured through the patio doors, sparkling on the crystal glasses and decanter on the sideboard, spreading itself like a honey-coloured doily over the table, lying on her neck like a warm massage. It was several seconds before Dawn realized that her e-mail inbox was up on the screen. *One new message*. The subject line read, *Matron Torridge, Forest Ward*.

The sender was Well-wisher.

Dawn put down her mug. That jerky frog-leap in her throat again. That was quick! He must have replied almost the minute he received the morphine. But what was there to worry about? This message would be no more than a confirmation to let her know that the package had arrived.

Before opening the e-mail, she paused deliberately to take another sip of coffee. She was the one in control here. She didn't have to be afraid. Whatever power Well-wisher had over her he had now well and truly lost. The internet connection was slow this morning. The text came blotching on to the screen in segments, like pieces of a jigsaw. There seemed to be quite a lot of it, too much for a simple confirmation of receipt of a parcel. Even when the entire text was in place, Dawn took it in only partly at first. There was the same disbelief that she had felt at the very first e-mail, the same conviction that this had to be a joke. The same heat in her cheeks and ears, the acid spasm behind her sternum as she tried to take in the words.

Dear Matron,
Well done for getting the morphine. I knew you
would succeed.

I can tell from your letter that you're getting tired of this. So you'll be glad to hear that I have only one last favour to ask you. It's a complicated one but I will try to make it simple for now.

Very soon, a patient – let's call him Mr F – will be coming to St Iberius for an operation. More details will follow, but for now there are only two things you need to know.

One is that he is being admitted within a couple of weeks. The other is that he must not leave the hospital alive.

You have done this before so I know you will find a way. Trust me, your method will be the kindest for him. Once it is done, I promise you won't hear from me again.
Sincerely,
A well-wisher

The mug of coffee was gone from her hand. She hadn't even felt it drop. *Must not leave the hospital alive.* Did he really mean . . . ? *You have done this before.* He did! He did mean it. The laptop, the sunlit table, the crystal glasses on the sideboard, all had started to wheel in circles about her with a whirring noise that grew to a roar. The carriage clock was still ticking in the next room, Milly's claws were pattering on the kitchen lino, Eileen Warren's lawnmower droned on across the road but the roaring noise overwhelmed them all.

Must not leave the hospital alive. God. Oh God. She had thought she knew what she was dealing with, but this . . . This was beyond anything she could have imagined. She was way out of her depth here. She looked at the sent date on the e-mail. One day ago. This message had been written yesterday. Before Dawn had left for London, she had checked her e-mail and there had been nothing there. So sometime during the evening, while she had been travelling up on the train in her glittery outfit, drinking wine, strolling with Will under the blue-lit trees, all the while blithely imagining that she had got the better of Dr Coulton, he had been hunched over his computer, tapping away with his pale, bony fingers, churning out this piece of evil, malignant trash.

Her hand and sleeve were soggy. The coffee had slopped over them as it fell. The chill of it slowed the spinning and roaring around her. She knew what she had to do. She would go to the police. She should have gone to them at the very beginning, at the very first e-mail, but she had panicked and posted the money on impulse. Why hadn't she taken the time to think things through? How would Dr Coulton have proved that she had killed Mrs Walker? Even if he had seen her with his own eyes, what proof did he have? Mrs Walker had been cremated. It would have been his word against hers. Dawn could simply have stood her ground and denied everything. She had been at St Iberius for almost twenty years; she had an excellent reputation there. Francine would have backed her up. The other ward sisters. Claudia Lynch. A creepy, arrogant loner like Dr Coulton wouldn't have had a leg to stand on.

Her face was hot, the blood rushing so violently in her veins that it took a moment for her to register the colder current sliding underneath.

If Dr Coulton had no proof when he had written the first e-mail, he did now. She had sent him the five thousand pounds, hadn't she? She had stolen the morphine from her ward and posted it to him. She had admitted her guilt as surely as if she had handed over a written confession.

The roaring again in her ears. Now she knew why the amount of morphine he had asked for was so small. It was to ensure it wasn't too difficult for her to steal, to guarantee that Dawn went ahead and compromised herself. But it never had been the morphine he was interested in. Nor even probably the money. All along, right from the beginning, this was what he had wanted. He had set this clever, simple trap for her and she had flown straight into it, like a fly crash-landing on a strip of sticky paper.

She made it to the bathroom under the stairs just in time. Vomit splattered into the sink. She hung over it, clutching the sides. The sour smell of wine rose from the porcelain. She retched again.

When there was nothing left to come up, she lowered the cover of the loo and sat on it. She was freezing cold, her skin covered in icy prickles under her gown. Yet the sweat was trickling down from under her arms. Her hands were clammy. All right. All right. No police. But if the police weren't an option, she would just ignore the e-mail. Wasn't that what she had planned to do all along? Hadn't she said that no matter what the blackmailer demanded this time she would refuse, because if all of this came out he had as much to lose as she had? Shocking as this was, why should it be any different?

Your method will be the kindest for him.

She pressed her knuckles to her teeth. What was that supposed to mean? Was it supposed to imply that if she didn't kill this Mr F he would be murdered some other way? A worse way? She couldn't ignore this. Not this! A doctor writing a message like that; he had to be insane. A danger to the public. She could not sit here knowing he was planning to kill someone and do nothing to stop it. She had to go to the police. She *had* to.

But the money! The morphine! If she reported Dr Coulton she would lose everything. She wrapped her arms around herself with a groan. Then her mouth filled with saliva and she had to stand up to the sink again. She retched but nothing came. She rested her forehead on the mirror. The coolness of it settled her again, helped her to think.

Mr F. Coming to St Iberius in the next couple of weeks. Well, if she couldn't go to the police and she couldn't ignore the e-mail, there was one other option left to her. As the Matron, with responsibility for beds and staffing, she had access to the names of all patients scheduled to be admitted to the hospital. Mr F, as a future patient, would have to be on that list. Whoever he was, wherever he was, she would have to find him. Track him down and warn him to stay away.

Mr F. It wasn't a lot to go on. No first name, no date of birth. No indication of what his medical condition was or which ward he was coming to. But if 'F' really was the first letter of his surname, it just might be enough.

Dawn went over and over all the possibilities as she changed into her Sister's uniform. It was only half past eleven and her night shift didn't start until nine, but leaving now would allow her to spend the afternoon uninterrupted on the computer in her office.

'Sorry, Milly,' she said as the dog bounced about at the sight of her putting on her jacket. 'No walk today. I've got to go to work.'

Milly barked, turning in circles inside the front door. Look! I'm back to normal! I'm not like I was yesterday. But it didn't do any good. Dawn took some biscuits and placed them on the step outside the porch. Along with two bowls of water, as she wouldn't be back until tomorrow. Milly whimpered, recognizing the signs. Dawn felt guilty. It was a very long time to leave her. Not just all today, but the whole of tonight as well. She crouched beside Milly, pulling at her ears, the old familiar routine that they both loved.

'We'll do something nice tomorrow,' she said. 'I promise.'

Milly gazed up at her, her ears cocked, her head to one side. The love and trust in the brown eyes was humbling. No matter what went wrong in Dawn's life, this kind, loyal, affectionate animal would always be on her side. She gave Milly's ears a final tug and stood up to leave. But as soon as she opened the gate, Milly squeezed in front of her and tried to force herself out on to the pavement. Dawn just managed to grab her and close the gate again. She was surprised. Milly had never been like this before. She seemed genuinely agitated: *Don't leave me. Please don't leave.* In the end, Dawn had to hold her back with one hand and inch past her on to the pavement. She shut the gate in Milly's velvety face.

'I'll be back tomorrow,' she told her. 'I'll see you then, OK?'

Milly stared after her through the bars as she walked up the road.

On the bus, it occurred to Dawn that the trembling of her hands and the dark blobs floating in her vision were not just due to shock but to dropping blood glucose. She'd had nothing to eat that day. She stopped at the hospital WRVS café for a coffee, added two heaped spoons of sugar and took a large gulp even before she left the counter. Coming out of the café, carrying her cardboard cup, she bumped into Francine.

'Dawn!' Francine stopped to greet her. 'I thought you weren't working until tonight?'

'I'm not,' Dawn said. 'I just came in to do some bits and pieces before my holiday next week.'

'Honestly, Dawn,' Francine gave a tut. 'The sooner you get away from here the better. I must say, you've chosen some lovely weather for it. I wish *I* was off somewhere nice.'

A vision of the week ahead rose before Dawn. Her, alone in her house, with no one to talk to and no idea of what to do or what might happen next. The sense of panic and claustrophobia made her close her eyes. She opened them again to see Francine staring at her with concern.

'Dawn, is everything OK?'

'Fine. Fine. Just felt dizzy for a moment.'

'Are you sure?'

When Dawn didn't answer, Francine put her hand on her arm and drew her in to the alcove where the telephones were, away from the crowds. She stood there in her white dress, her head tilted, her delicate face furrowed with worry. The shock and the low blood sugar had made Dawn emotional. Francine was such a warm, wise friend. Over the years they had grown very close. Through all the staff shortages and budget cuts and bed crises and consultant tantrums, Francine had been there, Dawn's staunch ally, the one person she could depend on for support, for brainstorming sessions, for laughs over a cup of coffee. Even when Dawn had got the Matron post, there had been no resentment or loss of goodwill. Francine's friendship had remained solid; she had wished Dawn every success, sent her flowers to help her celebrate, assured her of her support. And, despite her breathy, silvery voice and delicate dancer's frame she was, in fact, a much tougher person than Judy. Like most ward sisters, it took a lot to shock her. She was not one to sensationalize or to judge. She worked in an ITU, caring for the sickest patients in the hospital. She, of all people, would know why Dawn had done what she had. She of all people would understand.

Dawn opened her mouth.

'Sister Hartnett to ITU! Sister Hartnett to ITU!' Francine's pager was flashing red.

'Oh, now what?' Francine looked down and jabbed the Silence button. 'Honestly. I've only been gone for five minutes.' She looked up again. 'Sorry, Dawn. What were you going to say?'

'Nothing, nothing. You go ahead.'

'You're sure?'

'Yes. It was just . . . I skipped breakfast.' Dawn held up her coffee. The urge to confess was fading rapidly. What on earth had come over her? 'This will sort me out.'

'OK.' Francine was already moving down the hall. 'Call if you need anything. Otherwise – have a good night.' She smiled at Dawn and waved. A moment later she was gone around the corner.

In her office, Dawn closed the door and pulled down the blind. Then she switched on her computer. She brought up the details of all patients due to be admitted in the next few weeks. A long list appeared. St Iberius had nearly seven hundred beds. Name after name blipped up on the screen. All ages, specialities and dates.

Dawn put her hands to her head and took a breath. She was going to have to try to narrow this down. *Being admitted within a couple of weeks.* How many weeks was 'a couple'? Two? Three? Well, whichever it was, there couldn't be that many male patients whose surnames began with F coming in to St Iberius in the near future. She'd make it three weeks. No – a month, to be sure. If only she knew which speciality.

Endocrinology. Oncology. Gastroenterology. The e-mail again: *Coming to St Iberius for an operation.* An operation! That would put Mr F under one of the surgical teams rather than the medical.

Now she was getting somewhere. She pulled a sheet of paper from the printer. Scrolling through the names on the computer, she began to write down the details of all those patients who fitted her criteria. Mr George Furby, aged fifty, coming in on the twelfth for a hernia repair. Mr Amr Farooqi, aged sixty-nine, having a gastrectomy in three weeks' time. Mr Brian Foster booked for an arthroscopy as a Day case. Some of the names she recognized. Neil Foran, an elderly regular with bladder cancer. James Franks, aged thirty, a local drug dealer and frequent client of the St Iberius A&E department. Dawn scratched her forehead. So many names. So far she'd found at least forty and they were still coming. The next name appeared. Christopher Farthingale, due in next week for heart surgery. Aged nine months. Nine months! She closed her eyes. Surely Dr Coulton couldn't want her to kill a baby. But she couldn't rule him out. She couldn't rule anyone out.

Her neck ached from hunching over the keyboard. She tipped her head back to relieve the stiffness. *Mr F.* It wasn't enough. She needed more. Who was he to Dr Coulton? Why would he want him killed? She'd heard somewhere that most murderers knew their victims personally. Could this Mr F be a family member? A neighbour? The ceiling tiles were patterned with hundreds of tiny holes. She should look up Dr Coulton's address. HR would have it on file. It shouldn't be hard to come up with some sort of excuse as to why she needed it. Maybe if she asked around, one of the staff would know something. Dr Coulton didn't give much away about himself but there must be someone who knew about his background. People always knew things. There was always someone like Mandy who somehow managed to exhume all sorts of details and was happy to pass them along to anyone who asked. She looked at the list of names on her desk. What on earth did she plan to do with it when she'd finished? Phone all the patients up and ask if they knew of anyone who would want to kill them? 'Good morning. This is Sister Torridge calling from St Iberius. I have reason to believe that your nine-month-old has an enemy.'

But what alternative did she have? She sat forward again and took up her pen. If she had to rule out each and every patient, then that's what she would do. Name number forty-eight popped up on the screen. She pulled a fresh sheet of paper from the printer and kept going. There was a knock at the office door.

'Come in.' Wearily, she threw the pen down again. She arched her back and placed her hands on her head. It would be Mandy, calling in for a chat or to ask where the incontinence pads were.

But it wasn't Mandy.

'Good afternoon, Matron,' a dry, deep voice said.

Dawn spun in her seat, yanking her hands down.

'Are you busy?' Dr Coulton asked.

Dawn stared at him, her mouth open. Seeing him standing in her doorway . . . it was like chasing someone through a long, dark tunnel only to turn around and realize they had been right behind you all along. Dr Coulton's marble gaze slid over the room, pausing as it reached Dawn's lists of F names on her desk. Instinctively she lowered her arms to cover them. Dr Coulton's expression did not change.

'I have something to discuss with you,' he said. 'Something rather private.'

'I see.'

'May I?' Dr Coulton came further in to the office and closed the door. The only other chair in the room was stacked with documents and journals. Even if Dawn had been inclined to clear them for him, she wouldn't have been capable. He did it himself, picking the papers up and looking about for somewhere to put them.

'Just leave them on the cabinet,' Dawn said. She had to swallow between the words 'the' and 'cabinet'. The harsh daylight from the window made Dr Coulton's long face look more cadaverous than ever. *Dr Death*,

Danielle had called him. The name was more apt than she could ever have realized.

Dr Coulton sat down, rather fussily arranging his white coat around his trousers.

'You might not be surprised,' he said, 'to hear what it is I want to discuss.'

'No.' Dawn's voice was flat. Inwardly she wanted to shout, *Hurry up. Please. Just get on with it.* But she didn't. Something inside her warned, *Let him say it first. Don't give anything away you don't have to.* She sat, straight-backed, her hands in her lap. The Matron, graciously granting a few minutes of her time to the rather irritating junior doctor.

Dr Coulton said, 'It's about Mr Geen.'

Dawn blinked.

'Mr *Geen*?'

'Yes, Clive Geen. One of the nurses working on your ward.'

'I know who Clive is,' Dawn said shortly. What was Dr Coulton on about? What did Clive have to do with any of this?

Dr Coulton said, 'Well, have you noticed anything odd about him recently?'

'Odd?'

'Yes,' Dr Coulton said irritably, '*odd*.'

Dawn knew she was just repeating everything he was saying. But she couldn't help herself. Her brain wasn't offering any other options. She was having a completely different conversation than the one she had anticipated and her brain was still stuck on the other track, speeding off in an entirely different direction.

Now Dr Coulton seemed surprised. 'You *haven't* noticed.'

Dawn pulled herself together.

'I'm sorry,' she said coldly, 'but I seem to have completely lost track of where this is going. I would appreciate it if you could get to the point and tell me why you are here.'

'If I have to spell it out,' Dr Coulton said in an equally chilly tone. 'Mr Geen has been involved in the care of several of my patients and I take their welfare very seriously. Once I became concerned, I made it my business to observe him closely. And I am now convinced. He shows many of the signs.'

'Signs?' Dawn was bewildered.

He ticked them off on his fingers. 'Irritability, alternating with lethargy. Poor hygiene. Pupils that are enlarged on some occasions, then pinpoint on others.' When she didn't answer, he said impatiently, 'Surely that list rings a bell? They are the classic signs of opiate abuse. You are the ward sister, the Matron. I'm astonished you haven't picked it up.'

Dawn looked wildly around the tiny room. Of course she hadn't picked it up. Clive could have grown three extra eyes lately and she wouldn't have noticed.

'That break-in the other night,' Dr Coulton said, 'when the morphine was stolen from your ward. That has confirmed to me once and for all that Clive needs to be dealt with immediately.'

Dawn stared. 'You think Clive stole that morphine.'

'Obviously he did. He's an addict. An addict who has just recently started working at this hospital. Now drugs have gone missing. The police should be informed as a matter of urgency. I believe he was on your ward with a gun. He could have done someone a serious injury.'

Dawn almost wanted to laugh. This was nonsense. *Nonsense.* She knew perfectly well that Clive had not stolen that morphine. And Dr Coulton must know it too. What was the point of this pathetic charade? But still something held her back from confronting him. She didn't know why, but it had to be him who said it first. She gripped her thumb hard between her fingers to keep the words from pouring out.

Dr Coulton was saying, 'I could go straight to the Medical Director. But that would look bad for you, so I'm giving you the chance to deal with it yourself. I'm new here, but you have a good reputation amongst the doctors. Your ward is well run; the consensus is that the patients are in good hands. So I am surprised that you appear to have completely dropped the ball on this. Unless . . .' He paused. 'Unless, perhaps, you've got something else on your mind at the moment?'

He watched her, his cold, unblinking, snake eyes filled with meaning. Dawn straightened. At last. At last they were getting to the point. She fixed Dr Coulton's stare with a cool gaze of her own. 'And if I do?'

'Well, then for the sake of your patients I suggest that you sort it out.'

'Oh really?' She twisted her mouth. 'And how do you *suggest* I do that?'

Dr Coulton's eyebrows rose. His chin retracted, dipping and tucking in to his neck. His whole expression said, *I beg your pardon?* Suddenly Dawn couldn't stand it any more. The game-playing, the skulking, the hiding. He was taunting her. He knew that she knew, and that she knew that *he* knew. Well, enough of this. She wasn't going to put up with it for a minute longer. Yet even as she blurted it out she knew that it was as much because she was desperate to tell someone and couldn't keep it to herself any more.

'I'm being blackmailed.'

It was as if a catch inside her had been released. A trapdoor had burst open; the pressurized contents behind were pouring out, gushing down all over the desk and the papers between them. No going back. No going back now.

Dr Coulton's eyebrows rose even higher. His chin dipped further until it looked as if it was growing straight out of his neck.

He said, 'Blackmailed!'

'Yes.'

'Have you gone to the police?'

'No.'

'Why not?'

She wanted to scream, 'You *know* why not.' But her tongue stuck to her palate, refusing to form the words. Dr Coulton did seem *so* surprised. In those glacial eyes there was no spark of glee, no cunning flash of pleasure. Yet again, she felt herself backtracking. *Be careful. Be careful here.*

She said, 'It's a . . . a private matter.'

'I see.'

Dr Coulton was looking away from her now, seemingly fascinated by the pile of journals on the filing cabinet. Dawn wanted to fling them into his face. The way his nostrils flared, so prissy and fastidious, like a pair of umbrellas opening. He made it sound as if she was referring to some sordid sex issue. The unmarried Matron, gone and landed herself in something unsavoury. Christ. How had she got herself into this mess?

Dr Coulton, still studying the filing cabinet, said, 'I can understand why you might not want to say. But if you have no one else to tell, then I would advise that you go to the police. Your ward is suffering. You need to sort your staff out and you can't do that if you are distracted.'

So calm and rational. The male voice of Reason, rising above the female mess of disorganization and indecision and weird sex scandal. He seemed so earnest, so logical. So concerned about the patients. Could he really be faking it? Was it possible that he really *did* think Clive had stolen that morphine? But that meant . . . if that was true . . .

Despair filled her. If it was true. If it wasn't him. Whatever had made her so sure that it was? A random, throwaway comment about a window blind. That had been her sole basis for suspecting Dr Coulton above all the many other people who could have come on to the ward that day. She had leaped on his comment and seized it and twisted all the other evidence around to fit it because she had been so desperate to think that she could manage the situation, that she was in control. She had struggled and fought to outsmart him and had actually thought that she was getting somewhere. Only to find that not only had she got nowhere, but now she was in a far worse position than when all of this had started. Dr Coulton was right. Whatever his motive for saying it, he was right.

Her shoulders sagged.

'All right,' she said, 'I'll do it. I'll go to the police.'

Dr Coulton said earnestly, 'I think you're doing the right thing. Blackmail is a crime. You can't deal with this on your own.'

'No. No, I know.' She did know. It had been an enormous weight off her shoulders even to tell Dr Coulton as much as she had. Telling the whole story to someone in authority, handing over the problem to someone who would know what to do, would be a relief worth anything that might happen afterwards.

'The police see this sort of thing all the time,' Dr Coulton was saying. 'No matter what you've done, I'm sure it won't be as bad as you think.' He was standing up now, preparing to leave, straightening his white coat, brushing down his trousers.

At the door, he paused and turned.

'After all,' he said, 'it's not as if you've killed anyone.'

The sky was navy-blue, the horizon a deep orange flame. Out on the ward, trolleys rattled, collecting the remains of the evening meal. There was a smell of carrots and braised lamb. One by one the ward lights came on, making Dawn's office seem even darker. The F names on her sheets of paper were a mottled, fuzzy blur.

She had been so stupid. So stupid! How had she ever thought she could find Mr F on her own? The trouble was, she wasn't thinking straight any more. The more she had tried to pick her way out of the knot in her head the tighter it had twisted, until now it was a tangled mess with her trapped at the centre.

She needed help. Not right now – her shift was just about to start. But tomorrow morning, first thing, she would go to the police station on Latchmere Road just a couple of streets away. Ask to speak to someone there in private. She would sit down and tell them everything. Leave nothing out. And afterwards, whatever the consequences, she would deal with them.

But her job. Her *career.*

And Will. Will finding out. That look fading from his eyes.

Dawn put her head in her hands.

Chapter Fifteen

At ten to nine, Dawn switched off her computer. She rinsed her hands at the little basin in the corner and smoothed her hair in front of the mirror. Then she stepped out of her office. At the nurses' desk, Pam, one of their regular agency staff, was flicking through a copy of the *Daily Mail*.

'Another drug shooting in Bermondsey last night,' she was saying to Mandy with relish. 'I don't know how on earth they— Oh hiya, Dawn. Didn't see you there. Are you on with us tonight?'

'Yes, I am.'

'Lovely.' Pam turned another page. 'Oh, look! Yet another gullible woman conned out of all her life savings. Listen to this: "Dave seemed so lovely when we first started dating. I believed him utterly when he said he'd never met anyone like me. I felt so sorry for him when he said he needed money for his mother's life-saving transplant." Can you imagine? She actually ended up remortgaging her house to raise the cash.' Pam tutted with satisfaction. 'Don't these women have any brains?'

Clive appeared, clutching his backpack, wearing a tatty denim jacket over his uniform.

'Evening, Clive,' Pam said. 'All sorted for tonight?'

Clive muttered something. He looked terrible. His stubble was back, worse than ever, ringing his mouth like a fungus. A scaly rash flaked around the sides of his nose. He looked as if he hadn't washed in a week. Clearly he hadn't expected to be working with Dawn this evening.

Mandy, her shift over, was getting ready to leave. She pulled a pink cardigan on over her tunic.

'Should be a quiet one tonight,' she said, handing the morphine keys to Clive. 'They're all pretty settled. Oh – except for Lewis in the side room.'

'What's wrong with Lewis?' Dawn asked.

'He had his surgery this morning and he's been complaining all day of pain. But I've just given him another dose of morphine so hopefully that should settle him.'

'OK.'

'Funny how they all seem to be so sore lately,' Mandy said. 'That Danielle's been acting up all day as well. Though the last dose I gave her seems to have finally kicked in. And now Lewis has started up. Odd, because he's not normally one to grumble.

Anyway . . .' She flipped her hair out over the back of her cardigan. 'Hope it's a quiet one. See you all tomorrow.'

She left, carrying her grey slouchy bag over her shoulder. The doors swung and settled behind her. Dawn divided the patients up between the three night staff for obs and monitoring.

'Pam, can you take the top end? Clive, take the middle eight. I'll take the ones down this end, and the side room.'

'Right you are.' Pam folded up her *Daily Mail* and climbed to her feet. Clive took his list of patients and went off without a word.

Dawn did a quick round. Danielle Jones was asleep, curled up on her side, her blanket pulled right up so that just her hair was sticking out. Dawn examined the chart at the end of her bed. Danielle's vital signs were stable, the urine output for the past hour satisfactory. Dawn replaced the chart and moved on without disturbing her.

In the side room, Lewis was wide awake, sitting up with his light on. The cage-like metal fixator had been removed from his calf. The entire leg was now encased from thigh to foot in a giant white cast. Lewis was shifting in the bed, lifting himself up on his hands, then wincing and sinking back on to the mattress.

'Not too comfy, eh?' Dawn said. 'How did the surgery go?'

'All right.' Lewis shifted again. 'But I'm getting a lot of pain now.'

'The painkiller Mandy gave you hasn't helped?'

'Nothing's helped. I've been saying it all day but I don't think anyone believes me. But I'm not making it up, Sister. The last time was nothing like as bad as this. It's like I've had the op with no anaesthetic at all.'

'That last dose might just be taking a while to kick in,' Dawn reassured him. 'Just give it a chance and try to get some rest. I'll come back and check on you in a little while, OK?'

'OK.'

Dawn finished the rest of her round. Many of the patients were delighted to see her.

'On call this evening, Matron?' they said. 'Poor you. Stuck with us lot on a Friday.' One elderly lady gripped her hand and said, 'It's nice to see your lovely face. I'll know we're in good hands tonight.'

Afterwards, Dawn sat writing her report at the nurses' desk. The overhead lights had been turned off, the ward lit only by the glow from the nurses' lamp and from the individual reading lamps over the beds. Several of the patients had pulled their curtains round, transforming their cubicles into glowing blue squares.

From the side room, Lewis called out, 'Sister! Sister!'

Dawn got up again and went in to him. Lewis was sweating, still moving about in the bed.

'Can't I have something?' he pleaded. 'I'm in agony here.' His hair was stuck down flat to his forehead. His cheeks and eyes were scrunched up as if he was about to cry.

'Still no result from the morphine?' Dawn asked.

'No. It just seems to be getting worse and worse.'

He was actually shaking. His whole leg trembled in its bulky plaster. Dawn felt a stirring of unease. Even this soon after an operation, it was unusual to see someone in so much distress. Mandy was right: Lewis was not normally a complainer. Something was very wrong here.

She examined Lewis's leg. As far as she could tell through the heavy plaster, there didn't appear to be any bleeding. She touched the tips of his toes with her finger.

'Can you feel this?'

'Yes.'

'And this?'

'Yes.'

No nerve damage then. And his toes were warm. She reached her fingers up under the plaster to feel his pulse. The rate was up. She checked his BP: high as well, which pointed to the fast pulse being due to pain rather than to anything more sinister. Still, she didn't like the look of him. Inside her head, a red warning light had begun to blink. Dawn had a strong suspicion that she knew what she was looking at here. Lewis had Compartment Syndrome. She hadn't seen a case in years but it was the one complication every orthopaedic surgeon dreaded. If she was right, then Lewis was in serious danger of losing his leg.

She didn't let any of this show in her voice. 'I'll tell you what,' she said. 'Why don't I ask the surgical registrar to come up and take a quick look? Just to see. And in the meantime, I'll fetch some more painkiller for you.'

'OK. But please hurry.'

At the desk, Dawn paged the registrar. The surgeon on call was a girl called Katherine, pleasant and unflappable, easy to work with. Succinctly, Dawn outlined Lewis's symptoms.

'Shit,' Katherine said. 'Doesn't sound good. I'll come up when I can.'

Next, Dawn went to look for Clive to get the morphine keys. She couldn't see him at any of the beds. She checked the staff room. Normally Clive could be found there at every opportunity, watching Sky TV with his feet on the table, complaining about his ridiculous workload. But tonight his usual seat in front of the telly was empty. She tried the sluice room, the kitchen, the stock room. No sign.

'Seen Clive anywhere?' she asked Pam, busy emptying a urinary catheter bag.

Pam clambered to her feet, balancing her brimming plastic jug. 'I thought I saw him go out the main doors a while ago. Maybe he's gone to the toilet?'

'I'll give him a few minutes.'

Dawn returned to the nurses' desk and tried to continue writing her reports. But within minutes, Lewis was calling out again.

'Sister, please. You've got to do something. I can't stand this.'

'All right, Lewis. Coming now.'

She got up again. Where *was* Clive? Surely he couldn't still be on the loo? Dawn remembered his appearance when he had turned up earlier, his porridge-coloured face and bloodshot eyes. Even for him, he had looked appalling. Was there something more going on here than lack of hygiene? Could Clive actually be ill?

She went to the main doors and pushed them open. This night shift was beginning to fall apart at the seams. She went down the corridor to the male locker-room and knocked on the door.

'Clive?'

No answer. She knocked again.

'Clive, it's Sister Torridge. Are you all right?'

Still nothing. He must have gone elsewhere; maybe down to the main hall, to the vending machines. It wasn't illegal, but he should have told her or Pam where he was going. Wards shouldn't be left

331

under-staffed at night without the ward manager being made aware. She was just turning away from the locker-room when she heard something: a high, humming sound, emanating from behind the door. Or not a humming exactly – more a buzzing whine, like the drone of some tiny electrical instrument.

'Clive?' No response. The code for the male locker-room was the same as for the female. Dawn keyed the numbers into the pad and opened the door, tapping all the while as she entered.

'Hello? Hello?'

The buzzing whine grew louder. The light from the hall shone over the rows of metal lockers and slatted wooden benches. There was a strong smell of socks. The room was empty but still the buzzing noise continued. There was something familiar about the sound, but for the moment Dawn couldn't place what it was. She moved forward, turning her head from side to side, trying to gauge where the noise was coming from. It seemed to be loudest at the back of the room, just outside the door marked 'Toilet'. The door was closed but a narrow strip of light showed from underneath. Next moment, Dawn had tripped over something lying on the floor: a wooden theatre clog. The clog flipped into the air, ricocheting off the metal leg of a bench with a ringing clang. Instantly, the buzzing noise ceased.

'Clive? Is that you?'

Silence. But in the strip of light underneath the door, a shadow moved. Someone was definitely there. Dawn went to the door and rapped on it, hard.

'Clive!'

She pushed the door open. Inside was a tiny, square room with a sink and a single flimsy toilet cubicle. Clive was at the sink, his face ghastly white behind his stubble. As Dawn entered, he turned, quickly stuffing something underneath his tunic. His elbow brushed against something on the edge of the sink. It fell to the tiles with a tinkling sound.

'I'm sorry.' Dawn's gaze had followed the object to the floor. 'I did knock but there was no answer. Are you all right?'

'I'm fine.'

'When you didn't answer, I was worried. I thought you might be—' Dawn broke off. 'What *is* that?' she asked. 'That thing you've just dropped.'

Clive made a lunge for the object but Dawn was nearer. Before he could bend down she had stooped and brought it up, holding it between her finger and thumb. It was a small glass ampoule. Familiar in size and shape.

'What's this?' Puzzled, she turned it in her hands. The side of the ampoule was printed with red writing: *Morphine Sulphate 10mg*. The glass was unbroken. Yet, peculiarly, something was protruding from the bottom of it. A needle, sticking right through the glass, so that half of it was inside the ampoule and half out.

Clive stuck his hand out. 'Give that back to me. It's mine.'

'But isn't this a morphine ampoule? From the ward?' Dawn was still staring at the needle. Was she seeing things? How had a steel needle got through solid glass?

'It's not from the ward,' Clive said. 'It's my property, my business.'

The violence of his tone made Dawn look up at him. There was something strange about his eyes. The pupils were so dilated that the irises had almost vanished. His eyes were two giant, black discs, floating on a bloodshot base.

Irritability, alternating with lethargy . . . Pupils that are enlarged and then pinpoint.

Dawn had dismissed Dr Coulton's words as lies. Or the deluded ramblings of an arrogant know-all convinced he knew what he was talking about despite being completely on the wrong track. She knew that Clive had not broken into that safe the other night. Now, however, as she watched Clive's peculiar, jittery performance, suddenly an awful lot of what Dr Coulton had said began to make a lot of sense.

She said slowly, 'You've been taking it, haven't you?'

'Taking what?'

'Morphine. From the ward.'

Clive gave a scornful laugh. 'If you're talking about that burglary, I wasn't anywhere near here at the time.'

'I don't mean the burglary.' One by one, the pieces were dropping into place. Clive's attitude and behaviour. The way he seemed to hate the patients so much, yet still persisted in working there. 'I mean you've been taking it bit by bit. On the days you've been holding the safe keys, you've just walked in there and helped yourself.'

'That's crap. How could I have? Check the counts. No ampoules have gone missing.'

No, no ampoules had. Or none that she knew of. But he had been taking the morphine. And all of a sudden she knew how. She'd read about something like this happening elsewhere. There'd been a hospital in America . . .

'You've been draining the morphine out of the ampoules,' she said. 'Replacing it with something else so no one will know, then putting the ampoules back in the safe.'

'You're off your fucking head.'

In the American hospital, the thief had heated up a needle until it was red hot, then slid it through the glass. Afterwards, when the needle was removed, the hole had sealed up again and no one could tell that the ampoule had been tampered with.

But how had Clive done it? How had he made *his* little hole? The air in the bathroom was cold. He couldn't have been using any kind of heater. Dawn spun around, taking everything in, the cubicle, the sink, the bunch of morphine keys sitting between the taps. Then she looked at Clive again, still cradling the bulky object under his uniform, and she knew why the buzzing noise she'd heard had sounded so familiar.

'You've got a drill,' she said.

'What the fuck are you talking about?'

'Like a dentist's. To drill through the glass. A tiny one obviously, but it's there, isn't it? That's what you've been clinging on to, trying to hide it under your tunic.'

'This is bollocks. Bollocks! I don't have to explain to you what I—'

'If I hadn't interrupted you just now, you'd have taken the morphine out of this ampoule and replaced it with – what? Water? Saline? Then you'd have sealed up the hole . . . I don't know how, exactly, but we haven't noticed any leaks so you must have some way. Then you'd have put the ampoule back in the safe and no one would have been any the wiser. Except, of course—'

Dawn stopped.

'Lewis. Bloody hell! *That's* why his leg's been so painful. He's been getting doses of morphine all day but none of them have worked and no one would believe him. And he's not the only one, is he? Danielle, too, the girl who's had the surgery for her Crohn's.' Clive tried to speak but she talked over him, her voice rising with her anger. 'Lying there on the ward with that massive wound all down the middle of her abdomen. And she's been getting bloody *water* for it! How many other—'

She stopped again. A prickly feeling had risen in her face, hot, itchy dots spreading over the skin. Her ears tingled, filling with a rushing hiss, like the white noise from a TV, growing louder, drowning out the horror underneath.

Mrs Walker.

Mrs Walker, writhing in agony with a swollen, malignant tumour compressing her spine. Mrs Walker, shuddering and exhausted, getting all of that morphine, the maximum possible dose, yet all the while, hour by hour, her pain worsening and none of them able to work out why.

Dawn gripped the edge of the door.

'You bastard,' she said in a low voice. 'You bastard.'

'Hang on—'

'No. I will *not* hang on. I've let you get away with a lot of things. But by God, there's no way you're getting away with this.' The morphine keys were sitting on the sink. 'Give me those.' She snatched them up. As she did so, Clive made a grab for the ampoule in her hand.

'You give that to me, then.'

'You must be joking. Let me past, please.'

'You don't understand.' Clive's voice was hoarse. 'I've got to have it. Take the keys if you want to. Do whatever else you like. But I've got to have that ampoule.'

He did look unwell. His face was the colour of cement. The skin was sludgy and damp, like that of a patient having a heart attack. But all Dawn could see was Mrs Walker, her frail body contorted with distress, her cheeks drawn, her eyes stretched with misery and despair. Clive had known – all that time, he had known. A woman, dying in torment, had been getting nothing but water to ease her pain and Clive had stood back and watched and said nothing.

'I don't want to see you on my ward again tonight.' It was an effort even to spit the words at him. 'You can leave now, or I can call security and have you thrown off the premises. It's up to you.'

She turned to leave but Clive tried to block her way. 'You give that morphine to me. Or else—'

'Or else what?' Dawn swung back. She was so angry, she felt that if Clive had laid a finger on her right now she could have flattened him across the floor. 'Or else *what*?'

Clive backed off. He stood swaying by the sink,

his head down, like some scrawny, cornered animal, glaring up at Dawn through eyes that were slitted with hatred. The red rash on his forehead flared out like a traffic light.

'I think you know,' he said. 'You've had a taste of it already. But it'll be nothing to what'll happen if you cross me.'

'You don't frighten me,' Dawn said. She turned again to leave. She couldn't stay another second here with Clive in this tiny toilet, this fetid, sock-smelling air. That he could have done something like this! To a sick, defenceless patient. She could almost feel in her own body the agony Mrs Walker must have felt, the jolts of electricity, like long spears pushed down her spine. No wonder her dose of morphine had been smaller at The Beeches. They had been giving her the correct dose all along; a small amount had been all that was needed to keep her comfortable. But then she had come to St Iberius and got nothing at all. Dawn was sick at herself. How could she have missed it? How could she not have known? Her hands trembled as she went to the safe. She unlocked it and removed every ampoule of morphine from the shelf. None of them could be used now. There was no way of telling which ones Clive had tampered with. And that was another thing! Not only had he caused a great deal of suffering, he had actually put the patients' lives at risk. By tampering with the sterile seal of the glass he had risked introducing all sorts of contamination to the ampoules. For God's sake – he'd been doing this in the *toilets*! Dawn took the ampoules to her office and locked them in a drawer. In the morning she would hand them over to Claudia Lynch along with a full account of what had happened.

Lewis was still waiting for his painkiller. Calming herself, Dawn phoned ITU to ask if she could borrow some of their morphine.

'Run out, have you?' the ITU charge nurse asked chattily.

'Just think we might have a faulty batch.' No point going into details until the proper authorities had been informed. Dawn put down the phone and went to find Pam to ask her to nip down the hall for the morphine.

'Did you find Clive?' Pam asked.

'Yes. He's not well. I've sent him home.'

'Oh. Right,' Pam said. 'I thought he looked a bit peaky earlier.'

'We should manage with just the two of us for the rest of the night,' Dawn said. 'The ward's been pretty quiet.'

And now that all of the problems had been solved so suddenly, it *was* quiet. When Pam had left to fetch the morphine, Dawn stood in her office and felt the soft, beeping hush at her ears. And it was then, in the lamp-lit dimness, that Clive came back to her. Not to the ward, but to her mind. Swaying by the sink in the toilet, his vivid red rash shining out a warning. *You've had a taste already. But it'll be nothing to what'll happen if you cross me.*

Dawn plopped on to her chair, as limp as if all her strings had been cut.

The blackmailer. The blackmailer was Clive.

Chapter Sixteen

He had told her. Right there in that dingy toilet he had told her. Only she had been too caught up in her own anger and revulsion to listen. Dawn sat with her mouth open. How had it taken her this long to see?

Clive! He'd been the first person she had thought of, almost from the moment she had got the first e-mail. She had dismissed him because he had been gone from the ward that afternoon by the time she had killed Mrs Walker. But what was to have stopped him from returning? What was to have stopped him from coming back through those doors just as easily as anyone else.

His glare of hatred as he had faced her at the sink. *You've had a taste already.* A taste! Dawn wrapped her arms around herself, squeezing the skin on the backs of them until it hurt. Yes, by God, she'd had a taste. A taste of fear and humiliation and despair. How long had it taken him to realize exactly what he was seeing that day? He must have been thrilled. It would have been like all his Christmases arriving at once. Blackmailing her would have been sheer pleasure for him, quite apart from any financial or other rewards he might have got out of it.

Slow down, she told herself. *Slow down*. She was doing it again, leaping to preposterous conclusions at the drop of a hat. She had no proof it was Clive. Up until just a couple of seconds ago she'd been convinced the blackmailer was Dr Coulton. Why would Clive have come back to the ward that day? He had been so angry; if ever there was a time he would have wanted to get away from the hospital as quickly as possible, that would have been it. His threats just now might have been nothing more than bravado.

I think you know. You've had a taste already.

Dawn gripped the backs of her arms again. You could hardly get more explicit than that. It was completely different from Dr Coulton's random comment about the blinds. Clive might as well have admitted it straight out. She'd had him cornered in that smelly little room; he'd had no choice but to come out with it. Hit her with what he knew.

Her gaze moved sightlessly around the office. On the back of the door was the glossy poster for the International Research Conference. She'd never got around to taking it down. Something about it now struck her. Confused, she looked back at it, trying to focus. What *was* it? She must have seen that poster, or others like it, a hundred times in the past few weeks. The printed heading: *Sponsored lunch for all staff.* And below it, the list of lectures for the day. She was about to pass on when she saw it again. Perhaps it was because she had been thinking about him only moments ago that the name, previously hidden amongst the scores of others on the list, had jumped out and caught her eye:

Dr Edward Coulton, Speaker, Lunchtime Lecture: The Role of the Macrophage. 1-2pm.

Dawn couldn't take her eyes from the poster.

Mrs Walker had died at half past one.

The office door opened, swinging the list of names out of view.

'Dawn?' It was Pam, back from ITU. 'I've got you that morphine.'

Dawn shook herself. She took the ampoule. 'Thanks, Pam.'

'No problem. I'll get back to changing those urine bags, shall I?'

'If you don't mind, Pam. Thanks.'

Then, as her colleague went to leave the office, Dawn said, 'Pam?'

Pam turned back. 'Yes?'

Dawn nodded at the poster. 'Do you happen to know of anyone who went to that talk a couple of weeks ago? The one at lunchtime?'

Pam peered around at the back of the door.

'Dr Coulton's talk?'

'Yes.'

'Indeed I do,' Pam said. 'As a matter of fact, I went to it myself.'

'*You* did?'

'Yes. I'd just done a morning shift on Ocean Ward and decided to go along for the lunch. Free three-course spread from the Bengali Star!'

'And you saw Dr Coulton? You were at his talk?'

'Indeed I was.'

Dawn stared ahead, rolling the morphine ampoule between her fingers. So there it was. Dr Coulton was not the blackmailer. It was like doing a Sudoku puzzle that you had been stuck on for a long time, then suddenly having the right number light up in your head like a firework and finding that all the other numbers, *bam bam bam*, plopped into place, as plain as day.

'Boring bugger, isn't he?' Pam was saying. 'Likes his long words. I've never known anyone drone on so much. Half the audience was asleep by the end.'

Dawn said absently, 'Were they?'

'Oh, yes. Even Professor Kneebone. Clive spotted him nodding off in the front row. Gave me a dig in the ribs to point him out.'

Dawn's head snapped up. 'Clive?'

'Yes.'

'Clive was at the lunchtime talk?'

345

'Yes, he was. A couple of us met him in the hall as we were going in. We told him about the free lunch and he came along with us for the bhajis.'

'But . . .' Dawn looked wildly at the poster. 'But he couldn't have . . .' If Clive had been at Dr Coulton's talk, he couldn't have returned to the ward at the time Mrs Walker had died. Once again, the Sudoku number was wrong, the entire puzzle useless and destroyed. But how could it *not* be him? *You've had a taste* . . . What else could he have meant by that? What? *What?*

'Wait a sec, though.' Pam was holding a finger in the air. 'Now I think of it, Clive never actually made it to the lunch. He made some excuse or other and walked out after the first few minutes.'

Dawn was struggling to keep track of what was going on. 'Clive walked out of Dr Coulton's talk?'

'That's right. Said he'd left his pen on the ward. Like I say, purely an excuse. And he made the most dreadful fuss on the way out . . . trampling on people's feet . . .' Pam's voice faded. 'Dawn? You all right?'

'Sorry. Just thinking . . .'

The Sudoku puzzle was complete after all, the missing number finally stamped in place. The picture now was so clear; she could see everything as precisely as if she had been with Clive at every step. Clive, incensed after the row with Dawn, storming off Forest Ward. Bumping into Pam and the others in the hall, allowing himself to be talked into attending the conference. Realizing too late his mistake as Dr Coulton droned on about cytokines and interleukins, sitting there trapped and seething, then remembering his pen and deciding to get the hell out of there. Shoving past the audience, furious at having to return to the ward, more than likely hoping to just grab his pen and leave without having to face Dawn again. He would have barged through the doors of Forest Ward, his stubbly face suffused with temper, and then . . . what? How far had he got before he had seen it? The ECG over Mrs Walker's bed, flattening into the lethal rhythm that almost always meant imminent death. And Dawn, standing calmly beside her with the syringe in her hand. Perhaps he had known then and there what was going on. Perhaps it was only afterwards he had worked it out. Either way, she could imagine all too well his growing excitement, his malicious pleasure as he realized his chance for revenge.

And more than revenge . . .

Dawn's gaze fell to her desk. On it, her lists of F names, lying beside the keyboard. Looking at them again, she noticed something. One of the names stood out, almost leaping up at her from the page. The writing on this name seemed larger than the others, the print darker and bolder. Funny, she hadn't noticed at the time that she was doing that. Clearly, even as she had been copying the details from the computer, the name had meant something to her. She must have been struck by it for an instant – only without the information then that she had now, the true significance of it had passed her by.

James Franks. Aged thirty. Coming to St Iberius next week for an operation on his hand.

Nearly everyone working at St Iberius knew James Franks. A notorious local drug dealer and frequent Casualty attender, presenting regularly with various injuries: a fractured hand, a punctured lung due to a knife wound, a broken mandible. Once he had turned up with a whole crowd of injured gang members, escorted by a large group of armed police. One of the police, a girl who looked no more than eighteen, had sat on one of the plastic chairs outside a cubicle, cradling a rifle across her knee that was almost as big as she was. It had made Dawn uneasy. Did the police really think they were going to use those things in here, in a room full of patients and staff?

But if James Franks *was* supplying Clive with drugs, why would Clive want him dead? Drug addicts, surely, didn't go around killing their dealers. They depended on them remaining alive and well.

But then Clive didn't need a dealer any more, did he? Not now he had his own little supply set up at St Iberius. Perhaps James Franks had been hassling him, looking for money he was owed, insisting that Clive stay on as a customer. And so, when the opportunity had come along to get rid of him, Clive had jumped at it. It must have seemed so perfect. And now here was Dawn, threatening to ruin everything. Threatening to expose him, have him kicked out of St Iberius, cut off his supply. If she did that, Clive would have nothing to lose by telling the police everything he knew.

The morphine ampoule was cold and hard, like a bullet between her fingers.

Lewis, she thought suddenly. All day, sitting in that room, with a leg that had been freshly fractured and re-set, with screws and bolts driven into the bone. And the only medication he had been given was water. The pain must be appalling.

In the stock room, she drew the morphine into a syringe and wrapped a blue opiate sticker around the side. Then she took the syringe to the side room. Lewis was clutching the side of his bed, his other hand held in the air over his leg, the fingers shaped into claws as if somehow to rip the pain from under the plaster. His face was the same porridge-grey colour that Clive's had been.

'I thought you'd never come,' he said.

'I'm sorry.' Dawn was pulling the cap off the needle. 'I'm really sorry. But it's going to be all right now.'

'That stuff won't help. It's been tried already.' Lewis's pupils were black and dilated, so enormous you could almost see all the way into his head. Exactly the way Clive's had been.

'This time it will,' Dawn said. 'I promise. This time it's different.'

Lewis's distress and Clive's were due to different causes entirely but the remedy for both was the same. Dawn attached the syringe to Lewis's drip and pressed the plunger. The syringe emptied. The vein beyond Lewis's drip bulged as the morphine surged into his system.

It took less than a minute. Lewis's clawed hand relaxed, dropping away from his leg. He sighed and fell back against his pillows.

Dawn said softly, 'Better now?'

Lewis nodded. Out there somewhere, Clive was stumbling along some pavement or side street in the night, coping with his agitation and withdrawal the best way he could. It would be a long time before he managed to find any relief. But for Lewis, at least, the torment was over. His pupils shrank to their normal size. His eyes lost their eerie, translucent appearance; the porridgy skin pinkened to a more human shade. Lying with his head back against the pillows, he even managed a dreamy smile.

'Thank you, Sister,' he said.

Lewis slept soundly for the rest of the night. Dawn could only wish for such a luxury for herself. Several times she visited her office and sat staring at the drawer with the contaminated morphine ampoules wrapped in their envelope. The plan had been to take the ampoules to Claudia Lynch's office in the morning. Now what was she going to do? If she reported Clive, he would go straight to the police about Mrs Walker. Yet she couldn't pretend tonight hadn't happened. It would not be safe to simply replace the ampoules and use them on other patients. Discarding them wasn't an option either. Pharmacy would be up here like a pack of bloodhounds, baying to find out where they'd gone.

Why *shouldn't* she tell Claudia? If Clive counter-attacked by blabbing about Mrs Walker, all Dawn had to do was appear vehemently shocked and astonished. After all, who were people going to believe? Clive? A bitter, thwarted addict out for revenge? He would be laughed all the way to the police station.

The morning was a long time in coming. It seemed forever before Dawn was finally sitting down to lead the morning handover round with the day staff. At eight, she left the ward with the envelope of ampoules in her bag. Claudia's office was on the ground floor, off the main hall. To reach it, you had to go down the narrow side corridor near the entrance. Dawn slowed as she approached the mouth of the corridor. Nearer . . . nearer . . .

Then she kept on walking, right past the corridor entrance. Further on was the Pharmacy, with its large green cross lit up on the wall. Dawn went to the counter.

'Good morning, Matron.' Sally, the chief pharmacist, came smiling to greet her. 'What brings you down to us today?'

Dawn took the envelope of ampoules from her bag. 'Good morning, Sally. There's been a problem with this batch of morphine.'

'Really? What sort of problem?'

'It isn't working. It's had no effect at all on the patients.'

'That's strange.' Sally took the envelope and peered in at the ampoules. 'Unusual for that to happen with morphine.'

'Perhaps the ampoules weren't stored properly during transport?'

'But the storage wouldn't affect—'

'Regardless of the reason,' Dawn said firmly, 'the drug is ineffective. I would be grateful if you could remove these ampoules immediately from circulation. And send a fresh batch up to Forest Ward as soon as you can.'

'Of course, Matron. I'll arrange it this morning.'

Dawn left Sally, still perplexed, peering into the envelope. She walked through the hospital entrance and down the hill to the street.

She hadn't done it. She hadn't reported Clive to Claudia. She just hadn't been able to bring herself to take the step. Two streets from here, on Latchmere Road, was the Lavender Hill police station. Dawn's other plan for this morning had been to go there and tell them everything that had happened. All she had to do was take the next left turn.

She didn't take it. She walked on past the turn to her bus stop. It was a quarter to nine. The bus to Silham Vale was jammed with teenagers in ties and stripy blazers, shouting and jostling each other with their backpacks. Dawn sat on the front seat at the top, staring through the blur of trees and shops as they passed her by.

So. She had made her decision. She had not reported Clive. All morning he would be huddled by his phone, waiting to hear from someone at the hospital. By this afternoon, when no phone call had come, he would know.

So now what? They were at a stalemate. Neither of them could do anything without making things worse for themselves. Would Clive turn up for his shift tonight as if nothing had happened? And if he did, what would Dawn do? Treat him exactly as usual? Turn a blind eye while he continued to make his trips to the men's toilet with his morphine ampoules and his miniature dentist's drill?

At Silham Vale, she got off the bus. She bypassed

the Georgian terrace with its row of shops and take-aways, and turned down Crocus Road. She was so preoccupied that it wasn't until she had reached number 59 that she realized that the bars of the gate were empty. No dark, wet nose snuffling and poking through them to greet her. Normally Milly was ready and waiting when she arrived, alerted by the sound or smell of her from yards away.

'Milly?'

Milly wouldn't be expecting Dawn home at this hour of the morning. She was probably still fast asleep in the porch. Or too stiff with her arthritis to climb off her rug. Dawn lifted the latch of the gate and went up the path.

But the porch and the paw-print rug, slightly rumpled, were empty. The bowls of water, both still full, were outside the door. The pile of biscuits was scattered over the grass.

'Milly?'

Dawn paused on the step, looking around. She could see most of the garden from here. The neat box hedge along the wall, the narrow strip of lawn, the maroon and black tiled path to the gate. The gate had definitely been shut when she'd come home just now. Had Milly jumped out over it? She had been so anxious yesterday for Dawn not to leave her. But she had never jumped it before. And it would have been particularly difficult for her last night, with the state her hips had been in recently. Perhaps Will had called to take her for a walk. But it seemed unlike him not to have phoned to let her know.

She was still thinking this, gazing around her, when the shadow of a branch stirred under the box hedge. The ground beneath the hedge lit up in the sun, all except for one spot, far at the back. A dark mound, like a rock or an old coat lying on the earth. Dawn hurried to the hedge, knowing already what she was going to find.

'Oh Milly, Milly, my little friend. Please be OK.'

But the dark mound was stiff and very cold. It had been there for quite some time. A single brownish leaf lay on the coal-black fur.

'Milly!'

Dawn knelt on the grass. She took Milly up. She stroked her head and down her back in long, sweeping movements, as if by doing so she could start the blood flowing again. 'Milly. Milly.' The fur felt strange, too smooth and heavy, like artificial matting. The skin beneath had the texture of cool rubber, nothing at all like the skin of a real animal. When she lifted Milly's head, the front paws came too, sticking straight out into the air. Milly's eyes were half open, the exposed corneas covered with a dry film. How long had she been here? Had it been quick? A sudden heart attack? Or something slower, the pain and distress worsening as the hours had passed so that the long night had dragged like a chain? Why hadn't Dawn taken her to the vet long ago? Why had she thought she knew everything, that she was such an expert she could diagnose and treat Milly's illness by herself? This was why Milly had not wanted her to leave yesterday. She had known, had felt, that something was wrong.

'I'm sorry.' She rocked the stiff little body back and forth. 'I'm so sorry. I honestly didn't know.'

Her head felt full, too heavy to hold upright, but her eyes were dry. This was a dog. An elderly dog, who had led a long and mostly happy life which had now come to a natural end. In hospitals all over London, at this very minute, human beings were going through far worse. So Dawn waited, and after a moment the flare of emotion subsided. She lowered Milly's head to her lap. That was better. More natural now, as if Milly had come over of her own accord and put her chin on Dawn's knee. *Here I am.* Later, Milly would chase the magpies from the back lawn and they would go for their morning walk to the green. Milly would race ahead, then stop to pant and look back at Dawn, her triangular eyes bright with excitement. *Come on! Let's go!*

The grass was chilly under her knees. It was a warm day but the dew still lay on the ground under the hedge where the sun had not reached. Dawn lifted Milly's head again from her lap.

'Wait here,' she told her. 'I'll be right back.'

She lowered Milly to the ground. As she did so, something beneath her was dislodged and went rolling away from them, out over the lawn.

Dawn's first thought was that the object had come from her. She felt a flash of puzzlement, a sense of something being where it shouldn't be. Then the disorientation settled and she realized what she was looking at: an empty 5ml syringe with a blue opiate label stuck to the side. Lewis's morphine syringe. Of course. She must have put it in her pocket last night after giving him his dose and now here it had fallen out on to the lawn.

The syringe lay on the grass, its stubby, transparent barrel gleaming in the sun.

The thing was, she never did that. She never put syringes into her pocket after use. She always put them in the sharps bin. Every single time; the action was as automatic to her as turning off the water when she'd had a shower or locking her door when she left the house. And she had used a 10ml syringe to give Lewis his morphine. She always used a 10ml syringe to administer morphine. There was less chance of accidentally giving an overdose.

This 5ml syringe with its blue morphine sticker lay shining on the lawn. The same syringe that had lain in the darkness under Milly all night.

Another few seconds of disorientation before the message clicked home.

It'll be nothing to what'll happen if you cross me.

Dawn had made herself go to bed for a while. She had been up all night and she still had to work again that evening. She did not sleep, however, but lay and watched the light move higher and higher on her bedroom wall. At 5 p.m., she got up again. She sat at the kitchen table in her dressing gown, with Milly in her usual spot in the basket near her feet.

'I need to go, Mill.' Dawn swirled her mug of cooling coffee. 'I've got to get back to work.'

The kitchen was warm from having had the sun in it all day. The sun was shining through the glass back door directly over Milly's basket. Milly could not spend another full day here in this heat. Tomorrow, Dawn would have to do something about her. For now, all she could do was wrap her back up in her paw blanket and leave her for the night.

She knelt by the basket. Where had Clive injected the morphine? Had he used a vein or just stuck the needle in a muscle, anywhere he could reach? It wouldn't have been easy. Milly would have wriggled and moved about, displacing the needle before he could inject. How had Clive managed it, with his bloodshot eyes, his shaking hands? It was odd. Last night he had begged so hard for Dawn to give him the morphine. If he'd had a spare syringe of it lying about, why would he have wasted it on a dog?

It was when Dawn began to tuck the blanket back around Milly that she saw it.

A dark, clotted stain in the blue. The mark was new, Dawn was sure of it; she had washed that blanket only recently. She took the blanket back and examined the stain more closely. Maroon. No – dark red. She looked at Milly but could see nothing in the coal-black coat. She put the blanket to one side and ran her hands down Milly's sides, not even sure what it was she was looking for. There! There, on Milly's chest. A matted clump in the fur. Dawn lifted her hand and looked at her fingertips. More specks of red. She returned to the matted area of Milly's coat, exploring it with both hands, separating the thick fur until she found them.

Two wounds – two stab wounds – each about an inch long. One in Milly's side, just between her ribs. One further down in her abdomen. In both places, Dawn's finger went right through the skin and muscle and into the space beneath.

She lifted her head, gazing into the smooth blankness of the side of the washing-machine. No, Clive had not wasted a syringe of morphine on a dog. There had been no quick, friendly injection for Milly. Her end had been a lot more painful and brutal than that.

The empty blue-labelled syringe placed beneath her afterwards as a symbol only. A message. To make sure that Dawn understood.

It'll be nothing to what'll happen if you cross me.

The anger rose in her then. It sat in her like a thistle. When it was time to go, she wrapped Milly up again in her blanket.

'Goodbye, Milly.' She rested her hand on the dog's still head. 'I'll see you soon.'

She checked that there was a full bowl of water within reach, right beside the basket. A little pile of dog biscuits on the lino, the same as there had always been. It wouldn't have seemed right to leave her there with nothing.

With every step on her way in to work, Dawn felt larger and bulkier and more violent. Walking along the corridor to Forest Ward, her shoes seemed to punch holes in the floor. If Clive was here! If he *had* come in tonight! If she went on to the ward and saw his horrible bristly face and red, insect eyes twitching at her over the desk . . . She could hardly think. Her ears were ringing. Just as she had arrived at the bottom of the hill outside the hospital, a train had hurtled at full speed over the bridge. The deafening blast of it had smashed the circuit of her thoughts, driving them in twenty different directions. The noise was so loud that for a moment she was convinced the bridge was about to collapse. Surely it shouldn't be shaking like that? The air was so cloudy; it was like trying to see through a thick pall of smoke. Then the train had passed on, sucking with it the noise and the smoke and the shaking, leaving behind it only the relatively peaceful hoots and rumbles of the traffic below.

Clive was not on Forest Ward. When Dawn came through the doors there was just Pam, peacefully filing her nails at the desk, and Mandy buttoning up her cardigan, all ready to leave.

'Looks like it's going to be just the two of you tonight,' Mandy announced as Dawn appeared. 'Clive hasn't shown his face yet.'

'Must still be sick,' Pam said, holding her fingers out to inspect her nails.

Mandy sniffed. 'Well, he should have phoned to say.'

Dawn stood with the strap of her bag digging into her hand. Clive's presence had been so vivid in her mind that even now she could see him, hovering in the air beside Mandy like a dark, malignant cut-out.

'We'll manage.' She made herself sound calm. 'We managed last night with just Pam and me.'

Forest Ward was going through a peaceful phase. Danielle and Lewis were settled on their proper painkillers and well on the road to recovery. All the other patients were established on management plans that seemed to be working well. But long after Pam had finished seeing her half of the ward and gone to the staff room for her break, Dawn still went on prowling up and down between the rows of beds, tweaking a curtain here, an infusion pump there, letting the familiar routines and patterns ease the drumming of her heart, the sickening, acid hatred she felt for Clive. Had he sneaked up on Milly in the porch while she was asleep and simply rammed the knife into her side? Or had Milly heard him at the gate and come to greet him, wagging her tail, delighted to have a visitor in the middle of the night? Either way, her last moments: gasping in pain and shock, her eyes popping, her poor stiff hips wrenching and twisting as she struggled.

The phone rang. Dawn picked up the receiver.

'Forest Ward.'

'Dawn!' It was Francine. 'Thought I'd find you there. I'm on tonight too.'

'Right—'

Francine interrupted her. 'Have you heard?'

'Heard what?'

'Clive. Your nurse.'

A cold little clutch at Dawn's heart.

'What about him?'

'He's in A&E,' Francine said. 'Been brought in as an emergency.'

Further down the ward, an empty infusion pump began to beep a warning.

'He's taken an overdose of some kind,' Francine said. 'He was found a few hours ago, unconscious down an alley in Stockwell. The police reckon he was beaten up and robbed. He had no ID on him but the A&E staff recognized him. Apparently he's a user. Track marks all over his arms and groin. Did you know?'

'No.' It was the simplest thing to say.

'Well, you'd think he'd have more sense,' Francine said. 'Buying God knows what from some sleazy street dealer. He was seizing when he came in. A&E had to intubate him. He's stabilizing now, apparently, but I thought you'd want to know. Thought you'd want to go down and see him.'

'Yes, of course. Thanks Francine.'

Dawn put the phone down. The infusion pump was still beeping. It was several seconds before she could gather herself enough to go and look for Pam.

'Will you change that pump for me?' she asked. 'I've got to go down to A&E for a few minutes.'

'Will do, Dawn.'

Clive was in Resus Room Two, lying on a trolley under a powerful white theatre lamp. His T-shirt was slit down the front, hanging in rags at his sides. Giant, circular ECG stickers covered his chest like potholes. An endotracheal tube stuck out of his mouth, connected by a hose to a nearby ventilator. The bellows of the ventilator moved up and down *phht*, *phht*, in time with the rise and fall of his lungs. The A&E SHO was with him, young and nervous, a little arrogant to hide the fact that she wasn't quite sure what she was doing.

'Clive,' she was shouting. 'Clive, wake up.'

Clive's eyes remained closed but his jaw moved in a chewing motion around the ET tube.

'Coming round,' the SHO said with satisfaction.

'Hello, Matron,' Graham, one of the A&E nurses said. 'Come to see your favourite colleague?' He winked towards Clive.

'Yes, I have.'

Clive must have heard her because his eyes opened. His gaze slid to the side. His eyes met Dawn's and held them.

Graham said, 'Well, would you look at that! You've only been here two minutes and already you've got him awake. Go ahead, Matron – talk to him if you want to. I've got a couple of things to fetch so you can have a minute's privacy.'

He left the room, accompanied by the SHO. Now the only two people present were Dawn and Clive. Clive lay spotlit under the theatre lamp, like the principal actor on a stage, Dawn was in the wings, outside the circle of light. But she knew he could see her face.

'You bastard.' She spoke in a low voice. 'You bastard. You didn't have to kill her.'

A column of little wrinkles appeared in Clive's forehead. His eyes moved from side to side, as if he was searching for someone.

'Looking after him, Matron?' Graham was back. 'See, Clive. You're in good hands tonight.'

Clive seemed to be trying to say something but the tube was still blocking his vocal cords. His straggly hair lay like weeds on the pillow. More hair straggled on his chest, sprouting up between the ECG stickers. The SHO appeared, fiddling with something in her hand.

'Sorry, Matron,' she said. 'I just need to give him his antibiotic.'

She held up a large syringe filled with a yellowish liquid. The sticker on the side of the barrel read: *Augmentin*. At the sight of it, Clive's eyes grew round. He began to buck and heave on the trolley.

'All right, Clive,' the SHO said. 'Just let us take care of this.'

Clive began to claw at his chest. ECG stickers flew off all over the place.

'What's he doing?' The SHO stared at him.

The answer came suddenly to Dawn: Clive was searching for his silver chain and medallion. The one with the Penicillin Allergy warning on it. But the medallion was gone. Whoever had stolen his money and ID must have taken that as well.

'It's all right, Clive,' the SHO soothed him. 'This

won't take a second.' She attached the syringe of yellow liquid to his drip. Clive stopped clawing for the medallion and reached up to his face, trying to rip the ET tube from his mouth. 'Don't do that,' the SHO shouted, grabbing his hand. 'Someone – quick. A little help here.'

Two porters came racing into the room. They seized Clive's arms and legs and pinned him to the trolley.

'He's very confused,' the SHO explained. To Clive, she shouted, 'We're trying to HELP YOU, do you HEAR me? But you've got to COOPERATE.'

'Annoying when they put up a fight like that, isn't it?' one of the porters said. 'If they don't know what's happening, they should just cooperate and let you get on with your job.'

The muscles in Clive's throat were working. A clicky *ack-ack* sound came from around the ET tube. He was lying on his back, his arms immobilized. The other porter was leaning on his legs. Clive's eyes went to Dawn's and held them. *Please*, his eyes said. *For God's sake.* At his sides, his hands twitched. The sight of them gave Dawn a revolted feeling, of something crawling down her spine. Those were the same hands that had written those vile e-mails. That had yanked Mrs Walker up so violently that her head banged off an iron bedstead. That had driven a knife, twice, deep into Milly's side.

The SHO pressed the plunger of the syringe. The

movement snapped Dawn out of her mini-trance. She stepped forward. 'No—'

But before she could get the words out, there was a further commotion around the trolley.

'What's happening?'

'He's seizing again.'

'Where's the Lorazepam?'

The alarms on the ventilator were buzzing and shrieking. More people came crowding into the room.

'His BP's dropping. That shouldn't happen with a seizure.'

'It's not a seizure,' someone else said. 'It's the antibiotic. Look at him. He's having an anaphylaxis.'

A third voice shouted, 'No pulse. No pulse. V. Fib on the ECG.'

There were so many people around the trolley now that Dawn couldn't see Clive any more. There was a high-pitched whine as the defibrillator charged.

'Stand back.'

The crowd parted. As the current flowed through Clive's chest, Dawn saw him arching upwards, his body flipping into the air like a seal's. There was a crash as he landed back on the trolley.

'Adrenaline. Quickly.'

The A&E nurses were racing around, opening cupboards, emptying drawers. Dawn could do nothing to help them. This was their territory; they knew the routine here, where everything was, how the protocols should proceed. In this cluttered space, she was the one who was in the way. She went out to the hall to give them room. She waited by the door, listening to the terse instructions, the ripping open of packages, the further crashes as Clive's body landed on the trolley.

'Shock again, please.'

'And again.'

'And again.'

She lost track of the number of times they did it. Or of how long she stood in the hall with the A&E doors sliding open and shut behind her and the draught coming and going on her neck. Finally the crashing noises stopped. Dawn waited for someone to say, 'That was a close one!' or, 'Well done, Clive. You're back with us now.' But no one did. She listened for a long time into the stretching silence, and no one said anything at all.

Chapter Seventeen

She walked in her uniform in a light summer rain.

What would she do this afternoon? Where would she go? Not to the park; not without Milly, her faithful little shadow. She kept walking, away from the hospital, away from the stop where she normally caught her bus home. She walked northwards, over cobbled streets, under low, iron bridges, past the gold pagoda in Battersea Park. Then she was at the river, the chilly grey water reflecting the glass-walled tower blocks along the bank. She crossed the first bridge she came to, turned right, walked through a garden with leafy trees overhanging the river wall. It was only when she found herself up against a set of railings surrounding a high, yellowish building that she realized she had reached Westminster Abbey.

A line of people was filing through the black gates. Between the pillars, a sign propped on an easel read, *Evensong, 3 p.m.* The rain was coming harder. When had Dawn last been to church? Now was hardly the time for her to defile the place by her presence. If it felt wrong, she wouldn't stay. But the spacious, vaulted interior was more peaceful than she had expected. The other people had made their way to the top of the church, behind the ornate gold entrance to the choir stalls. Dawn was alone in the main part of the nave. The service had started. From behind the golden doors, a mournful male voice rose and fell. She stood, unsure. In the centre of the nave were several rows of straw-seated chairs which looked as if they had been placed there for latecomers. After a short hesitation, she sat down. A middle-aged couple came tiptoeing in, whispering to each other in some foreign language, and took their seats a few chairs along. Their disposable plastic raincoats dripped on the flagstones. Behind the choir stalls, the mournful chanting continued. The up-and-down cadence was soothing, slowing the ceaseless jumble and traffic in Dawn's head.

Clive was dead.

Clive was dead and she had killed him.

No! No, she hadn't! She had tried to warn the SHO. Was it her fault that the girl had been in too much of a hurry to give the antibiotic to listen? Behind the stalls, the choir launched into a hymn. The high, childish voices rose, chased each other across the high, Gothic ceiling.

She had killed him. Clive, lying there with his arms pinned, had sought her eyes and begged her for his life. She had been the Matron, the most senior nurse there. If Clive had been any other patient, it would not have happened.

When Mrs Walker had died, Dawn had said to herself, '*It's OK. It's OK.*' Because what she had done, she had done for Mrs Walker's benefit and for no other reason. There was no way she could say the same about Clive. There was no getting around it. What had happened last night had benefited nobody but herself.

The thin soprano voices echoed, eerie and discordant, like the cries of ghosts. Dawn put her fingers to her ears. She hadn't just done it for herself. She *hadn't*. What about all the people Clive had mistreated and abused? The vulnerable patients in his care whom he had made miserable? Almost certainly, Mrs Walker had not been the only one, nor would have been in the future. Clive had tried to make Dawn murder someone. He had savagely stabbed a harmless, elderly dog in her own garden. How would it help, for Dawn to lose her career and everything she loved because of a person like that? How would that benefit anyone in any way?

The grey walls rose around her. The statues and memorials between the pillars, the slabbed tombs on the floors, all in memory of prime ministers, scientists, beloved daughters. And most of all, soldiers. Everywhere you looked: the Vice Admiral of a British fleet, killed in 1716; a Major General, commemorated for services to the forces of the East India Company; a James Bringfeild, who had died in battle in 1706. All of these people had run wars or fought in them or died in them. Many of them had killed other people. Probably none of them had thought they were doing anything wrong. In fact, as the monuments demonstrated, they were now seen as heroes. If they had killed, it had been for the greater good. What was so different about this? With Clive gone, Dawn was safe, James Franks was safe, any future patients Clive might have treated were safe. Dawn could return to St Iberius and continue her job as if nothing had happened. She could go back to enjoying her work as before. Really, she could. Everything would be just as it had been.

The choir was swelled by an adult chorus. The deeper male tones mingled with the high ones, drew them down, anchored them in a long moment of unexpected sweetness. Then the music died away. There was a minute of silence. Then came the sounds of coughing, shuffling and footsteps as the congregation began to appear from around the sides of the stalls. Dawn stood up as well. Down the sides of the Abbey trooped the church-goers, goggling up at the carved pillars and statues, speaking in hushed tones that grew louder and more confident the nearer they came to the doors. How cheerful and carefree they all looked. Probably planning to move on to some other tourist attraction or stop somewhere for something to eat. Their biggest worry would be what topping to put on their pizza. They laughed aloud, walking in groups of three or four abreast. Dawn, the only person on her own, was obliged to step aside to make room for them. She kept to the walls, out of their way. She noticed how few of them seemed to see or notice her. If they glanced in her direction it was to look through her, to comment on some carving or monument lying directly behind her. As if all that there was of her was a dark shadow on the stone.

Will called her that evening.

'I was giving you a chance to get some rest,' he said. 'How did your night shifts go?'

Dawn had debated with herself through seven rings of the phone whether to answer it. But she needed someone to talk to. Someone to pull her back, to anchor her to the normal world. If she didn't pick up the receiver, it might be days before she spoke to anyone again. Hoping that Will would call tonight, she had practised her responses in advance, modulating her voice so that it sounded normal, or at least not so strained that he would wonder what was wrong.

'The night shifts were fine,' she said. 'But . . .' She

had practised this, too, and thought it would be easy to say, but at the last minute she had to pause to pinch the bridge of her nose. 'Milly died.'

'She what? Milly *died*?'

'Yes. I found her yesterday morning. When I came back from work.'

'Oh, Dawn. I'm sorry.'

She pinched her nose again.

'Was it an accident?' Will asked. 'Was she ill?'

'I think so. I think she might have had a heart attack.'

'I'm very sorry.'

'Well, you know. She was an old dog. Thirteen at least.'

Will said nothing but she could almost see him there at the other end of the phone, pushing his glasses up, shaking his head in consternation. She could feel him there with her, through the connection, right there in the hall.

'She's still here,' she said. 'In her basket in the kitchen. I didn't . . . I don't really know what I should do with her.'

'Would you like me to come over?'

'Yes. Yes, please.'

He was there in less than half an hour. There was the scrunch of a handbrake as his red Honda pulled up outside in the street. He had brought a long-handled spade.

'The best thing to do,' he said, 'would be to bury her. In your garden, if you want to.'

'Can we do that?'

'As long as you've got the space. And a suitable site.'

In the back garden, Dawn chose a peaceful spot: a small square of earth adjoining the back wall, under the hawthorn tree with its starry white flowers.

'Will that be big enough?' she asked. 'I don't know how . . . how deep it should be.'

Will said in a practical way, 'About four feet down, I would say. For a dog her size. You don't want the foxes to get her.'

The words were abrupt, callous even, but Dawn understood him. He had given her the necessary information, hadn't attempted to dodge or skip around the facts, yet in his tone were sympathy and understanding. He began to dig under the tree, scooping the earth out and placing it in a neat pile to the side. The recent light rain had been just enough to loosen the soil. When the hole began to look deep enough, Dawn went back to the kitchen to fetch Milly.

Will called after her. 'I'll bring her out if you like.'

'No. I'll manage.'

Before wrapping Milly up for the last time, she took off her faded red collar and placed it on the table. Then she wound her blanket tightly around her. She lifted her from the basket and carried her out to the garden. Milly was heavy but not unmanageably so; about the weight of a small child.

'It's OK,' she said as Will reached to help. 'I've got her.'

She laid Milly in her grave; a small, bulky bundle of fleece and pawprints. One sooty black ear stuck out from the top of the blanket. The damaged, lopsided one that had been bitten years ago. Dawn released the bundle and stood back. Will began to replace the earth into the grave. A couple of spadefuls later and Milly was gone from view. Will worked methodically, patting down each layer of soil as he went so that all of it would fit back in. Again that sense of his quiet intelligence, the knowledge that was hidden in him but there when it was needed. He had come straight away, had said little but had known exactly what to do, how deep to go. It was for that very reason that Dawn had made sure to handle Milly herself, keeping her well covered with the blanket. If Will had taken her, he might have noticed the red stains and matted fur and wondered what was going on.

And if he had?

If she had told him, Dawn couldn't help thinking – told him that night they'd had dinner on the South Bank – he would have known what to do. If she had asked him earlier for his help, things might never have ended up the way they had. But she had made her decision to say nothing and now it was too late to go back. At least now, as things were, Will never would have to know. Never would have to find out what she was really like. When the last spade of earth was patted on to the pile, she let out her breath and felt some of the tension inside her release.

The little heap of soil was higher and darker than the ground around it. The shadow from the hawthorn tree lay over it, spreading outwards to the lawn. Already the rectangle of earth had begun to blend with the surrounding space. Milly was a part of the garden now, as much as if she had never been separate from it at all. Without thinking, Dawn said, 'I feel so guilty.'

'It wasn't your fault,' Will said. 'She was an old dog. You said so yourself.'

'Yes.' Dawn caught herself. 'Yes, she was.'

'Don't be so hard on yourself.' Will tapped the spade with his foot to release the dirt. 'You can't help everyone.'

The sad little mound, darkening under the tree. 'I don't feel as if I've helped anyone.'

'Don't talk like that. You are worth so much. Remember that child in the café.'

Will spoke so agitatedly, thumping the spade on the grass, looking at Dawn, then away again, that she knew before he spoke that something important was coming.

'I'm moving back,' he said. 'Next week. To Keswick. I'll still need to travel between there and London for a while, finishing off contracts and that, but overall . . . that'll be it for me.'

She had been expecting it, but it was still a shock.

'Well.' She tried to smile. 'It was good to have had you down here with us. Even if it was just for a while.'

'I hope we can still see each other. I hope you'll come and visit me.'

'Of course I will.'

'They've got hospitals up there, you know.' Will was concentrating again on the spade, kicking hard at a stubborn clump of earth. 'I was looking into it. They need nurses. I know you'd never think of it in a million years – not a Matron as well-established as you – but . . .'

'I would,' Dawn said. 'I would think of it.'

'Really?' Will looked at her. His face had lit up. His cheeks were flushed and shiny, as if he had never ex-pected to hear anything so wonderful. 'Really?'

'Yes, really.'

And just like that, though she was surprised to have heard herself say it, it was true. She never would have thought of it, but now that Will had said it, it was the first thing in a long time that seemed right. St Iberius was poisoned for her now. Working there would never be the same. And what else was there to keep her in London? Cumbria might not turn out to be the answer either, but . . . She had a sudden vision of herself – her and Will – walking by the lake at Buttermere, climbing a slope through a green, damp wood.

'I'll make some enquiries,' she said. 'I don't know what might be available or what might suit, but . . . I'll certainly give it a try.'

The expression on Will's face told her what he felt. In that moment, she could almost feel it herself. Up there, at the Lakes, everything would be fresh and un-spoiled and new. She could be a new person; in time, perhaps, even be the person Will thought she was. If things worked out, in time, perhaps, she might be able to start all over again.

Will left her house early the next morning. He still had a contract to finish in town.

'I'll call and see you this evening.' He stood smiling down at her, messy in his rumpled shirt and small, kind eyes.

When he was gone, she fell into a deep doze. Even with Will there, solid and stable beside her, she had not slept well last night. Now, as if his presence was all that had prevented it, she found herself in the middle of a dream. St Iberius was on fire again. The patients were calling to her and she was trying to find them in the smoke. She pushed against the doors of the ward but they wouldn't move. Something was blocking them from the other side. She shoved as hard as she could, until her arms trembled with the effort, but the doors refused to budge. One by one, the screams from the other side faded, until there was silence. Only then did the doors swing open. Standing between them were Clive and Mrs Walker. 'You're too late,' they said, smiling at her through blackened teeth. 'Much too late. All of them are dead.'

Dawn woke with a start. The sun was white on the daisy-patterned walls. She lay there, comforted by the reassuring warmth.

It's over now, she told herself. *Time to move on.*

It would take a little while, she knew. In the meantime, today was Monday and she was on her holidays. No pagers. No phone calls. No worries about e-mails and wondering what might be in them. No paperwork even. Francine could deal with all of that now. Dawn would take a proper break, the first she'd had for a very long time. Concentrate on recovery and healing and new plans.

Downstairs, Milly's basket was still sitting by the washing-machine, the same spot where it had been since Milly had first come here as a terrified pup all those years ago. Dawn carried it out to the wheelie bin in the back lane. Also Milly's dog biscuits and water bowls and her remaining tins of dog food. The only thing she kept was Milly's faded red collar. She wrapped the collar in a sheet of tissue paper left over from Christmas and looked about for somewhere to put it. The odds-and-ends drawer in the kitchen was as good a place as any. She opened the drawer and tucked the collar in next to the bulky cardiac Resus kit, still awaiting its review.

Then she brewed herself some strong coffee.

The kitchen was too quiet. The only sound came from the intermittent hum of the boiler outside the back door. The space by the washing-machine where Milly's basket had been was marked by a greyish circle on the linoleum. In time, the sun coming through the back door would fade it, but for now it still looked very obvious. Dawn got up and took her coffee through to the sitting-room. But even there, sitting on the couch, she found herself staring at the sheepskin rug in front of the fireplace, flattened in the centre in a Milly-shaped dent. She got up again. Old habits died hard. With nothing else to do, and despite what she had promised herself earlier, she wandered in to the dining room to check her e-mails. She'd do one quick check, just to see if there was anything urgent to be forwarded to Francine. She wouldn't deal with any issues herself, no matter how pressing they were. She wouldn't even send anything to Francine that wasn't of absolutely earth-shaking importance.

The screen lit up. Dawn clicked through to her e-mail account. One new message. The subject line read, *Urgent. Matron Torridge. Forest Ward.*

The sender was Well-wisher.

Dawn had just taken a mouthful of coffee. The whole lot of it went straight into her lungs. She coughed and choked, jerking her chair back, almost tipping it on to the carpet. How could that e-mail be there? How could it be? How could Clive possibly have sent it?

A series of cold dots, like scrawny fingers, crawled on her scalp. She saw Clive again as he had been in her dream, smiling at her through his blackened teeth. She saw him climbing off his trolley in the Mortuary in the hospital basement, stealing down the hill to the railway bridge and through the darkened streets to her house. Creeping in here while she slept to leave this final gloating message on her laptop.

Then the cold spots vanished. For God's sake! Really, this holiday hadn't come a day too soon. It was blindingly obvious how the message came to be there. The last time Dawn had checked her e-mail was on Friday evening, before leaving for her night shift. Clive could have sent this to her at any time since then. Almost certainly he had done it sometime on Saturday, because by Saturday night, of course, he had been dead. He had probably sent this in response to Dawn's having kicked him out of the hospital on the Friday night. The only surprising thing was that he had been capable of it. He had been so agitated in the locker room, sweating, jittery, twitchy enough to leap out of a window at any moment. Obviously whatever he'd had to say had been important enough for him to make the effort. She could imagine what would be in the message. A venomous, vitriolic rant about how if she ruined his life he would make damn sure hers was destroyed as well. Perhaps even a detailed, gloating description of what he had done to Milly. Dawn gritted her teeth. Well, she would not read it. She would not give him the satisfaction. She raised her finger in the air above the Delete button.

But she did not press it.

She owed Clive. He had lain there, his arms and legs trapped, pleading with her, the one person who could help him, for his life. And she had stood there and done nothing. The memory of it made her shift in her seat. The least she owed him was some degree of respect. Whatever his intentions, he had felt strongly enough to write this final message to her. Well, then, whatever was in it, she would read it. Take the trouble to acknowledge what he had felt.

She opened the e-mail. Through the dust on the screen she read the words.

Dear Matron,
I hope you are well.
Following on from my previous message, the time has now come for an update. The name of the patient I mentioned to you is Gordon Farnley. I hope you remember what we agreed?
I can now confirm that Mr Farnley is being

admitted to St Iberius this morning. He will be going to Ocean Ward on the second floor.

Once again, I promise you, if you do this it will be over. When Mr Farnley is no longer with us, you will have paid your debt and you will not hear from me again.

Sincerely,

A well-wisher

The dust seemed to lift in a cloud off the screen. The air darkened, blotting out her vision. Dawn scrubbed frantically at her eyes. Gordon Farnley? Gordon Farnley? Surely he meant James Franks? She took her hands from her face and reread the words. *Being admitted to St Iberius this morning . . .* Clive must have written this on Saturday. There was no other day he could have done it. But why would this Gordon Farnley person have been admitted to St Iberius on a Saturday? Elective patients were never admitted on a Saturday. Weekends were strictly for emergencies.

She knew the answer even before she could admit it to herself. She went to check the timing of the message and her fingers bunched and fumbled like clumps of spaghetti, pressing several keys at once. She managed to scroll the message back up, her hands pawing at the keyboard.

Time sent, the message read: *10.25 a.m.*

One hour ago.

Chapter Eighteen

Not Clive! Not Clive! The coffee she had inhaled tightened her lungs, made her wheeze and fight for breath. The blackmailer was not Clive. The pounding in her head jerked every nerve in her body. Despite the crazy fluttering of her pulse, however, the odd thing was that her body on the outside remained completely still.

After a while, the stillness of her body began to spread to the inside. Not just the wheezing in her lungs, but all the colours and jumble in her head subsided until finally she sat there, empty. Ivy Walker, cold in her cheap coffin; Milly, struggling in the night with a knife in her side; Clive, pinned to his trolley, his thin hands twitching – all had left her, floated away. It was easiest just to sit there in her dressing gown, staring into the crystal sparkles on the sideboard. The one thing she knew now was that this would never be over.

She might have sat there for ever but for the thought that came swimming out of nowhere: *Now you know who Mr F is. He is Mr Gordon Farnley, a patient at St Iberius Hospital. And whether you like it or not, you are still the Matron there and he is your responsibility.*

She did her best to ignore the intrusion. What could she do about it anyway? If she interfered, she would make a mess of it, as she had of everything else. But the thought would not go away. *Mr Farnley is in trouble. His safety is in your hands. You have to warn him.*

It was like a painful pressure in her ears. Dawn turned her head to get away from it. All right, then. All *right!* She *would* warn him! Get up, go in there and make him listen. Tell him: 'Someone is trying to kill you. They are dangerous. They killed my dog.' She would stay until she was certain he was taking it seriously. She would say to him, 'Don't be alone with anyone. Get a relative in, a friend. Get the police. Let me be the last person you are alone with.' Only when she knew he was safe would she leave him.

And after that . . . then what? Then what?

It was three o'clock when Dawn walked through the hospital entrance. Several staff and patients greeted her at the glass doors but she barely noticed them. She walked with her gaze fixed straight ahead, her mouth stiff, as if her face had been anaesthetised.

Ocean Ward, the e-mail had said.

386

When Dawn came out of the lift on the second floor, two men were in the hall, working with a ladder. One held the base, the other was on the top rung, hammering at something near the ceiling. Jim Evans was watching from the side.

'Afternoon, Matron,' he called. 'You'll be glad to see we're getting those cameras in at last. Next time there's a break-in we'll have it all on record. We might even find that no-good who broke into your locker that time.'

Jim's voice was rising and falling, as though someone was turning a radio up and down. Beyond him was the set of white doors with 'Ocean Ward' printed in blue lettering above.

'I always did think it was strange,' Jim's radio voice was still rising and falling, 'the burglar flinging your stuff around like that and damaging your property. All the other robberies, they just took the money and scarpered. But with you, they went the extra mile. Like it was personal. But don't you worry, Matron. We'll find him.'

With you it was personal . . .

Of course. Of course it had been. Her locker had had her name on it. The break-in that afternoon, the vandalism of her coat – all had happened the day after her row with Clive. The day she had humiliated him in front of the ward for abusing Mrs Walker.

You've had a taste already.

So obvious. So obvious, when you were looking back and knew all the facts. But no time to think of that now. Here she was at Ocean Ward, and behind those blue and white doors, a man in great danger was waiting for her.

'Thank you, Jim,' she said.

She opened the doors and went in.

Ocean Ward, being in the tower block, was more modern than Forest: warmer, brighter, cleaner-looking. Each room had a maximum of four beds and its own bathroom and shower.

'Hello, Dawn.' Daphne, the orthopaedic sister, came bustling out of a side room, holding an IV tray. 'Here on one of your inspections?'

'Actually, I'm here to see a patient. A Mr Farnley.'

'Farnley. Farnley . . .' Daphne took her ward list from her pocket and opened it out. 'Oh, yes. Gordon Farnley. Admitted today. Having a hip replacement this afternoon. Is that the person you want?'

'I think it must be.'

Daphne waited, smiling, her head to one side. It was unusual for a nurse from another ward to come to see a patient. Dawn being the Matron of course, she could visit whoever she wanted; Daphne wouldn't have dreamed of questioning her. But it was natural to wonder.

'Bed management phoned,' Dawn said, when

Daphne showed no sign of moving on. 'They said they might put Mr Farnley on Forest Ward after his surgery. I just thought I'd come and check on his care needs.'

It was unconvincing to say the least, but Daphne didn't question it. 'Keen of you, I must say,' she said. 'Would you like to see his notes?'

'Please.'

Dawn followed Daphne to the chart trolley. 'Poor old chap,' Daphne said, riffling through the notes. 'If you ask me, a good holiday would benefit him far better than a hip replacement.'

'Is he a drug user?' Dawn asked.

'A drug user?' Daphne looked up. 'Mr *Farnley*?'

Dawn shrugged. She didn't know why she had asked. Whether or not Mr Farnley did take drugs was hardly relevant any more.

'Highly unlikely, I would have thought,' Daphne said, riffling through the charts again. 'Sure you've got the right person?'

'I think so.'

Daphne found the notes and pulled them from the trolley.

'Here we are,' she said. 'Room six. He's the only patient in there at the moment so you'll have some privacy.'

'Thank you.'

When Daphne had left, Dawn studied the notes.

The chart was very thin, just two pages, one printed with Mr Farnley's personal details – address, GP, next of kin – the other a single scrawled sheet from the admitting doctor: *Eighty-four-year-old male. Admitted for hip replacement. Alert. Vitals stable. Meds: Nil. Allergies: Nil.*

Eighty-four! Why would anyone want to murder such an elderly man? If the admission note was accurate, Mr Gordon Farnley was in good shape for his age. He didn't appear to have been an inpatient before – not at St Iberius at least, or the record would have been there in his notes. He had an address in Tooting. Dawn knew the street; she had often noticed the turn-off for it on her bus journey to and from work. Mr Farnley's next of kin was a Mrs Helen Cummings. That was it; that was all there was. Nothing whatsoever in the notes to suggest why someone might want him dead.

Room six, a two-bedded, was at the very end of the ward. The door was partly open. The bed nearest to the door was empty. A towel folded on the pillow and a blank set of notes on the locker suggested that an admission was expected but had yet to arrive. The second bed, next to the window, had its curtains pulled around. Dawn went to the cubicle.

'Mr Farnley?'

From inside the cubicle, she thought she heard a

snore. Lightly, she tugged at the curtains, deliberately rattling the rings to give the occupant a warning. Then she pulled the curtains back. Behind them, an elderly man lay dozing in the bed. He had a long jaw, thick, white, bushy eyebrows, a high, bald forehead. Most of what remained of his hair was concentrated in tufts above his ears.

'Mr Farnley?'

The man gave a loud snort and moved his head. Then he opened his eyes. He looked about him in a startled way. 'Who's that? Who's there?'

'It's only me,' Dawn said. 'Sister Torridge.'

Mr Farnley turned his head towards her. His vision didn't seem to be very good; he was clearly having difficulty focusing on her face. On his locker lay a pair of glasses, folded next to a plastic case.

'Edith?' he said, peering at Dawn in a hopeful way.

'No,' Dawn said. 'I'm sorry.'

Mr Farnley peered at her for another moment. Then he let his head fall back on the pillow.

'No,' he said. 'No, of course. I'm sorry. My wife died. A year ago . . .'

His speech was slurred, fading off at the end. Dawn's heart sank. She recognized the signs. Mr Farnley had been given a pre-med. This was going to make things a lot more difficult.

'Mr Farnley,' she said, 'I need to talk to you about

something very important. I need you to wake up and listen.'

'All right . . .'

'Is there anyone you know here who might . . . who . . .' She couldn't think of any other way to put it. 'Who might have a grudge against you? Someone who might want to harm you in some way?'

'No.' It came out as faint as a sigh.

'You're sure? Maybe someone you know from outside the hospital? Or who you might have met on a previous hospital visit?'

'This is my first time in a hop . . . a hop . . .'

'Mr Farnley, please. You must try to stay awake. Mr *Farnley*.'

It came out more sharply than she had intended. Mr Farnley flinched and opened his eyes. Then he sucked his breath in and grimaced, lifting his hand to his hip. Dawn winced too, guessing what he must be feeling. A sharp, scraping pain, like a knife running over the joint. When Milly's hips had been bad, any sudden movement like that had made her yelp and cringe to the floor.

'I'm sorry.' She put her hands on his arm. 'I'm so sorry. But this really is important. You've got to listen. I think you're in some kind of trouble . . .'

Mr Farnley nodded but he was starting to drift again. His eyelids were drooping. It was hopeless. If only there was someone with him. A family member or friend whom she could talk to and warn to keep an eye on him. But the only visitor's chair was sitting neatly under the window, undisturbed since the room had been cleaned. His locker was as bare as Mrs Walker's had been. The only personal objects on it were his spectacles and a set of dentures, floating at the bottom of a glass of water. The sight of the dentures gave Dawn a little squeeze to her heart. Patients in a hospital were so very vulnerable; she had often thought it. Their dignity stripped away, their belongings and clothes removed, all kinds of strangers coming in and out, doing things to them and ordering them around, and half the time the patients never had the faintest idea who they were.

Mr Farnley had begun to snore again. His breathing deepened, became more obstructed. On the fourth snore, he stopped breathing completely. His chest moved but no air went in or out. A second later, he gave another loud snort. His eyes flew open. At the sight of Dawn standing by his bed, he jerked back his head.

'Edith?' he said.

His tone was piteous. His blue eyes were watery. He was so frail. So very old and alone. What could a man like this possibly have done to anyone that would make them want to harm him? His pyjama jacket was frayed and missing a button. The material hung in loose folds around his shoulders. He looked to have lost quite a bit of weight recently. Older men often went like that when their wives died. They just couldn't cope with being on their own.

Dawn sat on the edge of the bed.

'It's OK.' She touched the long, papery hand on the blanket. 'It's nothing. You go back to sleep. Have a rest.'

Reassured, Mr Farnley closed his eyes again. Apart from his breathing, the room was quiet. From the far end of the hall came the distant sounds of voices and bangs and clatters. Daphne had arranged her ward in such a way that the post-ops, who needed the most care, were at the top end along with most of the staff. Down at this end were the pre-ops, bored and dozing, with an occasional nurse popping in to check that all was well. Another rattly snore from Mr Farnley. He was very tall. His large, knobbly feet stuck out over the end of the bed. The bones in his face were strong and sharp. He must have been a powerful man once. Now the effect of his pre-med, combined with the looseness of his pyjamas, underlined to Dawn once again how helpless, how vulnerable these patients really were. If someone were to come in here right now and do something to Mr Farnley – give him something, say, or press a pillow to his face so that he couldn't breathe – he would be utterly powerless to fight them off or to defend himself.

And if something like that *were* to happen . . . in a

quiet, isolated room like this . . . who would ever see or know?

The e-mail on her laptop that morning: *If you do this, it will be over* . . .

'*Hu*-llo!'

Dawn spun around on the bed. She hadn't heard the curtains pull back. Two large men in dark green scrubs were shouldering their way into the cubicle.

'Gordon Farnley?' one of the porters shouted matily. 'For theatre?'

'Yes.' Dawn got up off the bed. 'Yes, this is him.'

She must have stood too quickly. A cobwebby veil billowed inwards from the sides of her vision. She groped for the corner of the locker and pressed her hand hard down on it until the pain brought the bed back into focus. The porters were bustling about, helping Mr Farnley from his bed to the theatre trolley.

'All right, boss. That's it. Got you now.'

'Here you are, guv. A nice, warm blanket for the journey.'

In their casual, cheery way, they fussed around the old man until he was comfortable. The trolley wheels squeaked, *eek eek*, as they manoeuvred Mr Farnley out of the room. Dawn stood, still with her hand pressed into the corner of the locker, as the trolley made its noisy way up the corridor. *Eek eek*

eek the wheels went, all the way up the hall, until the squeaking faded, blending with the distant voices, and the cold, morgue-like silence closed back around the bed.

It was only when Dawn came out into the corridor herself that she realized just how stuffy Mr Farnley's room had been and how little air had been circulating. She shivered in the breeze from the ceiling vents. Strange, how dizzy she had felt in there. For a moment she had hardly known what she was thinking.

Daphne appeared.

'Hello, Dawn. Got everything you wanted?'

Dawn could still see Mr Farnley's bed from the door. The blanket gone, the sheets stripped right back so that the mattress was bare. The dentures in the glass on the locker, like the remnants of a skull.

She turned sharply to Daphne.

'I've got a favour to ask,' she said. 'When Mr Farnley comes back from theatre, could you arrange to have him moved further up the ward?'

'Don't worry, Dawn. We'll make sure he's kept nice and peaceful—'

'No! Not peaceful. He must be watched. He's got to be in a busy ward, with people with him at all times.'

Daphne frowned. 'Is there some sort of medical issue?'

'There may be. Promise me he won't be left alone. Not for one minute, not at any time during the night.'

'Well . . .'

'*Promise me?*'

'All right.' Daphne sounded startled. 'All right. I promise.'

In offended tones, she arranged for Mr Farnley to be moved to a bed in the room directly across from the nurses' station. Dawn watched as a junior nurse plumped up the pillows. There were three other beds in the room, all occupied. She breathed more easily as Mr Farnley's belongings were moved from his old wardrobe and locker up to his new. But it was a short-term measure only. She still hadn't warned Mr Farnley of the danger he was in. Now she would have to wait until he returned from theatre. The trouble was, he could be there for hours. And when he did come back, he would be drowsy and sedated from the anaesthetic. Even if she could manage to make him listen, there was a good chance he would remember none of it.

She tapped her thumbnail on her teeth. She could still remember Mr Farnley's home address from his chart. How many times had she passed that street on her way to work? The turn-off was just beyond Tooting Bec Common. What if she called round there? Now, while Mr Farnley was in theatre? There might be someone there that she could talk to. Some family member he trusted, someone whom she could persuade to keep an eye on him. The person might even know why he was in trouble. She could be at his house in half an hour, back at the hospital within two. It had to be better than hanging around here for the afternoon.

She left Ocean Ward and took the lift back down to the main hall. She had passed the green Pharmacy cross on the wall and was heading for the entrance when a voice called, 'Sister! Sister!'

Years of responding automatically to people calling her by her title meant that before Dawn knew what she was doing she had stopped and turned. A girl in a blue tunic came hurrying over from the fountain.

'Thanks for stopping, Sister. I was just about to try to find you on your ward.'

'You wouldn't have found me there,' Dawn said. 'I'm not actually working today. I came in to the hospital for something else.'

'Oh.' The girl's face fell. Dawn thought she recognized her. Wasn't she one of Francine's junior nurses from ITU? Salma. No – Seema. Timidly, the girl held out a green-covered ledger. 'It was just to ask you to sign this, Sister.'

'What is it?'

'Our drug book. We borrowed some medication

from your ward a couple of weeks ago, and I'm sorry, Sister, but we still haven't been able to replace it. Pharmacy says it's been discontinued.'

'What was the drug?' Dawn asked.

'Oh.' Seema looked down at the ledger. 'I'll have to check.' She began to flip through the pages. 'It's a funny one. Dip . . . Dipyrid . . .'

'Dipyridamole,' Dawn said. 'I never noticed it was missing. I didn't even know anyone still used it.'

'Neither did I, Sister. But Dr Carmichael came up to the ITU one day and got it into his head that he wanted to try it on one of his patients. He got very upset when we said it was obsolete and no one stocked it any more. Finally Sister Hartnett said she'd run down and see if you had any on your ward. Didn't she tell you?'

'No.'

'Because it was quite funny – we kept telling Dr Carmichael that Dipyridamole wasn't used at St Iberius any more and he said, you just try Sister Torridge's ward, I bet she'll have some. And of course when Sister Hartnett went down there, you did. Dr Carmichael was very triumphant and kept saying, See, I told you. I was sure Sister Hartnett would have mentioned it to you?'

'No,' Dawn said. 'She must have forgotten.'

'Oh.' Seema shrugged. 'Anyway, Pharmacy says that if you confirm you don't need it replaced, they'll strike it off your budget. If you could sign here – I've got the details filled in for you already . . .'

She was holding out the ledger, opened at a particular page. Dawn scribbled in the space indicated. The date at the top of the space caught her eye. April twenty-seventh.

She said absently, 'That date looks familiar.'

Seema leaned in to look. 'Wasn't that the day of the big research conference?'

'Yes, of course,' Dawn said. 'That's what it was.'

'Thanks, Sister. Thanks ever so much.' Beaming, Seema took the ledger and left. Dawn walked on through the glass doors, out on to the steps.

That date on the ledger. She had known, of course, as soon as she'd said it why it was familiar. April twenty-seventh. The day of the research conference.

The day Mrs Walker had died.

The day Francine had come to the stock room on Forest Ward to borrow some Dipyridamole and had never mentioned it to Dawn.

The sun was in her eyes. The tower block cast a sharp, black shadow on the hill. The car park smelled of traffic fumes and tar. And like a cool rain, the answer came dropping into Dawn's head.

Francine. Delicate, silvery Francine, rummaging around in the stock room with its bird's-eye view of the side room next door. Francine who had smiled and bought Dawn flowers when she had won the Matron post and assured her that she didn't mind. Francine, who looked as fragile as a porcelain doll but who always got her own way when it mattered.

Francine, who had said that if looks could kill, she would send a man to the bottom of the Thames.

Dawn turned her head to move the sun from her eyes. She felt nothing. What did it matter now? Whether Gordon Farnley was a shareholder in a crooked company, whether he was a monster responsible for job losses and misery who deserved his fate. He was her patient, and she had a mission to achieve. Until she had done it, she would allow herself to feel nothing. She could not afford to be sidetracked. Everything else she had got so wrong. This, at least, was the one thing she knew was right. The one thing she could allow herself to think about.

Yet as she walked down the hill, Francine returned to her mind. Francine, with her bright white dress and her bright white smile. Her serene, soothing manner that the patients loved. Her ITU credentials that gave her access to slip, unquestioned, into an isolated room at the end of a ward and to close the door softly behind her.

But it was all right. It was all right. Francine would not harm Gordon Farnley. For the next few hours at least, Mr Farnley would be safe. He would be in theatre for a minimum of three hours, constantly watched and accompanied. Then in an open room on Ocean Ward, surrounded by people. He would be attached to a monitor in full view; he would not be left alone for a second. Francine would not be able to get at him.

No one would be able to get at him.

Dawn walked on to the bus stop.

Chapter Nineteen

Laburnum Crescent was a curved cul-de-sac, lined with plane trees and red-bricked, medium-sized houses of mixed period. Most were Victorian terraces with front gardens about the size of Dawn's own. Some of the gardens were overgrown, with wheelie bins on the grass and bicycles chained to the gates, but the majority were neat and well kept. Number 18 had a black-and-white tiled path, similar to Dora's, edged with a scalloped stone border. The lawn was mowed, the conifer border neatly clipped. The flower bed along the wall bustled with red and pink and orange azaleas.

Dawn stood in the arched front porch and pressed the doorbell. The door was painted glossy black, with a polished brass knocker and letterbox and a window of whorled, yellow glass to the side. A hand-written card in the window read, *No Junk Mail*. Dawn pressed the bell again. No answer.

She walked backwards down the path, looking up at the house. The window blinds were all pulled half-way down in such a way that it was impossible to tell whether anyone was in there, or had plans to return for the night.

'May I help you?'

Dawn turned. In the garden next door, a woman was looking up from where she was kneeling by a flower bed. She appeared to be in her seventies, trim, with short white hair. She held a trowel and wore an expression of polite but suspicious enquiry.

Dawn went to the dividing wall. 'Yes,' she said. 'I'm looking to speak with Mr Gordon Farnley.'

'May I know who's asking?'

Dawn paused. She remembered Mr Farnley's words when he had woken up and peered at her with his hopeful, pleading expression.

'I knew his wife,' she said. 'Edith. Before she died.'

'Oh, I see.' Carefully, the woman placed her trowel on a square of matting beside her. Then she climbed to her feet, brushing the dirt from her trousers. 'Poor Edie,' she said, coming to the wall. 'A real shock. Were you a good friend?'

'Well – it was my mother, really, who knew her,' Dawn said, backtracking. She held her hand out to the woman. 'Dawn Torridge. I'm the Matron at St Iberius Hospital.'

As so often happened, the mere mention of the

word 'Matron' caused all doubt and mistrust to melt like an ice-cream in the sun. The woman's suspicion was replaced by a respectful, deferential look. She shook Dawn's hand. 'Helen Cummings.'

Helen Cummings! The next of kin listed on Mr Farnley's hospital chart. Dawn looked at the woman more closely. She was not as formidable as she had first appeared. Her face was round and friendly. She had chubby, hamster-like cheeks and guileless hazel eyes which gave her a youthful air.

'Are you a good friend of the Farnleys?' Dawn asked.

'Oh yes,' Helen Cummings said. 'For years. My husband and I.' She shook her head. 'Poor Gordon. He was always such a giant. Like one of those wrestlers you see on the television. But since Edie had her heart attack, he's shrunk to half the size.'

'I heard he was going in to hospital soon,' Dawn said.

'Yes. Today,' Mrs Cummings said. 'In fact, the taxi from St Iberius came to pick him up at five this morning, if you can believe that. It seems odd to me, expecting a person of that age to travel at that hour on the day of an operation. But then,' Mrs Cummings seemed to remember to whom she was speaking, 'I suppose the doctors do know what they're doing. And Gordon himself was quite happy to put off going until the last minute. He's always hated hospitals.'

Dawn pulled carefully at a tuft of moss on the wall. 'Why is that, do you think? Did he have a bad experience at a hospital in the past?'

'I don't think he's ever been to one before,' Helen Cummings said doubtfully. 'He's always been very healthy. But then, that's the very sort of person, isn't it, who most mistrusts anything to do with illness and doctors? Edie was at him for months to get his hip done but he kept refusing. But in the end he had no choice. The joint was all worn away. He was in such pain he couldn't even walk his dog. And if you know Gordon, you'll know what *that* meant.'

Dawn hazarded a not-so-wild guess, 'His dog is everything to him.'

'Oh, everything!' Mrs Cummings was much more chatty now. 'But then, their dogs always were like the children they never had. Although, between you and me, I think it was a mistake to get such a large breed again after Rupert. Rupert was a softie, but he was an old dog. It's different with a pup, isn't it? I think the new dog's been a lot for Gordon to handle by himself. But then, they weren't to know when they got him that Edie wouldn't be around.'

'It's so hard to manage when you don't have the strength.' Dawn remembered the loose pyjamas flapping around the wasted shoulders.

'Yes, it's been very difficult. Fortunately a young man Gordon happened to meet on the common has been helping out a great deal. Walking Boris for him. It's been a great help, because I don't know that my husband Martin or I would have managed. I've never been good with dogs, and Martin's emphysema lately has been getting worse and worse.'

The sun was disappearing behind the houses opposite. Time to come to the point.

Dawn said, 'Mrs Cummings, did Mr Farnley ever happen to mention anyone he knew working at St Iberius?'

'At St Iberius?' Mrs Cummings considered. 'Not that I recall.'

'You're sure? He never mentioned a nurse called Francine Hartnett?'

'He never mentioned knowing anyone who worked at a hospital,' Mrs Cummings said. 'Why do you ask?'

Dawn wondered how to broach the matter. How much she should say to this woman, who *seemed* to have Mr Farnley's interests at heart – but then, you didn't always know, did you? Mrs Cummings' chattiness could just as easily be due to nosiness and a love of gossip as to genuine friendship or concern.

'I'm sure,' Helen Cummings said, 'that if Gordon *did* know someone, he would have said. He was so nervous about going in. In fact, I'd go so far as to say that he has an actual phobia about hospitals. He was so worried he even made his will before he went. So that will tell you.'

'His will?' Dawn stopped pulling at the moss on the wall.

'Oh yes. And it just shows you, doesn't it, because he always said that with Edie gone and no children of their own he didn't care who got the house. But there. You can tell, can't you, that when it comes down to it, people do care. Don't want the state to get their hands on it, do they?'

Dawn followed Mrs Cummings's gaze to Mr Farnley's house, solid and pink in the evening sun. A spacious, well-built Victorian with its own garden in the middle of the city. Probably worth a good bit of money. Who had Gordon Farnley left it to? Helen Cummings and her husband? Given that he had put them down as his next of kin, the assumption was not unreasonable. But it was hardly the sort of thing Dawn could ask.

But she didn't have to. Mr Farnley's neighbour was of the Mandy breed, happy to tell all. Mrs Cummings glanced from side to side, then leaned towards the wall.

'And you'll never guess,' she said in a low voice, 'who he's left it all to.'

'Er – no?'

Mrs Cummings said triumphantly, 'His dog!'

'His *dog*!'

'Yes! Isn't that just typical of Gordon?'

Dawn glanced at her watch. She had been here for almost an hour. Mr Farnley would be waking up from his surgery soon. The softly-softly approach hadn't worked. She was going to have to be more direct.

'Mrs Cummings—' she began.

Helen Cummings waved her hand. 'Now, wait a minute,' she said. 'I'm being a little facetious here. What Gordon has done is actually quite sensible. He's left all the money to a dog charity. On the condition that if anything happens to him they'll take his dog in and make sure he's looked after properly.'

'I see,' Dawn said, 'but—'

'He and Edie were always so fond of their dogs,' Mrs Cummings said reminiscently. 'So in a way, it's exactly the same as leaving it to one's child, isn't it? Now, let me see – what was the name of the charity? Quite a small one, I believe. Not Battersea, but . . . Oh, what was it?'

'Mrs Cummings—'

'It's the young man he met who runs it. The one who helped him with his dog. Oh my word.' Mrs Cummings tapped her finger on her temple. 'It'll come to me in a moment. I don't know why I can't seem to—'

Her front door opened. A furry, orange blur came streaking out of the house, heading straight for the gate. Helen Cummings cried, 'Oh, there he is. Oh,

Martin – catch him. He's not supposed to go on the road.'

A red-faced man in a golf V-neck came panting out of the house but the orange blur was already on the pavement. Fortunately a crisp wrapper happened to blow past, distracting the dog from continuing straight on to the road.

'That's Gordon's dog,' Mrs Cummings said. 'We're looking after him while he's in hospital. Oh quick, Martin. He'll be killed.'

Martin made a grab for the dog's collar. The dog, bursting with energy, bounced out of reach. Martin managed a few steps in pursuit before he had to stop, bending over and puffing his cheeks out, his hands on his knees. The dog galloped off down the pavement, his feathery tail and gold-red coat burnished and shiny.

Chapter Twenty

By the time they had finally recaptured the dog –
bribing him back down the road and into the garden
with a piece of chicken – Dawn could stay no longer.
Any moment now, Mr Farnley would be waking up
from his operation and coming back to the ward. Also
it was clear that the Cummingses, rattled by the dog's
lunge for freedom, were keen to take him back into the
house and get on quietly with their evening. A final,
hasty couple of questions established that neither of
them had ever heard of Francine Hartnett. From what
Mrs Cummings had said, Gordon Farnley was badly
missing his wife and worrying about his dog and these
were the only issues recently to preoccupy his mind.
Dawn couldn't think of anything else to ask. None
the wiser, she was forced to leave the house and walk
back up the road to the bus stop. On her way, she
took her phone from her bag and called Daphne on
Ocean Ward.

'Is Mr Farnley back yet from theatre?' she asked.

'Just back in the past few minutes,' Daphne said. 'He's pretty out of it. Looks like he'll stay that way for the next few hours.'

Dawn tapped her nails on the side of her phone. If Mr Farnley was going to sleep for the evening, was there any point in her going back to try to talk to him?

'Are you watching him closely?' she asked.

'Yes,' Daphne said, rather stiffly. 'We are.'

'OK. Thanks, Daphne.'

Still thinking, Dawn clicked her phone shut. It would look odd, she supposed, to go in and hang around the bed of a comatose patient who wasn't even hers. The best thing now would be for her to go home. In a way, the decision was a relief. After that odd sensation she'd had at Mr Farnley's bedside earlier, she found she had a strong reluctance to visit him again. She crossed the road to catch the bus towards Silham Vale. But on the way home, she continued to worry. Mr Farnley would be all right tonight, perhaps – Daphne's team would keep an eye on him – but he couldn't be watched for ever. Sooner or later Francine would realize that Dawn was not going to kill him. And when she did – what then? Would she take matters into her own hands? It would would not be difficult for her to sneak in at some point and get him on his own. She had almost as much influence in the hospital as Dawn had.

Francine. Listlessly, Dawn gazed through the grimy window at a billboard poster advertising margarine. It was only now it was really beginning to hit her. Beyond everything that had happened – beyond the vicious e-mails, the danger Mr Farnley was in, what had been done to Milly – beyond all of these things was the fact that Francine had been her friend. Her *good* friend. That she could have done this . . . it was a far worse blow than if it had been any of the others. All the laughs they'd had. The merry conversations over horrible powdered coffee in the ward kitchens; the support Francine had given to her since she had become Matron; the way she had held Dawn's arm so tightly at Dora's funeral. And all the time – how she must have resented her. Dawn saw now how difficult it must have been; Dawn winning the Matron post even though Francine had greater experience; Dawn receiving the pay rise when Francine was the one in financial difficulty, with children who depended on her and a husband whose job was on the line. But she had never shown it. She had hidden her feelings behind her usual gracious smile. *How are you, Dawn? You look tired. Shouldn't you take a holiday?* Pushing her, Dawn saw now, to go on leave so that Francine could take over the Matron post while she was away and show everyone what an excellent replacement she was. Francine had been biding her time. Like all good managers, she was used to being pleasant with people

413

she didn't like. Hadn't Dawn seen her a hundred times, smoothing the ruffled feathers of senior surgeons at meetings, smiling courteously at the likes of Dr Coulton? Even the way she had gone to fetch the Dipyridamole for that crotchety old dinosaur Dr Carmichael instead of simply telling him that he couldn't have it and that was that. That mask of niceness which was, in reality, a form of ruthlessness, a way of handling people so that ultimately they would do what you wanted. Francine must have seen how stressed Dawn had been since Dora had died, must have guessed it was only a matter of time before she tripped up and made some kind of error – though just how spectacular an error it would be even Francine could not have foreseen.

The garden of number 59 was empty. No snuffle of welcome at the gate, no friendly patter of feet following her into the house. Dawn flung her keys on to the coffee table in the sitting room and dropped to the couch. She let her head fall on the back-rest. Something about the conversation she'd had with Mrs Cummings was bothering her. But she had too much else on her mind to wonder about it.

So now what? Being up against Francine was a completely different proposition from being up against someone like Clive or Dr Coulton. Francine would be taken seriously. People would believe her when she told them what she had witnessed. There would be far less chance of Dawn managing to deny everything and brazen things out. She closed her eyes. One thing was for certain: there was no doubt that she would hear from Francine again.

From the hall came the jangle of the doorbell.

Dawn opened her eyes again and looked at the ceiling. Eileen Warren, almost certainly. Dawn really wasn't in the mood right now to chat with her neighbour about tomato plants or how it was impossible to buy fresh leeks these days in the Somerfield. Wearily, she rolled her head to glance into the hall. But through the sidelight, instead of Eileen's thin frame and round, fuzzy perm, she saw a tall, bulky shape with broad shoulders that took up most of the glass. Will.

She was on her feet before she knew it. Part of her was saying, *Don't let him in. Don't see him tonight; you're too vulnerable.* In the mood she was in, she'd be bound to break down at some point, blurt out the whole story to him. Then regret it bitterly the next day. But the rest of her kept going to the hall. She would not break down. She would maintain her self-control. Will was the one person she could bear to see right now. He would ask no questions, make no judgements; he would simply be there, filling the void, his square, stolid face a relief and a comfort.

She opened the door.

'Hello there!' Will looked even more untidy than usual. His tie was half-undone and pulled to one side, his jacket off and crumpled over his arm. Sweat-circles spread down the sides of his shirt.

'I'm later than I expected,' he said. 'There's been an accident somewhere and the police are everywhere. Half the roads are blocked off. I've had to leave the car a couple of miles away at Norbury and walk the rest.'

His nose was shiny with sweat. His glasses slid down it towards the tip. He poked them back up again, in the manner, Dawn realized, that had lately become so dear and familiar to her. How many more times would she see him doing that? For how much longer would she have him? Her plan to go to the Lakes with him – would it ever happen now? No matter where she went, Francine would track her down. Sooner or later, if she stayed with him, Will would be bound to find out everything.

She forced herself to stop gawping at his nose.

'Come in,' she said. 'I was just about to make coffee, would you like some?'

'Yeah. Any kind of drink would be nice.'

In the kitchen, she boiled the kettle and took the coffee grounds down from the cupboard. It made things easier, having this ritual to perform, as if she was a normal hostess and this a normal, stress-free visit. It was like a dose of Valium, not eliminating the problem but putting it on hold for another time. The coffee filters were in the odds-and-ends drawer. She pulled the drawer open and saw Milly's faded collar, wrapped in its layers of tissue paper.

'You look tired,' Will said from the table.

Dawn paused. The contents of the drawer were blurred. She blinked to clear them.

'Someone let me down,' she said.

'Who?'

'A friend.' Unexpectedly, a sob clogged her throat. 'A friend at work for a long time.'

Will came to her. The warm, familiar smell of him. His sweat, the minty scent from his breath.

'Your friend Molly?' he said.

'Who?'

'The nurse on your ward? Frizzy blonde hair? Sort of plump?'

Dawn rubbed her eyes. She was so tired she couldn't think straight. Who on earth was Will talking about?

'Do you mean Mandy?' she asked.

'Mandy, yes. Sorry. That was it.'

The coffee filters and the tissue paper, poking from the drawer. Everything a mish-mash, all jumbled up together.

'How do you know Mandy?' Dawn asked.

'What?'

'How do you know Mandy? When did you meet her?'

Will went to reply. Then something seemed to catch in his throat and he had to stop to cough. He cleared his throat several times, patting his hand to his chest.

'I think you must have mentioned her,' he said when he had recovered. 'When you were telling me one of your nursing stories.'

'Oh.'

She had no recollection of it. It just showed the way she was so vague and distracted recently. She pulled the box of filters from the drawer. As she did so, Milly's collar was dislodged, poking out from its tissue covering. For some reason, Dawn saw again Martin Cummings, Mr Farnley's neighbour, grabbing at the collar of the excited dog on the road. The dog's red-gold coat, and the collar, standing out from it, a bright, distinctive blue.

Mrs Cummings saying: *Walking Boris for him.*

Dawn frowned and shut the drawer. She placed a filter in the coffee machine.

'How strong do you like your coffee?' she asked.

'I don't know. I normally drink instant, remember?'

'Oh, yes. Of course.' She was still distracted.

A young man Gordon happened to meet on the Common has been helping out . . .

Another memory: Will entering the café at Tooting Bec Common, the rain dripping from his hair. Boris bouncing ahead of him, his bright blue collar vivid around his throat.

He belongs to a friend. He can't walk him at the moment so I'm doing it for him.

Dawn turned. She hadn't noticed how dark the kitchen had become. In the gloom, Will was suddenly unfamiliar, a lumpy, distorted shape. She stood there, looking at him, the box of filters dangling from her hand.

Will's eyebrows bunched behind his glasses. 'What's wrong?'

Dawn went on looking at him. She said slowly, 'It's you, isn't it?'

'What?'

'You were there that day. On the ward. The day Mrs Walker died.'

As soon as the words were out, Dawn clicked her tongue at herself. This was ridiculous! She was starting to lose her mind. Was there anyone at all now that she didn't suspect? She was so messed-up and paranoid she hardly knew what she was saying any more.

'I'm sorry,' she said. 'I'm not feeling very—'

The words died as she saw his face.

They stood, inches apart, in the murky light. Apart from the motion of their breathing, both of them were still.

'Stupid,' Will said then. 'Stupid to think you didn't know.'

Dawn had to catch her breath. She had to feel

about her for support, to clutch at the handle of the drawer.

'I always knew you were an intelligent woman,' Will said. 'That day in Sussex. When you mentioned the limp from my hernia repair. You were telling me then, weren't you, that you'd seen me on your ward.'

The words were buzzing in her head. *Hernia repair.* Mandy in the Day Ward, her back to the side room, busy discharging a patient. A patient whose bed faced over her shoulder, directly towards Mrs Walker's ECG screen. But he couldn't . . . the bed must have been thirty feet away . . . From behind his glasses, Will's small eyes bored in on hers. His grey, northern eyes. *We can see further in the mountains than other people.*

Dawn said stupidly, 'You can read ECGs.'

'A bit,' Will said. 'Mainly just from what I've seen on the telly. Actually, at first I thought it must be broken. Then that ditzy little student nurse came running out of the room, screaming, and that's when I thought, *Hmm. Something funny going on here.*

She was having some kind of nightmare. She was imagining this. This was Will here. *Will!*

'How . . . ?' It came out as a whisper. 'How did you find me?'

He shrugged. 'Boris and I followed you from your

house when you were walking your dog. I would have found some way to talk to you eventually. Boris is a good conversation starter. But then that kid in the café inhaled his lunch and made things very easy.'

'I meant . . . I meant, how did you know me? Who I was?'

'Your tubby little blonde nurse . . . Mandy, is it? Never stops talking? I said you seemed very young to be a Matron and she filled me in on your life story. All about your parents and where you were from and why you'd gone into nursing. Bit of research took care of the rest.'

The kitchen looked so strange. The white surfaces too floaty and pale, the corners and ceiling too dark. Everything was strange. Gone was Will's meek, shambly air. He was standing straighter, his shoulders up and back. His voice had hardened. Even his accent had changed, the vowels shorter, the consonants glottal and staccato. This was not Will. This was a stranger, standing here in her kitchen. Oh, so easy to wonder how women could be so gullible, falling for the tricks and charms of a con man. How they could hand over their life-savings and self-respect to someone they knew nothing about. Someone whose friends they had never seen. Whose family they had never met. But this was different. She knew Will. She *knew* him! They had lived down the road from each other; they had known each other since they were ten years old.

'How could you do this?' She was utterly bewildered. 'We were at school together.'

Will made an impatient, clicking sound with his tongue. 'No, we weren't.'

'But . . .' The tall, fair boy in the playground, easing the cup from the hedgehog's nose. 'But *Will*.'

'What?'

'Will.' Fiercely now. 'The *real* Will. If you're not him, how could you know about him?'

The stranger in her kitchen was looking oddly at her. 'You told me.'

She stared.

'Everything I needed to know,' he said, 'you handed to me on a plate. All I had to do was agree.'

Our farm was a few miles away.

Will?

That's right!

She was sick. Sick at heart. The hedgehog. Will's hands that night, holding her face. Mr Farnley. Clive. Her hands slipped on the drawer, jerking it out a couple of inches.

'You never did have a fiancée with cancer. Did you?'

'No. But I do have an ex-wife, alive and well in Bromley.'

Will seemed to think this was funny. She didn't

have the energy to ask him his real name. No matter what he told her now, it would be meaningless. Yet another lie.

Will's manner had changed. Now the casual air became sharp and alert. 'What's the matter with you anyway? What's with all this prissiness? You did know, didn't you?'

'I didn't.'

'But you must have. The limp . . . my hernia . . . you must have realized . . .'

'I didn't know. If I did, why in God's name wouldn't I have said?'

There was a silence.

'Shit.' Will took off his glasses. He shoved his hair back with his hand. 'Shit.'

'If I didn't know,' Dawn cried, 'why would I have pretended? Why would I have let it go on for so long?'

'How the hell would I know?' Will snapped. 'To get more on me, to get me in deeper. I thought you must have been playing some kind of game. I never could figure out how much you knew.'

'You killed my dog. You killed Milly. Do you honestly think I would have stood back and let that happen?'

'I *had* to kill her. You were dithering so bloody much, you needed a push. Anyway, you said yourself, she was old.'

'*Old?*' Dawn shouted. '*Old?* Is that the same reason you wanted me to kill that old man? What the hell is wrong with you? You're sick. *Sick!*'

'Come off it.' Will's voice dripped with disgust. 'Don't come like that with me, all nursy and pure. Who are you to talk? You killed that old lady.'

'That was different.'

'No. I watched you do it. I saw your face. You liked doing it. You liked the control.'

She opened her mouth but nothing came out.

'Oh yes.' Will pointed his glasses at her. 'Don't pretend otherwise. She was a burden to you. A sign you and your precious hospital had failed. Lying there under your nose, taking up space. Like that old git, slowly crumbling away, sitting on a fortune someone else could make use of. You're a nurse, you know the score. People reach a stage where they'd be better off dead. Where they don't even want to keep going themselves any more. And what's so shocking about that? If they're on the way out anyway, what's the big deal with helping them to move on?'

He was pacing up and down between her and the doorway, still pointing the glasses at her. He didn't appear to have any difficulty seeing without them. 'You know all this. You *know* it. I saw it that day in your face, the day you killed her.'

Dawn couldn't argue. She was too unsteady, her

424

legs heavy, trapped in an invisible sludge. If she tried to move, she would fall.

'The two of us could work well together,' Will said. 'I bring them in, you finish them off. I've got a few lined up, ripe and ready to go. I'm good at that sort of thing. You'd be amazed how many lonely old people there are in this city, ready to clutch any stranger to their breast in exchange for a few cups of tea and a kind word. No one would make the connection between the two of us. It would be easy. Like I said – I always did think you were intelligent.'

His voice had softened. For a moment he was back, the old Will, looking at her in the old, admiring way. The shambly, eager Will who had walked with her in Sussex and held her face in the darkness. The shy, charming Will who had coerced a grieving elderly man into leaving him his house and all his money. Dawn's hands tightened on the drawer. Without the glasses, his face seemed emptier, the eyes taking up less space than usual. The tininess of them gave them a cruel look.

She managed to stand away from the sink. 'I'm calling the police.'

Will laughed. 'You? I don't think so.'

'Let me past, please.'

Will stayed where he was, blocking her path to the door.

'You're going nowhere,' he said, and his voice had

changed again. Ugly now, low and deliberate. 'Smug bitch. Who do you think you are?'

In the dark, his tiny eyes contrasted with his big shoulders and large farmer's hands. Through her daze, Dawn felt a sudden fear. None of her friends knew Will. No one she knew had ever seen them together. No one knew she was here with him alone.

He took a step towards her. She backed away. Something sharp poked at her back. The corner of the drawer.

The doorbell rang.

The deep jangle blasted into the silence. Dawn jumped against the drawer. Will didn't move. His gaze remained fixed on hers.

'Hello?' A tapping sound from the hall. 'Hello-o? Dawn?'

Dawn didn't have to turn her head to know who it was. Her neighbour, Eileen Warren. Peering through the window beside the front door, her hands to her face.

'Dawn?' she called. 'Is everything all right? I know you're there. I can see you standing in your kitchen.'

The dismay on Will's face brought Dawn to her senses. In a loud, defiant voice, she said, 'Just coming, Eileen.'

The relief of it! And the triumph. To stop her, Will would have to attack her right there and then, with Eileen watching the whole thing through the glass.

Deliberately, facing him, she marched past, pushing off his arm. His clammy skin recoiled from hers. He didn't like it one bit but he had no choice.

She flung the front door open.

'Eileen—'

'Oh, Dawn.' Eileen's voice quivered. 'Isn't it awful? Did you hear on the radio?'

Before Dawn could respond, she was aware of Will coming up behind her. And she saw, at the same time as he must, the dark, empty path stretching towards the gate. The only person on it this frail old lady, standing there alone.

She had a fraction of a second to decide what to do.

'I can't talk now, Eileen.'

'But—'

'Goodbye!'

She had never spoken so rudely to her neighbour before. She stepped back into the hall and went to slam the door but something was blocking it. Dawn looked down. Will's foot, planted in the frame.

'Hello, Eileen,' he said pleasantly. 'I'm Will. A good friend of Dawn's.'

'Oh.' Eileen grew flustered at the sight of such a very large man. 'Eileen Warren. From just over the road.'

'What were you saying was on the radio just now?' Will asked.

'Oh dear. The train crash at Clapham Junction. An

hour ago. The bridge has collapsed on to the road. Just outside your hospital, Dawn.'

'How terrible.' Dawn could feel Will looking at her.

'Lucky you're not working tonight, isn't it? You'd have been run off your feet.'

'Eileen,' Dawn's voice was high with panic. 'I really do have to go.' She tried to force the door shut again but Will's foot was still in the way. Bewildered now, Eileen looked back and forth between the two of them. Dawn signalled to her with her eyes, dipping her eyebrows, sliding her gaze sideways to Will and back again. *He's mad. Get help.*

Eileen's brow had lowered as well. She'd seen the message. She'd seen it. Thank God.

'Why do you keep doing that with your eyes?' Eileen asked.

'No reason. Nothing.' *Oh Jesus.* If Will thought Eileen knew, he would grab her there and then and yank her in. She could feel him deciding whether or not to do it; he was a hair's breadth from reaching out his hand.

A bitter, familiar smell wafted from the kitchen.

'Your coffee.' Frantically, Dawn turned on Will. 'It's ready. You should pour it before it gets cold.'

'But I don't know where you keep your cups.'

Dawn said desperately, 'Well, I don't know what sugar or milk you take.'

She tried to force him to keep looking at her, to lock him with her gaze. His eyes flicked from her to Eileen. Clearly he still hadn't made his decision.

Dawn made it for him.

'Eileen, sorry but I really have to go now. See you soon.'

She made one final attempt to close the door but she couldn't. She had no choice but to leave it. Turn her back and walk to the kitchen, hoping against hope that Will would let Eileen go and come after her. The back door was right there in front of her; he wouldn't want to risk her running out that way. She heard his footsteps approach. *Thank God! Thank God!* Now, at least, Eileen was safe. Now it was just her and Will. What would his next move be? Would he lunge at her, make some sort of attack? Would Eileen go home and think to herself that something hadn't seemed right and come back with someone? One of the neighbours? She had to have noticed how strangely Dawn was behaving. Not knowing what else to do, Dawn picked up the percolator and began to slosh the coffee into a mug.

Will's footsteps had followed her to the kitchen door. But there they stopped.

'Come on in,' Dawn heard him say. 'Join us for a cuppa.'

Eileen had not left.

Don't come in, Dawn kept thinking. *Don't come*

in. She saw now her mistake. She shouldn't have left the hall until she was sure that Eileen had gone. The coffee slopped from the mug into the open drawer in front of her. Slopped over Milly's collar in its tissue wrapping. Over the cardiac Resus kit, bulging with emergency masks and syringes.

And over something else.

Everything seemed to slow. It was like the time the child had been thrust into her arms in the café; like all the times she had ever dealt with an emergency at the hospital, where all the unimportant details around her faded and all she had to do was focus on what was under her nose.

Dora's extra-strength sleeping pills.

Nestled at the very back of the drawer, where Dawn had stored them after clearing out the sitting-room. The kind you could pull in two so that the powder spilled out. And that wasn't all. Dawn looked from the sleeping pills back to the Resus kit. Packed with every kind of drug that might need to be given quickly in a crisis.

Including a full syringe of Potassium Chloride.

Dawn jerked her head to glance at Will. He was still in the doorway, occupied with Eileen. She looked back at the Resus kit. A stinging heat was rising in her face. The sleeping powders first. Then, when he was ready, the syringe. A half an hour should do it, if only she could hold out that long. It would be as simple as that. No one had ever seen her and Will together. She doubted that he had mentioned her to anyone he knew. Eileen would not remember, or very little; she was so frail these days she could barely remember what she'd had for breakfast.

Even Will's car was conveniently abandoned a couple of miles away from the house.

Easy. So easy. After all, she had killed two people already.

She moved through her little bubble of calm. By the time the slowness around her had sped back up, the coffee was ready, the mug filled to the brim. Dawn took it and almost ran to the kitchen door. Eileen was peering anxiously from the porch. She had taken a couple of steps back, out of Will's reach. She did know something was wrong.

Dawn thrust the mug at Will. 'There you are.'

Too surprised to refuse, he took it from her.

'Go on.' Dawn put her hands on her hips. 'Taste it. See what you think.'

Both of Will's hands were taken up now, one with his glasses, one with the mug of hot liquid. To grab Eileen, he would first have to drop one or both of them, creating a great deal of awkward mess and noise. Reluctantly, he lifted the mug and took a sip.

'All right, is it?' Dawn asked.

Will made a face. 'Funny taste, isn't it? Sort of bitter.'

'It's the brand.' Dawn's heart was pounding. 'It takes a bit of getting used to.'

He shrugged. 'If you're thirsty enough, I suppose you'll drink anything.' He took another mouthful. Then a larger one, gulping it back. 'Actually,' he said to Eileen, 'it's not that bad. Sure you won't have a cup?'

Footsteps clacked in the street outside.

Dawn leaped forward. She shouted to Eileen, 'Come on. I'll walk you home.'

'What?'

'Come along.' The words came out almost as a shriek. The people passing the gate turned to look. Tim and Sue Rutledge, from number 46. Dawn hustled Eileen out of the porch. She caught a glimpse of Will's startled face, his open mouth above the rim of the mug, but there was nothing he could do.

'Evening, Dawn,' Sue Rutledge said as Dawn and Eileen hurtled past.

Dawn didn't look back. She kept going, almost shoving Eileen ahead of her. She didn't stop until they were across the road and inside Eileen's house.

She slammed the door behind them.

'Dawn?' Eileen's voice was trembly. 'Dawn, what's happening?'

Dawn was listening at the door. She was trembling herself. Will. Milly. The hedgehog in the playground. Again and again and again.

'Dawn?' Eileen was twisting at the buttons of her cardigan. 'Dawn? Is everything all right?'

Dawn was still listening, her ear pressed to the letterbox, her breaths coming in half sobs, her arms spread wide, almost hugging the door.

'I think so,' she said. 'I think now it might be.'

She gave it half an hour, to be sure.

She made a cup of tea for Eileen and herself. 'It's all right,' she told Eileen. 'Will's a distant cousin of mine. We've never got on. He won't be calling around again.' By next week, she knew, Eileen would barely remember what he had looked like. 'Look,' Dawn said, 'let's see if that crash you mentioned is on the TV.'

She turned on Eileen's black-and-white kitchen portable. On the screen appeared a familiar L-shaped tower block, high on a hill. In the foreground, a woman in a red jacket was shouting into a microphone, her hair blowing over her face.

'. . . latest reports . . . train derailed . . . hundreds injured. St Iberius Hospital overwhelmed . . .'

Dawn and Eileen watched in silence. Behind the woman were smoke and flames, glimpses of twisted carriages, the railway bridge partially collapsed, rubble all over the road. The camera moved back from the woman, panned over the people swarming everywhere: police with radios, men in orange vests and hard hats, hurrying with equipment.

When the news was over, Dawn returned home. The Rutledges had long since disappeared; the street was deserted. Warily, Dawn pushed open her gate. Almost on her toes, she walked up the maroon and black tiled path. The front door was ajar. No movement showed behind the glass. Dawn stopped to listen, almost feeling the bulge in her eardrums, her hearing so hyper-acute and attuned that she knew she would hear any breath, any creak. But there was nothing.

In the kitchen, she paused by the open drawer, dazed all over again at what had happened. But there wasn't time now to think about it. She had other things to do. She could still stop, still turn back. It wasn't too late to change her mind. But she could not let Will go. Clive had died because of him. Now that she knew who the blackmailer really was, why should he be allowed to get away with it when Clive had not? As long as Will was out there, she would never be safe. And nor would Mr Farnley, and nor would whatever other elderly victims Will might decide to target in the future.

Calmly, efficiently, she did what had to be done. It did not take as long as she had expected. Afterwards, she spent some time cleaning up the kitchen. She cleared away the coffee pot and filters, wiped up the spills in the drawer and on the floor. She washed

Will's mug thoroughly, making sure to remove every last mark and stain. She didn't want any trace of him left in her house.

When everything was spotless, she went upstairs to change. Before leaving the bedroom, she paused to check herself in the mirror on her wardrobe door. She smoothed down her navy dress, straightened her tights, fixed her ID badge on her pocket. She refastened her belt, positioning it so that the buckle sat dead in the centre. Only when she was satisfied that everything was exactly as it should be did she gather up her bag and jacket and leave the house.

The bus trundled on its familiar journey to the hospital. Will had been right about the traffic. The packed lines of cars moved barely an inch at a time. The few hundred yards from Tooting Bec to Trinity Road took twenty minutes to cover. At the corner of Trinity Road and Wandsworth Common, the bus was forced to stop. The road ahead was strung with blue and white police tape: *Do Not Cross.*

'Journey terminates here,' the driver shouted. 'Everybody off.'

In front of the blue and white tape, police in fluorescent yellow jackets stood directing cars and pedestrians down alternative routes. Dawn spoke to one of them.

'Is this because of the crash at Clapham Junction?'

'Yes, Madam. Roads need to be kept clear for emergency services.'

'I'm the Matron at St Iberius.' She lifted her badge from her uniform to show him. 'I think they're going to need me there tonight.'

The policeman examined the badge. He glanced at Dawn's uniform under her jacket. Then he lifted the blue and white tape. 'Go ahead, Matron. All right to walk the rest?'

'Of course.'

The common was empty of people, filled instead with shadows and deep hollows. On her soft-soled shoes, Dawn hurried between the trees, flitting through the violet glow. The brightness of the glow filled up her eyes, made her feel that something was about to happen. All her lethargy and confusion flew away. The nearer she came to the hospital, the more alert she became, the straighter she walked and the faster her heart beat in her chest.

Chapter Twenty-one

Before she had even reached the end of Northcote Road, she saw the rows of police bikes, ambulances, blue flashing lights. Falcon Road, below the hospital, was a mass of rubble and crushed cars. From the semi-collapsed railway bridge, a train carriage hung down, dangling above the road like a sheet from a washing-line. On the bridge itself, two carriages appeared to have met head-on and driven each other into the air. The shapes formed a triangle, like a smoking wigwam against the purple sky. The smell of smoke and diesel was everywhere. The most unexpected thing was the silence. No screams, no cries of panic or pain. Just some distant clanging and the occasional faint shout from a man in orange.

Dawn made her way around the rubble and began to climb the hill to the hospital. A group of men marched past, carrying a stretcher. One of the men held a fluid bag high in the air. Several of the injured came trudging up under their own steam, grey and ghostly in the dusk, their clothes ripped, their faces streaked with black or blood.

At the A&E entrance, Dawn had to show her badge again. A line of police was keeping out everyone who wasn't either staff or injured. Inside, the strange balloon of silence that had enveloped the bridge was abruptly punctured. The scene before her was like something from a Hieronymus Bosch painting. People lay everywhere, filthy and bleeding, some groaning on trolleys, many more sitting or lying on the floor. The tiles were littered with torn packaging, empty fluid bags, bloodstained dressings. Curtains whisked back and forth, revealing cubicles crammed with yet more bloodied and wounded. Alarms shrieked. Nurses rushed about, white-faced and frantic.

'Where's that O-negative?'

'We need more cannulas.'

The A&E doors crashed open. Another stretcher came barrelling through.

'Crush injury,' someone shouted. 'We've had to take off his leg.'

Maria, the small, round A&E sister, rushed at them, making slicing motions in the air with her hands. 'We've got no room. Take him somewhere else.'

'No time, love,' one of the stretcher-bearers said. 'He won't make it.'

Dawn spoke to him. 'Why are you still bringing

438

people here? You can see we're overwhelmed. There must be three hundred patients in this area at least.'

'There's nowhere else to go,' the man in orange said. 'The roads are impassable. We're doing our best to clear them, but for now you're all we've got.'

Maria's short, dark hair stood up in spikes, like a threatened hedgehog. 'We're almost out of dressings,' she pleaded to Dawn. 'And syringes. And staff. I don't know how they think we can take any more.'

Dawn eyed the carpet of blackened, bleeding bodies. 'Can't we move some patients to other parts of the hospital? Spread the load a bit?'

'We're trying to. But we've had so little warning. All the wards and theatres are full. There's nowhere for them to go.'

The doors crashed open again. Another casualty was helped through, his face streaming with blood.

Dawn said to Maria, 'Give me an hour or so. I'll see what I can do.'

She took the lift up to Forest Ward. After the chaos in A&E, the fifth-floor corridor was peaceful, more deserted even than on a normal evening. Every staff member was occupied elsewhere. The turmoil resumed as soon as Dawn entered the ward. Midway down, Elspeth, Trudy and Pam were huddled around a patient. The floor around them was spattered with blood. Frightened faces peeped around curtains as Dawn walked along the rows of beds. The whispers followed her down the ward. 'She's here . . . The Matron's here . . . Everything will be all right now.'

The patient, a young man in a filthy shirt, lay wincing on the mattress. His trousers had been slashed so that they only covered one leg. The surgical SHO, skinny and harried-looking with a pronounced Adam's apple, was leaning his full weight on the other leg, pressing a wad of tissue paper to his groin. Blood welled through the tissue, soaking into the sheets. Trudy, looking terrified, was rummaging through the drawers of the crash trolley.

'Gauze,' the SHO snapped. 'I need *gauze*, for Christ's sake.'

'What's going on here?' Dawn asked.

'Sister.' Elspeth swung to her, 'A&E sent this patient up a half an hour ago . . . They said he was stable but he'd only been here ten minutes when his wound burst open. We can't . . . the bleeding won't stop, and I can't find the type of dressing Dr Grove wants—'

'Bottom drawer,' Dawn said to Trudy. 'Big cupboard in the stock room. Wide gauze and Haemostat. Hurry.'

Trudy flew down the ward. Seconds later she was back, ripping open a package. The SHO took the gauze, folded it into a thick square and pressed it hard on to the patient's thigh.

'Bleeding's slowing,' he said with relief.

'Keep the pressure on it,' Dawn said. 'I'll call theatre and see when they can take him.'

She phoned theatre and got the bleeding young man placed on the emergency list. 'I don't know yet what time it'll be,' Dilly, the theatre manager, said. 'We'll get to him when we can but we're up to our eyes at the moment.'

Dawn led Elspeth to her office. 'OK. What's been happening here?'

'It's too much, Sister.' Elspeth was nearly crying. 'A&E sent up three patients all at the same time; we haven't had a chance to assess any of them properly. And then this happened. And they still keep on phoning us, insisting we take more, but we can't do it, we can't, we don't have the staff or the beds, we can't possibly—'

'We can do it,' Dawn said. 'We just need to prioritize.'

'But how—'

'The first thing is to free up as many beds as we can. Get the most stable patients dressed and taken to the relatives' room with their charts. The doctors can discharge them from there. As for the rest, essentials only for tonight. We don't wash anyone, we don't do any routine dressings. Here.' She was pulling her large red Disaster Plan folder out of her drawer. 'Put one of these stickers over every bed. Red for the sickest patients, green for the ones who'll manage with less care. Yellow for the people we can send home. Come on. I'll go through them with you.'

Around the walls of her office were the Disaster Plan guidelines she had drawn up a couple of weeks ago, stating in clear steps how to triage a ward in an emergency. Dawn unpinned them and took them with her. Between them, she and Elspeth quickly triaged every patient.

'You take the reds,' Dawn told Elspeth. 'Pam can take the greens and Trudy the yellows. At least that way you can each plan what you need to do. I'll be back soon to help. I just need to have a quick word with the other ward managers.'

She did a tour of all the surgical wards, handing out sheets of triage stickers and copies of her guidelines.

'Essential procedures only,' she told the staff. 'Vitals, meds, fluids. If you need more hands, call in your off-duty staff but remember it may take them a while to get here. In the meantime, use your students. Use the patients themselves. The alert ones can help to keep an eye on their neighbours.'

She pulled more pages from her red folder. 'Here's a list of what you're most likely to run out of: syringes, needles, fluids, dressings. Stick the list up on your stock-room door and put an X beside each item as you run low. I'll arrange for runners from Pharmacy and Central Supplies to carry stock around in bulk and check your lists regularly so you won't have to keep phoning to re-order.'

The ward managers almost fell on Dawn's pages of guidelines. Some had been handling the situation better than others but those who had been struggling were utterly relieved to find that they weren't on their own. On her way back to Forest Ward, Dawn stopped in to the ITU. Francine was grim but coping.

'A&E's just phoned,' she said. 'They want us to take three more. But we've only got two beds.'

'Any possibilities for discharge?'

'We've got one who could probably go. But I can't see any of the wards agreeing to take him. He was only extubated this afternoon.'

Despite the strain she was under, Francine's manner was still gentle and unflustered, her porcelain face smooth and serene. Dawn looked at her, remembering the thoughts she had been having about this woman only a few hours before.

'Send him to us,' she said. 'We'll have a bed in an hour.'

'Are you sure? What if he goes off again?'

'If he does, he does. We'll deal with it.'

Francine touched her arm. 'Bless you, Dawn.'

She hurried away. Dawn returned to Forest Ward. Things seemed to be more under control. Elspeth, calmer again, was hanging a fluid bag for a red patient. Trudy had made up two beds already and was starting on a third. Pam was helping a green patient to the commode. Dawn's phone rang constantly with queries from the wards and from Central Supplies. In between, she helped Elspeth with the red patients, monitoring obs, keeping fluids and feed and medications running. Francine's ITU patient arrived, a very relaxed-looking middle-aged man who, he assured Dawn, had never felt better in his life. She put a red sticker over his bed anyway. An elderly lady with a fractured humerus came up from A&E. Dawn's team processed her quickly and got her settled.

At midnight, Mandy phoned.

'I've just heard,' she said. 'I've been out all evening. How awful, Dawn. Should I come in?'

'No. Thanks, Mandy, but the best thing for you to do is get a good night's sleep. We'll need fresh staff for tomorrow.'

When the phone calls finally began to die down, Dawn paid another visit to A&E.

'It's getting easier.' Maria put her hands on her hips and blew out her cheeks. 'The wards are taking them now, so we've got more space. Oh, here comes another one.' A grimy stretcher was being manhandled through the doors.

'Resus room three.' Maria led the way. She and her team converged around the patient, hanging drips, cutting off clothes. 'Are there many more?' she asked the team of firemen who had carried the stretcher.

'No,' the lead fireman said. His eyes were streaming red slits in a soot-streaked face but he looked as if he hadn't enjoyed himself so much in years. 'We've been in and under every single carriage. This is the last one.'

'Thank God.'

The fireman looked at the two ward managers and tipped his hand to his forehead in a salute. 'We've done our bit,' he said. 'Now it's up to you.'

It was almost four o'clock in the morning. Nine hours since the massive pile-up had occurred. But at least now they knew what they were dealing with. Now they could take a deep breath and get on with it. Back on Forest Ward, Trudy was on her knees, cleaning up the mess from around the bed of the man with the bleeding groin. He had finally gone to theatre to have his artery explored. Trudy's thin face was white with exhaustion.

'Leave that,' Dawn said. 'Go and have a coffee.'

'But I've still got to—'

'No, you don't. You've been working flat out all night. Go and have a proper break.'

'OK. Thank you, Sister.'

Dawn felt her own fatigue in a mixture of exhilaration and nausea. Through her office window, a pale light was visible at the edges of the sky. On the bridge below, the pinprick lights of the searchers continued to bob and move. She went to the staff room and switched on the kettle to make a cup of tea. Just as she was pouring the water into her mug, an agitated voice called from outside: 'Sister! Sister!'

Dawn put the kettle down and hurried out again. Trudy was at the bed of the elderly lady with the fractured arm.

'I just saw her as I was passing.' She was ripping the Velcro ties from a BP cuff. 'Her resps are forty. I can't wake her up.'

'Mrs Rycroft,' Dawn called. Earlier the old lady had been alert, if traumatized. She had known where she was and what was happening. Now she was barely conscious, breathing in a deep, laboured way. Her eyelids flickered when Dawn called her name but that was her only response. Dawn pulled back the sheets. The first thing she noticed was that the right side of Mrs Rycroft's chest was not moving. She took the stethoscope from the crash trolley and listened. No question about it. There was no air entry on the right.

'It's a pneumothorax.' Dawn pulled the stethoscope from her ears. 'Do you know how to set up a chest drain?' When Trudy hesitated, she said, 'Just get the surgical set and a trolley. I'll show you the rest.'

While Trudy ran to the stock room, Dawn went to the desk and paged the surgical SHO.

'Grove.' It was the harried SHO from earlier.

'This is Sister Torridge on Forest Ward. We've got

a seventy-nine-year-old lady with difficulty breathing and decreased air entry on the left. I think she needs a chest drain.'

'I'm sorry,' Dr Grove said, 'but I can't possibly come up right now.'

'Her BP's right down. If she's not treated, she'll arrest soon.'

'I've got my hands full here.' Dr Grove sounded even more stressed than he had earlier. 'I've got seven urgent patients still waiting to be seen.'

'More urgent than Mrs Rycroft?' Dawn asked.

'They're younger.'

'*Younger?*'

'Yes. On a night like this, we have to prioritize. I'm sorry, Sister. I'll be up when I can.'

The line went dead. Dawn was left standing with the receiver in her hand. She looked over at Mrs Rycroft. The old lady breathed jerkily into her oxygen mask. Her clothes were stained and ripped but you could see how they had looked when she had first put them on. Neat brown skirt, pale lavender top, matching cardigan. There were traces of lipstick around her mouth. Mrs Rycroft might not be as young as the other patients Dr Grove had to see, but she was a woman who cared about herself and what she looked like. She had been going somewhere this evening, with plans to do something or meet someone. She had been in a major train crash and had survived it. She did not deserve to die now for the sake of a simple chest drain.

Dawn put the receiver down, then lifted it again. She paged the senior surgeon on call.

'Coulton here.'

Dawn sighed to herself. Could their luck possibly get any worse? She repeated the story anyway. 'I know how busy it is tonight,' she said at the end, 'but it's a simple chest drain. We'll have everything ready by the time you come. It will only take you a couple of minutes, but it could save her life—'

Dr Coulton interrupted her. 'Who is this, please?'

'It's Sister Torridge. On Forest Ward.'

'I'm on my way.'

To her surprise, he was there within minutes. Dawn and Trudy had the chest drain set up already. Dr Coulton listened to Mrs Rycroft's chest. Then he pulled on a pair of sterile gloves.

'Scratch coming up,' he warned the patient.

He took a scalpel and made an incision in Mrs Rycroft's chest, just under the armpit. At that, she flinched and gave a loud groan.

'OK. It's OK.' Dawn touched her arm. The groan was encouraging. It meant that despite the low BP, there was still plenty of blood flowing to Mrs Rycroft's brain.

Dr Coulton stretched and deepened the wound with

his fingers. Then he took the chest drain and slid it in. His movements were quick, yet deft and confident; it was plain that he had done this many times before. He attached the drain to a length of tubing, the other end of which was sitting in a container of water on the floor. The water in the container frothed and bubbled as the trapped air came whooshing out of Mrs Rycroft's chest.

'BP's coming back up,' Trudy said, listening with the stethoscope.

Mrs Rycroft opened her eyes. Then she started up from her pillows. 'What's happening? What am I doing here? Am I dead?'

'You're not dead,' Trudy assured her. 'You were in a train crash. But you're going to be fine.'

'My daughter.' Mrs Rycroft was struggling to sit. 'I was supposed to meet her. She'll be wondering where I am.'

'We'll call her,' Trudy soothed. 'Just as soon as we've sutured your chest drain. Try to lie as still as you can until it's done.'

While Trudy settled Mrs Rycroft, Dr Coulton got on with stitching the drain in place. Dawn handed him the bits and pieces he needed. She said quietly, 'Thank you for coming so quickly. I know how chaotic it's been tonight.'

Dr Coulton snapped off the end of the suture.

'It's thanks to you,' he said abruptly, 'that we've

been able to treat half the people we have. You've made an enormous difference to the A&E.'

He started on the next stitch. Dawn watched his fingers fly around the tiny knots. Did he feel any curiosity about what she had said to him the other evening? Did he wonder whether she had gone to the police about the blackmail? Or did he even remember the conversation? If he did, he gave no sign. All of his concentration was on the drain. They worked in silence, both of them so familiar with what they were doing that they knew without having to speak what came next, what was needed. When Dr Coulton had finished the last suture he glanced up for the dressing. The lamp over the bed shone full on his face. His eyelids were reddened with fatigue. Deep lines puckered the skin around his eyes, lay in grooves all down his high forehead.

'What time did you start?' Dawn asked.

He considered. 'Thirty-seven hours ago.'

A pager squealed. 'Surgical reg to A&E,' squawked a tinny voice from Dr Coulton's pocket. 'Surgical reg to A&E.'

Dr Coulton stood up, pulling off his gloves. 'I'd better go.' He nodded at Mrs Rycroft. 'She should be OK now, but any worries, give me a call.'

'I'll do that. And thanks again.'

He went off up the ward. Dawn watched his white coat disappear beyond the curtains. Beside her, Trudy was clearing up the discarded gloves and packaging.

'When you've had your coffee,' Dawn said to her, 'I want you to take charge of Mrs Rycroft for the rest of the night.'

Trudy looked uncertain. 'But she's a red patient—'

'She's *your* patient. You were the one who found her. If it weren't for you, things could have been a lot worse.'

Trudy flushed. She went back to settling Mrs Rycroft. Dawn watched her as she fixed the pillow, re-checked the BP, adjusted the oxygen mask, every action accompanied by a reassuring word or a gentle gesture. Where had the nervy, vapid young girl gone who had started on the ward only a few weeks ago? There was no sign of her tonight, that was for sure. That frightened child had vanished, leaving in her place this strong, competent nurse, this capable future ward manager in whose hands any patient could be sure of protection and safety.

'You've done extremely well tonight.' Dawn touched Trudy's arm. 'None of us will forget it. You should be very proud.'

Trudy turned an even deeper shade of tomato. Dawn left her to it and returned to the staff room for her cup of tea. On the way past bed sixteen she spotted old Mr Otway, grimacing as he tried to reach a glass of water on his locker. He was one of their less sick patients so Dawn hadn't seen much of him during the night.

She stopped by his bed. 'Thirsty, Mr Otway?'

'Oh, Nurse, I am. My throat feels like the Sahara desert.'

Dawn thought of her own drink, rapidly cooling in the staff room.

'Come on, then,' she said.

She sat beside his bed and held the glass to his mouth.

'Ahh.' Mr Otway gulped down the water. 'Lovely. Just what I needed. But I'm holding you up, Nurse. I'm sure you've got your job to be getting on with.'

Dawn tilted the glass again. She settled herself more deeply into her chair.

'This is my job,' she said.

Chapter Twenty-two

And then, at half past seven, when she was doing the morning handover round with Mandy and Elspeth, the heavy double doors to the ward opened and two men in dark jackets walked towards the nurses' desk.

Very calmly, Dawn took off her gloves and her plastic apron. She said to Mandy and Elspeth, 'I've got to go now. I'll leave you to finish up here.'

Claudia Lynch was with the two men. Most unusually for her she was not taking charge of the situation, bossing the men around and issuing orders in her sea-captain tones. In fact, she appeared bewildered, wringing her hands, looking much smaller and less intimidating than normal despite her violent royal blue skirt suit. As Dawn approached, one of the men stepped to meet her, holding up a badge.

'Matron Dawn Torridge?'

'Yes.'

'Detective Sergeant James Patterson.' His sideburns were long and pointed, like horns growing down his head the wrong way. 'And my colleague, Detective Constable Rowland. Is there somewhere we could have a word?'

'It's extremely busy here this morning as you can see.' Dawn looked about her. 'Perhaps out in the hall would be best.'

As they all trooped through the doors, Claudia caught her arm.

'I found your letter,' she hissed. 'In my office an hour ago. But it wasn't me who called the police, Dawn, honestly it wasn't. I would have come and talked to you first, you know I—'

'I do know, Claudia. It's all right.'

'But, Dawn.' Claudia's grip tightened on her arm. She hauled Dawn closer so that her mouth was almost brushing her ear. 'Dawn, why on earth would you *write* that? Killing a patient! And Clive! You know you couldn't possibly . . . You know you'd never . . .' She swung to the two detectives. 'There's been a mistake,' she said loudly. 'Sister Torridge has been under a lot of strain recently. I've known this woman for years. I know how utterly incapable she is of doing anything like . . . like whatever she might have said.'

'Claudia.' Dawn tugged gently at her arm to free it. 'It's all right. Just let me deal with this.'

'Sister Torridge.' Detective Sergeant Patterson

cleared his throat. 'Just to clarify the situation. Did you write two letters, one addressed to the CEO and one to the Director of Nursing of this hospital, and at some point during the past twelve hours, post those letters through the doors of their offices?'

'Yes, I did.'

'Letters stating that you are responsible for the deaths of Mrs Ivy Walker and Mr Clive Geen?'

'Yes.'

'And the contents of these letters? Are they true?'

'Yes, they are. Every word.'

Claudia's eyes were almost bulging out of her head. She had dropped Dawn's arm and was holding her hands to her mouth.

Detective Sergeant Patterson said, 'I'm sure you realize, Matron, that we will need to discuss this further. Is there any chance you could come with us now?'

Dawn looked back through the doors of the ward. At the nurses' desk, Mandy was standing, clipboard in hand, directing the staff to the various patients. Her blonde hair was in a cloud around her head; she looked pink-cheeked, cheerful and in control. A nearby patient said something and Mandy turned at once and sat down on the bed. She touched the patient's shoulder. Whatever she said to the woman, it made her sink back against her pillows and smile.

Dawn turned back to the two detectives.

'Yes,' she said. 'Yes, I can come.'

They waited for her to collect her bag and jacket. Then they accompanied her down the hall. Claudia followed them, every so often uttering gaspy little intakes of breath as if she was about to say something, but nothing came out. When they entered the lift, Detective Sergeant Patterson somehow managed to take up so much space inside the doors that Claudia dropped back and didn't attempt to join them.

When the doors closed, Detective Sergeant Patterson said to Dawn, 'Where is Will Coombs now?'

'Bearing in mind that's almost certainly not his real name,' Dawn said. 'He left my house shortly after nine o'clock last night. I don't know where he went after that.'

'We'll need to find him and talk to him.'

'Of course.'

Dawn leaned her head against the wall of the lift. She was tired now. Very tired. But things had worked out very well. Really, she couldn't have asked for better. She had worried when she had written the letters the previous evening that the police might come for her before the night was over, while she was still needed here. But as it happened, their timing was perfect.

Writing the letters to Claudia and the CEO was the task that had kept her so busy last night after she had returned from Eileen's to find the house empty and

Will gone. His disappearance was no more than she had expected. By now he was probably miles away. Funny – that crazy impulse she'd had to drug him with Dora's sleeping pills and inject him with potassium chloride. It never would have worked, of course. But it was the fact that she'd had the impulse in the first place that had made her sit down at her kitchen table yesterday evening, pick up her pen and write those two letters.

Will, holding her head in his hands that night, the night they had gone for dinner in London. Why had he done that? Why had he bothered to pretend? Why did she think! To gain her confidence, to keep an eye on her. To get to know her and to influence whatever she might decide to do. No wonder what they'd had between them had never seemed quite real. She had been a fool, plain and simple.

The lift doors opened. Dawn had never seen the main hall so empty at this time of the morning. The glass entrance doors were locked. Outside, on the steps, a huge crowd had gathered – relatives, journalists, reporters – all craning their necks, desperate for some sort of update. Harry Rowe, the CEO, was due at any moment to deliver a statement. Dawn and the two detectives avoided the main entrance, veering instead down the narrow side corridor past the HR and payroll offices.

'I've been told,' Detective Sergeant Patterson looked

at Dawn, 'that this route will bring us out at the back of the car park?'

'Yes, that's right.'

He was so polite. She wondered what he had thought of her letters. She had done her best not to leave anything out, to describe everything as it had happened, right from the very beginning. She had written a detailed description of Will and his red Honda; she'd even had a decent stab at remembering the registration number. She had added in all of Mr Farnley's details; it was possible that he might have other information about Will that might be helpful. Finally, she had been unsparing in the description of her own involvement in the whole affair. She had given an unflinching account of exactly what she had done to Mrs Walker and to Clive. At the top of each page, in block capitals, she had written, *Dawn Torridge. Full and Frank Confession.*

As it almost was. A full and frank confession. There was only one part of the story that she had left out. Because she could not bring herself to write it down.

Behind them came the sound of running footsteps.

'Stop!' a voice shouted. 'Stop! Where are you taking her?'

Dr Coulton, white coat flapping, was beside them, red-faced and out of breath.

'I saw you coming out of the lift,' he said. 'Are you . . . is this the police?'

He looked the two detectives up and down in his aggressive, surgical manner. Dawn answered for them. 'Yes, they are.'

'Well, you don't have to go anywhere with them.' Dr Coulton turned to Detective Sergeant Patterson. 'Excuse me, but have you actually arrested this woman?'

Detective Sergeant Patterson said, 'Sir, we'd prefer if—'

'She is a wonderful nurse,' Dr Coulton said. 'A wonderful person. Whatever she thinks she might have done. If you knew what this hospital owes her . . . what she has achieved here last night . . .'

'Sir—'

'Let me speak to her, just for a moment.'

They didn't try to stop him from drawing Dawn a few feet away, out of their hearing. It was Dawn herself who lifted her hand to stop him from saying any more.

'This is for the best,' she told him. 'There's a reason I'm going with them. I did something terrible—'

'You killed Mrs Walker.'

She looked at him in silent astonishment.

Dr Coulton moved between her and the detectives, deliberately blocking her from their view.

'I knew,' he said in a low voice. 'I always knew. When you got so upset about her that day, about the pain she was in. And then that row you had with

Clive. Of course I heard about that. Everybody did. And then her death was so unexpected . . . I'd seen her myself only that morning and I knew there was no reason for her to . . . I always wanted to talk to you about it, but I didn't feel I knew you well enough . . . I never knew how to bring it up . . .'

He seemed too agitated to continue. His white coat was stained and crumpled. A row of greenish smears was blotched all down one lapel. Dawn had never seen him look anything less than test-tube sterile and perfect before. The stains made him look . . . they made him look human.

'I should have talked to you,' he said. 'I shouldn't have let it come to this.'

His pager buzzed. He ignored it, still looking at Dawn. His eyes were grey, the deep grey of a snowy sky. Funny, that. She had often noticed how light his eyes were, but never before that they were grey. Northern eyes, like hers. Used to seeing in the dark.

'Dawn,' he said, 'Dawn . . . I . . .'

The pager in his pocket was still buzzing and flashing. Dawn pointed to it. 'Look,' she said gently. 'You'd better go back. You're still needed here.'

They left him holding the pager and continued on down the corridor. Dawn didn't look back. She knew by the silence, by the lack of footsteps, that he was still standing there, staring after them, right up until they turned the corner.

*   * .   *

Dawn sat in the back seat of the police car beside the silent DC Rowland. Northcote Road was deserted, all the shops and galleries closed, the tables empty on the pavements under the canopies. The street had an eerie, post-apocalyptic air, as if all of the citizens had somehow been spirited away in the night. The car radio crackled. Harry Rowe was live on the steps of St Iberius.

'. . . outstanding response by our hospital team . . . Death toll this morning far lower than initially feared . . .'

Dawn tuned out. She found that she was thinking again about her Full and Frank Confession. Or full and frank apart from the one thing she had left out. The one thing above all else that made her know, once and for all, that this had to come to an end.

It had been the moment when she had been alone with Mr Farnley in his quiet room at the end of the corridor. The moment when she had seen how isolated and vulnerable he was, and, just for a split second, had remembered the e-mail.

If you do this, it will be over . . .

If the theatre porters had not come in to the room just then . . . Would she really have done something? Could she really have harmed that defenceless, innocent man? She hoped not. She wanted to think that such a thing would have been genuinely beyond her.

461

But deep in her heart, perhaps she would never truly know.

Where would it end? Mandy had asked.

Dawn had thought she was in control, different from everyone else, immune to the dangers of the slippery slope. But sooner than she could ever have imagined, she had slid right down it; her foot, in fact, with what had happened with Clive, had actually ended up touching the bottom. Nursing was still her first choice, her beloved profession. She would always want what was best for it. And so had realized – thank God in time – that it was safer and better without her in it.

The car had reached Wandsworth Common. The road blocks were behind them now, the pavements populated and bustling again. The streets were clogged with traffic, the park yellow and alive with people. Children in school uniforms, mothers pushing prams. Ahead of them, a man swung a small child into the air. The sight of them gave Dawn a sudden pang. Not for Will, certainly. For Kevin then? No. She had not thought about Kevin for a long time. If anything, it was for the fact that she had driven him away, as she had driven so many others away. And for what? In the end, she had so little to show for it.

She looked out at the sunny common, filled with families and thought, *I've wasted my life.*

The car had drawn level with the man and child.

The man was tall, red-haired, with long, gangly limbs. The child's hair stood up in the breeze. His eyes were little slits of glee as his father swung him over his head. There was no doubt that the man was his father. Both had the same cheerful, good-humoured faces, the same russet hair, almost orange in the sun. Unusual to see a father and son so identical. Dawn turned to look at them more closely but already the car had passed them by. Now the rest of the park was spread out before her. An elderly woman pushing a shopping trolley. A man carrying a shopping bag. A boy spinning past on a bicycle. It was a beautiful morning, a morning to which no train crash or deaths or any suffering could ever belong. Everywhere you looked, there were people. Dawn sat up straight, gazing at them through the window. Her fingers touched the glass, her hands encircling the park. Enclosing them, all of them, guarding them, keeping them safe.

Have you read Abbie Taylor's *Sunday Times* bestseller?

That was how she saw him, mostly, in the weeks that followed. Standing there in the doorway with his toothy little grin, his crooked fringe, his blue fleece with the smiley elephant on the front.

Life as a single mother is hard. Emma loves her thirteen-month-old son Ritchie, she really does – but sometimes, she dreams about what life would be like without him. But when Ritchie is abducted from the London Underground, Emma's dream becomes a nightmarish reality.

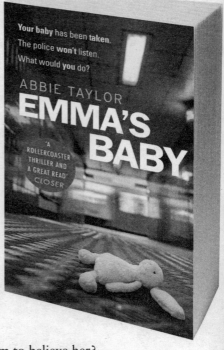

So why don't the police seem to believe her?
Why do they think that she would want to harm her son?

If Emma wants Ritchie back, it looks like she'll have to find him herself. She hasn't been the best mother in the past – but she's willing to go to desperate lengths to bring her little boy home . . .

Available now in paperback and ebook